A Matter of Time

LOVE COMES WHEN LEAST EXPECTED

MARGARET LOCKE

For Ellie, my very own little spunky sunshine.

CHAPTER 1

December 31, 2011

Eliza James smoothed her hands over the cream-colored, empire-waist gown. The dress was a bit small, straining at her chest too much for her liking, but that didn't dampen her joy at being in full Regency garb. Tingles raced up and down her arms. *Tonight! It was happening tonight!*

"We're beautiful."

Eliza threw a grin at her best friend, Catherine Schreiber, as they studied their reflections in the mirror. "Yes, we are. There's something to be said for emphasizing the feminine form, isn't there?"

She'd never felt so gorgeous in her life. Sure, men hit on her often, complimenting her sapphire eyes and flaxen blonde hair, but now, standing here, dressed as if she could have walked out of a *Pride and Prejudice* movie set, she believed it—despite those pesky twenty extra pounds.

"At least the boobs," her friend said. "They haven't seemed this perky in years. I actually have cleavage."

Eliza elbowed her. Cat may envy Eliza's curves, but Eliza would trade for Cat's tall, lean frame in an instant. Until now, perhaps. Her boobs *did* look particularly appealing, squished up in the low-cut bodice as they were. She just hoped they didn't escape the dress at an inopportune time.

"Look at us, Eliza. Really look at us." Cat's hand grabbed hers. "I'd like to think that if we had lived two hundred years ago, we still would have been best of friends. You mean the world to me, and you always will, even if tonight is the last night we are together."

Eliza's eyes welled up. She wiped away the tear that escaped, and gave Cat an impulsive hug. Their last night together. It didn't seem possible. Maybe it wasn't possible. But Eliza hoped it was.

Tonight was her fairytale ball, her chance at being Cinderella, and ending up with her very own Prince Charming. Well, not a prince, but a duke, if all went right.

It was crazy, this plan she and Cat had hatched to launch Eliza back to the early nineteenth century. The Regency period. In England. If any of their friends knew, they'd say the two ought to be committed.

But nothing seemed crazy anymore, not after Cat had found a medieval manuscript left to her by her father, plus old love stories Cat had written but forgotten about, and strange things had started happening. *Make that strange men.*

They'd come out of nowhere, these men asking her friend out. No one had paid attention to Cat in years, which was exactly as Cat liked it. Then suddenly, she'd had three guys hot after her. And not just any three guys—guys exactly like the ones in Cat's stories.

Eliza almost cackled out loud. It still amused her to know that Cat, who'd teased Eliza mercilessly for *years* about her reading genre of choice—romance novels, when not Jane Austen—had secretly written her own stories about the fantasy men she'd longed for. The men who'd appeared, one by one, this fall.

The only explanation was magic. Well, that, and Cat's manuscript, which claimed its owner had the power to turn words into flesh. Her friend hadn't believed it, had fought against it. Who wouldn't? The whole idea was insane. But when Cat had changed a story and it'd changed reality, they'd known: Cat could bring fictional men to life.

That's when Eliza had come up with this nutso idea: to throw a Regency-themed ball in the Treasure Trove, Cat's downstairs bookstore, in order to bring an English duke, one Cat would create for her, forward in time to find Eliza—and take her back with him.

Over the last two weeks, the friends had played around for hours on the British Museum's online site and on Pinterest, researching and plotting and drafting to their heart's content, until Eliza was satisfied with her dream duke—someone she envisioned as a cross between Hugh Jackman, Colin Firth, and the hero of every romance she'd ever read.

Her heart swelled with the idea that she would be meeting him tonight. So did her anxiety levels. Because, really, even if this duke, this Deveric Mattersley, as Cat had named him, *did* show up and whisk her back two hundred years, who was to say he'd actually fall in love with her, Eliza James, twenty-nine-year-old widow, perpetual grad student, a woman too fond of brownies and not fond enough of exercise? She wasn't exactly ideal duchess material.

She shook off those thoughts. Who was to say she'd fall in love with *him?* Love was a two-way street, after all. And it would work out as it should. It would. She had to believe that.

"I'm sorry for leaving you, Cat. I love you like the sister I never had. Thank you for understanding … and for letting me go."

"I'm not letting you go. I'll just have to meet you in a difference place." Cat backed up a step. "If this works, that is. May I admit I'm secretly hoping it won't?"

"You may," said Eliza. "But if it doesn't, I know you were willing, and that means everything to me." She wiped more tears off her cheeks. "Thank goodness most Regency women didn't wear mascara," she said, "or I'd resemble a raccoon right now."

She breathed in and out, in and out, working to calm herself. This was going to work. This had to work. There wasn't much here for her, anyway, besides Cat. Eliza'd lost her husband ten years ago, and then her parents. She loved her best friend, but she wanted more. Now that Cat was hopefully on the verge of her own happy-ever-after, it was Eliza's time for more, right? She lifted her chin up, adjusting her breasts in her dress a final time before pulling on her evening gloves. *Start as you mean to go on, girl.* She sniffed as she checked one last time to ensure her jewelry and phone were tucked in the hidden pocket she'd added to the costume.

Cat handed her a Kleenex. "C'mon, Miss Austen, let's go greet our guests."

Chapter 2

Deveric strode into the room, adjusting his shirt cuffs under his navy-colored tailcoat, satisfied he'd intimidated his brother into staying away from the gaming tables later that evening. Now to dress for his mother's blasted ball.

Shaking off thoughts of Chance, he paused. An eerie wave of dizziness washed over him, and he closed his eyes, fighting for balance. Upon opening them, shock shot through him, sending frissons of unease racing around his whole body.

He'd been heading for his study to join his friends, Arth and Coll, for a quick drink before the evening's activities. Now, he was in a different room entirely. A ballroom, from the looks of it, but not *his* ballroom. People filled the space, but none of their faces were familiar. *What the devil?*

He stood stock still, as if his Hessian boots were rooted to the floor. What had happened? How did he get here? Where *was* here? Everyone was staring at him, scrutinizing him from head to toe. He scanned the room, senses alert. No one appeared armed or threatening, but he wished he had his pistol, regardless. Who were these people? Their hair and garments looked foreign, not quite right in cut or style.

His stomach lurched as the room spun around him. The strains of a waltz tickled his ears, but no musicians were in sight, even as a few couples moved in awkward steps around a small open area. Attuning his senses, he sought out the source of the music, his eyes zeroing in on a black box perched on top of a bookshelf. On it sat a small, rectangular item somehow illuminated from within. Echoes of Mozart bounced through the room. There was no other conclusion he could draw than that the box with the lit-up object on it was making the noise.

His eyes bulged and his jaw dropped. He could almost hear his mother chiding him to stop making such a spectacle of himself—there was the family reputation to uphold, after all, and a Claremont did not panic—but he couldn't stop his gaze from darting around the space in which he found himself. It was an odd ballroom, undersized and lined with bookcases at its edges, each filled with numerous volumes.

A ball in a library?

Everything was all wrong.

Black dots swam before his eyes as he looked up, attempting to regain his composure. Simple glass-covered globes, not the grand chandeliers of Clarehaven's ballroom, hung at regular intervals from the ceiling. The candles in them weren't lit. The warm glow from the fire in the fireplace and a few thick, flickering, pillar-shaped candles on the tops of the bookshelves were the only sources of light.

Suddenly, two bright lights shone through the front window, brighter than anything he'd ever seen. They moved at an incredible rate of speed, flashing by in an instant, and Deveric raced toward the door, pushing past a dancing couple as he tried to determine the source.

"Hello. I'm Eliza, Eliza James," came a voice from his right. He looked down as a young woman hooked her arm through his and smiled up at him. Perhaps not so young, he amended, noting the small lines starting to form around her eyes. But she, at least, looked properly attired, more so than anyone else in the room, though the bodice of her dress was perhaps overly snug. He stared a moment too long before quickly moving his eyes back up to her face, his ears burning. *Gentlemen do not openly ogle women's bosoms, even ones as plentiful as this one.*

She was a beauty, with eyes of a startlingly deep blue and hair a fine straw-colored blonde. He fought the inexplicable urge to touch one of the tendrils hanging down near her delicate ear.

No woman of good breeding would ever approach a man on her own and introduce herself, much less slip her arm through his in such a familiar manner. His eyes flickered down to her bosom again. The dress was no lower-cut than those worn by his sisters, and yet the mounds straining against the bodice definitely sparked a very unexpected, very non-familial response.

His mother would be appalled at the way this woman so brazenly presented herself. Was she a member of the demi-monde, a woman well-versed in the art of seduction? That would explain her unusual behavior.

"Mattersley. Deveric Mattersley." Damn, why had he introduced himself with his full name? He hadn't made that mistake in years, not since he was a child. *Simply not done, Claremont*, his mother would say. Even his mother always called him Claremont.

The woman nodded, still smiling. Her grin was unnaturally wide, showing a large amount of teeth. Startling. At least they were straight, and white. He pulled his eyes away. Why in God's name was he noticing a woman's teeth?

No recognition showed in the woman's eyes. She didn't know the Mattersley name?

"Duke of Claremont," he added to fill the stilted silence. He pulled at his cravat, which suddenly choked him, acutely aware all eyes were on him and the woman. People were whispering to each other and pointing. Pointing? No one of his association was so vulgar as to point. He lowered his voice. "Where am I? What is this place?"

For Deveric Mattersley, seventh Duke of Claremont, was now absolutely certain he was no longer in his own ballroom, but was, somehow, somewhere else.

The woman pulled gently on his arm, leading him toward the back of the room. Still smiling that strange smile, she replied, "This is a New Year's ball."

"But it's March." He fought to retain his composure—*a Claremont did not panic*. He surveyed the crowd once more. Another thought hit him. "And you speak oddly. American?"

Rather than answering, she turned away. A woman across the room nodded in their direction as this Eliza James pulled on his arm again. He followed her without thinking, his mind racing. Who was that other woman? What was happening? He fought to breathe. *A gentleman does not show confusion, or fear.*

Suddenly, a rather heavyset woman held a black rectangle to her eye, similar to the one on the mysterious music box, and yelled, "Say cheese!" A flash shot out from the rectangle.

"What the devil?" Deveric reacted instinctively, throwing his arm in front of his face and stepping in front of Miss James to shield her from whatever weapon this was.

Miss James, however, ignored his question and the

flashing object, grasping his arm tightly as she guided him through the doorway from which he had entered into a small room off the corridor beyond.

"What are you doing? Where am I?" He fought to control the churning in his stomach as everything swirled around him. "This must be a dream. A bizarre dream, where music plays without an orchestra, and where lights flash by at inhuman speeds ..." His voice trailed off. He thought he might faint. How embarrassing. He, Claremont, succumbing to a fit of vapors. It was almost enough to make him laugh. *A Claremont most assuredly does not faint.*

The woman said nothing, those impossibly blue eyes wide as she stared at him. It was almost as if she were as perplexed by what was happening as he was. Except no, she'd led him here. She must know what she was about.

He could hear people counting down, and then the blare of some sort of horn instrument. As the off-key strains of people singing *Auld Lang Syne* filtered around the doorframe, the woman pulled his head down to hers, kissing him with those rose-hued lips. Even in his bewildered state, his body reacted instantly to the female form pressing itself against him. How peculiar. It'd been years since a woman had sparked such an intense, burning response.

As her lips danced over his, he murmured, "A dream." Yes, he had to be dreaming. Nothing else made sense. And if it were a dream, why not indulge? He couldn't hurt anyone in a dream, after all. Intensifying the kiss, he stroked her lip with his tongue. "A very satisfying dream, with my very own goddess to entice me." His hips pressed into hers, and he leaned her back against the door, anxious to continue this now very pleasant fantastical interlude.

Then the world turned black.

CHAPTER 3

January 1st, 2012. Or not.

*It is a truth universally acknowledged that a woman
who's just traveled across an ocean and back two
hundred years in time might find herself in a bit of
a pickle. Unless that woman discovers herself to be
trapped in the arms of a man in possession of a good
fortune ... and in want of a wife.*

Eliza blinked her eyes as that corny perversion of
Jane Austen's opening line to *Pride and Prejudice*
flitted through her mind. She looked down at
the man in whose arms she was awkwardly wedged. He was
half-sitting, half-leaning on a settee sofa, out cold. His arms,
however, held her firmly, and even as she attempted to shift
to survey her surroundings, he clutched her to him. His
warmth and size enveloped her, a strange energy humming
between them.

Peeking out over her left shoulder, Eliza could see she was

in a library of some sort. Not a public library, but rather an old-fashioned personal library, like the ones she always read about in her novels. Built-in bookcases lined the two walls, filled with volumes of books in antique-style bindings—only in pristine condition. A fireplace separated the shelves on one wall, and a large portrait of an older gentleman in a white curly wig hung on the oak panels over it.

Turning to the right, she lifted her head a bit in order to see over the back of the sofa. A large, heavy, ornately carved desk, which was covered with papers, sat near a back wall containing more bookcases. A real inkstand rested on top of the desk, and next to it, several quill pens. An old clock ticked forlornly from the wall behind the desk. She couldn't see the entryway into the room—it must be behind her—but the distant strains of a violin and the low murmurings of conversation drifted in from somewhere close by.

She closed her eyes. If the furnishings were any indication, she was in Regency England. For real. It'd worked. It had actually worked.

The man shifted beneath her, but didn't relax his grip. Eliza's eyes flew open again as the enormity of the situation hit her. She was trapped in the arms of a duke. A duke her friend Cat created for her. An authentic Regency duke.

She whimpered, panic rising in her throat. Her stomach flopped and her head swam, as much from the weirdness of the situation as from the champagne she'd imbibed earlier.

Searching for calm, she focused on the man in whose arms she lay. He was handsome, all right—no surprise, considering she'd described to Cat exactly what she wanted when they'd concocted this crazy scheme. Dark brown hair cropped closely at the sides, though a bit longer at the nape, accentuated his high cheekbones, while a longer lock fell over his forehead, drawing her attention to the small scar cutting through his left eyebrow. His eyes were closed, but she knew they were a brilliant green, a vibrant shade she'd thought only achievable with colored contacts. Clearly she was wrong. Well, not really; Cat had added that in on purpose, knowing Eliza's weakness for green-eyed men.

She couldn't believe it. She was here. It was happening, exactly as Cat had written.

Eliza sucked in a deep breath. She'd read the story Cat had written for her so many times, she didn't need to see the paper anymore; she'd committed it to heart.

It was fairly short, more a rough sketch of things to come than a true story, but Eliza had wanted it so, had wanted it vague enough to not guarantee the ending, to have a chance at everything feeling natural, real, rather than predestined.

The words her friend had drafted warmed Eliza's heart like nothing else, a testament to Cat's love for her, as well as a blueprint for Eliza's grand romance to come:

Deveric Samuel Alexander Mattersley, seventh Duke of Claremont, Marquess of Harrington, Earl Thomas, born to Samuel Mattersley, sixth Duke of Claremont, and his wife Matilda Mattersley, nee Lady Matilda Evenston, will absolutely, irrevocably, intensely, and forever be attracted to one Eliza Anne James, for her vivacious spirit and energy, her incredible intelligence, her generous heart. He will not be able to resist Eliza's stunning face and glorious figure, despite the fact that said Eliza believes she overindulges in sweets.

Deveric needs Eliza to help him, to heal him, to love him, for like Mrs. James herself, Deveric has suffered loss. He is a widower, as she a widow. Though surrounded by family, he often feels alone, remote, separate. He needs to learn to love again, and Mrs. James is the best teacher he shall ever have.

Likewise, Eliza needs to be loved, to be the center of someone's existence, to have an outlet for all the passion and devotion she harbors in her heart.

It shall be as if from a Jane Austen novel, with Eliza as Elizabeth and Deveric, her Darcy. Or, as I prefer to imagine, a Disney movie, and Eliza the fair Cinderella. Deveric and Eliza shall find each other at a ball, with a kiss at midnight leading them magically back in time, into each other's arms. Eliza shall pull said duke to the Treasure Trove's storage room before completing this kiss, lest she freak out everyone around her by suddenly vaporizing.

I shall be crossing my fingers that this works, that my powers extend to time-travel, that love trumps scientific reality and launches my real friend back with her once-fictional, now real duke to his estate in Regency England.

Deveric shall not care that Eliza is an American of allegedly no standing (the author does not agree with the social distinctions of said period in England, but acknowledges and includes them, per Eliza's request for authenticity); all that matters to him is her character, her soul, who she is as a person. Well, and her boobs. Ha ha ha.

Deveric's many sisters shall also, I hope, come to view Eliza as a sister, as well, for she deserves that, to be surrounded by love on all sides.

Deveric Mattersley, Duke of Claremont, shall be tall, muscular, heavily masculine, garbed in Regency *attire far exceeding anything Colin Firth has worn in terms of attractiveness—with Hessians, of course, and breeches that shall make Eliza salivate whenever she sees him in them. His eyes shall be a vivid green, his face shall have a hint of Hugh Jackman to him. Because who doesn't think Hugh Jackman is wildly sexy? At least without the Wolverine hair.*

While I, Catherine Abigail Schreiber, do declare Eliza and Deveric shall fall for each other, any relationship shall evolve through choice. Should obstacles appear, Eliza and Deveric must resolve them themselves—I am no fairy godmother weaving together something no one but God can tear apart. That is for marriage vows, and Eliza and Deveric must find their way to love on their own, commit to each other on their own. The attraction I decree, the outcome I do not.

Should Eliza Anne James ever wish to return to her best friend, in the present time, she need only find the monolith on Deveric's estate (because I can't resist a good mini-Stonehenge, or the chance to pay homage to one of Eliza's favorite romances, Outlander*), need only sit on the stone at the center and wish with all her might, all her heart, all the love in her body, to be back in 2012, back with the fictional man on whom I told her to fix her attention (for I fear this Escape Clause shall not work without a man I've created as its focus, given the limitations we've discovered regarding my weird powers). Then, I do declare (and seriously hope) she will return, but only if she truly wishes to do so.*

Also, I decree that Eliza James shall have at some point the opportunity to meet Miss Jane Austen in person. (Not that I have any power to guarantee that, as Eliza well knows, but I figured it would amuse her.)

God bless and Godspeed, Eliza Anne James. You are and will always be my best friend. I shall miss you more than you can possibly imagine. Thank you for bringing zest back into my life when I thought all was lost, and for showing me now, in the midst of all the bizarre happenings of the last several months—yeah, creating people, anyone?—that I do actually know who I am, and what I want. And whom. I owe it to you, Eliza. And so I give you this gift.

Go forth, and fall in love with your Regency duke, the stuff of your beloved romance novels. As Shakespeare said, "The course of true love never did run smooth," but I hope for you, the waters never cease flowing between you and the ones you love.

You deserve that happy-ever-after, dearest friend. I wish you the greatest luck in pursuing it.

As it is written, so let it be.

Catherine Schreiber, signed this December 25th, 2011.

Her friend's words echoing in her head, Eliza studied Deveric's lips—those rich, full, sensuous lips. The memory of them moving over hers, surprisingly gently, given his rather rugged demeanor and large size, sent tingles racing through her. She nearly kissed him again, but reached up instead to rub her fingers over the faint hint of stubble on his cheek. Before she could touch his face, a hand flew up and grabbed her wrist.

His eyes were wide open now, and firmly fixed on her. They pulsated, those magnificent emerald orbs, pulling her like a magnet.

"Who are you?" he demanded. "Why am I lying down?

What happened? What was that place?"

His body tensed before he pushed her off of him and stood up. He grasped the edge of the settee, as if fighting dizziness, and cast his gaze around the room. After a second, his shoulders visibly relaxed. "Thank God. This is my study. I'm in my own study. It *was* a dream. An extraordinary dream."

Study? Not a library, then. Eliza wasn't sure what to say or do, her own nerves having her clutch at the edge of the sofa, herself. What was the protocol for time-traveling situations? Besides absolute bewilderment it'd worked in the first place.

"But you're here. You're here," he continued, whirling back toward her. "So it couldn't have been a dream." He grabbed her shoulders and shook her. "Who are you? Who put you up to this? Was it Arthington? I'll kill him."

"Ow!"

He immediately dropped his hands, his face wrenching in dismay. "I'm sorry. I—"

"It's okay. I get it."

"Oh—kay?" His brows wrinkled in confusion.

"Yeah, it's all confusing for me, too. I was hoping you'd show up, but a part of me didn't think you would, so I was making the most of it, figuring it'd be the only Regency-type ball I'd ever get to attend. And then, *boom*, there you were!" She raised her hand to her head. "Ugh. My head hurts. Guess I drank too much. Or maybe it's from the time-traveling …" She broke off, biting her lip.

His head spun as she spoke. Funny, that: unlike the woman, he hadn't yet had a drink. His eyes fell to her lip, the one she was still chewing, so plump and full. A stunning American, but lacking in manners. Definitely not a lady of refinement. She resumed talking, so he tried to focus on her words.

"And I told Cat even though *she* had clearly created those guys for her it was okay if it didn't work for me. I mean, what kind of broke grad student would ever really land a duke anyway, right? That'd be like winning the lottery."

He couldn't understand half the words she was saying. Oh-kay? Grad student? Wait—time-travel? Was the woman a lunatic?

She rubbed her hands up and down her arms as if to warm herself. "Wow, it's cold."

"Since no one was expected in here tonight, the fire wasn't drawn." He couldn't believe how calmly he'd spoken those words, given his bewilderment as to who this woman was, and how she'd got into his study. Or what had happened just before that, for that matter.

He eyed her gown, his gaze lingering on her impressive chest. His groin tightened and he clenched his fists, determined to ignore his extreme, and inappropriate, reaction to her. "You women, dressing in those absurdly thin gowns. You'll catch your death."

She muttered something about Regency styles imitating classical styles.

With her finely etched features and well-formed body, she did somewhat resemble a Greek goddess. Aphrodite, perhaps.

At that thought, his mind flew back to the last thing he could remember before all had gone black—of him calling her his personal goddess, of her kissing him with that sweet, succulent mouth.

What had come over him, kissing an unknown woman

21

like that? He hadn't allowed passion to rule him for years, even before Mirabelle died. The guilt was too strong. He'd tamped down that side of himself in atonement for his sins.

Yet this woman, this unknown, fired his blood like no one else had in a long time. If ever. He cleared his throat. He didn't even know who she was. Some tart Arthington had arranged as a practical joke? He and Collinswood did often heckle Dev for "not taking advantage of the bounty before him."

"And I agree." Her words pulled him out of his head and back to her. "I always thought these dresses, although beautiful, did seem impractical for an English winter. Though I suppose they'd make sense in a warm climate like Greece or Italy. I'd much rather be in my sweats with a thick sweatshirt, and maybe even a coat."

"In your what?"

"Oh yeah, sorry. Never mind. You wouldn't know what sweats are. I've got to be more careful in what I say."

She visibly steeled her shoulders, pasting that toothy smile on her face again as she dropped into a rather awkward curtsy. "Let's start over. Hi. I'm Eliza James."

He couldn't take his eyes off her exquisite mouth. "Who *are* you?"

"I just told you, I'm Eliza. And I know you're Deveric."

His eyes widened at her use of his first name. Only his sisters and his closest friends, James Bradley, Duke of Arthington and Morgan Collinswood, Marquess of Emerlin, called him thusly. Everyone else addressed him as Claremont.

"Oh, I'm sorry. I forgot," she offered, her cheeks pinking adorably. "I should not use your Christian name until you give me leave to do so. My pardons, Your Grace."

His brows wrinkled, although he supposed it understandable an American wouldn't know the ins and outs of the peerage. Surely even in America, however, new acquaintances did not stoop to such intimacy as Christian names on a first meeting.

Voices echoed from down the hallway, catching his attention. Someone was close by. Good God, if he were discovered here with this female, alone …

"Quick, hide behind my desk," he commanded.

"What?"

"Go on, hurry. I don't plan on being caught with an unmarried woman in my study." He glanced at her gloved hands. "You *are* unmarried, I assume, given your advances earlier?"

"Advances?" she squeaked. "I merely kissed you. Cat said I had to, to make it work." She arched an eyebrow. "And it's not as if you were complaining."

"Who is this cat to which you constantly refer?" Was she a witch, with a feline as her familiar? She didn't *look* like a witch. Not that he knew what one would look like, even if he believed in witchcraft. Which he didn't. He was far too enlightened for that. Still, a niggle of fear rooted itself under his skin. If not a witch, who—and what—was she? A succubus? She certainly had his blood running, every inch of her calling to him.

Her other words suddenly registered. "Make *what* work?"

"Me. Coming here. To Regency England. In 18-whatever it is." She cocked her head. "What year *is* it, anyway?" she added, as the voices in the hall drew closer.

"You don't know the year? 1812? Are you mad?" He shook his head. "I can't make sense of you. I can't make sense of any of this. I must have struck my head. Or you, yours." Yes, that was the only logical explanation.

As he reached up to check for a lump, the door to the library flew open, and a woman and a man fell in, enveloped in each other's arms and laughing. The woman pressed her lips against his throat as the man fastened his hands on her derriere, pulling her closer into him.

Fury rose in Deveric, blocking out all thoughts of the delectable Eliza James.

"Amara!"

CHAPTER 4

The woman broke away from her companion with a start, whirling to face the occupants of the room. She was gorgeous, Eliza noted, with that honey brown hair and fiery hazel eyes. Drop-dead gorgeous.

"Dev?" the woman said with a gasp. "What are you doing here? And who is that?"

Jealousy tickled at Eliza's insides. Which was ridiculous, considering she'd known Deveric, what, all of five minutes? Still, he was *hers*. Who was this woman, this dazzling creation, to address Deveric with such familiarity? Though she kind of liked that little nickname: *Dev*.

"I could ask the same of you!" Deveric barked.

"I'll be going now." The man hurriedly straightened his waistcoat before scurrying out the door.

The woman sighed.

"So much for chivalry," Eliza murmured.

"That was Lord Hodgins, wasn't it?" said Deveric. "I should

demand satisfaction!" A muscle ticced in his jaw. "He's courting Lady Mary Wemple, Amara. Why would—?"

"Please. You know you needn't defend my *honor*." The woman's cheeks flushed crimson red, even as she spat the final word.

Anger? Or embarrassment? A surprising spark of sympathy flickered in Eliza.

"At least he wasn't married this time," Amara went on. She gestured toward Deveric. "You're one to talk, cavorting about in your library with this ... this ... courtesan, whoever she is."

The flicker went out. Before Deveric could respond, Eliza pushed forward until she was nearly nose-to-nose with this Amara person. "I am not a courtesan!" Settling her hands on her hips, she thrust her elbows out in indignation. "I've hardly even *kissed* anyone since my husband died. Just because a woman goes on dates—er, I mean, has gentleman callers—and maybe kisses a few guys—oops, I mean men— *doesn't* mean she's a sl—a harlot."

Amara looked down her nose at her. "Real ladies don't use such language. And they certainly don't kiss a variety of men."

"Truly, Amara?" Deveric asked, his voice taking on an unexpected hint of amusement. "That, from you? I think you could outcurse me some days."

Amara glowered at him. "I've kissed far fewer men than everyone thinks," she said with a huff. "As you well know. And if I know any less-than-proper language, it's because I learned it from *you*, brother."

Brother? This Amara was Deveric's sister? Eliza exhaled in relief. Now that she thought about it, there *was* something similar in their eyes ... and their outthrust jaws.

"Wait. You're a widow, Eliza?"

Eliza turned toward him at his words. Deveric was frowning.

26

Amara gave what Eliza could only describe as a snort. *So much for delicate Regency feminine sensibilities.* "Eliza? You address her so familiarly?"

Deveric settled his arms across his chest, his eyes narrowing on his sister.

Amara ignored him. "Who are you?" she said to Eliza. "I've not seen you before today."

Eliza jumped as Amara reached out and caught up the edge of Eliza's skirt near her hips, rubbing the fabric between her fingers. Surely this wasn't normal, a woman touching another woman's clothing? Eliza might have done it to Cat, but, hey, they were *friends.* This woman was quickly becoming an enemy.

Amara released the skirt before Eliza could yank it away. "You're well-dressed, and yet your gown looks ... strange," she said, almost to herself. "I've never seen cloth of this type." She leaned over to investigate the embroidered edge of Eliza's bodice. "The stitching is amazingly even, close. And yet the gown doesn't fit you all that well."

It was Eliza's turn to snort. The woman was downright rude. Yet Eliza needed to tread carefully. This was Deveric's sister, after all. Alienating her would not help Eliza's cause.

She fought down a sudden wave of nausea. Could she pull this off? Could she get not only Deveric to accept her, but all the people around him?

Oh, my God. What was I thinking? I can't do this! She clutched her middle, willing herself not to vomit. *Cast up your accounts,* said a small voice in her head. *No puking or vomiting in these days.* An idiotic voice, that was, to be worried about exact period phrases at that moment.

"I think it fits her very well," Deveric countered, a catch in his voice.

Eliza let out a nervous giggle. Amara's eyes looked as if they were about to burst out of their sockets as she stared at her brother. The blush creeping up Deveric's neck gave Eliza a much-needed boost of confidence. If nothing else, Deveric Mattersley was definitely attracted to her. It was a start.

"Who *are* you?" Amara demanded again.

Eliza opened her mouth, but Deveric interjected. "Amara, this is Mrs. Eliza James. Our … cousin. From America."

Both Eliza and Amara gaped at him.

"Cousin?" Amara repeated.

"I am?" Eliza said. "Yes, yes, I am." She plastered a grin on her face, determined to make peace with this Amara. "Nice to meet you, Lady Amara."

Amara ignored her, her stare fixed on her brother. Eliza perused the bookshelves, unsure what to do next. The tension in the room nearly choked her.

"Yes," Deveric affirmed. "Our cousin from …"

"Virginia," Eliza said.

Dev exhaled. Was that relief on his face? "Of course. That's where our distant relatives lived, if you remember, Amara."

"You told us not two months ago they had all perished in a fire."

Deveric adjusted his cravat. "That is what I had thought, as indicated in the letter I'd received. Only this week, a notice from Eli—uh, Mrs. James' family solicitor arrived, informing me of her fortuitous survival—"

"—I was staying with a family friend," Eliza interjected, warming to his tale.

Deveric was lying for her. That had to mean something, right? Some level of interest, some desire to protect her? *Unless, of course, Cat wrote this part, too.* Eliza's smile faltered. That hadn't been in the story; was it possible Cat had written details Eliza never saw? *No. My friend wouldn't do that to me.* Deveric was covering for her of his own accord.

"Since Mrs. James is without a husband and now without family, the solicitor hoped we could find a place for her here."

Eliza managed to nod in agreement. "Yes, yes, I'm afraid I have no one back home." Her eyes filled with tears at the thought of Cat, the friend she'd left behind. One teardrop spilled down her cheek. *Good. Maybe that would convince Deveric's sister.*

Amara's eyes narrowed and she crossed her arms as she studied the two. "And she is completely without funds, unable to survive on her own? How convenient." She paused. "You shall have to do better than that if you're going to convince anyone else of this mad tale. For one thing, she's not wearing mourning dress. Odd for someone who's just lost her entire family, don't you think? Are you *sure* she is who she claims to be, Dev?"

Deveric shifted from one leg to the other, pulling at his cravat. His face, however, was a thundercloud. "You dare question—"

Eliza cut him off. "All of my things were lost at sea."

"Except a *ball gown*?" Incredulity was written across Amara's face.

"Well, um, what little I had—jewelry—is sewn into a pocket and the hem of this dress, so, um, when the Captain warned the seas were getting rough and we might need to toss cargo overboard to stay afloat, I changed into this dress, to keep the jewelry safe." Sweat trickled down Eliza's neck, in spite of the cold. *Good Lord, I need a donut.* What was she going to do if Amara refused to believe her?

Amara burst out laughing. "Most certainly, you need a better story."

Voices drifted in from down the hallway again. Amara's face sobered instantly. Deveric swallowed and ran his fingers through his hair, distinctly ill at ease.

"Why, I do believe that's Mother I hear coming," Amara said. "Good luck with your story."

"Back me up," Deveric offered through tight lips, "and I will never breathe a word about Hodgins to anyone."

Amara flinched in surprise. "You would lie, not once, but twice, in the same evening?" From her tone, Eliza could tell Deveric was not one to normally fudge the truth. *Score One for my Prince Charming.* Honesty was a valued trait, and one Eliza had seen far too little of in the twenty-first century, at least among the jackasses who'd tried to get her into bed.

Deveric's eyes darkened and a not-completely-unattractive scowl twisted his face, but he said nothing. *Score Two for not lying about lying.*

"Fine. This ought to be good." Amara waved dismissively as the door opened behind her.

A tall, regal woman swept into the room, bedecked in an ornate gown, back ramrod straight, two younger women at her side. "Aha—I knew I'd find you here, Claremont. Too busy with your papers to properly host your own ball." She stalked toward him with a ferocious swish of her skirts. "Goodness gracious, you are not even dressed!"

The confidence Eliza had channeled for her interactions with Amara dissipated completely in the face of the formidable figure in front of her. A sudden image of Maleficent from Walt Disney's *Sleeping Beauty* popped into her head. All that was missing was a staff and a raven. Even the woman's bonnet was pointy. And maybe … *were* those raven feathers peeping out from the swathes of fabric?

"Mother," Deveric said, tipping his head to her. "My

apologies; I have not had time to change."

The woman stopped in front of Eliza, drawing her chin up high as she stared down her long, aristocratic nose. "Who, may I ask, are *you*?"

Eliza wilted under the withering glance from the ferocious woman standing less than two feet in front of her. *Mother. This dragon is Deveric's mother? Oh, heaven help me.* She took an involuntary step backward. If Deveric's mother were living in 2012, Eliza was sure she'd be commanding an army. Or two.

Eliza opened her mouth to speak, but Deveric beat her to it. "Mother, this is Mrs. Eliza James, of our Virginia cousins. Mrs. James, my mother, the Dowager Duchess of Claremont."

The Dowager's lips narrowed at his announcement. "Cousin? You informed us all had perished."

Eliza watched Deveric as covertly as she could. If this woman intimidated him, he certainly didn't show it. He gave off an air of ease, as if used to being challenged by her.

"She survived the fire that took the rest of her family, our Virginia cousins," he said. "The solicitor … erred in saying all had died."

Did the Dowager hear the slight pause in his sentence? Eliza wanted to move closer to him, to seek out his protection—and frankly, his warmth, as she was shivering again. But she stood her ground.

"Mrs. James." The woman's eagle eyes burned into her. "Did your husband survive, as well?"

"No, ma-Your Grace. He died more than ten years ago."

"More than ten years?" gasped one of the young women standing to the Dowager's side, the one with ebony hair and striking blue eyes. "How old *are* you?"

As the other girl, a blonde beauty, elbowed her in the

side, Deveric's mother turned to the dark-haired woman and snapped, "Lady Rebecca Adelaide Mattersley, one *never* questions another lady as to her age."

Rebecca blushed. "My apologies, Lady James. I meant no offense."

Eliza's cheeks bent up in a smile. "It's quite all right. I'm actually Mrs. James, not Lady James. No titles in my family."

Deveric's eyebrow went up in warning.

"N-not in my immediate family, that is," she stammered. She clasped her fingers together, pinching her thumbs tightly.

"Regardless, my apologies, ma'am," Rebecca said, casting a nervous glance at her mother.

"I'm twenty-nine. Still a little young for the ma'am's, aren't I?"

The other young lady, the blonde not yet introduced, wrinkled up her forehead. "You were married, were you not? Therefore, you are a ma'am."

Dang. Another faux pas.

The Dowager actually rolled her eyes, which made her slightly less dragon-like.

Deveric cleared his throat. "Mrs. James," he said. "These are my sisters. You have met Lady Amara. As you heard, this is Lady Rebecca." He gestured toward the young woman with the black hair. "And this is Lady Emmeline." He nodded toward the blonde.

Addressing his mother again, he said, "Her family's solicitor sent a letter asking that we provide for Mrs. James. She has no other relations left in the world."

At his words, tears welled up in Eliza's eyes again. *That was certainly the truth.* And had long been. The euphoria over the success of Cat's and her wild time-traveling plan, as well as the final dregs of her champagne buzz, deserted her. She *was* all alone, suddenly dependent on this man and his family, none of whom seemed exactly accepting at the moment.

Not that she could blame them. What had she been thinking? This whole thing, her whole plan, was nuts. She patted her side, the one with the pocket containing her jewelry and phone. She wasn't completely out of options if this all went south. She hoped. Her stomach flipped. *What I wouldn't give for a piece of cheesecake about now. Or some Tums.*

"Why is this the first I'm hearing of this? When did she arrive?" The Dowager popped an eyebrow at her son. Eliza could see from where Deveric got that.

"You were busy with your preparations for the ball. It wasn't worth disturbing you over. She is, after all, my concern, not yours."

"Nonsense. If a young woman comes to stay under our roof, of course it is my concern. Propriety must be maintained. We do not need any more tarnished reputations in this family." At the last, her gaze darted to Amara, who stiffened visibly.

Pangs of sympathy hit Eliza. What had happened to Dev's sister to earn such reproof from her own mother?

"Mother," broke in the blonde. "Would it be possible for Becca and I to return to the ballroom? I do not wish to miss the opportunity to dance with Lord Derbourne; he's signed to my card for the next cotillion."

The older woman nodded in assent.

"But I don't need to go back," cried Rebecca. "I don't give a fig for dancing, and I find Mrs. James much more interesting!"

The Duchess pinched her lips, her nose arching even higher, if that were possible. "We shall continue this discussion later. We need to return to the ballroom and our guests. Perhaps you wish to dress first?" She waved a hand toward Deveric's boots.

"Not now. Our guests shall have to forgive me," Deveric said. "And because I am their gracious—and generous—host, they shall. I am not the first to wear Hessians to a country ball, Mother, I am sure."

His mother tsk-tsked, but held out her elbow to Deveric, who took it automatically. "Lady Amara," she said, "you may walk with our *honored* guest."

Amara grimaced, but fell in line behind Deveric and her mother. Leaning over to Eliza, she whispered, "Welcome to the family. Whoever you really are."

Deveric peered over his shoulder, giving Eliza a look that said, *This isn't over yet.*

Eyeing the way his coattails moved over his firm backside, Eliza grinned, in spite of her inner turmoil. *No, it's not. It's only just beginning.*

Chapter 5

Walking alongside Amara through a long corridor, Eliza did her best not to gawk at everything. It was as if she were on one of those old mansion tours she'd taken while in London a few years ago. Wooden floors gleamed under thick carpet runners. *Were these carpets Aubusson?* She'd read the term in countless romances. The walls featured numerous portraits spanning several historical periods—of Claremont ancestors, she presumed. She briefly fingered a doorknob, wondering what lay beyond it, but removed her fingers at Amara's sharp look. *She probably thinks I'm going to steal something. The silver, perhaps?*

And then there was no more time for thought, as Deveric threw open the doors to the ballroom and strode through, his family following behind. Deveric's mother headed toward two older women beckoning her with their fans, and Emmeline and Rebecca joined a group of young women at the edge of the room.

Eliza froze at the ballroom's entrance. *I've walked into a Hollywood production. This can't be real. Is this* real? The room was packed with people of all ages; young women tittering with each other behind fans, older matrons observing the figures on the dance floor. Men, young and old, a number of them looking as if they'd prefer to be elsewhere, stood aimlessly around the perimeter of the room. A few watched several of the younger ladies with hungry eyes. *Well, no change there from modern times.*

A small group of musicians in the corner was playing a lively tune. How different the music sounded—how much richer—than any speaker system she'd ever heard. She watched the violinist's fingers fly over the strings, marveling at his skill.

The people on the dance floor worked their way through an intricate set of steps. Oh Lord, she was completely out of her element. She'd watched *Pride and Prejudice*—the Colin Firth version, of course—a million times, studied Regency dances on YouTube, even gone to one of the Regency Society of Virginia's balls, but always found the great variety of dances and dance steps confusing. There's no way she could learn to dance like that, was there?

A panicked giggle finally escaped. How could she *not* be out of her element? She'd walked through history. She was a foreigner in a foreign land in a foreign time. Duh.

Amara gave her a sideways glance, suspicion in her eyes.

"I'm sorry," Eliza said. "I've never seen anything so grand." That was the truth. The "ball" she and Cat had thrown was an embarrassment compared to everything and everyone before her.

Amara smiled at that, a brittle, close-lipped smile. "I suppose not … in America."

Eliza bristled at her tone. *It's only natural, that dig.* It hadn't been that long since the Revolution, after all, as weird a thought as that was. And it being 1812, the two countries would soon be at war again. Not that she remembered many details of that conflict. Military history had never been her thing. Gosh, she hoped people wouldn't be hostile to her because she was from across the pond.

As she followed Deveric and Amara farther into the room, she chided herself. *I should've paid more attention to the actual events of this period, not just its literature.* She closed her eyes briefly, willing calm to come. She could do this. She could do—She bumped into Deveric, who'd stopped ahead of her.

"Oh, uh, sorry," she stammered, as he turned to her. He said nothing, but his eyes, those green drops of heaven, didn't leave hers. She fought the urge to leap at him, to cling to him, as if he were a port in this storm of her own creation.

His eyes darkened and his hand touched her elbow briefly. "Are you all right?"

She merely nodded, unable to form words with those emerald orbs consuming her. *So far from it. And yet so very close.*

A gaggle of young women startled her as they threw themselves at Deveric. "Your Grace," one of them gushed, "I thought you had forgotten our promised dance."

Deveric's shoulders tensed, but he bowed politely. "Never, Lady Harriet. I shall be pleased to partner with you. We were to dance the cotillion, were we not?"

"Oh," pouted the woman. "I was hoping for a waltz. I have promised the cotillion to Lord Mackleston." Several of her companions tittered, their cheeks coloring, but the woman stood her ground, actually moving a few inches closer to Deveric.

She can't be more than, what, twenty? Practically jailbait. Eliza nearly stepped in front of Deveric to claim him as her own. *Ridiculous, Lizzie. He's not yours.* Yet.

"The waltz is not a dance of which my mother approves. There shall be no waltzing here tonight." He took a step back.

Good for you. Let her go play with the boys. Leave the man to me.

Lady Harriet—Harlot, now, in Eliza's mind—tipped her head down. "Shame. Perhaps a different dance, then?"

Deveric gave her a tight smile. "I shall have to refuse. I am promised the rest of the evening to my cousin, Mrs. James, newly arrived from America."

"What?" Eliza and Amara gasped simultaneously.

The young woman scrunched her nose, as if she smelled something rotten. She said nothing, but turned away from Eliza in an obvious fashion.

Eliza's hackles rose. Reading about the cut was quite different from experiencing it.

If Deveric noticed Harlot's rude behavior, he didn't acknowledge it. "Mrs. James, this is Lady Harriet Templeton."

The group of girls around Lady Harriet watched their leader to gauge her reaction. Harriet gave Eliza a stiff nod, her lips pinching into the semblance of a smile. As she turned back to Deveric, an innocuous, pleasant expression covered her face. Her eyes flashed, though, betraying her anger. "I understand your obligation to *family*. I look forward to our next encounter, however, Your Grace."

She curtsied to Deveric, using the pose to push her bosom forward. Eliza narrowed her eyes. If the girl dipped any lower, her boobs might just spill out of that dress. *Two can play at this game.* Grateful for her own ample proportions, Eliza threw her shoulders back in order to emphasize her assets, but quickly adjusted her posture as Amara coughed at her side.

Harriet and her minions sidled away, for which Eliza was thankful. A moment later, Emmeline approached, her eyes sparkling and her face open and friendly. Perhaps here was a potential friend.

"Do you enjoy dancing, Mrs. James? The music is so lovely." The way Emmeline's eyes were scanning the crowd, Eliza wasn't sure if she wanted an answer, or had just searched for something polite to say.

"I, um, do not know these dances."

Emmeline's head whipped around. "No?" She looked at Deveric. "You are in the right hands, then. You could have no better teacher than my brother, cousin. He's quite good. All the women want to dance with him."

Eliza thought she heard Amara cough again, but Emmeline's face reflected only innocence.

Yeah, that's why they want to dance with him, girlfriend. Because he's a good instructor. It had nothing to do with the way he looks in that dark blue tailcoat. Or that waistcoat, elaborately embroidered with blue and green flowers. A bit like the purple and green blooms decorating Eliza's own gown. *Good thinking there, Cat. We already match. We belong together.*

Her eyes trailed over him. An immaculately tied cravat encircled his high-collared, perfectly starched shirt. Snug, buff-colored breeches encased firmly muscled thighs that Eliza itched to touch. *Scandalous, Mrs. James!* But he was so utterly scrumptious, like a fashion model come to life. In period clothing. She moved her gaze back up, lest he catch her ogling certain parts of him.

The mussed hairstyles of the day certainly suited him—

she loved the longer pieces threatening to spill down into his eyes. And then there was that face. He did look a bit like Hugh Jackman—kudos to Cat for that—but perhaps a dash more rugged, that aquiline nose well suited to his noble breeding.

No, all the ladies wanting to dance with him had nothing to do with those fierce eyebrows, framing those hypnotizing green eyes. Nor did his title play into anything. A duke. A real duke. Nothing at all, right?

Deveric had the grace to look mildly embarrassed at his sister's compliment. He straightened as something caught his attention from across the room. He turned to Eliza, his green eyes boring into hers. "I shall return to you, as promised," he said "I have some matters to discuss with my brother. It shall not take long. I beg your pardon."

Eliza's cheeks tingled under the intensity of his gaze. *At least he doesn't seem interested in that Harriet chit ... I'd be so disappointed if he were, what with her practically still in the cradle. And because he's mine.* At that thought, her face burned even hotter. *Not mine yet,* she reminded herself. And there was no guarantee he would be, no matter what Cat wrote.

"Y-yes, Your Grace." She reached up, twirling one of the tendrils hanging near her face, until Amara gave her a look. Drat. It was an old habit, one she used to comfort herself, but a ball was apparently not the place for that. Or perhaps the nineteenth century wasn't the place.

Deveric swallowed. "Amara, will you stay? Chance needs me, whether he knows it or not."

Concern creased Amara's face. "Of course."

As Deveric strode away, Emmeline also took her leave, announcing she was in need of refreshment, though she trailed after a handsome young man who'd wandered by seconds ago.

Left in silence with Deveric's sister, Eliza's mind reeled. Since when did Deveric have a brother? Cat hadn't written anything about a brother, she was sure of it. Unease snaked through her veins. What other surprises awaited her?

Half of her wanted to go home. Maybe this was too much. Maybe one's ultimate fantasy coming true wasn't all it was cracked up to be. How ironic; that's exactly what Cat told her after they'd figured out Cat's new magical abilities. Eliza figured there could be nothing better than being able to create one's Perfect Man, but Cat had insisted there were side effects one needed to consider, a notion Eliza had blown off.

Well, Eliza was considering those potential side effects now. For, really, how could a twenty-first century American, even one fairly well-versed in the Regency literature of the day, ever hope to blend in with the nineteenth-century *ton*? These people were born to the manor, raised in the intricate etiquette and manners needed to move about successfully in polite society. Eliza was just a regular old Virginia girl, raised on fried chicken, McDonald's, and Diet Coke. Sure, she'd looked through *Debrett's* and studied up on titles and forms of address in the past two weeks, but how could she have thought that was enough?

Plus, who was she to think she would *ever* have a shot with a duke? It was like believing she could get a billionaire to fall in love with her in her own day. Her chances of failure here—with Deveric, and with society as a whole—were devastatingly high.

No. Don't think that way. You've been here, what, an hour? Start as you mean to go on. You can do this, Eliza James. You can.

Now if only she believed herself.

Amara remained silent, which rather surprised Eliza. She

41

figured Deveric's sister would grill her, now that they were alone and she had the chance. Maybe that just wasn't done, no matter how much one might want to. Or maybe, Eliza thought, as she caught the miserable expression on Amara's face, *she's going through something, and I don't register on her scale right now.* She almost wanted to hug the woman, but that likely wouldn't earn anything but scorn, so she refrained, instead choosing to study the people around her.

Many were looking in Amara's and her direction, though if Eliza tried to meet any of their eyes, they averted their gazes.

She wished Deveric would return. Being the object of everyone's attention—everyone except the one whose attention she wanted—sucked.

After a few moments, two gentlemen—one a tall, lanky fellow with a mop of black hair, the other a bit shorter and more muscular, with sandy blonde hair and a square jawline—approached.

"Lady Amara," the blonde one said. He nodded toward Deveric's sister, but his sky-blue eyes fixed on Eliza.

Wow, they really knew how to grow them in the Regency.

His exquisitely carved lips parted into a snaggle-toothed smile that somehow rendered him even more appealing; men with perfectly straight, obsessively white teeth always seemed unnatural to her.

She peeked at the taller one. He was perhaps not quite as classically handsome as the blonde, but his wide-set blue eyes crinkled as he greeted Amara, his lips cracking into a grin that revealed dimples to die for. *Heaven help me, Cat. Did you have to make them* all *so good-looking?*

Then again, *had* Cat drafted these fellows? Eliza had no clue. It was hard to fathom, her friend's power. Neither one of them knew exactly how it worked, beyond that Cat could write a love story and bring the hero to life. Once real, though, he had his own complete life story, back history, family ... as evidenced in the men Cat had dated, and now Deveric's family.

Her head ached. She'd been awake for a good eighteen to twenty hours or so, and that, combined with the champagne and, well, the time-travel, had her longing for a bed to crawl into. Where would she sleep? And when would she get to go to bed? Balls often lasted into the wee hours of the morning; not exactly ideal for her morning-person self.

"Gentlemen!" Deveric said as he approached again, addressing the blondie, then the dark-haired fellow. He smiled broadly at the men. *His* teeth were quite fine, actually. Considering some of the tooth situations she'd seen happening with other men and women here in the last few minutes alone, she should give thanks for a full set of pearly whites that actually looked clean.

The blonde gave a pointed look first to Deveric, then Eliza.

Dev gave him a nod. "Mrs. James, may I present the Duke of Arthington and Marquess of Emerlin? Arthington, Emerlin, my cousin, Mrs. James."

"A pleasure to meet you, Your Grace and, er, Lord Emerlin," Eliza said. She dropped a quick curtsy, hoping she'd gotten both that and the titles right.

At her words, Arthington raised his eyebrows. "An American cousin? You have family in the colonies?"

The colonies? It's 1812, dude.

"Distant relations," Deveric said.

"The pleasure is ours." The Marquess of Emerlin had a pleasant lilt to his speech. *Irish?*

"Will you be joining us for that drink at last, Claremont?"

Arthington said.

"Oh," Amara interjected, a smirk playing at the edges of her lips, "my brother has promised to stay at our cousin's side all evening, seeing how she is newly arrived and all."

When both men focused those blue eyes on her at once, Eliza wanted to melt into the floor.

"Your husband is not here?" Emerlin's voice was soft.

"I'm a widow."

At her response, Arthington's lips curved up.

"Off with you," Deveric said, his voice affectionate in spite of the harsh words. "Go mind that my scamp of a brother doesn't spend all of the Claremont fortune, will you?"

Arthington looked as if he wanted to say something else, but Emerlin grabbed him by the arm. "Come now, you must obey a duke's command."

"*I'm* a duke," Arthington grumbled, but after bowing to both Amara and Eliza, he wandered off with his friend.

Amara straightened her shoulders. "Excuse me, dear brother and dearest *cousin*, but I believe I shall find Aunt Josephina and engage her in a rubber of piquet. No better way to make up for having to attend a ball than by trouncing persons at cards." With that, she turned and pushed her way through the crowd toward a doorway off to the left.

"She doesn't enjoy dancing?" Eliza said to Deveric.

There was a small, stilted silence. "She is not often asked."

"Why not?"

Deveric's jaw clenched. "I understand Americans are quite forward, but seeing as we have just met, and you are not truly family, I do believe I've said quite enough."

Eliza wasn't sure what to say after such a reprimand, so she simply stood next to him. Curious glances flew her way often, but no one approached them. Looking at Deveric out of the corner of her eye, she could see why; his face was tight, closed, his eyebrows dark over his eyes. Downright formidable, in fact, as he shot a heated glance in her direction. Was that anger? Or something else?

"I'm sorry," she offered.

His eyebrows rose in surprise. "For what?"

"For … I don't know—for being too direct? Causing problems in your family? For all the confusion? For kissing you?"

His pupils flared as his gaze dropped briefly to her lips. "I can't exactly say I'm sorry for the kiss. It was magnificent." He cleared his throat as if embarrassed by that admission.

The orchestra struck up a new tune.

"Are you sure you do not wish to dance?"

Eliza snickered. After all the crazy events of the evening, this duke was asking her to dance? "You needn't be so polite. I promise you, I don't know the steps. Even if I did, I'd likely trod on your feet and crush you."

"You'd hardly crush me," he answered. "You are quite small."

Small? He thinks I'm small? Glancing down at her dress, in which she felt a bit like a stuffed sausage, she murmured, "I disagree, Your Grace. I think there's rather too much of me."

"Oh, no," he said. Why did it sound as if he were choking? "You are perfect. Absolutely perfect."

As her eyes flew to his face, he cleared his throat again, looking away. Was that red on his cheeks? *This is a good sign, Cat. The physical attraction between us is real, if nothing else yet.* It was a start, right?

She nearly grinned, until he whipped his head back around, his green eyes piercing her blue ones. "Who are you, in truth?" All signs of flirtation had fled from his voice—if, indeed, they were there to begin with.

"I told you. I'm Eliza James. I'm from Charlottesville, Virginia. I truly am a widow." *Might as well get it out in the open now.* She sighed, glancing around quickly to ensure no one was within earshot. "And … I'm from the year 2011."

Deveric jerked, the muscles in his jaw ticcing. "I beg your pardon," he demanded, incredulity written across his face as he leaned closer to her, fixing her with that intense gaze.

Eliza shrank back, longing for a chair in which to sit. Exhaustion and nervousness were setting in with a vengeance. She didn't blame him for his reaction; it was hard enough for *her* to believe it, and she was the time-traveler, from an era in which time-travel, while not possible—at least not until now—was routinely discussed and depicted in books and movies.

She took a deep breath, forcing herself to stand tall. *Start as you mean to go on, girl. Sure, he's wigging out, but don't let him intimidate you.* "I'm from 2011. Or I guess 2012, now, since today is New Year's Day. At least it was, for me. I, um, traveled back in time to get to you. Well, except that first you came forward to me." *She wasn't about to tell him her friend had created him. No-sir-ree, Bob.*

Deveric ran his fingers through his hair and closed his eyes for a moment. "You're telling me that earlier this evening, I was in *2012??* Two hundred years from now? With *you?*"

"Yes."

"I should escort you to the door right now. You're a madwoman. Or someone put you up to this. Either way, this is insane. Yes, I should remove you from my presence at once."

Frissons of fear snaked up Eliza's spine. *If he kicks me out, what will I do? Where will I go?* She forced herself to breathe, struggling to present a calm demeanor. She and Cat had prepped for such an emergency, after all. She patted the pocket holding her jewelry. Surely she had enough to survive for a while, at least until she could use the escape plan Cat had written for her.

But she didn't want to use it. She didn't want to. This ferociously handsome man was her duke, and she wasn't giving up that easily. No romance heroine would. That's not how the stories worked.

Showing him the phone would convince him, wouldn't it? Or would that just make it worse? This was the Enlightenment, but there were still those who believed in the supernatural, in witchcraft. Had she just leapt from a twenty-first century frying pan into a nineteenth-century fire?

She bit her lip, hard. She wasn't reading a novel. This wasn't fiction, not anymore. No, she was standing right in front of a living, breathing duke, and he was a real person. One currently staring at her as if she'd grown a third eye.

"You could," she agreed. "I probably would want to, if I were you." She closed her eyes, steeling her shoulders. "Go ahead."

Chapter 6

*D*everic made a sound under his breath, not sure what to do. That was a feeling to which he was unaccustomed, and one for which he didn't care. He'd always been certain of the world and his place in it. He was a duke, for goodness' sake. One step below royalty. Always in control.

Until tonight. Until he'd heard music from a box, until he'd seen brighter lights than could possibly exist, moving at speeds faster than anything could move. Until he'd kissed this woman.

It couldn't be true, her wild claim. People simply could not travel through time. But *something* had happened. He'd been here, and then elsewhere. Could it have all been an illusion, some sort of magic trick? His mind refused to consider something otherworldly. That was as preposterous as this woman's assertions—despite what Rebecca might say, with her penchant for indulging in Gothic novels.

No, something had definitely happened. Something he

didn't understand, but desperately wanted to. Needed to. He needed to know what had happened this evening, needed to understand Eliza James, to comprehend this pull toward her that had his blood racing through his veins, his hands itching to touch her.

He couldn't dismiss her, even if he wished to. Not yet. "That would be difficult to explain, now that I've introduced you as our cousin."

"You could admit you lied. Or say I did, I guess."

He stiffened. "I would never impugn your honor in such a way. And I never lie."

Eliza laughed out loud. "You look like a scared, angry cat with your fur all ruffled up. And what do you mean, you never lie? You lied to your family not fifteen minutes ago!"

He opened his mouth to retort. How dare she? As he was about to lay into her for comparing him to a feline—a *feline!*—a voice broke in from behind him.

"Good evening, dearest brother. Once again, you have found the most beautiful woman in the room. May I beg an introduction?"

A young man stepped into view, flashing a smile at Eliza, a wide cheeky grin with more than a hint of seductiveness to it. Eliza coughed, her own cheeks turning a rather becoming apple red.

Deveric scowled at his brother, but dutifully performed the introductions. "Mrs. James, this is my brother, Lord Chance Mattersley. Chance, this is *Mrs.* Eliza James," he said, emphasizing the Mrs. It delighted him to see Chance's grin falter. "She's our cousin. From Virginia."

"It's a pleasure to meet you," Eliza said, dropping a curtsy.

Chance extended his hand. Eliza's eyes flashed to Deveric, confusion in them, but she stuck her hand straight out. His

49

devilish brother grasped it and turned it so he could press his lips to her knuckles. Deveric wanted to strike him.

A titter burst out from Eliza as his brother released her hand. Did she just bat her eyelashes at the scamp?

Women had always thrown themselves at his younger brother. Emmeline said it was Chance's devil-may-care attitude: "He's all rake and roué." Perhaps. He certainly lived life to its fullest—if one could consider those habits fulfilling.

The idea of Eliza succumbing to his brother's seductive ways sent waves of alarm—and jealousy—crashing through Deveric. It was all he could do not to wrap his arm around Eliza's waist and pull her to him, claiming her for his own. *Good God, man, what was happening?* Possessiveness had never been his nature.

Until now. It made no sense.

"Cousin?" Chance said. "We have cousins in America?"

"Surely you jest." At Chance's blank expression, Deveric heaved a sigh. "Too busy gallivanting about Town, gambling away your inheritance, and chasing every damsel who crosses your path to attend to family matters?" He stopped himself. What was he doing? *A Claremont did not spill family secrets.* No matter how irritated he was to see Eliza responding to his brother's infernal flirting.

A wounded expression crossed Chance's face, but he replaced it instantly with an insolent grin. "Someone's got to do it, brother—might as well be me."

"I can think of far better ways for you to be spending your time."

"I'm sure you can, but right now I'd like to spend my time dancing with our new cousin here," Chance answered smoothly, offering a hand to Eliza as he made a bow.

"I'm sorry," she offered, "but I have a headache."

Deveric frowned. Did she? He should have attended her better.

"Perhaps a lemonade would help. I'll be happy to fetch you one." Chance took off across the room before Eliza could say anything.

"You certainly have my brother under your spell," Deveric muttered as he watched Chance push his way through the crowd.

"Please don't say that." Eliza twirled that adorable tendril again, her eyes troubled. "I promise I'm not supernatural."

"No," he replied wryly. "Just a woman of unknown origin and unknown connections who claims to be from two hundred years in the future. And for whose sake, for reasons unknown to me, I lied to my family."

Deveric prided himself on his honesty above all else. It was a value he held dear, and yet he'd broken it the minute this woman had landed, literally, in his lap. It unnerved him, his willingness to lie for her, almost as much as the earlier events of the evening did. He would get to the bottom of this, get to the bottom of the mystery of Eliza James. And then he would be free of her, of this incomprehensible allure she held for him.

Except he had publicly claimed her as a relative. Damnation.

Chance returned almost as quickly as he'd left, proffering a drink to Eliza. "Here's your lemonade, Mrs. James."

"Chance!" called a voice, as Eliza took a sip. Chance searched for the source, and then rolled his eyes. "It's Emmeline. She probably wishes to introduce me to another of her cloying friends."

"Probably," answered Deveric. "But it would be most rude to ignore her. Off you go."

Chance raised a brow at him, but Deveric ignored it. He didn't want to examine why he felt so territorial about Eliza, even as half of him wanted to never see her—or hear her ludicrous claims—again.

Chance flashed Eliza another grin, and then with a "Pardon me," crossed the room to their sister. Tugging at his shirtsleeves near his wrists, Deveric studiously avoided Eliza's gaze.

A Claremont always knows what to do. Except when he doesn't.

"You must wish to be alone with me, the way you keep running everybody off," Eliza teased, nursing the rather bland lemonade. When Deveric stiffened, holding his back perfectly erect, she winked at him.

She didn't know what had gotten into her. Normally, she wasn't this forward with men. She couldn't even figure out why she wasn't freaking out more, considering she'd left everyone and everything she'd known and traveled back in time to be with a man. *This* man.

Except that a part of her—a big part—wondered if it all weren't a dream. A lucid dream, perhaps, in which she could control the action, but a dream just the same. For no one could *actually* travel through time, could they? And if they had, would they be calmly standing next to a duke, wishing to waltz with him? Wouldn't they be in meltdown mode? Or something?

She shrugged. If this was a dream, she might as well enjoy it. Only in her dreams would she be dancing with a duke anyway; in real life, she had two left feet.

A yawn caught her by surprise. *Did one yawn in dreams?* Apparently.

Deveric's lips flattened into a line. "You are tired. Perhaps you'd like to be shown to a chamber, and we can discuss this further in the morning?"

"Yes. Please." As much as she didn't want everything to end, she was about to fall over. If one slept in one's dreams, is that what Poe meant by a 'dream within a dream?' Not that anyone here would know Poe—he was too late for this period.

"Very well." Waving a hand, Dev called a footman over. "Please have one of the maids escort Mrs. James to a chamber."

The footman scampered off to attend his command.

"Couldn't you just take me? I don't want to bother anyone else."

"Certainly not," Deveric replied, indignation in his eyes. "Whatever you may be, *I* am a gentleman. Escorting a lady to a private chamber is not done."

"Okay. Settle down. I wasn't planning on jumping you," she retorted. Not that half of her wouldn't like to, but she *was* tired.

"Oh-kay? Jumping me?"

She wanted to laugh at the perplexed look on his face. *I must be more careful in my word choices.* "I guess those are American expressions. I meant I have no intention of impugning your—or my—honor."

"My apologies, Your Grace," the footman said upon his return, "but I am told there are no more chambers free." His eyes darted to Eliza.

"Good God. Mother must have invited all of London to this house party." He gave the footman a curt nod. "Then have someone escort Mrs. James to the Duchess's chamber. I assume you can quickly ready it for a guest?"

The footman's mouth fell open, but he immediately closed it. "Yes, Your Grace." He turned to Eliza. "If you could follow me, my lady?"

Eliza blinked. The Duchess's chamber? She had to room with that dragon? "Why am I going to your mother's room?"

"Not my mother's. My wife's."

"Your wife's?" Eliza's heart fell. It didn't make sense. Cat said he was a widower. Had he remarried? What was going on?

"My deceased wife," Deveric bit out, eyeing the footman, who was watching the exchange with barely concealed interest. "We will talk more in the morning, Mrs. James. Go now," he said, before turning and striding across the room without a backward glance.

Brandy. He needed a drink. Make that several.

Dev stalked out of the ballroom and back to his study, not caring whether or not his mother would approve. He was the Duke; he could bloody well leave his own ball if he wished. It wasn't *his*, anyway; it was his mother and his sisters who'd insisted on this final party before removing to London for the Season.

Grabbing the brandy off the sideboard, he sank into his chair with gusto, uncorking the decanter and taking a drink without bothering to fetch a glass. Hardly the behavior of a gentleman, but he didn't feel like a gentleman tonight. He was a caged beast, a tiger wanting to lash out at everything and everyone around him, not understanding how he'd got himself trapped to begin with.

For he felt caged. Caged by society, caged by expectation. Even caged by his inexplicable reaction to Eliza James. He wanted nothing more than to follow her up to his wife's chamber, to peel that dress from her shoulders, to bury himself in her lush body.

And he didn't like it. All it took was a few hours and one woman—granted, one incredibly beautiful, intoxicatingly sensual, intriguingly mysterious woman—and he was ready to disregard the self-control he'd worked so very hard to cultivate?

No. Simply unacceptable. A man ought to retain control of his physical passions at all times. Especially a man like Deveric. For passion could bring tragedy, and he wouldn't endure that again, no matter how appetizing Mrs. James appeared in that overly snug bodice.

He raked his fingers through his hair, willing his body to calm down. What *had* happened tonight? It was beyond his comprehension, a frightening prospect in and of itself. This Eliza James claimed to be from the future. Claimed to have come back in time. For him.

Why? Even if he accepted her time-travel assertion—which he most decidedly did *not*—why would she say she had come back for *him*?

Goosebumps raced along his skin. Ridiculous. Goose-bumps were for women. He took another swig of the liquor, grateful for the calming sensation the fiery liquid produced.

What could he do? This wasn't a situation he could discuss with Arth and Coll. "Excuse me, gents, what would you do if a woman dropped into your lap, claiming to be from 2012?" No, that would never do. He must reason this out on his own.

He stared at the sofa, the sofa on which just hours earlier he'd awoken to find the delectable Mrs. James wrapped in his arms. His body ached to hold her again. His mind demanded answers.

Images flashed through his head, images of bright lights and flashing boxes and mechanical music.

He shut his eyes.

Tomorrow. Tomorrow he would get to the bottom of this. Tomorrow he would question her and solve this mystery. Logically. Rationally.

But for now, he would let his mind wander … over her form. For while he'd never indulge in reality, fantasy was a perfectly fine arena in which to let his passions run free. And his passions—intellectual, emotional, physical—all centered on one maddening woman.

Mrs. Eliza James.

CHAPTER 7

*E*liza rolled over in the bed, burrowing deeper beneath the covers, refusing to open her eyes. *Ugh. I bet the alarm is going to go off any minute. This is going to be a three cups of coffee day, at least.* Especially given the excruciating headache pounding through her temples. Yuck. She hated hangovers.

"Good morning, my lady," a voice called.

"Cat? Is that you?" she slurred, trying to rub the sleep out of her eyes. She heard a scraping noise, and then light suddenly flooded the room.

"I'm Betsy. I've come to help you dress."

Eliza sat straight up, her eyes rounding at the sight of a young woman standing at the foot of the bed. She clutched the blanket to her chest as she took in her surroundings. She was in a sumptuously outfitted chamber, lying in a plush canopied bed with curtains tied back on all sides. A tall, sturdy oak table stood to the side against the wall between two windows, which were flanked by velvet-looking drapes.

The drapes. The woman—Betsy—must have opened the drapes.

Across from the bed was a fireplace, with a fire crackling brightly. On the right side of the bed against the interior wall sat a gorgeous, intricately ornamented desk-like piece of furniture. Eliza stared at the lion's heads brass drawer pulls. *Oh my God. It isn't a dream. It isn't a dream. I'm here. I'm really here! Wherever here is …*

Hearing soft splashing, Eliza looked back over to see Betsy pouring water out of a large pitcher into a basin. "You may perform your toilette here, my lady, and then please let me know when you're ready to dress."

She curtsied to Eliza, and then walked to the desk and lifted its lid, revealing a mirror on the underside. A chair to the side of the desk looked remarkably like an antique chair her grandfather had had in his study, complete with the green velvet seat covering.

"Thank you very much. I appreciate all of your help. I'm Eliza, by the way."

Betsy's eyes widened. "Yes, my lady. It is no trouble."

"Please, call me Eliza."

Betsy looked down, twisting her thumbs around each other. "I don't think that would be appropriate, my lady."

Eliza blinked. It was one thing to read about servants always *Yes, My Grace, no miladying* everyone in this time period, but quite another to hear a person insist they couldn't address her as an equal. She didn't particularly care for it.

Shifting in the bed, Eliza suddenly realized she was clad only in the slip—*chemise, it's called here*—she'd worn under her dress the night before. At least it covered her modern bra and undies; she didn't want to see what kind of reaction those would get.

Betsy walked over to an armoire next to the fireplace and

pulled out a long-sleeved, high-necked white gown. "Lady Amara has lent you this morning dress until suitable clothing can be found for you. She said you lost all your possessions at sea, my lady."

Eliza nodded. Fighting the small panic in her throat, she said, "May I ask, Betsy, where my gown from last night has gone?" She vaguely remembered a maid helping her out of the dress, but not what happened to it afterward.

"It's here in the cupboard, my lady."

Eliza breathed a huge sigh of relief, ecstatic her safeguard remained hidden. Heaven forbid someone found her phone. That could only bring more trouble down on her head, having to answer questions she wasn't prepared to answer. To anyone except Deveric, at least.

"I, um, have a little jewelry. Is there a safe place to store it?" She hoped Betsy wouldn't assume Eliza was accusing her of potentially stealing, but she had to ask, had to protect what little she'd brought with her.

Betsy nodded. "The Duchess, she had a small lockbox. Let me see." Betsy bent down and rummaged in the armoire before pulling out a beautifully carved cherrywood box. "Yes, here it is." The maid set the box on the table to the side of the bed.

Eliza was grateful her request didn't seem particularly out of the ordinary. Standing up, she walked to the washbasin, accepting a cloth Betsy dampened for her. As she washed her face, her arms shook. She couldn't believe she was here in a nineteenth-century bedchamber, a maid waiting upon her next command. She wished Cat were here to see it.

It had taken Cat a while to come to terms with her turning-fantasy-into-reality power. Not Eliza. She'd known instantly what she wanted. She'd dreamt for years about finding a hero, about experiencing a grand romance like those in her beloved novels, despite the fact few people she knew had found a love like that.

It was what had sustained her through her lonely childhood as an only child, especially when both her parents worked long hours. It was what had sustained her through losing her husband, Greg—because he'd made her promise if he should die in the line of duty, she'd find someone else. She deserved that kind of love, he'd said.

And as long as she was creating a fantasy, why not add a duke? It was the obvious choice, given Eliza's obsession with Jane Austen and all things Regency. Might as well aim for the top of the top, if one were going to give this insanity a whirl.

She handed the cloth she was still holding to Betsy, and then sat down on the edge of the bed, staring into the fire. If the maid thought her actions odd, she kept quiet about it.

It was what Eliza'd held on to after her parents died, too— this idea that something big, something better, something life-long was waiting. What else was there to live for? Sure, she'd enrolled in grad school under the pretense of becoming a professor, but deep down she knew she studied Jane Austen not for her literary merits—which were immense—but because of her promises of second chances in love. Even if Jane had never had a second chance herself, her characters did. Elizabeth got her Darcy. Anne her Wentworth. Surely someone was out there for Eliza?

Cat teased her constantly over her unfailing romanticism, but Eliza never doubted she'd find her prince, in spite of the fact she kept ending up in pools of frogs, all looking to be kissed—and more.

She wasn't about to make love with just anyone, though. Not because she didn't enjoy it—Lord knows she did, and missed those intimate moments with her husband. But that was exactly why she wasn't into casual sex. For her, those moments were *intimate*, meant to be shared with someone with whom you could entrust your soul, not Joe Schmo from some bar.

She sighed. Surely there were still people in the world who wanted only one other person, who wanted a true, deep, passionate, lasting love.

Was Deveric one such person? Cat had written he'd always be attracted to Eliza. But she hadn't said *only* Eliza. Eliza blew her hair out of her eyes. She rather wished Cat *had* decreed he'd be forever faithful, knowing how important that was to her.

Then again, had she known this would actually happen, that she'd be sitting here now, on the end of a nineteenth-century bed, staring into a nineteenth-century fire, with a nineteenth-century maid ready to wait on her, maybe she *would* have asked for a longer, more detailed story, one which told her exactly what to do, and exactly what would happen.

No. That's not what she wanted. Not in her heart. She wanted any relationship to evolve naturally, to be a choice on both their parts. Otherwise, how could she ever trust it?

Her eyes filled unexpectedly with tears. Contemplating a real relationship, one that could be permanent, could lead to marriage, admittedly frightened her, as much as she longed for it.

What if she lost a husband again? Deveric's green eyes flashed before her. She didn't think she could bear it, losing love a second time. She hadn't truly considered remarrying, despite her numerous dates and indulgences in flights of fancy over a forever love. In many ways, it was too scary, too painful, to think of having to endure such pain again. It was why she'd only had one true boyfriend since Greg.

Hearing Cat admit she'd walled herself off too long to

avoid hurt had jolted Eliza from her comfort zone, though. As much as she'd thought she'd been living her life, she hadn't—not when she wasn't opening up her heart, opening it truly, to what could be. That was what had motivated her to ask for it all, to reach for the highest brass ring she could, to launch this crazy scheme.

And here she was. Trying to get a Regency duke to fall in love with her. Insane.

She flopped back on the bed, the motion sending her head pounding again. Lord, how much champagne had she had last night? What she wouldn't give for some ibuprofen. And a regular toilet. Chamber pots were much better when only seen in a museum, not used, as she'd discovered in the middle of the night.

A snicker escaped her lips. It was all too much to believe, like a cheesy Hollywood rom com. *Except that it was happening to me. It* is *happening to me.* If only she knew whether this would have the "and they lived happily ever after" ending she craved, the kind people went to the movies for.

"My lady?" Betsy's voice was hesitant.

"I'd love for you to call me Eliza. Or Mrs. James, if you insist."

"As you say, my lady. Are you ready to dress?"

So much for that. My lady did feel better than ma'am, at least.

Betsy aided her into a set of stays—a half-bra, half-corset deal Eliza would rather have avoided. She still had her bra on underneath her full slip, but she'd keep that information to herself. Besides, maybe all the support would rein in her breasts better.

After Betsy helped her into the morning gown, Eliza examined it with interest. She was rather surprised it wasn't exceedingly tight on her, given that Amara, while curvy, wasn't as padded as Eliza was. Perhaps the few inches difference in height helped—or had Amara once been heavier?

More solidly made than the gown Eliza'd worn the previous evening, the dress was pure white in color, with ruffles at the wrists, and a long ruffle down the whole front of the dress. More ruffles adorned the bodice and capped the shoulders. It reminded her a bit of Seinfeld's puffy shirt. She stifled the snicker threatening to emerge.

Given the gown's warmth, she assumed it was made of wool, for which she was grateful. Even with the fire, there was a noticeable chill in the air. *Oh Lord, I miss central heat already. I wonder if my toes will ever feel warm again.*

"I'm afraid we only have your ball slippers, my lady. I will see if I can find walking boots for you."

"It's fine, Betsy," Eliza answered, grateful the ballet flats she'd worn had passed muster. "I'm sure they will do."

"But surely you will want to walk the grounds, my lady? There may also be lawn games for the ladies this afternoon. You would not want to muddy your slippers."

Eliza nodded. She should have thought of that, though the idea of going outside, where it was undoubtedly colder, wasn't exactly appealing.

"Here is a cap, my lady."

Eliza took the knitted cap; perhaps it would help against the chill. Her mother had always said ninety percent of body heat escaped through the head. Spying herself in the dressing table mirror, she grimaced. "I can't say I find this particularly flattering, Betsy." She pulled the cap back off and set it down.

Betsy's face reddened. "I can see if I can find something else, my lady, but this cap came from Lady Amara."

Eliza could have kicked herself. "I'm sorry, I meant no

offense. It's just … different from the American fashions I'm accustomed to. I think I'd rather leave it off."

Betsy nodded quickly, ducking her head. *She's probably expecting me to wear it.* Women of a certain age or marital status wore caps constantly. But Eliza couldn't relegate herself to being a wallflower widow yet—not when there was a duke to entice.

She studied herself in the mirror, dressed in this foreign garb. The high-throated, long-sleeved dress made her feel downright dowdy. She glanced at the various powders and items Betsy had laid out on the dressing table. *What I wouldn't give for a bit of mascara and some lip-gloss.* She smoothed her tongue over her teeth. *And a toothbrush.*

"The tooth powder is there on your right, my lady."

Seriously? Mind reader. How strange to have someone shadowing her, especially someone anticipating her needs. It was kind of fun this morning, but would it get old soon?

She wished she had time alone to sit and absorb her surroundings. And think.

"Let me fetch the boots. I shall return shortly." Betsy ducked out the door.

Eliza took advantage while the maid was away to empty the contents of her dress pocket into the lockbox. For a moment, she held on to the pocket watch Cat had gifted her last Christmas. It'd looked Regency-esque to Cat, in spite of the more modern numbers on its face, and she'd decided Eliza needed it. The watch wasn't particularly valuable, but Eliza had wanted it with her, anyway. She rubbed her fingers over the inscription on the back: *Friends for all time.* Indeed. Setting the watch in the box, she closed the lid before her watery eyes spilled over. No need for Betsy to catch her crying.

She could move the remaining jewelry hidden in the

dress's hem later; the bulk of her fortune, if one could call it that, as well as her phone, had been her greatest priority. She was grateful the lockbox's key was on a chain that fit easily around her neck. *There. Safe.*

Betsy popped back in, a pair of fawn-colored boots in hand. "I'll set these here." After placing the boots at the base of the armoire, she looked at Eliza. "Shall I guide you to the breakfast room, my lady?"

So much for more alone time. Eliza sighed and stood up. "I'm ready, Betsy."

I think.

Deveric lay abed far longer than he usually did, and not just because of the excess brandy he'd imbibed.

Sleep had eluded him, his mind buzzing with images: images of what he'd seen from wherever he'd been, and images of Eliza James. Eliza, the very first time he'd seen her, less than twenty-four hours ago, those sapphire eyes seducing him within ten minutes of their acquaintance. Eliza, lying atop him on the sofa settee, those same eyes wide as she'd taken in her surroundings. The memory of her soft, pliant body, so deliciously bountiful, so sumptuously curvaceous, pressed so intimately against his, had tormented him through the night, his head filled with visions of the things he'd like to do to her, with her, for her, his body rigid with desire ... and denial.

To know she slept mere steps away was almost more than he could bear. At least his late wife's bedchamber didn't directly connect to his, as was typical for a married couple. Mirabelle had insisted on her own room across the hall, saying she needed a space she knew was truly her own. Deveric had acquiesced, figuring he could visit whenever she wished him to. Which, of course, had been never.

At first, the hurt of knowing his wife didn't want him had run deep. Though theirs hadn't been a love match, he'd done everything he could to please her, in and out of the bedroom. It hadn't been enough. She'd complained he was too much—too large, too demanding, too lustful.

Eventually, he, too, had been grateful for the distance, for the separation, his wife's constant coldness scalding his heart. A man had needs, though, and at times he'd still requested a more intimate connection. Mirabelle always complied, had said she knew her duty, but she hadn't enjoyed it, had said he caused her discomfort. Guilt over those furtive, rushed encounters had never fully left him.

Amara insisted it wasn't his fault his wife didn't love him—she was certain Mirabelle was incapable of loving anybody. Deveric, however, had seen how his wife was with their son. She'd doted on Frederick, even more than Deveric had. How sad that poor Freddy barely remembered his mother now; it was Frederick whose heart had broken when she died. Not his.

Since her death three years ago, Deveric had avoided the room in which his wife had spent far too much time, had forbidden anyone to do much with it, in fact, its mere presence a painful reminder of his failures. He'd preferred to view it as a door to nowhere, a door to a past he'd rather forget. That's why no guests had been in it until now. Which is why his family, his friends, hell, even the servants had reacted last night to his command Eliza be given the room.

He'd told himself there were no other options; that since all the other bedrooms were occupied, she had to use that one. It wasn't true, of course; he could have asked one of his sisters to share a room. They would have. But he hadn't asked. Why? Why open the door to Mirabelle's ghost?

But it wasn't Mirabelle in that chamber now, it was Eliza. He groaned, flipping over and pressing himself into the mattress, wanting to assuage the ache, ignore the desire coursing through him. He must get up, get away, put space between him and the mysterious American. He had so many questions, needed so many answers.

Bounding out of bed, he stalked to the washbasin, drenching his face in cold water as he willed the rest of his body to cool down. Normally, he ate breakfast before his morning ride, but today his hunger was not for food, and the possibility of running into the entirely too tempting Mrs. James in the breakfast room was more than he could handle. He needed time and space to comprehend yesterday's events and decide his future actions.

Yanking on his riding clothes without bothering to call for his valet, Deveric exited the room and made his way outside, the cold morning mist the perfect companion to his miserable mood.

Eliza James—and all she brought with her—was a complication he couldn't afford. He preferred his life orderly, predictable—or, as Arth would say, boring. Better boredom than pain, and that's what his previous marriage, his previous investment of emotion, had brought him: pain.

"Good morning, brother." Amara's voice startled him out of his sorrowful reverie.

"Amara." He tipped his hat to her. "You are out early."

"And you, late," she responded, giving no reason for her atypical behavior. He didn't press her; both had had unusual evenings the night before, to say the least. Was it so surprising their mornings were off, as well?

"I was … contemplating last night's events."

"Our American *cousin?*"

"Among other things." Like musical boxes and flashing candles and lips more succulent than any fruit of temptation …

"Tell me truly, brother—who is she? What is she about?" The protective edge to her voice moved him. Amara had seen her own share of scandal, had weathered her own fair share of hurt. And yet here she was, looking out for him, her older brother.

"I wish I knew." At Amara's knitted brows and wrenched mouth, he added, "But she is as bewildered as we are by the recent changes in her life. I will give her the benefit of the doubt." *Until I can question her, that is.*

She studied him before nodding. "Then I shall give her the benefit of the doubt, as well. If you vouch for her, I trust your judgment. Do you continue to insist she is a relation?"

"I insist you give me time to determine the appropriate course of action." His voice was firm, though he gave her a smile.

"Understood, brother. But if she tries to hurt you or take advantage of you …"

A true chuckle escaped. "You shall what?"

Amara's eyes narrowed. "Never underestimate the power of a female. Particularly any to whom you're related."

"Indeed."

He certainly shouldn't underestimate Eliza James.

CHAPTER 8

"**G**ood morning, Eliza!"

Eliza gave Becca a grateful smile as she entered the breakfast room, happy to hear a cheerful, welcoming voice.

"Rebecca! You address our guest as *Mrs.* James," her mother chided. "You have not been given leave to use her Christian name."

Eliza bristled at the cold tone, wanting to slink under the table in face of the Dowager's withering stare. *Begin as you mean to go on, Lizzie. As Eleanor Roosevelt said, "Nobody can make you feel inferior without your consent."* At that thought, Eliza threw her shoulders back and returned the Dowager's gaze, even as she swallowed the lump in her throat.

"I would like to thank you again, Your Grace, for allowing me into your home. I understand my arrival was a surprise, but I will endeavor not to be a burden on your family. I am ready and able to work to assist you." There. That sounded confident. Right?

A glimmer of surprise and then respect flashed in the Dowager's eye, but before she could respond, Becca cut in. "I'm sure you could hardly be a burden, Mrs. James. Please, sit here, and have some breakfast. The footman will bring you a plate and pour you coffee."

Well, at least Becca didn't seem intimidated by her mother. And coffee? The word was heaven to Eliza's ears. She sank into the chair next to Emmeline as a small plate heaped with eggs, cheese, and toast was set in front of her. *Not quite an Egg McMuffin, but thank goodness for familiar foods.* "Thank you very much," she said automatically to the footman, who looked at her in surprise.

Everyone at the table stilled, including the footman.

"We do not thank servants, Mrs. James," intoned Deveric's mother in that condescending voice.

Oops. "My apologies; I did not mean to err. My mother taught me the kind thing to do is thank people who perform a service for you."

All eyes flew to Eliza. She wanted to clamp her hand over her mouth. Why had she said that? She'd tried to justify her faux pas, but instead sounded like she was schooling the Dowager. Definitely not her intent; she didn't need to get into a war with this fierce old biddy, whether Eliza thought thanking servants was appropriate or not.

"It is simply not done," the Dowager said after a pause, her voice pure starch.

Eliza took a bite of the rather over-brown piece of toast from her plate, determined to not let that woman get her down. The toast was dry in her mouth; she missed the big, sugary muffins she used to get from the coffee shop across from the bookstore already.

"Do you not care for it, Mrs. James?" Emmeline asked.

Eliza was unsure of her tone; it was neither welcoming nor unwelcoming. Disinterested, perhaps. That was better than openly hostile, was it not? It would not surprise her if the whole family had doubts about her this morning.

"No, no, it is delicious."

After a moment, the Dowager set down her tea cup, her eyes fixing on Eliza. "Tell me again, *Mrs.* James, what is the connection between our two families?"

Eliza's forkful of eggs stopped in midair. The Dowager was openly challenging her. According to what Deveric had said last night, the family had known of their American cousins, though distant. She'd have to be careful what she said.

"To be honest, I am not quite sure. My father always said we had relatives in England, but I did not know much beyond that."

"You are from where in Virginia?"

"Charlottesville. Home of … Thomas Jefferson." She'd nearly said the University of Virginia, but it hadn't yet been built. What a bewildering thought.

The Dowager sniffed. "I am no great admirer of the rebellious upstart."

Eliza had to bite her lip to keep from retorting. She wasn't here to win over the Dowager. She was here to win over Deveric. Though it'd be a lot easier if everyone else liked her, too. Tears prickled behind her eyes.

Emmeline broke in. "Would you like a tour of the house today, Mrs. James?"

"Yes, that would be wonderful." She breathed out a sigh of relief. *Thank you, Emmeline, for putting an end to that particular conversation.* "I am surprised Deveric and Lady Amara are not with you all this morning."

The Dowager drew herself up in her seat, impaling Eliza

with a baleful glance. "You may do things differently in America, *Mrs. James*, but here in England we expect people to address their betters properly. It is inappropriate for you to address the Duke by his Christian name."

"My betters?" The words slipped out before Eliza could stop them. But, dang, this woman raised her hackles. Why did she hate Eliza so? *Because you don't belong, and she knows it.*

"Indeed," answered the Dragon, as Eliza decided she would now call her. Internally, at least.

After a moment, she exhaled and gave the Dowager Dragon a wan smile. *You win this battle. I retreat. For the moment.*

Rebecca reached over and put a hand on Eliza's, which Eliza had unconsciously clenched in a fist. "I don't mind if you call me Becca; everyone in the family does. And you're family. Right, Mama?" Becca's face expressed only guileless cheerfulness, but rebellion flamed in her eyes.

An ally. Thank God.

"Perhaps," the Dowager answered after a moment. "That remains to be seen."

A short time later, Deveric's mother left the room, announcing she had matters to attend to regarding the afternoon plans for the guests. As she exited, Becca relaxed in her seat and Emmeline sighed.

Eliza chewed the inside of her cheek, which she'd been doing ever since the Dragon had made that crack about Jefferson. She'd wanted to retort Thomas Jefferson was one of the greatest men who'd ever lived. Er, was living.

Her eyes narrowed. She could hold her own against that

Dragon; she refused to let the woman cow her. Outwardly, at least. The woman *was* rather terrifying. But making enemies with the Dowager was ill advised, especially if Eliza hoped to be Duchess herself someday.

Still, the interaction stung. She'd read about the class system in England in both her academic realm and her romance novels, of course, but it was certainly different to be confronted with it face-to-face. Eliza suddenly wanted to hug Betsy and apologize for everyone who'd ever made a servant feel inferior.

"We're sorry about Mama," said Becca. "She is quite lovely much of the time, truly, but fiercely protective of the family name and, well, of our brother, considering everything he's gone through."

Emmeline gave her sister a sharp glance.

"Everything he's gone through?" Eliza couldn't help but ask, before taking another bite. The eggs, at least, were delicious.

Becca's eyes darted to her sister.

Emmeline answered after a moment. "My brother's wife died in childbirth three years ago. His newborn daughter, too. And these past few months, his son, Frederick, has been quite sickly."

Eliza's mouth fell open. Wait, what? None of that was in Cat's story. Not that it had been detailed enough to account for everything Eliza would face here, but first Deveric had a brother, now a son? And he'd lost a daughter? What other unexpected surprises lurked in her future?

Her heart squeezed at the thought of all Deveric had gone through, even as her stomach knotted with anxiety. She set her fork down, appetite gone. Eliza had lost a spouse, and then her parents. That was awful enough, almost beyond bearable. But losing a child—she couldn't fathom that pain. "Oh, my God. The poor man."

Both sisters nodded in agreement.

"He bears it well," Emmeline continued. "He never shows sadness."

"He never shows much of anything," Becca interrupted. "I'm far younger than he is, but I remember he used to laugh and play a lot more. With me. With Freddy. Now it's all duty, even with his son."

"How old is he?"

"Thirty-two."

Eliza chuckled. "Okay, that's good to know, but what I meant was, how old is his son?"

Becca wrinkled her nose in confusion. "What is this oakey? Why do you address us as such?"

"Oh, I'm sorry." Eliza was trying so hard to blend in, to not to mess up language-wise—at least she hadn't yet said *awesome*—but okay was such an integral part of her vocabulary, she didn't notice when she said it. She'd have to try harder. "It's an American expression, I suppose. It means something like 'all right' or 'good', or even maybe 'I agree.'"

"Very good," said Becca. "Or maybe I should say 'Very oakey?'"

Eliza laughed.

"And Freddy's just turned five," Becca added. "He is such a sweet boy. I do wish Deveric spent more time with him."

Emmeline cleared her throat, her lips pinching in silent reprimand. *Not supposed to be telling me so much, I guess.*

It was hard to imagine Deveric with a five-year-old son, given in her mind he was the devilishly romantic hero Cat had conjured up for her. A son. So she was to be a stepmother. She choked on a sip of coffee. *That's quite a leap, Eliza*

James. You're sitting here, a penniless distant relation whom the Dowager Dragon clearly doesn't like, and you've already married yourself off to her son.

Well, a girl could dream.

CHAPTER 9

"Clarehaven was built sometime in the sixteenth century," Becca said as she led Eliza through the house. "Legend has it that when the original Duke showed the land to his new wife, who was of Scottish descent, she declared it to be 'Clear Heaven.' The architect accompanying them misunderstood, thinking she'd said 'Clarehaven.' He assumed it went with the ducal name of Claremont, and wrote it down on the plans. The moniker stuck. This estate has been known as 'Clarehaven' ever since."

Eliza fingered the heavy wooden bannister of the stair railing as they passed through the main hall. "It's marvelous. I can't imagine growing up in a place so grand. I can't believe I'm standing in one, to be honest."

Marble columns flanked the hall, and an intricate, inlaid mosaic of birds and flowers covered the floor. Eliza half-expected a museum guide to pop out. She stuffed down the urge to ask where the gift shop was.

Becca swished her dress from side-to-side, eagerness

radiating from her. "Would you like to see the stables now?"

"She's seen but one wing, Becca. Patience," Emmeline said. "Your horse will still be there."

Becca's lip jutted out in an adorable pout, but she trailed after her sister as Emmeline led them into another room. "This is our drawing room, though we rarely entertain morning callers in the country," Emmeline said. "That's why it's such a delight to have so many guests here at the moment; Clarehaven is quite dull otherwise. I cannot wait to remove back to Town."

Eliza couldn't imagine ever finding such a magnificent home dull. These sisters didn't know what they had. Several of the rooms were nearly the size of Eliza's apartment.

Emmeline's last words suddenly registered. Eliza stopped walking. "We're not in London?"

The two sisters gaped at her. "You must be teasing," Becca said after a pause.

Great, Lizzie. Way to keep suspicion away from you and blend in. Eliza's thumbs wrestled with each other as she fought back a nervous giggle. "Um, well, of course." She wanted to kick herself. Not that she'd been near many windows this morning—and last night was dark—but surely *something* should have clued her in that they were not in the city. The lack of outside noise, perhaps. On the other hand, Clarehaven was so monstrous, and so solidly built, was she wrong for assuming it insulated them from everything? "I, uh, slept some in the coach yesterday. I must not have realized how far we traveled." How far *were* they from London?

"You must have been quite exhausted to be able to sleep in a traveling coach," Becca said. "I never can."

"You would have been, too, had you just spent weeks on a ship," interjected a deep voice as Deveric strode into the room.

It was all Eliza could do to keep her mouth from dropping open. Damn, the man could give Colin Firth a run for his money when it came to sex appeal. Regency sex appeal, that was. He wore buckskin breeches, a shade darker than those of the day before, perhaps, but still molded to his thighs, and high riding boots—top boots, Eliza recalled, the type modern English riding boots liked to imitate, with that distinctive brown upper, black lower half. She loved them. His tailcoat was less formal this morning, cut of deep rich forest green velvet that made his eyes pop, his waistcoat ivory underneath. All was immaculate. And, oh, that wind-blown hair.

Drooling. I'm drooling. Reading about a hero in a novel was nothing compared to the sheer physical impact of standing face-to-face with one. Though she wasn't truly face-to-face with him; he was across the room. And likely didn't think of himself as a romantic lead. He cocked an eyebrow at her and shot her a smile. *Or maybe he does, given that smug look on his face.*

This man? This vision of perfection? I'm supposed to get him to fall in love with me? Little old pudgy Miss Nobody me? Eliza's heart raced, nervousness feathering out over her skin. She tugged on one of the tendrils hanging near her ear and stared at the floor. When she peeked up again, his eyes were fixed on her.

"Oh, were you riding, Deveric?" Becca exclaimed, her eyes lighting up.

"You know I ride every morning. I'm sure you're chafing at the bit—no horse humor intended—so go and change into your habit. I shall continue the tour with our … cousin."

Becca gave a little excited hop and raced from the room. "Thank you!" she called as she left.

"I have never known any woman to be so besotted with

horses." He strolled across the room. "Do you like to ride, Mrs. James?"

Was that a suggestive undertone in his voice? Surely not. "No. To be honest, I've never been on a horse."

Both brother and sister stared at her. "What? You've never ridden a horse?"

"Well, no. They scare me, actually."

Emmeline clasped her hands together. "I fell off my pony when I was ten. Ever since, I've been nervous, as well."

"They don't have horses where you're from?" Deveric's tone assured Eliza he hadn't forgotten their conversation the night before—and that he didn't believe her claims.

"Oh no, they do. Most people just, um, don't ride them anymore. We, uh, walk or … use other means."

"Other means?" Deveric challenged.

Shoot. How am I going to get myself out of this one?

"I mean, we often use a … wagon."

Emmeline nodded, satisfied. "Frankly, I prefer to walk; coaches and the like can be so jarring. Our curricles and rigs are well-sprung, so they're not bad, as long as my brother doesn't make us go too quickly."

"What can I say? I like speed."

Eliza grinned at him. *Oh, if only you knew.* A horse was nothing compared to zipping down the interstate at seventy miles an hour. Or flying across the ocean in a matter of half a day.

His eyes twinkled. He seemed … relaxed. How could he be, when every inch of her was aware of him, of how immensely attractive he was? *This isn't fair.* Self-doubt crept in again. Maybe she wasn't his type. Maybe he preferred tall, willowy brunettes. Ones bred for the role of aristocrat. Crud.

Nope. Not going there. Cat said he'd be attracted to you, and last night, you could tell he was. Yeah, but that was last night, the other side of her screamed. Maybe today he's decided you're a nutter, and he's calm because he's about to toss you out on your ear.

"Emmeline?"

Eliza turned to see a dark-haired woman enter the room.

"Oh, I'm sorry—I didn't mean to intrude."

"Nonsense, Grace," said Deveric. "I'm glad you are here. Are you feeling better? Amara said you had the headache last night."

Emmeline's lips tipped up in a grin. "More likely she was reading that book again and didn't care to make an appearance at the ball."

"It's a wonderful book," protested Grace as she walked farther into the room. "I quite like the character of Elinor."

Eliza couldn't help herself. "Are you talking about *Sense and Sensibility*?"

Grace's eyes lit up. "You have read it? Is it not delightful?"

"It's wonderful. I adore Jane—," Eliza answered automatically, and then bit her lip, hard. Jane Austen originally published her works anonymously. Few of the general public knew her as an author until after she had passed away. *Crap. I've got to stop messing up like this.*

Grace looked at her. "Jane? I don't recall that character."

"I must be mistaken. I meant the … younger sister."

"Marianne? Truly?" Grace wrinkled her nose. "Think you not she's a bit rash, hasty to action?"

Yes. Much like me.

"You've read the novel already? In America?" Emmeline's face reflected her puzzlement. "My brother procured Grace a copy in November and said it had only recently been published."

Deveric said nothing, his eyes watching her intently.

Way to help me out, dude.

"Uh-h," stammered Eliza. "Two women on the coach yesterday discussed it at length."

"When you weren't sleeping, of course," said Emmeline, her brows knitting together.

"Yes, exactly. Perhaps one of the ladies in the coach was a Jane and I confused her name with the book. I was quite tired and often dozing, of course." Sweat pooled in her armpits. Thank goodness the dress and undergarments were thick enough to hide it. *Antiperspirant. Another thing I took for granted.*

Grace looked first to her brother, and then dipped her head toward Eliza.

"My apologies," Deveric said, taking a step closer. "I forgot you had not yet been introduced. Grace, please meet Mrs. Eliza James, a Virginia cousin. She survived the fire, and is to stay with us for … a while. And E—Mrs. James, this is Lady Grace, my sister."

He'd nearly called her by her first name. Again. No one else had noticed, but it pleased Eliza for some stupid reason, that slip. At the same time, she'd noticed his hesitation at "a while." Panic seized her again. He *did* mean to get rid of her.

"It's a pleasure to meet you, Mrs. James," said Grace, her voice shy.

"You, too, Lady Grace." She wanted to say, "Call me Eliza," but refrained. She needed to do a better job of adhering to protocol, whether she wanted to or not. Her eyes drifted to Deveric. "How many sisters do you have?"

She supposed that was likely a rude question, but what the hell. At this point, what did she have to lose?

"Five. And one scamp of a brother, whom you've already met. Lady Cecilia is now at Cove Lawn with her husband, the Marquess of Amsfordshire."

"And their darling daughter," added Emmeline.

"Yes. Their daughter." Pain creased Deveric's face momentarily.

Emmeline's hands flew to her mouth. "I am sorry, Dev. I wasn't thinking."

"I rejoice in their healthy daughter," Deveric said, his face once again a stoic mask. "Please never think otherwise." He stiffened his shoulders, his back unnaturally straight, his gaze not quite meeting anybody's eye. "If you'll excuse me, I have business to which I need to attend." With that, he strode out of the room.

Emmeline's face crumbled. "I didn't think, Grace."

Grace took her sister's hand and rubbed it lightly. "You were not inappropriate, Emme. Our brother truly does take joy in little Mary."

Emmeline shot Eliza a glance. "Shall we continue?" she said, beckoning Eliza forward, clearly eager to drop the topic of their niece.

Eliza would much rather have gone after Deveric, but turned to follow Emmeline, leaving Grace to submerse herself in the book she pulled out from under her shawl.

Just wait until she reads Pride and Prejudice. Eliza was ecstatic to meet a fellow Austenite and bookworm, even if Lady Grace was rather shy. Cat was an introvert, too. Eliza could deal with that.

What woman wouldn't fall in love with Darcy? At that thought, an image of Deveric in those breeches and boots, his face remote, his attitude arrogant, leapt into Eliza's mind. *What woman, indeed?*

Deveric paced his study, the study to which he'd retreated for the second time in twenty-four hours. *Coward.*

Both times were on account of a woman; the first, in an effort to dampen his desire for Eliza James—an effort that had failed miserably, given his reaction to seeing her this morning. His whole body had lit up, an unusual feeling of happiness infusing him upon seeing her delicate face. The second, however, had been in a desperate attempt to stem his emotions, lest his sisters witness him lose his composure.

Guilt consumed him over how little he'd seen Cecilia and his new niece, Mary. But in truth, he couldn't bear it, couldn't bear to see those chubby little cheeks, those sparkling eyes, so full of *life.* Of course he didn't begrudge his sister her happiness. She deserved it, deserved that darling little girl.

But for Deveric, Mary was a nearly unbearable reminder, a painful contrast of glowing health in comparison with his little Louisa. So pale, so lifeless. His daughter had never drawn a breath, never looked at him with those impossibly small eyes, never grasped his finger with her tiny one. He'd held her, held her for hours, tears streaming down his face. Until the doctor had come, told him Mirabelle was gone, too.

He hadn't been with his wife, as he ought. Relations had long been strained, to be true, but he should have attended her, not just their daughter. His mother had insisted it wasn't his fault; that it would have been unseemly for him to be there as the doctor had attempted to stem the bleeding, to save her life.

But Deveric knew. The guilt gnawed at his heart. He hadn't given a thought to Mirabelle; the grief over his daughter had been all consuming. He would forever carry that burden, knowing that not only had he caused his wife's death, but he hadn't been there, hadn't even thought of her while she lay dying.

He took a swig from the nearly empty brandy bottle. It was early, but he didn't care—plus, nothing worked better to cure a hangover than a bit of the poison that ailed him. Nothing worked better to ease pain than drowning it.

At that thought, he set the bottle back down. He'd almost gone down that path, almost given himself over to the darkness of his despair. Until Cecilia had come to him, had reminded him his son needed him, his *family* needed him. She'd pulled him from the depths.

And so, he'd thrown himself into managing the estate, into improving the lives of those dependent on him, into strengthening the land and increasing profits. If he couldn't save his wife and daughter, by God, he'd make sure no one else in his care suffered.

That was why he must steer clear of Mrs. Eliza James. He couldn't risk it, couldn't risk her. Even if it were an option, she was not the kind of woman he could tumble, a woman he could bed and forget, like the occasional mistress. No, in his bones he knew she'd never be as simple as that. And so he had to stay away.

After he got answers, of course.

CHAPTER 10

"It's a bit chilly, but I find a walk in the gardens refreshes me and prepares me for the day ahead," Emmeline said, as Eliza trailed behind her through the back hall. They'd finished the house tour and Eliza, frankly, was overwhelmed and exhausted by it all. This was not a house. It was a castle.

How could she ever hope to fit in here, she of no financial means who'd only lived in rented apartments her whole adult life?

And she wasn't just aspiring to fit in, she wanted the role of duchess. The highest female title next to royalty? Whom was she kidding? Being a duchess was no light undertaking. A duchess had to manage the household, had to supervise servants. Had to know the ins and outs of the peerage—with whom one should associate, with whom one shouldn't. A duchess had to raise children in the principles of the British ruling class. Eliza was sure there were probably numerous other activities a duchess was expected to undertake, duties to perform about which she knew nothing.

Knowing all those things from her studies was quite different from facing them in reality.

She wished she could lie down for a while and take a nap, but didn't want to be rude to Emmeline, who'd been surprisingly friendly and accepting that morning. As had most of the family. Well, except maybe the Dowager Dragon. And Amara. And, well, Deveric. Perhaps not most, then. The thought depressed but didn't surprise her. *Nobody falls in love in a day, Eliza James, whether with a lover or with a friend.*

Except she and Cat *had* clicked instantly, all those years ago. What she wouldn't give to be sitting in the coffee shop with Cat right now, nursing a mocha and a piece of Crumb Cake. Her stomach growled at the thought. *But only for a moment—because Cat is finding what she needs, I'm sure, and I'm here to do the same.*

"Do you have a pelisse?"

Emmeline's voice startled her back to the present. Or should she say past? "No."

"I shall have a maid fetch you one of mine. We are of similar size, I see."

Eliza smoothed her hands over her hips as Emmeline signaled to a maid. *Similar size, my ass.* She snickered inwardly at the bad pun. She and Emmeline might be of the same height, but she was sure she had at least twenty pounds on the girl. Maybe thirty.

"I should like to hear more about this Virginia," Emmeline said. "Is it as wild as they say? Were you ever attacked by Indians?"

"Indians?" Eliza answered. She fought the urge to correct the word to Native American. At least Emmeline hadn't said savages. "Uh, no. There are not many near where I live." *Not to mention we decimated them.*

"Truly?" Emmeline's mouth tipped down in disappointment.

The maid appeared with the requested pelisses, and Eliza was grateful for the interruption. As she pulled on the long, red, woolen garment, she heaved a sigh of relief that it was not as snug as she had feared. She couldn't fasten the front buttons, but she didn't mind.

Emmeline looked her over, and then handed her a pair of kidskin gloves. "We shan't stay out long. If you get cold, please inform me."

Get cold? She was already cold. How much worse could it be outside?

"Oh, it's lovely," Eliza exclaimed, as they reached a garden threaded through with well-organized paths lined with numerous plants, most of which were foreign to her. Not that she'd paid much attention to the flora and fauna in Virginia, either. She was rather an inside girl, content with a book or a screen, and something to munch on.

This area, however, made her understand why people would like to stroll here. Evergreens and other small trees—fruit trees, perhaps—dotted the landscape, and here and there charming stone benches provided spots for respite. She bet when flowers were in full bloom, the area was even more spectacular. A row of tall hedges lined the back, preventing her from seeing what lay beyond.

"Shall I show you the maze? It is quite popular with our guests," Emmeline said, her face glowing pink in the cold.

Eliza pulled the pelisse closer around her midsection. She'd prefer to troop back to the house, perhaps warm up with a hot drink, but she didn't want to disappoint Emmeline. Eliza needed all the allies she could get in this bizarre situation. "Um, sure."

The two women meandered toward the hedge. Upon approach, Eliza could see the small break marking the opening to the maze.

"I love to walk here. It feels as if I'm in my own private world," Emmeline said. "Not that I don't love my family …"

"But sometimes one needs a bit of space to oneself."

Emmeline's face flushed.

"There is no shame in that; it makes sense to me. It must be weird to have people around constantly—especially servants."

Emmeline stopped walking for a second. "You didn't have servants in America?"

Eliza chuckled. "Definitely not."

"How did you dress on your own?"

Eliza looked down at her gown. It *would* be difficult to don the undergarments she was wearing, much less secure the back of the dress she had on, without assistance. Cat had helped her the night of the ball, and a servant had been there to aid her this morning. Could one do it alone? How silly, to design clothing that necessitated aid to get in and out of. A hallmark of wealth, she supposed.

"My … sister." Cat had certainly been the closest thing to a sister Eliza had ever had—it felt right calling her that. A wave of longing for her washed over Eliza again.

"Oh, how tragic, to have lost a sister. I cannot imagine." Emmeline's eyes clouded, but she resumed her leisurely pace. "You must miss her."

Eliza nodded, hugging her pelisse close. "Yes. Very much."

"Emmeline!"

Eliza and Emmeline turned around, searching for the source of the booming voice.

"We are here, brother!" Emmeline called cheerfully, as Deveric's head poked around the side of the hedge near which the women were standing.

"My apologies, I did not realize you were still with our guest. Lady Penelope is looking for you."

"Oh, hurray. We are going to look at the latest *Belle l'Assemblee*. I need new gowns for the Season." Emmeline wrinkled her nose. "Why did you not send a servant for me? I'm sure Lady Penelope did not mean to inconvenience you."

Deveric shifted from one leg to the other. "I was … on my way to the stables anyway. Thus, it was not an inconvenience."

Emmeline turned to Eliza. "You are likely chilled; let's return to the house. I hope you don't mind that I wish to spend time with my friend."

"Not at all," Eliza said. "I understand the value of friendship."

"Do not concern yourself with Mrs. James," interjected Deveric. "I will be happy to escort her back to the house."

Emmeline's brow rose. "I thought you were going to the stables?"

"Indeed. But Mrs. James and I have some business matters relating to her father to discuss." His eyes bore into Eliza's.

Emmeline headed toward the house, waving gaily to Eliza and her brother. "I shall see you soon," she called as she picked up her pace.

Deveric pulled Eliza back around the edge of the hedge,

so that they were enfolded within the greenery around them.

"What are you doing?" Eliza shook his arm off her elbow.

"My apologies. But I want answers. Who are you? And don't give me that nonsense about being from the future."

Eliza chewed on her lower lip. She didn't know whether to laugh or cry. *Shall I tell him I'm here because he is my soul mate and we are destined for a great love affair? It's not like he would believe me.* Maybe it wasn't even true. Eyeing the angry Duke in front of her, Eliza regretted the lack of a sure happy ending to their tale. Although if the outcome were predetermined, it wouldn't feel legit, right? That's what Cat had decided for herself.

Yes, but I'm not Cat. And I want the fantasy—the whole thing. I just want it to be real. Like Cinderella at the ball, but, well, true. Is that too much for a girl to ask?

"I'm waiting, Mrs. James." He tapped his boot on the gravel path.

She ran her tongue over her lip to soothe the spot she'd bitten. Deveric emitted a noise. A growl? A groan? What was up with him?

"You can believe what you wish, *Your Grace*," she returned, irritated with his commanding tone. Did he expect her to fall at his feet in submission? The drill-sergeant approach never had worked well with her; it always roused rebellion. That had tickled her husband, who'd often said she wouldn't last a day in boot camp. It was true.

Deveric stared at her, his eyebrow rising. He was not used to people challenging him; that much was clear. Narrowing his eyes, he moved a few steps closer. "You insist you are from two hundred years in the future? That I was there with you last night? And that now you have followed me through time to the present? Or the past?"

"Yup." She refused to back up. Not that there was much space—she was almost against the hedge itself.

"And you say that in order to travel through time, you had to activate whatever magic was involved by kissing me, correct?"

She swallowed as he moved even closer. Hedge needles pricked her back. "Um, yeah."

"Then obviously there's only one thing to do." A wolfish grin broke out on his face.

"Wh-what's that?"

"This," he answered, and lowered his lips to hers.

Eliza closed her eyes and leaned into the kiss. She hadn't expected it, but that didn't mean she wasn't going to fully enjoy it. She opened her mouth and slid her tongue along Deveric's lips. He paused, as if surprised, but then widened his own lips and met her tongue with his, dueling with her as they each pressed harder into the other.

This is a battle I don't mind waging. She wound her hands up through Deveric's hair, pulling him closer. He enthusiastically complied, reaching around and clasping her to him as if he feared she'd disappear at any second. For a moment, there was nothing but sensation, the delicious taste of each other among the scent of the evergreens, the feeling as if all were right, as they stood enfolded in each other.

Suddenly, Deveric broke off, leaning back and staring at her. He didn't remove his arms from around her waist, but his gaze was no longer hot; instead, he looked troubled. His eyes darted around, as if ascertaining their surroundings.

"We're still here. If kissing you brought us here, it should have sent you back," he said.

Eliza gasped. "That's ... that's why you kissed me? Because you wanted to send me *back?*" She thrust her arms up, breaking the embrace. Deveric let her.

"You told me you had to kiss me to travel here; it only seemed logical to try the reverse," he mumbled. He ran a hand through his hair, confusion furrowing his brow.

Eliza's cheeks burned with shame. "I had thought—" She broke off, studying the stone path at her feet. "I wish to return to the house."

"You thought what?" Deveric reached for her arm, grasping her hand and pulling her back toward him. "That I kissed you because I wanted to? Because I haven't been able to stop thinking about kissing you since I met you? That I'd like nothing more than to keep kissing you, because your lips taste like nothing I've ever known before, a taste of which I can't get enough?"

Eliza stared up at him. *Those eyes. Oh my God, those eyes.* "Well, a girl can dream, right?" she stammered, attempting a weak smile.

Deveric's pupils flared. He leaned toward her, his lips parting. Just as she was sure he was going to kiss her again, he backed up a step, exhaling loudly as he tugged at his overcoat.

"Perhaps you *are* a witch," he muttered. "I can't think straight around you. You make me *feel*, you make me *want*." He looked off into the distance, not meeting her eyes. "I don't understand. I've been in complete control since …"

Eliza's insides warmed as she watched this man, a powerful duke used to commanding every situation, fumble with his words. *He may not believe me yet, he may not trust me—heck, he certainly doesn't know me, but I'll take desire. Better than nothing!*

It was hard to believe a man as immensely attractive as Deveric could desire her. To be fair, she'd had her share of male attention, in spite of her penchant for brownies and cheesecake. But she'd known she wasn't the ideal woman by twenty-first century standards. She was too soft, too curvy. "Too much junk in the trunk and too much boob in the bosom," she'd joked to Cat.

"You were just born in the wrong century, Lizzie," Cat always asserted. "Look at the paintings of the masters and you'll see. As Sir Mix-A-Lot said, 'Baby Got Back!'"

"It's okay, Dev," she whispered. "It's all very confusing. I get it. Believe me, I'm confused, too." She smoothed his hair back from his forehead. He closed his eyes at her touch.

After a moment, he stepped back, gesturing around them. "We're still here. In my gardens." He eyed her. "But you maintain you're from two hundred years in the future?"

"Yes," she said calmly, her eyes not leaving his. *Start as you mean to go on.* Honesty was the best policy, even in a situation as bizarre as this one.

He watched her a long while. "Some part of me must believe it, too. I've considered every option I can think of— that I hit my head and this is all a dream; that something otherworldly is going on, that you're an actress hired by my brother, or perhaps Dawes."

"Dawes?" Eliza's voice cracked. Cat had created a man of the same last name: William Dawes. What was going on? Dawes couldn't be *here*—could he?

Deveric's eyes grew cold. "You know him? Did he put you up to this? He did, by God, didn't he, as retribution for me outbidding him for that horse last month. Some friend." He stalked back and forth along the garden path.

"No!" she exclaimed. "I only reacted because that was the name of one of the men Cat created. He did say he had ancestors in England. But the William Dawes I know is from 2011, and he's an American. I swear!"

Deveric continued pacing. "Earl of Stoneleigh," he muttered. "Everett Dawes is the Earl. His estate borders mine—Pierfield." He stopped and looked at her again. "William is his youngest brother." His eyes bore into hers, as if looking for some sign of recognition.

Eliza returned his gaze, taking a step closer.

"A moment," he said, holding his hand out as if to ward her off. "You said men that this Cat *created*?"

CHAPTER 11

He made the sign of the cross over his chest, his face deathly white. "You *are* a witch, with a cat as your familiar." He backed up several steps.

Crap. No, no, no. Eliza rushed toward him, setting her hand gently on his chest. "Of course not. There are no such things as witches. Well, at least not how we picture them, with their pointy hats and wicked spells." She pulled the pelisse more tightly around her midsection. "Why don't you let me tell the story from the beginning? But can we walk a little? I'm freezing."

Deveric offered her his arm, no doubt on account of the courtesy bred into him. His rigid muscle tone testified to his suspicion, and nervousness. "I would escort you inside," he said, "but I cannot guarantee privacy in conversation there."

"It's all right. I didn't need my toes, anyway," Eliza teased. As they strolled, she gave him the gist of Cat's experiences with the men she'd dated, and answered his questions as best she could about the things he'd seen. She tiptoed around the issue of Cat creating Deveric for her, talking more generally about her love for this time in English history, and how her desire to experience England in the Regency period prompted her to ask Cat to write her here. Nothing would send him running faster than her assertion that he was her soul mate—her first fictional, now real soul mate—she was sure.

He didn't ask about the kissing requirement again, and she didn't volunteer.

They spent the better part of an hour walking the garden—they left the maze, so as not to be caught in a private space together, alone. Eliza talked all about living in twenty-first century Virginia. Well, not all; even if she'd had the time, she didn't want to overwhelm him. But she picked things she thought might interest a speed-loving duke: cars, airplanes, computers, the Internet, cell phones. To his credit, Deveric didn't bolt, but instead listened with avid interest, peppering her with questions, his eyes burning with intellectual curiosity in the midst of his doubt. She answered as best she could, certain she was getting the technological details wrong.

At one point, she rubbed her hands up and down her arms, her teeth chattering. She should have accepted Amara's blasted cap. At least her ears might not be half so frozen if she had.

Deveric immediately apologized for not thinking of her comfort. "We should return to the house. Mother is likely fretting over where I am, as I'm to lead the men in the hunt this afternoon."

"You could skip it." Eliza was loath to end her time with him, no matter how cold she was.

"Skip?" he said, a corner of his mouth turning up. "One

does not skip about during a hunt. The horses would not comply."

"That's not what I meant. Wow, it's hard to know which expressions are in use by now, and which yet to come."

"You likely have much to learn about my time, as I do about yours."

"So you believe me, then?" she asked, her heart pounding.

"I am not certain yet. However, these machines of which you speak, these jets and space-ships and cars—they fascinate me. I want to hear more."

"Such a man." She rolled her eyes. A second later, she stopped in her steps, unlinking her arm from his. "Wait. I can *prove* it to you. I can show you my phone! Why didn't I think of that immediately?"

"Phone? Oh, the talking device you described?"

"Yes! I have pictures on it—of Cat and me and the bookstore, but also of our trip to the Air and Space Museum in D.C.! And maybe more." She clapped her hands, hopping up and down. "I'll go get it!"

She turned to run into the house, as they'd reached the back portico, but Deveric pulled at her arm. "As much as I'd like to see this ... phone, I'm still waiting for you to explain what *I* have to do with all of this."

Eliza stumbled at his words, the ones she'd dreaded. He'd been so patient, listening quietly as she'd told her wild tale. He hadn't fled, or clapped her in chains to haul her off to the madhouse. But how on earth was she to explain that he'd been created *for* her? That he hadn't existed until her friend Cat had willed him into existence for her—Eliza James.

She worried her bottom lip. Perhaps it was more complex than that. Maybe Cat just managed to match people together somehow, rather than truly creating them? When Cat had given Grayson a sister, she'd suddenly appeared—but maybe that sister had existed somewhere else? Or maybe it worked differently with the past, rather than the present—incorporating real people, rather than fantasies?

Eliza's head throbbed, angry echoes of the stress and confusion inundating her, and she clasped her hand to her temples. Deveric remained silent, waiting for her answer. One of the portico's doors sprung open and Becca came skipping out, her eyes sparkling and cheeks ruddy.

"You must have enjoyed your riding." Deveric's eyes softened as he looked at his sister. Eliza liked how much his fondness for her showed.

"Oh, yes. Thank you so much for Otto. He is simply the best horse ever!" Becca flicked an errant strand of curls back from her forehead before turning to Eliza with a wide grin. "Would you like to meet him?"

Not exactly. Horses always sounded romantic from a distance, but up close, they terrified her. But she'd do anything at the moment to get away from Deveric's overly inquisitive stare.

"Yes, that would be great." The words tumbled out in a rush. "Surely you don't mind, De—I mean, Your Grace. I've monopolized your attention for long enough."

He gave her a wry smile, bowing before arching that infernal eyebrow again. Clearly he knew her motive, but was willing to let her flee for now.

Becca clapped with glee. "Oh, you're going to *love* him, Eliza—I mean, Mrs. James!"

"Please, call me Eliza, if you would; Mrs. James makes me feel so old."

"I suppose Christian names are appropriate," said Deveric. "After all, we are family—are we not?" He gave a short bow to Eliza. "I shall be waiting to finish our … business." With a meaningful glance, Deveric walked into the house. He did not look back.

Twice. Twice in the space of twenty-four hours he'd kissed that woman. And it wasn't enough. It wasn't nearly enough. What *was* this powerful energy between them? Did she feel it as much as he? Or was he imagining her responses to be as ardent as his own, because he wished them to be?

He stalked his way to the kitchens, his stomach rumbling. He was grateful not to encounter anyone; he didn't want to have to speak, to go through polite niceties, when his mind was overloaded to the point of collapse.

That he'd sunk to accusing her of witchcraft mortified him. He was a man of science, a man of logic. Others may believe in sorcery. He did not.

Though given all she'd told him after that second kiss, perhaps he should. Surely the tales she told couldn't possibly be truth. And yet, she spoke with such conviction, so matter-of-factly, it was hard to believe she could create such fiction from her head. He'd pressed for more details a number of times, asked varied questions, challenged points, all in an effort to trip her up, and yet her descriptions remained consistent, her voice confident, her attitude very nearly relaxed as she talked about satellites and a box with moving pictures—tele-vision, she'd called it—and something called a Ferrari. She'd assured him he would like one of those very much, as it could travel speeds in excess of one hundred miles per hour.

He grabbed a roll out of a basket on the sideboard, giving the cook a brisk nod as he exited, making his way back to the lawn to gather the men for the hunt.

His head ached, as much with desire as with confusion. Befuddling, maddening, and, yes, sexually bewitching—such were words to describe Eliza James. Also, intelligent, loving, loyal—he'd seen from her tone how much she loved this Cat. Yes, Eliza was a woman of great depth of feeling, emotions dancing across her face whenever she spoke.

It was refreshing, that, to see someone so open, so engaged with the world and the people around her. It was so different from most females of his acquaintance, women who modulated and modified everything they said and did, until it seemed there was little left to them that wasn't artifice. It was so different from Mirabelle, from his mother.

Was it any wonder he couldn't resist her?

But he had to. For her sake. And for his.

As they neared the stables, Eliza's anxiety rose. Did horses bite? She hoped not. Becca chattered at her side, talking about Otto and Charlemagne and Henry and Charles, obviously referencing horses, not medieval rulers. Eliza pasted a smile on her face as Becca pulled open the door to the stables. The stable hand inside tipped his hat to the girl in casual familiarity.

"Back again, Lady Rebecca?" he asked.

"Of course. I would stay all day if I could."

He looked briefly at Eliza and then cast his eyes down to the ground. "My lady," he said, pulling the hat off his head.

"Hi!" she answered brightly in an effort to put him—and herself—at ease. One of the horses in a neighboring stall nickered and Eliza jumped.

Becca laughed. "You act as if you've never seen a horse before!"

"Oh, I've seen them." *On television, at least.* "I just wasn't expecting one to talk to me."

"That's Otto—once he sees me he won't leave off until I give him a treat." Becca fished an apple out of the small bag hanging off her right wrist and handed it to the horse, which chomped on it with glee. *I swear that horse is smiling at her.*

Eliza eyed Otto, her stomach dancing with nerves. Up close, a horse was quite massive. And smelly. She wrinkled her nose.

"Sorry, my lady," the stable hand offered. He must have noted her reaction. "I was getting ready to muck out the stables again." He grabbed a shovel and headed to the back of a neighboring stall.

"How do you stand the smell?" she asked Becca, who was petting the horse's nose fondly.

Becca shrugged. "I'm around the horses so much I hardly notice it anymore. Besides, it's only bad in here. Out in the meadows, all you smell is the grass and the air. There's nothing like it, riding out on your best friend, exploring the forest and galloping across the dales." She sighed, fingering the horse's mane.

Eliza grinned. She liked this Becca Mattersley, liked her openness and friendliness and willingness to show her passion for horses to the world. Much better than the Dowager's uptight, closed-off demeanor ... not to mention Deveric himself.

Except his lips moving over yours were hardly reserved— they tried to suck your mouth right off, girlie.

Eliza's cheeks flooded with heat at the memory. Becca didn't notice, thank goodness; she was busy feeding the horse another apple. "Here, would you like to give him one?" she said, handing a small red apple to Eliza.

Eliza scrunched up her mouth. "Will he bite me?"

"No, you goose. Just hold it out flat in your hand." She clapped her fingers over her mouth for a second. "I'm sorry, I shouldn't have called you a goose. Mama says I often speak without thinking. It's what I call Emmeline, and, well, it slipped out."

"I'm flattered you would address me as you do your sister," Eliza said with a rush of feeling. "I do hope we can become friends."

Becca gave the horse a final pat. "I hope so, too. You seem more fun than most of the women I know. Even if you are terrified of horses." She linked her arm in Eliza's. "We shall have to remedy that."

"I don't know if *terrified* is the right word," Eliza protested. "More like … unaccustomed." She could learn to ride, right? Of all the things that could intimidate her in this century, a horse shouldn't be one of them.

"Not for long." Becca turned away from Otto, reluctance emanating from every part of her. "We must return to the house now. Mother has requested I help entertain our female guests this afternoon. Not that they want to do much beyond walk the rooms and talk about men. As if there weren't things in the world infinitely more exciting." She sighed, sounding so forlorn that Eliza nearly burst out laughing.

Together, they exited the stables.

Eliza's mind boggled again at the grandeur of the huge house as they approached it. She could hardly believe this was a family home, rather than a fancy museum or a hotel.

Men and women milled about on the back lawn, grouped according to gender and not interacting all that much, though occasionally some of the women cast flirtatious glances toward the men. One young, fashionably dressed gentleman winked at a darling little brunette who looked all of sixteen. The girl turned away, flushing, but by the way she raised her hand to her mouth and glanced back at him, it was clear she was interested. Evidently flirting methods hadn't changed that much in two hundred years.

"Oh good, the men are about to leave for the hunt. At least we will not have to listen to odious conversation about how many poor animals they plan to kill." Becca's nose wrinkled as she said the words.

Grace pulled away from a small group of women and walked over to Becca and Eliza. "Mother has been looking for you, sister. She and Amara need help setting up the scenery for the play."

Becca's eyebrows wrinkled. "A servant cannot aid them?"

"She also wishes you to run your lines. You know how forgetful you are."

Becca let out an exasperated harrumph. "I am *not* forgetful. I'm merely more interested in other things."

Grace gave her a soft smile. "You are right in that, Becca." She looked over at Eliza. "Would you like to come? We are practicing *The Sailor's Daughter*. Our performance is tomorrow night, at the end of the house party."

Becca crossed her arms. "I'd rather do one of *your* plays, Grace. They are so much better than the ones Amara chooses."

Grace's cheeks colored. A writer as well as a reader. Cat would like her.

"If it's all right with you, actually, I'd like to rest for a bit," Eliza said. "I'm quite tired from my … travels."

"Quite understandable, Mrs. James. I find traveling exhausting, as well," said Grace. "I will have Sally show you to your room."

Eliza wanted to protest she didn't need a servant, uncomfortable with the idea of stopping someone else from what they were doing simply to help her, but in truth, she wasn't sure how to get to the chamber in which she'd slept last night. "That would be wonderful, thank you."

She shot a quick glance toward the men to find Deveric, to see what he was doing. He stood amidst a group of men who were talking animatedly, but he was staring at her, his face intense. Noting her look, he put his fingers to the brim of his hat and gave a crisp nod.

Shivers raced up her spine. She felt almost his prey. Or perhaps it was the other way around.

CHAPTER 12

everic pretended to listen to Arthington prattling on about an ancient sword he'd acquired, but in truth, his attention was on the woman who'd just disappeared into Clarehaven.

His mind swam. The machines she described piqued his curiosity, he had to admit. He'd long admired Watt and Boulton's steam engines, had read with interest of Robert Fulton's steam-powered boat, and had seen Richard Trevithick's London Steam Carriage in person. The machines appearing with increasing frequency in the cotton factories in the north operated on steam power—inciting riots by workers angry at being replaced by machinery. "The Luddite Rebellion," Eliza had said, nodding her head when he'd mentioned that to her. Eliza had talked of railroads, advising him to invest in those, of automobiles and even vehicles in the sky. Airplanes, she'd called them. He'd seen hot air balloons in Paris, but these were different; enclosed, capable of unheard of speeds. According to her, man had even landed on the moon. *The moon.*

If one could fly through the sky, if people could travel into space, was it possible, remotely possible, a person could move through time itself?

He shook his head, which still ached from last night's overindulgence. Or perhaps from everything he'd heard.

She'd told him so many things, so much that sounded impossibly fantastical, and yet she had spoken with confidence, no doubt or subterfuge evident in her demeanor. Either she was telling the truth, or she was a master liar worthy of the Regent's special service.

Either way, she aroused something in him he didn't want to acknowledge. Curiosity. Fascination. Desire. Fear.

"The dogs are ready, Your Grace," broke in the huntsman from his right. Deveric forced himself back to the task at hand. He had duties here in the nineteenth century. Eliza James, and her magical 'phone,' would have to wait.

After a delightful snooze snuggled under as many blankets as she could find in the room, Eliza rose, glad to be alone and able to explore without eyes upon her. She picked up items—a book, quill pen, comb—and inspected them closely, marveling at the workmanship. One couldn't find items of that quality at a Walmart, for sure. She ran her fingers along the wooden posts of the bed, admiring the intricate carvings and solid feel of the thing. Every piece of furniture in here was of top quality: no pasteboard or partial veneers in this era. Spying herself in the dressing table mirror, she attempted to adjust her hair, which her nap had mussed, before crossing to the armoire. She might as well secure away the rest of her jewelry.

From outside the room, she heard a giggle, then the pattering of feet running down the hallway. The door to the chamber flew open, and a small, reddish-haired boy ran in, breathless and laughing, as a large dog almost the same size as the boy followed him, bouncing up and trying to lick his face.

"Master Frederick!" cried an exasperated voice. "What would your father say? You should be abed. The fever has only been gone a day. Such exertion is not good for your lungs."

The boy's face paled as a whale of a woman pushed her way into the room. Clad entirely in black, with buttons that strained across her front, she regarded the child with an expression so stern, Eliza felt as if she herself should bow her head and apologize.

The boy, however, straightened his shoulders and answered her calmly. "I'm tired of being in bed, and Racer wanted to play." The dog, a big, funny-looking brown thing with curly hair, turned and looked at the grouchy servant, his tongue lolling out of his mouth, his ears up as if he wanted to make amends.

The nurse's face purpled. "I'll box that dog's ears if I catch you behaving in such a fashion again, I will! He ought not be in the house as it is, the dirty creature."

The boy threw his arms around the dog and squeezed it. "He will behave, Nurse Pritchett. I promise he will. I will, too."

"See that you do. You know His Grace doesn't like disturbances, and a boy and a dog are prone to creating just that." She shook her head as she turned, catching a glimpse of Eliza, who stood in the corner, observing these events with amusement. Kids weren't so different in this century, apparently.

The nurse flushed and her face slackened. "I'm sorry we bothered you, my lady. I had no idea … no one has been in this chamber for so long." She ran over to the dog and pushed on it to move. Her efforts didn't seem to faze the canine; he stood up and slowly padded his way out of the room. "Come, Master Frederick," the nurse said. "We oughtn't to be disturbing this lady."

"Who are you?" the boy demanded, eyeing Eliza with a mixture of curiosity and disapproval etched across his small, if handsome, face.

"Master Frederick!" exclaimed the nurse, visibly more frazzled by the second. "That is *no* way to address an adult, much less a lady."

"But I want to know who she is!" He plopped his hands on his hips, and jutted out his chin. "And I want to know why she is in Mama's chamber!"

Ah. So this is Deveric's son. Sympathy flooded through Eliza for such a small child willing to face down that hulk of a nursemaid to know who was in his mother's place.

As he lifted an eyebrow and growled, "I demand to know who you are and by what right you are in the Duchess's chamber," the sympathy dissipated.

He was his father's child, all right, already used to high-handed ways of behaving. Could she blame him? He'd been raised since birth to believe himself deserving of all sorts of things, given that he was the heir to a dukedom. Modern kids, who often annoyed Eliza with their senses of entitlement, could learn a thing or two from this one.

Crouching down in front of him, she looked him directly in the eyes, eyes a lighter shade of green than his father's. His reflected doubt mingled with angry curiosity.

"I'm sorry if I startled you by being here. I'm your cousin Eliza, from America." She stuck her hand out so that he could shake it. He crossed his arms, giving her an uncertain glance. "And you are?"

The nurse looked back and forth between the two of them, seemingly unsure of what to do. "Master Frederick, His Grace's son," she said to Eliza.

"Ah. A pleasure to meet you. Your daddy put me in this room." Eliza moved her hand back to her side, curbing the impulse to hug him. She wanted to reassure the boy, such a mix of haughty arrogance and uncertainty. She knew what it was like to put on a brave face; she'd been doing it since she arrived.

"My *father* never puts people in this room," he insisted. How was it he was managing to look down his nose at her when he was shorter than she was? "It's Mother's room."

He looked to the nursemaid for assistance, once more the unsure child.

The nurse's face softened. Maybe she loved the boy, for all her chastisements a few moments before.

"I'm sure the chamber is only being used because all other rooms are full," Nurse Pritchett said. "And it's not for you to question the decisions of your father." She crossed the room, taking the boy by the hand. "My apologies again, my lady," she said to Eliza as she led him toward the door.

"It's quite all right," Eliza said. "It was pleasure meeting you, and Racer. I love dogs."

Frederick gave her a crisp nod before marching proudly out, his nurse behind him.

Eliza crossed to the doorway, watching his small form disappear down the hall. "A regular little prince. Great. Now

I have two men to win over."

She lay back down on the bed, reluctant to face the people below. Had it really been such a short time ago that she was standing in the Treasure Trove, talking with Cat about this impossible dream? Now here she was, and yet she was less sure than ever. Deveric had responded better than she'd anticipated to her discussions of the future—meaning he hadn't immediately tossed her out on her ear—but he still wanted answers, still wanted to know why she was here, at Clarehaven, with him, as opposed to somewhere else. She'd have to think up an answer. Nobody wanted to hear they were a figment of someone else's imagination, a fictional hero brought to life. He didn't need to know that, either.

If only it were as easy as waltzing one time at a ball, and falling instantly in love. Cinderella didn't know how good she'd had it. She'd won over her prince with one look. The tale said nothing about Prince Charming having a suspicious mother or a handful of sisters. Much less a recalcitrant son.

Cinderella may have occupied the bottom rung in the world in which she lived, but at least she'd been familiar with all the rules, had known the ins and outs way better than Eliza did, no matter how much she'd thought she'd known before coming here.

Eliza sighed. She'd always liked Belle better, anyway. Belle hadn't given a fig for what society thought, and ended up with that amazing library of books. After taming the Beast, of course. Ah, the Beast. He hadn't really been a beast at all, just a wounded man looking for love … and acceptance. Okay, maybe he *had* been beastly, at first, in human form; but it was Belle's love that had transformed him, had healed him, had accepted him, and allowed him to open his heart again.

Cat had known *Beauty and the Beast* was Eliza's favorite

story; had she been thinking of that when she'd drafted Deveric's tale? Was Eliza Belle, Deveric her wounded Beast? And Regency society the mob of angry townspeople she needed to appease?

Eliza touched her lips, relishing the memory of Deveric's mouth on hers. Prince Charming, a Beast, or just plain old human, she liked him. She liked how he interacted with his sisters, the obvious affection he showed them. She liked how he treated his mother respectfully, but was no mama's boy. She liked his intelligence, readily on display as he'd drilled her about the machines she'd described to him in the garden. Yes, she liked Deveric Mattersley.

A hint of guilt nibbled at her conscience. She still felt a little as if she were betraying Greg any time she showed interest in another man, even ten years later, even now, after she'd wished for exactly that. Eliza had pledged her love and fidelity to Greg. They'd only been married three months, and they'd been so young, but she'd taken her vows seriously.

Not that she'd lost interest in men; far from it. It'd just become easier to admire them from afar, to make them fantasies, to make them like the heroes in her romance novels—unreal. Unattainable. It was safer emotionally, safer physically, safer all the way around.

Yet here she was. In like with a man she could see herself in love with, a man she *wanted* to fall in love with. But love brought complications. Love brought intimacy—physical and emotional. Love brought the possibility of hurt, of loss.

Eliza thought she was ready, but was she? It was one thing to moon over someone like Deveric on a surface level. It was quite another to actively build a relationship with him, to open herself to him, to reveal to him who she was, flaws and all—and to be willing to accept him for who he was, as well.

"Good Lord, girl. Cart before the horse, much?" she muttered as she pushed herself up off the bed and paced the room. Liking him was a solid start. The rest, if it came, would take time.

She walked to the closet and pulled out the lockbox. Retrieving her phone, she cradled it in her hand. She turned it on, needing to see Cat's face. At the selfie of them in their Regency garb, laughing as they tried to fit themselves and their dresses into the picture, tears slipped down Eliza's face. She touched her finger to the screen, to Cat, then turned the phone off again. She was grateful she'd sprung for the back-up battery case, but even so, the phone would eventually run out of power. She needed to conserve it as much as possible, so that she could show everything to Dev, but more than that, she wanted to be able to look back at her past every once in a while, to see her friend.

Once the phone was completely dead, she guessed she'd have to destroy it—too risky to keep it around forever. Or—could she hide it? Maybe take a few pictures here, and somehow get it back to Cat in 2012? Would the phone even make it that long? Perhaps its innards would corrode over the two-hundred-year span separating her from Cat.

With a sigh, she tucked the treasured phone back into the lockbox and stashed the box away before collapsing on the bed again.

Eliza'd been kidding herself into thinking this wouldn't be so bad. Cat had warned her, but Eliza hadn't wanted to listen. Cat was right. Traveling to a foreign country was often disorienting enough, traveling to a foreign *time* was another thing entirely. She thought she'd read enough to know what life was like here, but she was wrong. For one thing, romances never mentioned bathroom issues, or how deucedly uncomfortable wool could be. Romances didn't focus on feeling cold, or weird foods, or servant-ducal relationships. Even in Jane Austen's novels, Eliza had read for the romance, not for the reality.

And what she wouldn't give for a good old-fashioned Coke. *Old-fashioned, Lizzie? The stuff hasn't even been invented yet!*

She dropped her arm across her forehead, closing her eyes. She'd been insane. She'd been deluded. How was she ever going to blend in here, much less make a duke fall in love with her?

Why had she assumed it'd be easier to create a soul mate than to find one in real life? This *was* real life, and she still had to go through all the effort, all the beginnings, without the promise of the happy-ever-after.

And she was doing it at a severe disadvantage, considering how much a stranger in a strange land she was. She fingered her dress with her free hand. She was drowning in it, this heavy garment full of nips and tucks and ruffles, layers on layers of fabric, a far cry from her favorite T-shirt and jeans. She understood why the woolen layers were necessary, for although embers glowed in the fireplace from that morning's fire, the room had taken on a noticeable chill.

With a sigh, she stood up, smoothing down her dress. *Eliza James, you asked for this. This is what you wanted, and you're not going to find love by hiding in this room.* Because that's what she was doing. Hiding.

How was she going to pull this off? Even if Deveric eventually accepted her for who she was, how was she going to move in this society with any degree of finesse? Manners, social grace, and social status were crucial in this era, taught from birth, ingrained on one's consciousness. If she blew it, she faced serious ostracism and loss of social position. Not that she had a position right now. God, she prayed Cat was right that she could return home if she needed to, for she faced a very uncertain future were things not to work out with Deveric, and the escape clause failed.

There were few options for unmarried women without family in this era, and the relatively respectable ones—milliner, seamstress, cook—Eliza held no qualifications for. She might perhaps pass as a governess, or a lady's companion, if push came to shove, and opportunities arose. If she really mucked up here, if she couldn't make it work and the Dowager Dragon dispensed of her, she would be up a creek. Many women in this era had turned to prostitution to survive. Eliza shook her head. She would never—*never*—be one of them.

She tucked a tendril of hair behind her ear, releasing a heavy sigh. Rome wasn't built in a day. Neither was love. Patience. She needed patience. And a plan.

And, well, hiding out until tomorrow seemed a good enough start. Facing Deveric's dragon of a mother, kissing Deveric in the gardens, meeting Deveric's son … that was enough for anyone to deal with in one day, right?

She crawled back into the large bed. Too bad there was no Do Not Disturb sign to hang on the door. Would anyone come looking for her?

She clutched the covers up to her chin, a wave of loneliness engulfing her. A tear slipped out of her eye, and she wiped it away. No one said this would be easy. But she'd been alone before, for long periods of time. She was strong.

And, as Scarlett O'Hara had said, tomorrow was another day.

CHAPTER 13

Eliza woke to the sound of Betsy laying the fire.

"Good morning, my lady," the maid said, her cheerful face warming Eliza's heart. "I came to check on you last night, but you were fast asleep. I didn't wish to disturb you."

Eliza yawned, stretching her arms. "I feel so much better, Betsy. Traveling really takes it out of a girl." Especially time-traveling.

Betsy nodded. "I suppose so. You overslept and missed breakfast, but I brought you a tray. I thought you'd be hungry, having missed dinner."

At that, Eliza's stomach rumbled, and she gratefully took the tray, on which Betsy had piled eggs, a chunk of cheese, toast, and … wait, was that chocolate? Hot chocolate? Eliza picked up the steaming cup and sipped. Definitely chocolate, but rather bitter. On the other hand, bitter chocolate was better than no chocolate. She sipped again. Not quite the same as the drink from The Grounds, the coffee shop she and

Cat frequented, but it would do. It would do, indeed.

"Thank you, Betsy. This is heavenly."

The maid beamed and bustled about the room, straightening items already straight while Eliza ate. When Eliza had finished, Betsy helped her into a new gown, one quite similar to the one she'd slept in. After securing Eliza's hair in a simple but elegant-looking style, she curtsied. "I must go help downstairs, my lady. The guests have gathered outside for games. Would you like me to escort you?"

"No, no. I'd like a few more minutes here, if you don't mind. I can find my way, I'm sure."

Refreshed from more than a full night's sleep, Eliza was ready to face the day—and the people—but figured this was a good time to explore the house and hopefully pick up more clues about the formidable Mr. Mattersley. *Oh, excuse me—His Grace, the Duke of Claremont.* She wasn't snooping if she didn't get into anything, right? She just needed a little time on her own to soak in this Regency experience, to gather her bearings, to … okay, yeah, to snoop on the Duke.

She wandered from room to room, unnoticed, occasionally glancing out a window at the people gathered on the lawn. Most of the guests, as well as the Mattersley family, were outside, playing badminton. No, wait: it was battledore and shuttlecock, an earlier iteration of badminton. She stopped to watch for a moment, thankful for the time alone; it gave her space to breathe. Besides, exploring Clarehaven was a joy in and of itself. Everything was bright and vibrant, not faded from time, and, unlike in a museum, she could touch things.

She ran her hands along the silken fabric wallpaper in another parlor, noting the rich yellow colors, the different fabrics of the papers giving the walls a striped appearance. It was higher quality than anything she'd ever seen on modern walls, for sure. Against the back wall sat a small reclining sofa with intricately carved feet. Two long windows let in a great amount of sunlight, warming the room considerably. Eliza ran her fingers over the wooden surface of a small cherry desk in the corner—a writing table, she figured, noting the inkstand at its top end.

"What are you doing in here?"

Eliza's head jerked up at the voice. Deveric's sister crossed the room from the doorway, the corners of her mouth turning down.

"My apologies, Lady Amara," Eliza said. "I wasn't sure what I should do or where I should be today. I didn't want to disturb anyone, so I thought I'd, uh, read a book." A small lie. But she couldn't exactly admit she was spying, right?

Amara looked down at Eliza's noticeably empty hands.

"I couldn't remember where the library was." Eliza's cheeks burned, but she did her best to project openness and friendliness, despite Amara's suspicious expression. She could win this woman over. She could. "I wanted to thank you for loaning me this dress. I greatly appreciate it." Eliza smoothed her hands down over the fabric at her hips. "It's grander than anything I've ever owned."

"Grander than the ball gown you were wearing the other night?"

Eliza sucked in a breath. "Well, that technically isn't mine. A ... a dear friend gave it to me, figuring I would need it here in England." She looked down at the floor. Raising her eyes again, she gave Amara her warmest smile. "I miss her. It would be nice to have a friend here, too."

Amara's mouth turned down even further. "You mean *me*?" She walked slowly around the room. Stopping in front of the window, she set her fingertips against the glass as she looked out. "Who are you, truthfully?"

Eliza gulped. "I am who I said I am: an American widow looking for a new life here in England." *That much was the truth.*

Amara looked back at her, raising a brow. "And you are cousin to one of the wealthiest dukes in the country? How convenient."

Eliza met her gaze, refusing to let Deveric's sister intimidate her. "I am sorry you find my motives suspect. I assure you, I did not expect to be in this position, either. My friend helped ... fund my passage to Clarehaven. She knew there was nothing left for me in America after losing my husband and then my parents. I had nothing. I was ... lost."

Amara jerked her head toward the window. "I often feel the same way," she said after a minute. The words came out in a whisper, and the minute she said them, she ducked her head and looked in the opposite direction from Eliza, as if embarrassed by the admission.

Eliza walked over to her, stopping a few feet away. The two women watched as Emmeline whacked the shuttlecock into Rebecca's face.

"I'm a good listener," she offered to Amara. "If you need an ear, that is."

Amara's shoulders stiffened. "You think I would share intimate secrets with a stranger?"

Eliza shrugged. "It's up to you. Loneliness hurts. I could use a friend. I thought maybe you could use one, too." Amara's walls were high, and icy. If she could befriend this woman, she could conquer anything. Anyone. Right?

Dev's sister studied her. "I admit, I appreciate your bluntness, Mrs. James. It's a nice change from constant pleasantries, especially from people you know speak about you behind—"

She stopped talking as a maid walked in. "I'm—I'm sorry, Lady Amara," the maid said upon seeing the two women. "I weren't expectin' anyone to be in here." She started to back out of the room.

"What's your name?" Eliza called.

"M-Mary, my lady."

"Hello, Mary. I'm Eliza. I'm sorry if we're keeping you from your work. We can go elsewhere, right, Lady Amara?"

The maid gulped. Her cheeks flushed red as she glanced uncertainly toward Amara.

"Mrs. James and I shall leave you to your duties," Amara said after a moment, her eyes fixed on Eliza as she spoke the words. She walked toward the door, beckoning Eliza to follow. As Eliza obeyed, she could have sworn Amara muttered "benefit of the doubt" under her breath. *Huh?*

Once in the hallway, Amara pressed her finger against her mouth. *Wait, was she smiling?* "That is possibly a first for me."

"What is?"

"Vacating a room for a servant. Mother taught us to ignore the servants. They are to do their duties without comment, and are not to disturb us while doing so."

No wonder Mary looked so nervous. "Gee whiz, that's a snobby approach," Eliza exclaimed before clapping her hand over her mouth. She really needed to think more before she spoke. It was a habit that often had gotten her into trouble in her own time, and it wasn't doing her any favors here. She braced herself for Amara's response, sure she was about to get a major set-down.

Amara choked back a laugh, instead, the edge of her lips curling up. "I should be offended," she said, "having been called a snob by an American. And yet I find it rather amusing. Refreshingly honest."

Eliza exhaled in relief.

"A duke's family is expected to be, as you put it, snobbish. We *are* of a higher station than others, of course."

"You really believe that?"

"It is what I have been taught from birth."

"Well, *I* believe all men are created equal."

"How … American." The words were sharp, but Amara's eye held an unexpected twinkle.

"Women, too, for that matter," Eliza said, as they moved down the hallway together. In for a penny, in for a pound. Something about Amara's feisty character suggested to Eliza that Amara wasn't truly enamored of the way her society functioned.

Amara stopped midstride. "You believe men and women are equal?"

"Absolutely."

"My mother undoubtedly deems herself equal to any man who might cross her path." Amara smirked. "And I, myself, like the idea. Unfortunately, the rest of society does not. Men may be free to pursue what—and whom—they wish; women certainly are not."

"They are where I come from. At least in principle."

"Mr. Jefferson did not include women in his Declaration of Independence," Amara pointed out. "All *men* …"

"No, he didn't. But that will change, I'm certain of it. Same with slavery. The end of that can't come soon enough for me."

Amara nodded. "You and I are in agreement on that, at least."

"Heaven forbid we agree on something," Eliza dared to say, relief flooding through her at Amara's laughing response.

"Amara! Cousin Eliza. There you are!" a voice called from down the hallway. Becca scurried toward them. "I'm to tell you Mother wants you with us on the lawn."

"She does? Whatever for?"

"I don't know." Becca shrugged. "She told me to come find you both; that is all."

"Maybe she thinks my American ways will corrupt you," Eliza said to Amara, her lips pinching together in amusement.

"More likely she's worried about me corrupting you." Amara heaved a sigh, ignoring Eliza's questioning glance. "We are coming, Becca. You may tell her."

"Yes, sister," answered Becca, before she skipped back down the hallway and out a door at the far end.

"She is so young," Amara said. "To be that innocent again."

"Agreed."

Amara gave her a shrewd look. "Perhaps—" she started, before cutting herself off.

What had she been about to say?

"Come." Amara made her way to Clarehaven's back entrance, Eliza trailing behind. Accepting woolen pelisses from a maid, Amara handed one to Eliza. As they donned the warm garments, Amara gestured to the door. "Shall we?"

It wasn't a declaration of friendship, to be sure, but that Amara was willing to stay in her company was a beginning, right?

Together, they walked out into the cold sunshine.

Chapter 14

*D*everic's attention flew to Eliza as she and his sister walked out onto the lawn. He'd tried to convince himself he wasn't thinking of her, wasn't wondering where she'd been yesterday evening and what she'd been doing, wasn't wrestling with everything she had told him the previous morning. Whom did he think he was fooling? How could his mind be anywhere else? Not only were the things she'd told him so wondrous they couldn't be ignored, but she herself called to him like a siren to a sailor.

That in and of itself was disconcerting. He couldn't remember having a stronger physical reaction to any female—and it's not like he hadn't had plenty of opportunity. Being a duke attracted women in droves. Being a youngish duke in possession of all of his teeth and, according to what a number of women implied, being of fine countenance, meant he never lacked for opportunity. Just interest. Until Mrs. James had appeared.

Part of him couldn't help but still wonder—was he under some sort of spell? Who knew of what people were capable in this future of hers? She'd insisted she wasn't a witch—but was it possible she had other sorts of powers, powers against which a man like him had no hope?

He shook his head. It couldn't be. And yet, he couldn't keep his eyes off of her. In truth, it wasn't her physical person alone that drew him to her, though Lord knew he found her wildly, intoxicatingly, frustratingly attractive. No, though he'd only known her a few days, he already admired her spirit, her energy—and her keen mind. It was obvious from speaking with her this was no empty-headed, simpering miss. Indeed, she'd told him she'd been at university, working on being a doctor of literature, before she'd come to this place.

Women at university. It was hard to fathom, though he'd never held to the beliefs others of his ilk did, that women were naturally inferior to men. He'd seen the strength in his sister Amara as she'd weathered scandal, he'd seen the ferocity in his mother when she defended her family, seen the brilliance in Grace, with her literary creations he thought rivaled Ann Radcliffe or Fanny Burney. But his sisters at Cambridge or Oxford?

Eliza laughed openly at something Amara said, and the joy on her face brought an ache to his stomach. Or perhaps higher. Eliza was full of life. She was zest and exuberance and vitality. The opposite of how Deveric had felt for years. The opposite of Mirabelle, of many of the women of his acquaintance, who, if they had such vibrant personalities, dulled them down for the sake of decorum. This Mrs. Eliza James was a breath of fresh air in a very stale existence.

She drew him to her like a magnet.

Several times that afternoon, Arth and Coll had ribbed

him about his head being elsewhere. They'd trounced him at bowls. A number of the young ladies had pouted openly that the Duke and his friends were paying them no attention, earning the women scoldings from their mothers.

It was true; he wasn't paying attention. To anything. Thoughts of Eliza, this mystery woman, consumed him.

As the women neared, it surprised him to see Eliza link her arm with his sister's. It shocked him even more that Amara didn't resist, especially given her hostility that first evening. As far as Deveric knew, it'd been some time since Amara had shown interest in any female outside the family. And she well knew, if no one else did, that Mrs. James was no relative. How had Eliza won Amara over so quickly? Unease licked at his skin. What kind of magic did the woman wield?

No. No magic. No witchcraft. Those things were illogical, absurd. She was just a woman. A regular woman. He nearly snorted at that thought. Eliza James was anything but *regular*.

"Where have you been?" he blurted out when they were within earshot, his voice sharper than intended. Several guests looked at him. He shouldn't be surprised at their interest, he supposed. A gentleman did not call loudly after women. He walked a few steps toward the women to ensure their conversation would not be overheard, glowering over his shoulder in the guests' direction, lest they entertain the idea of eavesdropping. With satisfaction, he noted many of them moving away, before he turned his attention back to Amara and Eliza.

"Did you miss us, dear brother?"

"I merely wanted to check on our guest. She was not at dinner last night." He hoped his tone conveyed polite disinterest. *Nor breakfast*, but he wasn't going to admit he'd noticed. Amara's sly grin and steady gaze told him he hadn't fooled her.

"I'm fine. I was merely exhausted from … traveling," Eliza said. She leaned in and whispered to him. "I met your son."

"Freddy? When? How?" What was the boy doing out of bed? He was in no condition to be up. Deveric's heart constricted, his breath catching. Would Frederick worsen now? Sink back into delirium? "Is he all right?"

"Yes, he's fine; he was hiding in my chambers yesterday afternoon, attempting to escape the nurse. Not that I blame him—once I met his nurse, I wanted to escape, too."

His lips turned up in amusement. He'd often thought the same of Nurse Pritchett, but she was a fixture at Clarehaven. She'd been Deveric's nurse when he was a small lad, and was terrifying then, as well. He was sure one of the reasons he'd been so healthy all his life was his fear of being physicked by the nurse.

Eliza returned his smile. "He seems like a nice boy. Not too fond of me, though."

He lifted an eyebrow.

"Seems to think I'm trying to take his mother's place."

At that, his eyebrow shot up even farther. Amara made a noise in her throat, and Arth, who, *damn him*, had moved closer, noticeably stumbled at her words. Whispers echoed behind him. Others must have heard her, too.

Deveric studied the luscious woman before him. There was no comparison between Eliza and Mirabelle. His wife was as different from Mrs. James as night from day. There were times he could hardly recall his wife's face, much to his shame, but he'd never forgotten her frailty. So small, so thin. He'd often worried he'd snap her in half.

"I'm sorry, I didn't mean that like it sounded," Eliza stammered. "I just meant he was disappointed to see me in his mother's chamber." Her cheeks flushed a becoming pink.

The whispering behind him increased, but he quelled it with one backward glance. He knew why they talked, knew everyone was aware no one used Mirabelle's chamber, ever, but no one should dare gossip in his presence. He was the Duke, after all.

His eyes returned to Eliza, and then fell to her full bosom, his loins tightening. He liked her rounded figure, liked that she was more a sunflower than a reed, all full blossom and heavier shape. She was sturdy, solidly built. She would never crumble, not the way Mirabelle had. In the short time he'd known Eliza, he'd witnessed the fire in her spirit, and optimism to her outlook, that he sensed were hard to dim.

"Are you o—are you all right?" she asked.

He nodded, a sharp motion, trying to douse the desire running through his veins. He was no school lad, incapable of controlling himself. With great effort, he slowed his breathing, his eyes now anywhere except on the tempting widow.

"A pleasure to see you again, Mrs. James," Arthington commented from his side. "You are looking *well*." The words were innocent, but the tone was not. Before he knew it, Dev edged closer to Eliza, in front of the other man, as if to shield her from Arth's view. Arthington might be one of Deveric's closest friends, but he had quite a well-deserved reputation as a rake, and a young widow such as Eliza would be easy prey. It was Deveric's duty to protect her. Was it not?

Arthington coughed, acknowledging the strangeness of Deveric's behavior. Eliza moved out from behind him to his side.

"Pay no attention to my brother, Your Grace. He seems not quite himself today," Amara said, her lips twitching.

"We have something in common," Arthington drawled to

Eliza, disregarding Deveric. At her confused look, he added, "James. My given name. A fine name. I am the seventh James in our family." He paused, his eyes falling to her mouth. Deveric stiffened as Arth's lids lowered, his mouth pulling to the side, revealing that snaggletooth. Deveric knew that look, had seen Arth use it on numerous women, to great effect.

Arthington stepped closer to Eliza, ignoring Deveric's glare. "Would you like to stroll with me in the gardens? Perhaps with Lady Amara and Emerlin? I'd love to hear more about the wilds of America. I've never been."

"She's promised a walk to me," Deveric bit out. Amara's mouth fell open.

"I di—" Eliza began, but Deveric grabbed her by the elbow, leading her away before she could finish her protest. Over his shoulder, he called out, "Coll is over there surrounded by debutantes. He could use some rescuing." He didn't look back to see Arth's response.

"Where are we going?" Eliza stumbled to keep up with his large strides. "And you don't have to be so rough," she snapped, pulling her arm free from his grasp.

He slowed. "I'm sorry," he offered, taking a deep breath. What was wrong with him? He never behaved this way. Who *was* this woman, and why did she have this effect on him?

Undoubtedly Amara and the others were wondering the same thing, having never seen him drag any woman off from another man, not even his wife. Not that many men had wanted Mirabelle; she hadn't exactly been a beauty.

His marriage had been a marriage of convenience, a union agreed on between his father and his father's neighbor as a way of consolidating wealth and property. Because of their marriage, Clarehaven now extended as far as the eye could see.

Deveric understood why his father had made such an arrangement. He'd gone along with it, figuring one woman was as good as another. He certainly appreciated a fine figure, but had never had romantic notions about marriage. *A Claremont does his duty.* He'd expected to marry someone of appropriate rank and rearing, regardless of attraction or affection between the two of them. And Mirabelle had been kind-hearted at first, if nothing else.

Of course, kind-hearted hadn't proven enough. Watching her turn away from him after they'd consummated their marriage had told him it wasn't enough for her, either. They'd got along tolerably well, as long as he hadn't pressured her in the bedroom. He'd learned to sublimate his baser instincts.

His thoughts were anything but pure now, he admitted, looking down at Eliza's bosom, which was rising and falling rapidly due to her efforts to keep up with him.

"My apologies again." His friends would wonder if he'd gone mad, offering two apologies in the space of less than a minute. "I felt you might need protecting from a man like Arthington."

She laughed out loud. "You think I haven't encountered men like him? I know perfectly well he's a player."

"A ... player?"

"Yeah. I guess you'd say rake or rogue. Or roué? A charmer. Rapscallion."

Deveric nearly choked on his own laughter. Player. How perfectly that encapsulated his friend.

He looked back at Arth, who was winging toothsome grins at the women surrounding Coll in an attempt to woo them away. "Good to know you are not some doe-eyed female likely to fall under his spell, then," he said.

"Nah, he's not my type."

"Your type?"

She looked at him. "Yes, type. You know, the kind of person you tend to be attracted to. Maybe tall redheads, or short brunettes. What do you call that here?"

He stared at her. "This is hardly appropriate conversation."

"Oh, come on. Play along. What's your type, Deveric?"

Hearing his Christian name on her lips was delicious, though in truth they oughtn't be so familiar with each other. She wasn't family. He didn't know what she was. Beyond … his type.

His eyes trailed over her figure. How could she look so delicious in that silly morning gown? Amara had surely been only too willing to rid herself of the dress; it was the one his mother insisted his sister wear often after her scandal. Covered from head-to-toe, as if clothing itself could keep one from temptation.

This American tempted him, whoever she was and whatever she was wearing. The fabric of the dress stretched tightly over her breasts, emphasizing them in a way he could hardly complain about. He ran his fingers through his hair.

"A gentleman of good breeding doesn't think in such ways."

"Oh, baloney," Eliza said. "You can't tell me that out of that gaggle of girls over there, not one of them interests you more than the others? Come on, I see a couple of blondes, a brunette, a redhead …"

Why was she pushing him on this? Was that a gleam in her eye? Was she deliberately provoking him?

The only woman here who interests me is you, he wanted to shout. *You, with your strange ways and odd manner, with your lips that make me long to taste them again. You, with that delicate bit of flesh showing between that ridiculous dress's neckline and your ear, you with the bluest eyes I've ever seen.*

"This is a pointless, and inappropriate, conversation."

"Who knew you'd be so stuffy? Are all dukes this stuffy? I should have told Cat, no stuffy guys."

"Stuffy?"

"Yeah, stuffy. Pompous. Rigid. Uptight. Overly proper."

"You think I'm *stuffy*?" His blood burned, his eyes searing hers. He pulled her into the garden and around the hedge, in the place they'd stood the previous morning, out of sight of the other guests.

His hand reached up and hovered in mid-air, over her breasts, without touching them, before he put it back down, clenching it in a fist at his side.

"Do you have any idea how far from stuffy I feel at the moment, Eliza James?" he ground out. "I'll tell you who's my 'type,' as you put it." He ran his fingers up into her hair, fixing her head between them. "Bizarrely endearing widows with unusual ways of speaking." He swooped in to kiss her. "American women who claim," he nipped at her chin, "to be from the future, who bewitch me with their flashing blue eyes and swishing derrieres and lovely breasts." His mouth found hers again, and his tongue traced a path across her upper lip. "Who make me doubt my own sanity. But if this is madness, I want—" He pulled her face toward his again. "—it all." He took her mouth with his in a fierce duel, lips meshing against lips, tongues exploring, tasting, testing.

The chatter of voices approached, but he ignored it, wanting to lose himself in this woman, to give in to whomever, and whatever, she was, without thought, without remorse, without consequences.

There are always consequences. His mother's voice rang in his ears. He pulled back from Eliza, fighting to catch his breath. She stared at him with those big, wide, impossibly sapphire eyes, and he wanted to immerse himself in her again, pull her down to the ground, bury himself in her depths.

A man of high station had to watch every step he took, however, lest he be trapped, or entrap others, by his own foolish actions. Panting, he retreated further, running his hands along his waistcoat and through his hair, endeavoring to regain his composure, and an appropriate distance, before anyone found them.

Amara's tinkling laughter hit him first. "I'm sure they're not far, Mother," she said as she entered the maze. "See? Here they are."

His mother whipped around the corner, all ferociousness and fire.

CHAPTER 15

"Claremont." The Dowager spat the word, Amara beside her. "This is beyond the pale. A gentleman of your breeding does not dilly-dally with a … *lady* … in the gardens."

Eliza tensed at the derision in his mother's voice.

"I am not dilly-dallying with *anyone*," Deveric snapped. "I am discussing with our *cousin* her plans for the future."

Eliza's eyes flew to his face, her cheeks draining of blood. *Oh God.* Had she pushed him too far just now, in her desperate attempt to ignite a spark between them? Would he send her away?

"I have told her she is, of course, welcome in our household for as long as she wishes to stay. Family provides for family."

Eliza nearly threw her arms around him. Gratitude churned through her veins, warring with surprise over his passionate response to her. She'd been goading him, after all, testing to see if the attraction was one-sided. His response, both physical and verbal, proved it wasn't. Thank God, it wasn't. *This is working, Cat.*

Though desire alone was not enough to build a strong foundation for a relationship, much less a life-long marriage, Eliza well knew.

But he'd defended her again to his mother, and declared she had a place with him, always. Well, okay, with the family. Whatever. Knowing she wouldn't end up homeless and destitute on the Regency streets released a torrent of emotions in her—gratitude, peace, hope, and … longing. For more than just a place with the family. For her place. With him.

The Dowager turned her disapproving gaze on Eliza, judgment written across every feature on her face. "Of course," she ground out. "A Claremont should do no less for his people. Perhaps Mrs. James will prove useful in some way."

Eliza had to stop herself from moving behind Deveric to use him as a literal shield against his mother. Instead, she drew up her shoulders and faced the matriarch head on. *Thank you, Mrs. Roosevelt.* "Rest assured, Your Grace, as I said yesterday, I do not wish to impose. Had I anywhere else to go, I would have gone."

That wasn't exactly true. This was the only place she wanted to be. Heat radiated from Deveric, who stood close behind her. Too close for propriety, surely, but she didn't care. She wanted to melt into him. She didn't know how or where things would go forward from here, but she was grateful at least the man was attracted to her. Yes, she was exactly where she wanted to be. Well, okay, not at *this* precise moment, not with the fearsome figure in front of her.

"Perhaps I could tutor young Freddy," Eliza said. *What the heck? What do I know about kids?* She smoothed her hands nervously over her hips. *It's not like you have many other applicable skills in this period, Lizzie. Nobody needs a doctoral student in literature, much of which hasn't even been written yet!* Her eyes slid to Deveric, who was glaring at his mother, his mouth tight. *And maybe win over the son, win over the father?*

The Dowager Dragon's lips turned up, a victorious expression settling on her face. "You wish to serve as *Master Frederick's* governess?" She emphasized the young boy's name. Clearly Eliza was not supposed to call the poor kid by a nickname. "Do you have the appropriate qualifications? Or references?"

Deveric interrupted her. "Eliza does not need to work for a position in our household, Mother."

"*Mrs. James,*" his mother emphasized, "seems more aware of practical matters than you, dear son. Frederick is five. Ready to begin his education. You said you would find instruction for him once he had recovered, yes?"

"Yes, but—"

"It seems Providence has stepped in here," his mother continued, ignoring his attempts to speak.

Ha, you have no idea, lady.

"We shall discuss this at a later date, in private." He stared his mother down. She returned his gaze for a few seconds, and then nodded in assent. "The huntsman is looking for you to discuss today's hunt," she said, before walking away.

Deveric sighed. Amara, who'd remained silent through the whole exchange, patted him on the arm. "You've survived." Bitterness echoed in her voice. "Is this where I admit it's nice to have someone else be the object of her wrath?"

"No. It isn't." He turned to Eliza. "My apologies. Again. I—" He broke off. Lifting his chin, he smoothed his waistcoat.

"Amara, would you escort Mrs. James back to the house? I have duties to which I need attend."

"Of course."

"For Pete's sake, I don't need someone with me every second." Eliza crossed her arms, letting out a huff. "I promise I'm not going to steal the silver." Reading that young women could hardly do anything in this era without someone in attendance, even if only a maid, was a far cry from actually experiencing it. And she was a widow; weren't they supposed to have more freedom?

Amara snickered.

"I'm not worried about what you're going to do," Deveric said as all three exited the maze. "I'm worried about them." He gestured toward the group of men across the yard.

Arthington tipped his hat in their direction.

Deveric's lips pressed into a thin line. "On the other hand, all of them shall be hunting with me by my order. A duke's decree does come in handy sometimes." He nodded to Eliza and his sister as he made his exit, his eyes lingering on Eliza's.

Eliza watched him walk off to round up the young bucks. She admired the close fit of his breeches, the way they showed off his thighs. The tall boots he wore somehow enhanced the whole masculine effect. And why *were* cravats so damn sexy? Butterflies erupted in her stomach.

"Come," Amara said, linking her arm through Eliza's, a small smile playing at the edges of her mouth. Had Amara noticed the way Eliza couldn't take her eyes off the woman's brother?

Amara gestured with her free hand toward the men. "Let us go find something to do that is unlikely to get both of us in trouble. Cards, perhaps?"

Crap. She had noticed.

Was that good thing? Or a very, very bad one?

Deveric couldn't resist one last look as Eliza and his sister strode off together. He'd definitely have to keep an eye on the two of them. Amara on her own was a spitfire enough; Amara with Eliza had the potential for disaster.

Coll approached him, having finally extricated himself from his passel of female admirers. A grin cracked his face as he followed Deveric's gaze to Eliza.

"It's good to see you acting as if you are human." His mild Irish brogue laced his words, despite the fact he'd lived in England most of his life. Coll's father's estates were in Ireland, but his English mother had wanted him educated "like a true Englishman," Coll once said, his eyes bitter, "though I'm not." Deveric wondered if Coll held on to the accent just to spite her.

Last night, over several rounds of brandy, Coll confessed he'd traveled to Clarehaven with Arthington to escape the long arm of his father, who was pressuring him to marry— and bring his bride home to Armagh.

"You certainly aren't lacking in options," Arthington had griped. "The ladies prefer your combination of dark hair and light eyes."

"And you are?" Deveric teased. "You spent time on the balcony with at least two different ladies at the ball."

"Spying on me, were you?" Arth had retorted. "And I'll have you know that … yes, well, that was me."

Arthington sauntered up now, joining Deveric and Coll. The three had been friends since their days at Eton, when

Deveric and Arth had pummeled a viscount hounding Coll about his Irish heritage. Deveric's mother had been friends with Arth's since they'd debuted in the same season, before Arth's mother had died, and Deveric viewed him almost as a brother. Not that he didn't love his own scamp of a brother, Chance, but with eight years separating them, their relationship resembled more one of father-son, especially with Samuel Mattersley having been dead more than seven years. Someone had to rein in the wild younger son.

"You know if Dawes were here, he'd have left none of the women for you," Deveric said. "So, Arth, it could be worse."

Everett Dawes, Deveric's neighbor and Earl of Stoneleigh, made up the fourth in their group. Everett's sober demeanor matched Deveric's, which was one reason they got along so well, and a reason they needed Coll and Arth to drag them back to the light when darkness called.

Dawes's mother had taken ill all of a sudden, though, which was why he was absent. He'd sent a note that he hoped to join the house party before its end, but if not, he'd meet up with them again during the Season.

"Say now, I thought we were to hunt foxes today, but if you'd prefer a different kind of sport," Arthington quipped as he pivoted to see what, and whom, Deveric and Coll were watching.

Deveric yanked on his waistcoat and turned the other direction, heading off toward the stables. "Not at all, my friends," he called over his shoulder, as the two men raced to keep up with him. "Just ensuring my sister is behaving."

"Lady Amara?" Arthington said. "Not bloody likely."

All three laughed.

"Did you enjoy dancing with every debutante who could get her hands on you, Coll?" Deveric said, wishing to change the subject from Amara, and the delectable Mrs. James.

Collinswood shrugged good-naturedly. "I have to at least pretend I'm looking for a wife. No doubt someone here will report back to my da."

Deveric chuckled as he opened the stall in which his horse, Lightning, was anxiously pawing the straw. The horse was as ready as he was to get away, to race without care or consideration of anything but the feel of the wind and the lure of the vixen in front of him.

Funny how it was Eliza, not the fox, who came to mind.

As the men lined up, anxiously anticipating the late morning's adventure, Arthington eased his horse closer to Deveric's. "You're not going to get off that easily, you know. Coll may be too otherwise occupied to notice—Lady Agnes is remarkably persistent—but I've seen the way you look at that new woman. Frankly, it's a way in which I've never seen you look at any woman before."

Deveric avoided his friend's eyes. "I don't know what you are talking about. She is a cousin, a *relation*, from America, newly arrived and grieving for the loss of her parents. I'm merely helping her adjust."

Arthington grinned, flashing that snaggletooth that drove women wild. "Methinks he doth protest too much," was all he said before he kicked his heels into the side of his horse, racing off with the rest of the riders at the sound of the huntsman's horn.

Deveric leaned over Lightning's saddle, encouraging him to faster and faster speeds. There was nothing better than this—the thrill of the race, the scenery whipping by in a blur, the air on his cheeks and the power between his legs. Suddenly Eliza's description of—what had she called them?—cars jumped into his head. It was hard to fathom the speeds of which she spoke. What would it feel like to move along at fifty, sixty, seventy miles per hour? The distances one could cover. He'd wondered before if the steam-powered vehicles he'd seen in London could eventually travel at speeds greater than a horse, but never would he have believed man would be capable of covering the distance from Winchester to London in an hour or so's time. It was nearly incomprehensible.

And she had insisted that these autocars—no, wait, automobiles—were covered carriages capable of producing cooled air in the summer and warmed air in the winter. It was all too fantastical to believe, but she had described it in such detail, such familiarity.

He needed to see this tele-phone of which she spoke, the one she claimed carried portraits of these items within it. He'd demand she show it to him this evening, after the hunt. He wanted proof.

She appeared no more than a regular woman, if one with odd speech patterns. No trace of madness was evident in her eyes, her bearing. But if it hadn't been for his own memories of the ballroom—the *wrong* ballroom—he'd have dismissed her as a lunatic. For what person could possibly travel through time? And for what purpose? He wasn't convinced her story about wanting to experience this period was true, or at least that it was the full story. Why *was* she here? With him? And what did she intend to do?

His horse leapt over a fallen trunk, and Deveric's body moved agilely in the saddle with it. He gripped the reins, pulling Lightning to the left, where he could hear the hounds howling. They must have caught sight of their quarry. The other riders were behind him, their mounts not as fast as Lightning—and likely not as skilled, Deveric thought with satisfaction.

As host of the hunt, it would be rude for him to capture the prize, so he pulled back. A few seconds later, several gentlemen raced by with calls of "Huzzah!" Arthington looked over his shoulder for a second, taunting, "Will you cede your vixen as easily as you've ceded this fox?"

With a snarl, Deveric once again leaned in and let Lightning give chase. Cede his vixen, ha! She wasn't a vixen. But, he realized with a startling surge of protectiveness, he did rather feel she was his.

Chapter 16

Eliza stood on the edge of the circle of women, listening to their chatter. The other Mattersley sisters weren't there—Becca had gone riding, Emmeline was walking in the gardens with her friend Lady Meade, and Grace, unsurprisingly, had opted to stay inside and read, according to Amara.

After an unsuccessful attempt to teach Eliza whist—she never had been good at picking up rules to games—Amara had suggested they return outside to try their hand at battlecock. Eliza was happy, at least, to learn she was decent at that.

All the women had ceased physical activity, however, and now were talking amongst themselves. It wasn't so different from modern chatter; the young ladies avidly discussed current fashion, hair products, shoes … and men. Evidently Regency ladies were as obsessed with the opposite sex as any of her twenty-first century contemporaries had been, although here the focus was on marriage, not hooking up.

Out of the range of the matrons, who'd gathered in lawn

chairs near the garden, undoubtedly enjoying being able to relax their vigilance over their charges since the men were away, the young women talked of stolen kisses and attempts to escape the eyes of their mothers or maids. Most of the girls were better versed in the mechanics of the bedroom than Eliza expected. Another twenty-first century bias to fall by the wayside, the idea that young gentlewomen of this period were ignorant about sex, though from their conversation, Eliza gathered none of them had yet done much more than kiss.

It did surprise her they felt at ease talking in front of her, a stranger, but then again, since she was standing to the side, listening rather than participating, perhaps they'd forgotten she was there.

"What's it like, Lady Amara?" Lady Harriet asked, a noticeable smirk on her face. Eliza definitely did not like that woman; she reminded Eliza of the mean girls from high school.

"What's what like?"

"Oh, come on … *it*. My married sisters won't tell me any details. They say I shouldn't worry about it until I'm married, but I say that's ridiculous. Shouldn't a young woman know what it's all about before she gets into it?"

Amara didn't act disturbed by the question, but Eliza was sure sadness flashed across her eyes. *Good God, I want to claw that harlot's eyes out, and I don't even know the full story here.*

"*It*, as you put it, is not something to be bandied about in light conversation, as you well know, Lady Harriet. I'm surprised your mother lets you come near me, being the fallen woman I am."

The other women tittered at this declaration. *Fallen woman?* Eliza's empathy for Amara jumped a hundredfold, as did her understanding of Amara's standoffish demeanor.

"You're likely correct, but I do believe she is napping under the shade of that umbrella and isn't paying the least bit of attention to me. Is it true you were caught *in flagrante delicto?*"

The girls around Lady Harriet gasped. Amara's eyes blazed brightly and two pink spots infused her white cheeks. Eliza put her fists on her hips, anger surging through her, but before she could open her mouth to defend Dev's sister, Amara spoke, her voice calmer than Eliza expected. "My situation is old news and hardly fodder for public consumption."

Harriet had the grace to at least look embarrassed. "I'm sorry. I meant no offense, truly—I merely hoped you could share details with us."

"Here's what I can share, *Lady* Harriet: be on your guard. Know what kind of man you're dealing with before you go off anywhere with him. In fact, don't go off with anyone ever. Don't do anything ever. Live a boring, obedient life, until you find yourself nodding off under an umbrella at a house party, safe in the conviction that your daughter would never do anything untoward, because you never did."

Eliza nodded along with Amara's words, glaring at Lady Harriet. She couldn't resist adding, "Lady Amara has more class in her little finger than you in your whole little self. No woman should diss another woman like that."

At that, Amara turned and walked off, shoulders straight and head held high.

Harriet sputtered as her friends looked at her. Ignoring the brat, Eliza chased after Amara, wanting to hug her to death after that strange, wretched, painful conversation.

"Oh my God, are you all right?" Eliza said as she caught up to Amara in the front parlor. Amara started at Eliza's voice. She sniffed once quickly, running a finger along the underside of her left eye, as if brushing away a tear.

"Yes, fine. I thank you for coming to my defense. You'd think I'd be used to it by now. It's been five years." She walked over and sat down on a green armchair, but kept her back erect.

That hardly looks comfortable. Eliza slouched down into a chair next to her, but immediately sat up when her stays pressed into her sides. No wonder everyone had such good posture here.

"That girl was awful to you. I am so sorry, Amara."

Amara snorted, but didn't meet Eliza's eyes. "I'm surprised you didn't hear about my ruin in America. My mother seems to think it was scandal enough to cross oceans—a nine day's wonder multiplied tenfold, in her view."

"Surely it can't be that bad."

"Yes, actually, it can." Amara traced her finger along the edge of the armrest. "I was twenty-two. Old enough to know better. Old enough to be considered halfway on the shelf, as a matter of fact. I'd had several offers over the previous seasons, but I'd always had eyes for only one man: Lord Drake Evers." At Eliza's blank gaze, she added, "Viscount Monteith. Do you know of the family?"

Eliza shook her head. The only Monteith she'd ever heard of was Cory, of *Glee* fame. Not that she had a chance of knowing any American families from this period, besides the presidential ones, perhaps.

Amara sighed as she smoothed her hands over her skirts. "I thought he only had eyes for me, too, with the way he'd flirt, the attention he paid to me. But one season turned into two and two to three, and no offer came. Mother told me to move on, that he was a rake, but I didn't want to believe her."

Plucking at an invisible thread, she continued. "He went

away to America for a year. His uncle had plantations there in Carolina—South, I think—and his father thought it'd be good for Drake to see how they were run, or something."

Eliza sat quietly, watching pain work its way across Amara's face.

"When he came back, he flirted as much as ever. One night at a ball, he asked me to go into the gardens with him. He told me he loved me. I thought a proposal was forthcoming. I let him … I lay with him. Right there, in the gardens. Like a common trollop."

Amara shook her head, her mouth twisting. A lone teardrop traced its way down her cheek. "When I happily asked when we would be married, he just looked at me, a cross of pity and I don't know what on his face. I remember his exact words. I'll never forget them. 'Sweetling,' he said. 'I'm already married. That's why I went to America—my father arranged for me to marry my cousin years ago, before he died. It was a promise he'd made to his brother, to ensure the American holdings remained in the Monteith name. I have to return next month.'

"I yelled at him, beating on his chest. 'You never told me! You let me think you were honorable, that your pursuit was honorable!'

"'Shh,' he said. 'Someone will come. And I know. I'm sorry. I wanted you so much. I love you. I've always loved you. Nobody knew about the contract besides my uncle, but I'd agreed to it at eighteen, out of loyalty to my father. Once I met you, I thought maybe I could get out of it.'"

Amara made a derisive sound in her throat, clutching her arms across her body. "Of course, my yell brought people running, and yes, they discovered me there, half-undressed, in a daze." She stood up and paced across the room. "Drake, well—he fled to America, but I, I got to bear the brunt of the scandal here at home."

She sniffed. "Deveric tried to call him out, but the coward slipped on board a ship that night and hasn't come back since. The truth came out about his deceptive behavior, but it was too late for me."

"No wonder you and your mother dislike Americans," Eliza muttered. Her heart broke at the travesty Amara had described. They might call such a man a scoundrel here, maybe even a bastard, but he was flat-out an asshole, no matter what the century.

Cat's fiancé had ditched her at the altar for another woman. How often had Eliza worked to convince Cat she wasn't at fault? Now here was another poor woman, blaming herself for the despicable actions of another. "But you did nothing wrong." Eliza ran her hand across Amara's back. "All the fault lies with Drake. That jerk."

Amara tensed at Eliza's touch. "Jerk? I don't know this word."

"Uh, a blackguard, a bounder, a …"

"I get the idea." A wan smile crossed Amara's face. "I was at fault. For being free with my affections. Not that I wanted to marry, but after being publicly ruined, no man of status would consider me. Though a number propositioned me, of course."

"Ruined? That's absurd. Having se—having relations with someone doesn't ruin you, for Pete's sake."

Even as the words came out of her mouth, Eliza recalled all the books she'd read that stated exactly that—if you slept with a man before you were married in this era, you were toast. Eliza had always been conservative in this area, a testament to her overly romantic heart, perhaps. She'd only been intimate with her husband, and one other man. And the second one wasn't because she'd wanted to, but because he'd put on pressure and she hadn't said no. But at least the worst she'd faced from that was her own self-recriminations. No one else had batted an eye. In fact, many of her friends thought it weird, her reluctance to hop into bed. At least Cat had understood, had agreed that kind of intimacy wasn't to be taken lightly.

Eliza's thoughts flitted to Deveric. He aroused her like no one else, even more than Greg—though it felt a betrayal to think that. Then again, she and Greg had been young, new, inexperienced. Their first encounters had been half-fun, half-fear. It had gotten better, their lovemaking, but, truth be told, Eliza had always wrestled with the naked part of physical intimacy. It was difficult for her, to be so fully exposed to another person, to face their judgment, and potential rejection. Not that her husband had disliked her body. But he *had* made the occasional comment about her level of sweets consumption.

"Do you really need that second piece of cake?" he'd said to her on her eighteenth birthday, a month before their wedding. She'd been self-conscious after that, wanting to only make love in the dark, lest he see her rounded thighs, her not-exactly-flat stomach, and be turned off.

Images of Deveric and her naked, entangled, flooded her mind. She was sure her cheeks flamed brighter than a fire truck, and was almost grateful Amara had her hands over her eyes, so she didn't see. Eliza swallowed.

It was one thing to admire Deveric's physicality from afar. What would it be like to be in bed with him? To be intimate with him? Panic flared, even as her skin tingled and her pulse raced at the mere thought. It was clear, thank God, that Deveric was physically attracted to her, but would that attraction dim if he saw her in the nude, saw how her skin dimpled and curves existed where they ought not be?

Better not to think of that right now. She'd deal with that if and when the time came. Perhaps everyone in this time period preferred intimate relations to occur in the dark.

"You are not ruined, Amara," Eliza repeated, her hand making circular motions across the other woman's back, desperate to imbue some calm into Deveric's poor sister, whose shoulders shook as silent tears fell. She knew, however, her words weren't true, by Regency standards. Anger and frustration flared at all Amara had had to endure. It wasn't right. It just wasn't.

"You're telling me it's different in America? That young women are not judged on their virtue?" Amara narrowed her eyes, her mouth pinched tight as she wiped the tears from her face. She stood up and paced the room. "Here, ironically, you can be intimate with whomever you want—*after* you're married. People turn a blind eye to affairs and trysts all the time among the married or even widowed set. Mama certainly did to Father's. But be less than virtuous once as a debutante, and your reputation can never be restored. The taint of scandal forever remains, even for the daughter of a duke."

"That sucks." *Deveric's father had cheated on the Dowager?* Maybe that explained the Dragon's sour disposition. *Deveric wouldn't do that, would he?* Eliza'd mentioned specifically to Cat an unfaithful husband was one of her greatest fears. Surely Deveric was the loyal and true type, right?

A choked laugh burst forth from Amara. "That *sucks*? I'm not sure what that means, but it sounds apt."

Eliza rose and walked with Amara, glad to see a spark

return to Deveric's sister's eyes. "Do you *want* to get married?"

Stopping at the window, Amara stared out at the lawn, where the other young women still meandered back and forth, talking. "It hardly matters; I am not marriageable. Oh, Mother found men willing to take me after the … incident. A large enough dowry wins out over soiled goods. But I refused. I was, stupidly, still in love with Evers. I couldn't imagine giving myself to another man. Now, I am past my prime."

Eliza snorted. "Um, how old are you?"

"Twenty-seven."

"Twenty-seven? Honey, you are hardly past your prime. You're just getting started. Besides, Anne was twenty-seven when she found Wentworth, and love, again."

Amara's brow furrowed. "Who is this Anne?"

Drat. Persuasion hasn't been written yet. Jane Austen's novels had been such a part and parcel of Eliza's life for so long, it was hard, not to mention a bit bewildering, to realize most of them didn't exist yet. "A … friend. I myself am twenty-nine, and still hope my great love is out there." *Out hunting right now, as a matter of fact.* "But if you don't want to marry, you must have other interests."

A harsh cackle escaped Amara. "What shall I do? I live off my brother's largesse. There are few options for spinsters. Unless I serve as a lady's companion, or perhaps a governess." She threw her hands in the air. "I sew fine stitches; perhaps I shall become a seamstress. Or an actress. Or perhaps courtesan, to match others' opinions of me."

"I'm sorry. I wasn't trying to upset you further." And women thought they had it bad in modern America. Sure, ageism was rampant, but at least there were many more options from which to choose than here.

Amara didn't answer, but rather traced her finger along a pane of glass.

Eliza fell silent, as well. Her options, were Deveric and she not to fall in love, weren't much better. She was a widow, at least, so she had more freedom, even in potential dalliances, than Amara did. But regardless of whether widowed or never married, being a single woman in the Regency was not desirable in the least, unless one was perhaps rich. And rich she was not.

Crossing her fingers, Eliza sent up a mental plea that should, heaven forbid, she need to use Cat's escape clause, it would work. She'd been so swept up in the fantasy, in the absolute belief Cat could make her dreams come true, that she hadn't wanted to face the very real possibility this could fail, and she could be trapped—permanently—in the past. Deveric had promised she'd always have a place here, but would he stick to that if they had a falling out?

After a moment, Amara turned toward Eliza. "No, I should apologize. That was untoward of me. I'm frustrated that women of my position are expected to do nothing. Throw balls and soirees, maybe play an instrument. Dabble in painting. But express too much of an interest in, say, reading, or heaven forbid, science, and one gets labeled a bluestocking."

"I can think of worse labels. Is that what you want to do? Study science?"

Amara looked up and out at the brilliant blue sky. "I've always been fascinated by the stars," she admitted. "They are so beautiful. Fixed. Familiar. And yet unknown at the same time. I want to know more about them. I want to visit the Royal Observatory, look through a giant telescope. I would love to meet Mr. Herschel, and his sister, Caroline, perhaps some day be elected to the Royal Society." She tucked her head down. "I've never admitted that to anyone before. Those aren't things a duke's daughter does."

"I'm honored you shared with me," said Eliza, truly touched that this woman, who two days ago seemed a certain enemy, now felt more like a friend. "It's a shame the universities here don't admit women."

Amara gave her a wry grin. "Here? They do in America?"

"Uh, well, not yet …"

"Not yet? America may not have the same social restrictions as here in England, but I highly doubt the day will ever come when women are valued as equally as men, no matter what Mary Wollstonecraft preaches."

Eliza considered Amara's words. While she'd never been as career-driven as other women she knew, she'd had friends who railed against the glass ceilings in their corporations, against the miniscule maternity leaves granted to women and the difficulties in reentering the workforce after having kids, especially if one worked in a high-intensity, highly competitive field such as law or medicine.

"Maybe we're not there yet, but much will change. I'm sure of it."

Amara eyed her curiously. "You're different. I'm surprised to find I rather like your American frankness."

"Thank you," Eliza said. "I would so love to have a friend here. I miss mine from back home." Heart pangs struck. What was Cat doing right now? Who was she with? Was she okay?

"Why did you not stay, then?"

"There wasn't much left for me, without my parents and husband. And I was hoping for better fortune here."

"Better fortune?" Amara's whole body tensed as her brows narrowed.

"No, no. I don't mean it in that sense." Heaven forbid Amara think her a fortune hunter. "I mean—I guess I mean family. I don't have anyone anymore. I'd like family here, whether that be … cousins, or yes, eventually a husband and children of my own."

"I have noticed you watching Dev. Are you after my brother's title and wealth?" Suspicion emanated from the woman who moments before exhibited friendliness, the bluntness of her question catching Eliza by surprise.

"No!" Eliza's face sizzled, her thoughts on the passionate kiss she'd shared with Deveric in the garden. Make that kisses. "I will only follow my heart, and if it doesn't lead to true, reciprocal love, then, well, I don't know. But I assure you, I am not after your family's money."

"But you are penniless, correct?"

Eliza's eyes stung with tears, though she was glad Amara was so protective of her brother, of the Mattersley family; loyalty was a quality she admired. She couldn't fault Amara her accusations, either. Wouldn't Eliza think the same thing of a strange woman showing up in a rich man's household?

"Not exactly," she said. "I have a few jewels and gold I managed to bring with me in my dress. But you're right; it's probably not enough to live on long-term. That's why I offered to serve as Fred—Master Frederick's governess—to earn my keep here."

Amara's shoulders relaxed. After moment, her eyes softened. "I must apologize, Mrs. James. I tend to expect the worst in people."

Eliza didn't respond, her emotions awhirl from Amara's accusations and her uncertainty over her own future.

"I *have* seen how you look at him, though," Amara said. "There is something you must know. Even if my brother were to remarry, he would never marry a governess. Nor an American cousin, for that matter. It's not fitting for a man of his station." She tapped her fingers to her lips. "But in truth, none of those things matter. Deveric has sworn never to marry again."

Chapter 17

Amara's words knocked the wind out of Eliza. Never marry again? Never consider her? *Was this too big a social gulf to bridge?*

Eliza hadn't fully taken that into account, though she should have, of course. Cinderella went from rags to riches, but that story was notable exactly because it rarely, if ever, happened. Just like the multiple tales of marquesses with maids, earls with vicars' daughters, and dukes with governesses in Eliza's romance novels. They were fantasy. Fiction. Fiction that allowed Average Janes like her to believe, if only for a few hundred pages, they, too, could land a man of wealth, power … and impossibly good looks. Like Deveric.

Perhaps she *should* have asked Cat to write in a title for her, make her a duchess in her own right, or something. Except that wouldn't have worked—through trial and error, they'd deduced Cat could only bring fictional people to life; changing existing people wasn't possible. *Curse me and my impulsive nature, leaping from frying pan after frying pan into the fire.*

Despair settled on her shoulders like an unwelcome yoke. She swallowed, hard.

Empathy shone in Amara's eyes. "Believe me, as you now know, I understand what it is like to be in an impossible situation. To have feelings, even in such a short time, for someone that can never be."

Tears pricked Eliza's eyelids, but she refused to let them fall. Amara was not the master of her fate. She was. Just because Amara said Deveric would never remarry did not necessarily mean it was true. She squared her shoulders, willing her confidence back. Besides, Amara did not know of Eliza's secret, of Cat's story, of the power of Deveric's and her connection.

And I will never tell her. Or Deveric. He may perhaps accept my time-travel tale, but to reveal he himself was a fictional creation? Not in a million years. Besides, he was one hundred percent real now. As was the rest of his family. *It is no different than if we had met in some regular way.*

She fought back a painful snort. *Yeah, you keep telling yourself that, girlie.* Still, there was hope. Cat's story brought her hope—as did its promise that anything that did develop between Deveric and Eliza would be by choice.

"May I ask you something?" Amara's voice was gentle.

Eliza nodded, optimistic determination warring with misery.

"You said you've been a widow for ten years. May I ask what happened?"

The last thing Eliza wanted to do was talk about Greg, not with Deveric so heavy on her mind. But Amara had been honest with her; Dev's sister deserved the same in return. "He was my childhood sweetheart; our parents were friends. We were married only a few months before I lost him."

"How did he die?"

"Trying to save others during an attack." Her mind raced unwillingly to that day and the horror of the Twin Towers.

"Commendable. A military man?"

"Yes," Eliza whispered. She didn't like to think of it, of the what-ifs. What if he hadn't been visiting his brother? What if he'd gotten out, instead of staying to help others? What if?

"I am sorry. Truly."

"Thank you."

Amara walked back to Eliza. "Come," she said.

Eliza stood up, unsure what Dev's sister wanted, but Amara merely hooked her arm through Eliza's, pulling her into a stroll about the room. "As a widow, you have more freedom. If you want to dally with my brother—"

"—I don't want to 'dally' with anyone." Eliza's voice was sharp.

"Forgive me. I did not mean to disparage your character. Whereas you came to my defense upon learning of my indiscretion, I did not give you the same benefit of the doubt, and now I stand guilty of assuming you would commit improprieties. Not all are like me, I suppose." Amara gave a self-deprecating snort. "Let us begin again, if you are willing. I should also like a friend. Few people beyond my family have kept up connections with me."

"Well, that's ridiculous." She patted Amara's arm, the one hooked through her own. "I firmly believe *you* committed no improprieties, Lady Amara. You were with the man you loved. There is nothing wrong with that. It is he who committed improprieties, and worse, against you."

Amara's eyes shone with unshed tears. "In truth," she said, "I *would* like to see my brother happy. He has closed himself off for so long, though at least his retreat was his own choice."

She broke off. "What is it about you, Mrs. Eliza James? It's as if I've known you forever, as if we were destined to be friends, and it's only been two days. If I'm not careful, I will have spilled all of the family secrets to you within the space of an hour."

Warmth flooded Eliza's veins. "I feel the same way. I'm glad you can talk to me. I've been lonely." She may only have been gone from 2012 and her friend Cat for a few days, but it felt much, much longer than that. Two hundred years longer.

"Come, let's retire to our rooms," Amara said, formal demeanor back as she released Eliza's arm. "It's time to dress for dinner."

"Um, okay." Eliza had been hoping for another nap—the events of the last few hours, the last few days, of switching centuries—were getting to her. "But I'm not sure I know how to find my room again."

Amara led her down a corridor. "It *is* rather a maze, is it not? Clarehaven is not my favorite of the family homes for that reason; too many past dukes have added on too many rooms over the centuries. I myself have got lost many a time."

"Homes?" Eliza gulped.

"Yes, of course. We have an estate in Yorkshire, as well as here. Claremont owns a townhouse on St James's Square for when he's in London. The family has a separate space near Grosvenor—a place for the women to stay while in Town. Deveric does not care for the social chaos when we are all in residence at once."

"Good Lord," was all Eliza could think to say. Her parents had proudly bought a house when she was a child, but it'd been a small one, perhaps the size of the ballroom and her chamber here combined. Cat had shared her small apartment above the bookstore. Eliza loved it and was grateful to call it home, but she didn't own it.

It was one thing to wander through this majestic house as if a tourist. It was quite another to imagine it as a regular home. Was there a room somewhere where the family could let their hair down and relax? Everything to this point was exceedingly formal. It exhausted her.

As she watched a maid exit a room and skitter down the hallway, a thought hit her again. A duchess was expected to competently run a household of this size—or several households, as Amara had just said. How could she ever hope to do so? How could she ever learn all the rules, the ins and— *No! Stop that! Whatever comes your way, you can handle it, Eliza Anne James.* Doubt and fear never helped anything, and neither would succumbing to them now. *Start as you mean to go on.* And she meant to go on with confidence.

"I expect we'll journey back to London in the next week or so for the Season," Amara commented as they strolled down yet another hallway. Did this house never end? "Although I suppose you will stay here, if you are to tutor Frederick."

Freddy got left behind? Eliza shouldn't be surprised; she knew many a wealthy, noble family sent their children elsewhere for education in this era. Still, sadness swept through her at the thought of the little boy alone in this huge house. Servants were no substitute for family.

Where did he play? Did he get to play? Were there other children around for him to associate with? If there weren't, he must be dreadfully lonely. *Perhaps he and I do have something in common.* Eliza knew what it was like to be the only child of busy parents.

She couldn't resist asking. "Does he have anyone to play with?"

Amara paused. "In truth, I don't know how he spends his

days. I hadn't thought of it, really."

"He's your nephew!" *Oops.* Way to solidify a friendship, Lizzie—by chewing someone out.

Amara's cheeks pinked. "Yes, but I haven't much of an affinity for children. I don't think I'd like to be a mother. Though I suppose if I ever were to marry, it would be expected of me."

"Perhaps that's why you haven't."

"What?"

"Perhaps that's why you haven't married. Easier not to have children if you don't have a husband," Eliza said. "Though I guess that's not a guarantee against pregnancy."

Amara flushed. "Are you suggesting … ? I have never, not since Drake. People think, but …"

"No, no, I was not referring to you specifically. I'm sorry!"

Amara waved a dismissive hand. "In truth, I have considered it." She grimaced. "I cannot believe I admitted that." A heavy sigh escaped her. "I am tired. Tired of waiting, tired of behaving. I have spent years being on my best behavior after Evers, but it doesn't matter. I'm twenty-seven years old. Am I to have no fun in my life because of a mistake made long ago?"

"I certainly hope not. I mean, I certainly hope you are."

Amara gave her a tender smile, her eyes moistening.

She wasn't Cat, but it was a start.

"Here you are." Amara stopped in front of a chamber. "I'm still surprised he put you in this room." Her eyes swept across to the chamber door on the other side.

"He said all other rooms were full."

"Perhaps. But he could have put you in with one of us— Emmeline or Becca or me."

"Oh, I wouldn't want to burden you like that."

Amara said nothing, looking back and forth between the

two sets of doors. "Be careful," she finally said. "I wouldn't want anyone to take advantage of you. Not even my brother."

"Ha, I should be so lucky," Eliza muttered, then clapped her hand over her mouth at realizing she'd said that out loud.

Amara burst out laughing. "Oh, I like you, Mrs. Eliza James. I like you, indeed." She swept an errant curl away from her forehead. "Not that I should worry. As far as I know, Deveric has lived as a monk these last few years. Perhaps we are just not passionate people."

"Ha! I don't think so. I saw you with Hodgins, remember? You weren't exactly having a bad time."

"And I have found you alone with my brother, not once, but twice. We are not so unalike, perhaps. But do mark my words, Eliza. Be glad it was I who stumbled upon you. Widow or not, being caught in a compromising position with Deveric would not end well for you, especially if my mother heard of it."

"Duly noted," Eliza said as she opened the door to her room. Heaviness and doubt struck her anew at the reminder once again of the challenge she faced. Half of her was convinced she could pull this off, that the fairytale Cat had drafted for her could come true. The other half wondered if she were insane, expecting a man of Deveric's status to ever truly consider her as wifely material. Deveric's responses to her attested to his attraction—thank God. But was that enough? She'd be nobody's mistress, not even Deveric's, as wildly attracted to him as she was. This was an all or nothing deal—his whole heart, or nothing at all.

"Thank you," Amara added.

"For what?"

"For your unexpected kindness and understanding. And for one of the most entertaining afternoons I've had in years."

Chapter 18

*D*everic was breathing hard by the time he and Lightning returned to the stables. It hadn't been enough to race Lightning to the brink of his capabilities; at one point, when he'd realized the horse was tiring, he'd leapt down and run as hard as he could through the woods, pushing his legs almost past their endurance. It had felt exquisite to pound it out, the confusion, the anger, the desire, the yearning …

It was strange to feel that much at all. Over the years, he'd polished his days and his interactions to avoid emotion. Such was expected of a man of his position, but beyond that, it felt safe, it felt good, it felt necessary to keep everything contained, regimented, tucked away. Avoiding pain was so much better than experiencing it. *A Claremont retains control over emotions at all times.*

Then again, as Collinswood had pointed out one evening last month over cards, locking out emotion to block out pain also meant locking out pleasure.

"I find pleasure enough in cards, in horses, in passing time here with you fine fellows," Deveric had said, gesturing around the room at White's.

"Shallow pleasures, perhaps."

"Is there any other kind?"

"I hope so." Coll's blue eyes had locked with his over the table. "Surely this can't be all there is."

"Oh, ho, ho," Arthington chortled. "Do tell, Coll. Have you figured out the meaning of life?"

Collinswood glared at them both. "Weren't you urging him to stop avoiding life not five minutes ago?"

"What I meant was, he should seek out *pleasure*. No doubt the fine ladies at the White House could draw him out of his shell." Arthington waggled his eyebrows in comedic fashion, wrenching a slight grin from Dev.

Coll threw down his cards in disgust.

"What? Don't tell me you, too, have forgone the divine pleasures of the flesh?"

Coll's cheek quirked up in a devilish grin, those dimples out in full force. "You know me too well for that, friend." He looked over at Deveric. "I just meant, I hope there is a grander plan to life, a destiny, if you will, awaiting me. I'm twenty-eight years old. I'm getting bored."

"Bored?" Deveric sipped from his brandy. "Perhaps we should head to Tattersall's tomorrow and pick out a new racer for you. A filly of that type always pleases me."

"Not that kind of bored. It's as if … as if …"

"Something's missing?" Arthington's face grew serious.

"Yes. I just don't know what."

Arth's words had hit Dev like a blow to the gut. He hadn't wanted to admit it, the emptiness that had overtaken him. Days felt routine, nights endless. He enjoyed Freddy, of course, but sometimes the boy reminded Dev too much of all he had lost, all the suffering he had caused, and Deveric had to shut it off. To avoid.

Guilt ate at him for how little time he had spent with Frederick of late. He'd once sworn not to be like his father, to always openly show his love for his children, despite what anyone else might think. Before he'd realized how destructive love could be, at least. Or not love, perhaps—he hadn't loved Mirabelle, not in the way a husband ought to love a wife.

Connection. That's what led to destruction. Had he not sought, had he not needed physical connection with someone, Mirabelle would still be alive. And Louisa never would have died.

Yes, better to remain with friends and avoid that kind of intimacy all together. Love hurt. Loss was excruciating.

And yet … *was* this all there was? He'd studied his brandy, desperate to keep his friends from noticing his sudden somberness. He didn't need more questions.

"Me either." Arthington had taken up his cards again, shaking off the intense moment with a toothy grin. "Unless it's a blonde chit with big, you know, brains." They all knew of Arthington's fondness for well-endowed, flaxen-haired women.

"You wait," said Deveric, grateful as always for Arthington's light-heartedness. "'Twill be a brunette, a flat-chested one, who'll snare you some day."

"The horror!"

The men had chortled and continued on with the game. Several rounds of brandy ensured no other maudlin conversation made an appearance that night.

Thinking of big-bosomed blondes brought one in particular to mind now. As he removed the bit and bridle from Lightning's mouth and handed the reins to a stable hand, his mind roamed freely over one American widow's body. If only his hands were roaming, too. *Cool down, Dev, or walking is going to become quite difficult.*

After the stable hand removed the saddle, Deveric checked Lightning's hooves for stones, and then took up the grooming brush, pulling it in long, even strokes over Lightning's sweaty sides. The stable hand could have done it, of course, but Deveric always enjoyed the task. It was only fitting he give back to his faithful horse, Lightning, who always gave his best for Deveric.

If only his wife had done the same. Mirabelle had preferred to leave him alone so as not to disturb him, she'd said. He'd known, however, what she hoped was that he not disturb her. Connection was not something she had needed—at least not with him.

Some had urged him to take on a mistress, find love elsewhere. Many men of his station did, of course. But he'd seen how his mother had suffered over Samuel Mattersley's public indiscretions, had heard her weeping and railing at his father's portrait in his absence. Deveric had sworn never to do that to a woman.

When he'd kissed Eliza, she'd responded eagerly to his embrace. She'd not been frightened, had in fact pushed him for more. She seemed as aware of him as he was of her, sparks flaming between them whenever they were in the same space. Their attraction was mutual, he was sure of it. But would she turn away from him, be repulsed by him, as Mirabelle had been, if things went farther in the bedroom?

His heart tore at the thought, of seeing the desire in those deep sapphire eyes turn to rejection, even as his pulse raced and parts of him throbbed at the image of Eliza underneath him. Perhaps most men were unconcerned with whether or not the woman found actual pleasure, considering it a triviality. But it mattered to Deveric.

He liked Eliza. Truly liked her, as well as longed for her more than he'd ever longed for any woman.

Was it possible he could find true emotional and physical satisfaction with her?

He paused in the grooming of the horse, a sudden thought hitting him. This Cat of whom Eliza spoke, she wrote stories. Love stories, Eliza had said, had she not, stories in which men had come to life for this Cat, men meant to be suitors? Eliza claimed only that she'd wanted to come to England during this Regency, but Deveric felt she was concealing something, something more. He'd thought at first it pertained to her claims of being from the future. But maybe … Had this Cat written a love story for Eliza? For Eliza to come here, to be with him?

And if so, did this mean Deveric was a fictional creation?

The idea was so preposterous, he actually snorted out loud. Lightning turned his head and nickered in response.

"It's not you, old chap," Dev murmured, dismissing the idea. He was no more fictional than Lightning was a unicorn. Of that, he was sure.

But *could* this Cat have chosen him, somehow, as Eliza's destiny? Were they, could they be … soul mates? He'd never believed in the idea, had figured it for emotional rubbish best left to poets and actors. And yet, the idea sparked hope like he'd never felt before. His insides were on fire, every inch of him burning for it to be true, to be a possibility, at least. For life, for God, to let him atone for his sins, to give him something to believe in, someone to live for.

Good God, what was *wrong* with him, indulging in such ludicrous, maudlin fantasies?

"It's me. I'm as mad as she is, thinking someone would come back two hundred years from the future, just to love *me*."

To *love* him? When had love entered the picture?

Lightning whinnied.

"That's right. It's all a bunch of—" He sighed as Lightning released the contents of his bowels. "Well, yes, but I didn't need such a graphic demonstration."

He handed the brush to the stable hand. One advantage of being a duke was not having to deal with horse manure. "Finish grooming, and then muck out that stall."

The lad nodded and ran to comply.

Deveric strode toward the house. Between the smell of the manure and the sweat he'd worked up that afternoon, he needed a bath.

Entering the house, he bade the servants to draw one. He'd had a tub installed in the dressing room off his main chamber several years ago, which drained right down out of the house—a miracle of modern plumbing. He often soaked for great lengths of time, letting the heat and salt ease the aches and pains of the day.

Striding up to his chamber, he glanced across the hallway. The door to his wife's chamber was closed. Was Eliza within? He stood for a moment, a vision of her in his tub springing to mind, with her blonde hair down and eyes welcoming, those luscious blue eyes that had pulsated when he'd pulled back from kissing her that morning. She hadn't wanted to let go, and he hadn't wanted to let her go.

His breeches grew uncomfortably tight. It was astonishing to be led more by his cock than his head. *A gentleman of good breeding maintains control over his physical person at all times.*

As if he could control it, this response to that damnable American. She'd thrown his whole life in chaos.

Opening the door to his chamber, he stomped in and flung it shut. The servants rustled about in the adjacent room, and he could hear the sounds of pouring water. Good. They were fast today.

He pulled off his cravat and then sat down on the bed to remove his boots. His valet, Myers, entered the room to assist him, carefully setting the boots aside while tsk-tsking at the scuffs. Deveric allowed him to remove his riding jacket, and then sent him away. He knew Myers wished to perform more services. "But, Your Grace, a valet is to serve in all ways," the man often lamented. Dev had never enjoyed others dressing and undressing him, though. Many of his friends gave no thought to parading about in front of servants. They were part of the wallpaper. But not to Deveric. Not when he was naked.

Pulling off his shirt and breeches, he laid them to the side, and then peeled off his smalls. He looked down. Apparently his mind was still on Eliza. Hopefully the bath would, er, soften him a bit. Walking into the next room, now empty of anyone, he climbed into the water, hotter than most people could stand, and slid down into it with a large sigh.

He'd let the water wash all thoughts, all those damnably tempting images, of Eliza James away.

CHAPTER 19

ootsteps echoed outside her door. The forcefulness of the stride let her know it was Deveric—what other man would walk with such assurance in this grand cavern of a house? Suddenly, the noise stopped. *What was he doing?* She resisted the urge to peek out. *Nothing to see, Lizzie. Nothing to see.* After a moment, his door opened and then closed rather forcefully.

She paced about in her room, not sure what to do. She needed help to get out of her dress. It was embarrassing and frustrating that she couldn't undress herself in gowns like these, but it was the reality. She wasn't sure how to call for a maid; Betsy had always just appeared. Maybe if Eliza quickly asked Deveric, he could send someone up.

Her mind made up, she opened her door and walked across the hallway. She knocked on his door. There was no answer. He was in there, wasn't he? She knocked again, more loudly this time.

"Come in!" His irritated voice sounded farther off than

she expected; perhaps this chamber was particularly well insulated. Opening the door, she walked in. And had to stop and gape. The giant bed encompassing the center of the room was the most magnificent piece of furniture she'd ever seen, all heavy wood, masterfully carved, of a deep, deep mahogany. She wandered over to run her fingers along one of the posters, tracing her thumb across an intricate leaf, marveling at the craftsmanship.

"Bring it in here," came the voice again, and she followed it without thinking. Walking through a small connecting door, she found herself in another chamber–and face-to-face with Deveric. Naked Deveric. In a bathtub. She shrieked as his face purpled.

"I'm sorry! I'm so sorry! I had no idea! I just, um—" Turning back and forth, she couldn't decide whether to run or stay.

"What are *you* doing in here?" he demanded, sinking lower in the tub. "I thought you were Myers with my shaving soap."

It was a large tub, almost the size of a modern Jacuzzi, but it still couldn't hold all of him, and his shoulders rose above the water like icebergs. They made her feel anything but cold, though, reminding her as they did of the statue of David she'd seen in Florence. How did a man get so muscular without being a weightlifter? It's not as if he did manual labor. Did he?

"I, uh, I needed assistance. Um …" She looked at the ceiling. "Amara told me it's time to dress for dinner, but I, uh, can't get out of this dress on my own."

He cocked an eyebrow at her. "You're asking me to get you out of your dress?"

"*No!*" she shrieked, her eyes flying back to meet his. "I mean, yes. I mean, no, not *you*! But I, um, don't know how to call for help." She turned away and stared at the wall, twisting her fingers together.

She should leave. At once. She knew it. And yet, she couldn't. She bit her lip, peeking at him over her shoulder before yanking her head back to the wall in front of her. *Holy cow, the man was magnificent.*

Deveric was starting to enjoy this. Clearly she was even more discomfited than he was, and he was the one who was naked. She wasn't close enough to see down through the water, was she? If so, she'd realize just what his reaction was to the idea of undressing her.

Her eyes darted to him, even as she pretended to focus on the wallpaper in front of her. *Does she like what she sees? She hasn't run. And she's peeking at me, those cheeks burning so prettily.* Maybe he should stand up and give her the full view.

The smile left his face as he pictured what she might do. Run screaming, as Mirabelle once had? He couldn't help that he was so … large in all areas. Many women preferred the more effete, lean dandies of the day, but his broad shoulders and muscled thighs precluded anyone ever calling him fashionable. That was of no matter to him. He dressed as befitted his status, but wasn't as consumed with finding the proper waistcoat, much less being a pink of the *ton,* as a number of his acquaintances were—Arthington, in particular.

"In this century, a woman isn't to enter a man's bedchamber unless she is his wife." He sluiced water casually over his shoulders. Better not to let her know how off-kilter she'd set him upon appearing in his room.

"Oh God, I'm sorry. I didn't think. I wasn't sure what to do and I heard you in here. I'm sorry, I'll go." Her voice trembled as she spoke to the wall. Desire? Fear?

"No, no, we will have to check first to ensure no one sees you. It would not do for us to be caught in my private chambers alone together. Especially with me in this state of dress. Or undress, rather. Hold on."

Reaching over, he grabbed a large towel sitting on the chair next to the tub. "Close your eyes!" he commanded, lest she peek again. Though Lord knew he wanted her to, so he could gauge her reaction. If it were the one he wanted, however, if her eyes burned as hotly as he hoped, there'd be no turning back. A man only had so much restraint, and a woman in his bedchamber while he was naked—no, *this* woman in his bedchamber—was too much for it.

Eliza did as told, squeezing her eyes so hard she saw dots. Did he think that would erase the memory of those lovely shoulders, or of his strong neck rising from the water? Dear Lord, the man was gorgeous. She even liked the hint of five o'clock shadow gracing his face. He must have a lot of hair, to need shaving twice a day. He was all man, no doubt about it.

She heard the water sloshing around in the tub as he rose, and her ears burned. She may not be watching, but she wasn't having a hard time imagining what it would be like to see the water sliding down across his chest, down his belly, over his … She shivered. Oh, to be that water. She needed to get a grip. *What I'd like to grip*, her belligerent mind said, and she had to clasp her elbows firmly with each opposite hand to keep herself from turning around.

This was real. It wasn't a fantasy, wasn't a daydream. She was standing in Deveric Mattersley's private dressing room, and he was naked.

Footsteps approached. "Here," he said, his voice suddenly tickling her neck as he loosened the back straps of her gown. Gracious, he was right behind her, the heat of his body radiating into hers.

"What are you *doing?*" she yelped, jumping and coming down on his foot.

He didn't move. "Thank goodness you're a tiny little thing, or that would have hurt."

Eliza had been about to apologize, but his words stopped her short. Tiny little thing? He thought she was tiny little thing? She grinned, in spite of the awkward situation. How nice to have a man who didn't object to a little extra padding.

As his fingers traced their way down her back, his touch raising goosebumps even through the layers of clothing under the dress, she remembered where she was—in 1812, not 2012, and in a man's bedroom, where she shouldn't be, no matter how much she wished to stay. Not if she wanted to avoid a scandal, at least. The Dowager Dragon would kick her out on her ass in an instant if Eliza were discovered in the Duke's chamber. Much less discovered with him naked.

"Stop it! You can't, you shouldn't—" Without turning around, she fled, racing across his room, although she was careful to peek out the door before darting across to her own chamber. Thank goodness no one was there.

Dev ran his fingers through his hair, standing at the edge of his dressing room, water pooling beneath him on the floor. What had got into him, touching her in such an intimate manner? He knew better. Though he'd just loosened the dress, as she'd requested, nothing more. He would have sent her away once the task was done. Wouldn't he?

He was a man of principle. A man of honor. He wasn't the type to seduce young women, or even a slightly older widow, in his own bedroom. No matter how much certain parts of him wanted to.

He glanced at his bed, imagining Eliza spread out on it, naked, those glorious breasts on full display. He pictured her beckoning to him, acceptance and desire radiating from her brilliant eyes as she opened her arms, and legs, to welcome him in.

It was too much to bear.

He closed his eyes and let out a sigh of frustration. Dropping the towel, he prepared to dress, though the bath hadn't softened his desire for her one bit, hadn't slaked the thirst apparently only Eliza James could quench.

Good God, what was wrong with him? He'd kept this side of himself under control for years. Two nights with this woman under his roof, and he was ready to abandon it all, ready to risk everything, just to taste her again.

Who was she?

Eliza leaned back against her door, her heart thumping. Closing her eyes, she tried to catch her breath, but nothing could calm her down from the image she'd just seen: Deveric

Mattersley, naked, in the bathtub.

Sure, she hadn't seen down through the water—trying to get a glimpse would have been too obvious—but Oh. My. God. He put most modern men to shame, and that included the gym rats she'd seen while occasionally working out at UVa's Aquatic and Fitness Center.

What did the man do? How did he stay that fit? In spite of the hunks peppering the pages of her romance novels, she'd assumed in real life most members of the peerage never had to lift a finger for anything, and were therefore likely to be on the softer side.

This one broke the mold.

Thank God for that. She grinned. If this all worked out in the end, she'd write Cat a big old thank you letter, and figure out a way to get it to her friend. A man with shoulders like that. Yowza. If only she'd been able to see his thighs under that towel. If only she'd been able to see …

She wanted to touch him, to run her fingers through the hair on his chest, to trace the elegant expanse of his shoulders, feel the contours of his body. Heat flamed out to her breasts and the lower half of her as she imagined lying underneath him, his hardness pressing into her, being enveloped by all man.

His responses to her were assuaging her self-doubt, whittling away at her fears about her own body far more quickly that she ever would have imagined. With him, with the way he looked at her, she felt desired, truly desired. *All* of her seemed to please him, not just her pretty face. To be accepted for who she was, emotionally *and* physically—that was the ultimate dream. A dream more and more within reach, given the obvious chemistry raging between them. *Thank you, Cat.*

Shaking off the image of Deveric buck-naked as best she could, Eliza pulled her arms from the sleeves of her dress. At least this afternoon encounter had accomplished something; she could escape the layers of clothing she had on. These dresses were warm, true, but the fabric constricted her arms and shoulders, especially since the dresses had been made for Amara, not her. What she wouldn't give for a T-shirt and jeans.

She strolled over to the fireplace, where a fire blazed merrily. Someone had refreshed the logs. She froze. Betsy? Had Betsy known where she was?

A knock sounded at the door. Eliza quickly threw her arms back into the gown. Was it Deveric? Surely it wasn't Deveric. *Even though you want it to be Deveric.* "Who is it?"

The door opened and Betsy walked in, holding a pitcher of water. She dropped a curtsy upon seeing Eliza, and then strode to the sideboard, setting the pitcher into place.

"I brought some fresh water, milady, in case you want to wash before dinner."

"Thank you, Betsy."

The maid walked over to Eliza, moving around to her back. "Who undid your laces?"

"Um." Blood rushed to Eliza's face, setting it on fire. Thank goodness Betsy was behind her. "Amara did, after she walked me back to the room."

"Hmm."

Was that doubt in the maid's voice? If so, she said nothing else.

Betsy removed the morning gown and laid it carefully across the bed, then held up Eliza's twenty-first century imitation of a Regency ball gown she'd worn that first night.

"This is a pretty gown, my lady," said Betsy as she helped Eliza into the dress. "It's different. The fabric isn't like anything I've ever felt before."

Eliza wasn't sure what the dress was made of. It looked silky to her, but she guessed maybe rayon or polyester. That wasn't something she wanted to explain to a nineteenth-century maid. "Perhaps it's an American style." *You know, two hundred years in the future.*

"Shall I do your hair?"

Eliza nodded, taking a seat in front of the dressing table mirror. Although the pampering was fun, it still bothered her to have someone wait on her hand and foot. She wished she could offer Betsy some form of payment. Not that that would be appropriate, or that she had anything to offer.

In fact, how *could* she turn her jewelry into money? Being entirely dependent on others didn't sit well with her; she'd prefer to have funds of her own ready at hand. *Hmm.*

As Betsy pulled the brush through her hair, Eliza closed her eyes, letting her thoughts drift. *What is Cat doing right now? Well, obviously not* right *now, not in 1812.*

She missed her friend. It'd been easy, too easy, to take their friendship for granted when they'd been together so long. Cat had tried to talk her out of this madcap scheme, tried to keep her with her. Their separation was so much harder than Eliza had imagined. She'd been so focused on where she was going, she'd ignored the reality of what she was leaving behind. Namely, the best friend a girl could ever have.

Should she have stayed? She'd made progress with Amara today, she was sure, and it seemed as if all were going well with Deveric. But was it? Was this going to work out?

She sighed.

"Are you all right, my lady?" Betsy fixed a pearl hairpin into the hair she'd arranged on top of Eliza's head. "Did I pull too hard?"

"No, no, Betsy, you're fine. And my hair … my goodness, it looks wonderful!" And it did. Eliza stared at her reflection. Betsy had braided her hair, and then fastened it into an elaborate bun before weaving pearl hairpins through it that glowed in the light. She'd left two thick tendrils hanging down around Eliza's ears, which tickled her neck as she turned her head to and fro, sending shivers through her.

Betsy gave her a bright smile, evidently pleased at the compliment. "Do you want a hint of rouge? You looked a little pale when I first walked in. Emmeline likes this Pear's Liquid Blooms of Roses." Betsy held up a small bottle she'd plucked off the dressing table.

Pale? She'd been on fire. Deveric's green eyes flashed before her. "Thank you, Betsy. Though it's not as if I have a gentleman to impress, right?" She gave a high-pitched, fake giggle—the kind she hated. Thank goodness the maid said nothing about Eliza's suddenly odd behavior.

As Betsy deftly applied the cheek color with a light hand and then set about cleaning up the hair implements, Eliza lost herself in daydreams again, fantasizing about what London looked like in this era. Amara had told her it was doubtful Eliza would accompany them into Town for the Season— as governess, she'd stay with Frederick—but Eliza hoped otherwise. She'd visited London with her parents while in high school. The Tower, St. Paul's and Westminster Abbey were amazing, of course, but her favorite memory was the afternoon when she'd wandered around Mayfair, Piccadilly, and Hyde Park, trying to imagine them as they might have been in Jane Austen's era.

How far to London was it from Clarehaven? For that matter, where was Clarehaven, exactly?

"Betsy, what's the nearest city?"

"City? Why, Winchester. My ma and da live there."

"How far away is it?"

"Not far at all; four or five miles. An easy walk."

Nobody walked four or five miles in modern Charlottesville, unless they were doing so for fitness. How times changed.

Eliza pursed her lips, picturing her wall map of England in her head. "If we're near Winchester, we must also be somewhat near Chawton, correct?"

"Yes, my lady. I think it's about twice as far. I've never been there. It's only a small village."

Eliza fought to keep her outward demeanor calm, but inside she bounced up and down. *Jane Austen! I'm near Jane Austen! Right now!*

She knew Jane had moved with her sister and mother to live in a small cottage on her brother's estate in 1811. That cottage was where Jane did the majority of her writing— or would do, Eliza corrected—until her death. *Maybe she's writing right now!*

"You may go down now, my lady."

Eliza wanted to race around the room, so excited she was to know she was *this close* to Jane Austen. *The* actual Jane Austen. Instead, she gave the maid a nod before making for the door.

Shivers of delight teased her skin as she passed Deveric's chamber. Meeting Jane Austen had long been her ultimate fantasy. Until the spectacular sight of one naked duke in a tub, that is.

CHAPTER 20

*D*everic's head rose as Eliza walked into the parlor, her slightly too-tight dress from that first evening pushing up her breasts in far too enticing a fashion. *Damn.* He'd barely managed to get himself under control before coming down for dinner, and here he was, every part of him instantly aware of every part of her. Especially the most luscious parts.

Numerous house party guests milled about, waiting to proceed into dinner. He hadn't noticed their comings or goings, much to the matrons' dismay, several of whom had overtly nudged their daughters to walk near him, casting eyes.

But enter one Eliza James, and everything in him stood to attention. It was disconcerting, this constant reaction. It was exhilarating. She looked stunning. The gown was the same as her first evening—*he'd have to remedy that*—but her hair was swept up in a far more elaborate coiffure, and the two tendrils that fell down below each ear framed her face, drawing attention to the curve of her neck.

He wanted to touch her there, to trace his hand along its creamy expanse, to drop kisses on her warm skin and hear her sigh in delight.

He shifted positions, willing his pantaloons not to betray his reaction to the delightful, perplexing, and extremely alluring mystery that was this American "cousin." She moved further into the room, scanning the crowd. Suddenly, she smiled and walked away from him, toward the opposite corner. *Who had she seen*? He craned his neck.

"Looking for someone?" Arthington clapped a friendly hand on Deveric's shoulder. "Let me guess, it's not me."

Deveric gave him a wry grin. "Just seeing to where my sister had gone. She does like to get into trouble."

"Which one?"

A chuckle escaped Deveric. "True. Although in this instance I was thinking of Becca." He barely tripped over the words. "I'm hoping she changed for dinner and won't walk in with the stench of horse dung on her slippers."

"I believe she's over there," Arth said. "With Grace. And it looks like your cousin has joined them, as well." He gestured across the room, where Eliza chatted animatedly with Grace. His normally shy sister's face glowed with excitement; what could they be talking about?

Casting one last quick glance their direction, he forced his attention back to Arthington. Collinswood made his way over to them a moment later.

"I don't supposed either of you would like to take one of these sisters off my hands?" Dev quipped, desperate to discuss anything but Eliza.

Coll grinned while Arth snickered. "Not on your life," Arth said. "First off, we've got our hands full just trying to handle you. Second, you'd kill us if we laid a hand on any of them. Besides, they're like sisters to us, too."

That was undoubtedly true; Coll and Arth had known the girls practically since they were in the nursery. Becca had fancied herself half in love with Coll at one point—on account of his magical dimples, she'd said—but he still called her 'Little Scamp', much as he had when she'd followed him around as a toddler, whenever he'd come home from school with Dev. Which was often; venturing to Ireland was too far for the holidays.

"You two are too old for any of them, anyway. Except perhaps Amara." Deveric was not thinking of Eliza James. He was not. Definitely not.

"Too old?" Coll arched a fine eyebrow. "My mistress would tell you otherwise."

"You're acting as if we—and you—have one foot in the grave!" Arthington exclaimed.

"For all your talk about marrying, I'm starting to wonder if you two are going to grow old together, rather than commit to any one woman." Deveric raised his own eyebrow. "Now that would cause conversation."

Arth elbowed him good-naturedly. "Coll is like the brother I never had. The one I can tease mercilessly all day and carouse with all night. But have no doubt, there are women involved. Definitely women."

"Did I imply otherwise?"

All three men laughed as the butler announced dinner. Men and women lined up as they were accustomed to enter the dining room. Deveric couldn't help but look back at Eliza, who was wandering about, twirling a tendril, clearly unsure as to where she belonged. She started toward the back of the line.

His mother expected Deveric to escort her. He'd done

so since Mirabelle died. He headed toward Eliza, anyway. "Escort my mother, will you?" he threw back at Arth, not waiting for an answer.

"Allow me, Mrs. James," he said as he reached Eliza's side. He offered her his elbow, smiling as she took it.

Murmurs echoed around them in response to his unexpected actions. Deveric didn't care. He looked back at his mother. A hint of disapproval crossed her otherwise expressionless face as Arthington politely extended her his elbow. With a pointed look at her son, the Dowager took the proffered arm.

"Did I commit another faux pas?" Eliza whispered to Deveric, her brows crinkling in the most delightful way.

"No." He led her toward the front of the line. "I did. Traditionally, as Duke and host, I escort my mother, the Dowager hostess, into dinner. But she and our guests understand that making a new family member comfortable in unfamiliar surroundings ought to be my highest priority." His mother understood no such thing, he was sure. He'd hear about this later.

"Oh my. I don't think this is going to endear me to her." She folded one arm over her stomach, her cheeks white.

He held her other arm in his, keeping her steady. Ushering her forward, he led her to a seat next to the head of the table. "Never fear. I shall keep you safe."

Eliza's shoulders tensed as the other guests rather awkwardly adjusted their seating arrangements. This was causing quite a stir. People were looking at her, some with open disdain.

On the other hand, Lizzie, he's paying attention to you. A lot of attention. In front of everyone. *This is a good sign. Right?*

Or maybe not. Maybe he wanted to ensure she didn't babble to the other guests her crazy notions of being from the future. Easier to keep her under tabs if he kept her close.

She sighed. Figuring this out was exhausting. One the one hand, he was made for her. Literally. And he'd shown interest, that much was clear. Sexual interest, at least. But could she trust that? Could she trust that whatever was going on between them, whatever might be developing, was real, not pre-programmed? She understood Cat's dilemma more fully now, that's for sure—it *was* hard to accept that a man created specifically to love her could do so of his own accord.

On the other hand, she'd told Cat not to make it predestined, to give both Deveric and her a choice, and Cat had done so. In that way, this wasn't much different than finding your "perfect match" on a website, right? You entered what you were looking for, you were given a match, you gave it a go, but there was no guarantee it would work. And if it did, that didn't devalue the feelings that developed, just because they were helped along by technology. Right?

But this was different than any dating website scenario. There were so many more hurdles. If, by some miracle, Deveric did fall in love with her, would it be possible to go from American "cousin" to Duchess of Claremont? The social opposition she'd face was obvious, as evidenced by the pointed looks guests were throwing her way. And this was a mere fraction of the *ton*. Panic clawed at her throat. She couldn't pull this off; she'd never blend in.

She fingered the edge of the tablecloth as she surveyed the table. The Dowager Dragon stared at her from the other end, her eyes ice, even from this distance. Eliza was thankful so many feet separated them. On Eliza's end, Deveric sat to her left, and Lord Chance, whom she hadn't seen since that first night, to her right. Across from her was a young lady Eliza had seen, but not yet met. From the way the lady—girl, really, she looked all of eighteen—was making moony eyes at Deveric, it was clear she relished sitting next to the Duke.

Jealousy furled low in Eliza's belly, greener than Deveric's eyes. Why couldn't one of the older, far less attractive women have been seated next to her duke? This girl, whomever she was, had radiantly red hair and delicate ivory skin, accentuated by her mint green dress. With her huge eyes, she reminded Eliza of Ariel. The Little Mermaid's Ariel. Compared to her thin frame, Eliza felt like Ursula—all bosom and derriere, and not a chance of snaring Eric. Er, Deveric.

Chance spoke to Eliza in low tones, disrupting her depressing train of thought. "So nice to see you again, dearest cousin. I have wanted to spend time with you, but alas, my brother has suddenly found a never-ending list of tasks for me." He flashed her a winsome grin. "I can see why he wants to keep me away."

Well, he certainly is a charmer. She smiled more widely than she should, glad to have a friendly face near. Out of the corner of her eye, she noted Deveric's scowl as he stared at his brother. *Good.* If she could instigate a little jealousy on the Duke's part, distract him from the confection to his left, that couldn't hurt, right?

At that moment, the footmen set shallow bowls of soup in front of the guests, working with brisk efficiency and in better synchronization than many a swimming team. She studied the bowl. The famous Regency white soup, she guessed. It looked innocuous enough, so she took a bite. *Not bad. A hint of almond.*

Chance sipped from his wine glass. "How are you finding Clarehaven?"

"It's magnificent," Eliza replied without hesitation. "Beyond anything I've ever seen. I feel as if I'm visiting a museum, with how splendid the house is."

He winked at her. "A museum? We need to liven things up, in that case."

"Oh, I'm having adventures enough already." She didn't answer his quizzical look, instead taking a drink from her own glass. The wine was rich and heady, and tasty, but she would have preferred a glass of ice water with lemon, or even the mildly bitter hot chocolate Betsy had brought her before.

She eyed the small finger bowl of water near her plate. Would anyone notice if she drank it, rather than rinsed her fingers in it?

"And here I thought we were in the middle of a rather dull house party." Chance's words pulled her out of her musings. His eyes sparkled. "With the men away for the hunt, what fun could you ladies have possibly had?"

"Yes, because women ought only think of men all day?" Her tone was sharper than intended. She was hardly one to criticize, considering she'd traveled through time for a man.

"Isn't that as it should be? After all, we only think of you," he countered smoothly.

Oh, he would be dangerous in a few years. Right now he was a puppy—an adorable, floppy-eared, fun-loving one, but a pup all the same.

"I thought you were hunting foxes."

"Foxes, vixens: one brings the other to mind."

"I should hope not—lest you want to skin us for our pelts." She spoke the words before realizing how suggestive they sounded.

Chance choked on his wine. Deveric, who'd been conversing with the enamored young woman at his side, broke off to watch them.

"I've never heard it put so boldly before," Chance whispered, his lips twisting into a leer. "But I would love to see your pelt."

Eliza's eyes widened. That had crossed the line. Had they been in the twenty-first century, in a bar, she'd have been tempted to throw her drink in his face. Here, she said nothing, but turned pointedly to Deveric, to let Chance know he was barking up the wrong tree.

"Ah, the cut direct." The side of Deveric's mouth quirked up. "Nothing more than my impudent younger brother deserves. What did he say?"

"Nothing important," Eliza said. "I hope I did not interrupt your conversation." She nodded at the girl across from her. The girl narrowed her eyes a touch before pasting a fake smile across her face.

"Not at all—" began Deveric.

"—We were discussing plans for His Grace to visit us in the coming weeks," the woman broke in. "I would love to welcome him to Crestville." Her eyes flashed triumphantly.

"Well, please, don't let me keep you." Deveric had agreed to visit this chit? So much for the jealousy game. She'd lost; it was eating her alive. "By the way, I'm Eliza James." Cat would be proud of the polite indifference she'd infused in her voice, an indifference she certainly didn't feel.

"Forgive me for not providing a proper introduction," Deveric said. "Lady Parcine, this is Mrs. James, our cousin visiting from America. Mrs. James, this is Lady Parcine."

"Ah, *Mrs.* James. Is your husband here, then?"

"No. He passed away years ago."

Deveric's eyebrows puckered as he watched Eliza. What was he thinking?

"A fellow widow. My condolences. Are you returning to America soon?" Lady Parcine asked, her face hopeful.

"Uh …" Lady Parcine was a widow? She looked barely old enough to be legal.

Deveric broke in. "Having lost her entire family, Mrs. James will be with us for as long as she wishes to be."

Lady Parcine approximated a sympathetic look. "It is so kind of the Duke and his family to provide for the less fortunate." Her smile didn't reach her eyes.

Witch. Dang, these women were cutthroat. Thank goodness Deveric's sisters were kind, lest she think all women of the *ton* so vicious. Perhaps when the only option for a woman of rank was marriage, the competition did what it took to win. Mean girls from her century could learn a thing or two from *Lady* Parcine. Lady Harlot, too. Eliza was thankful, at least, that Harriet was at the other end of the table, flirting outrageously with a popinjay to her side.

"Yes, it is," Eliza managed to respond, her own mouth tight.

Deveric looked as if he was about to speak, but the Witch quickly interjected. "I do hope, Your Grace, you have saved a dance for me."

Deveric's eyebrow popped up. "My apologies, but there is no dancing this evening, Lady Parcine."

"I meant whenever we next meet. Please say you will remember you are promised to me."

Damn, but the chit was good.

"May I serve you?" broke in a voice from Eliza's right. Chance's sheepish smile indicated his desire to make amends.

Eliza scanned the table. All of the men were serving the

women food, as she knew was custom. Eliza couldn't decide whether she found that sexy or sexist. Perhaps a little of both, if Deveric had been the one serving her.

Lord Chance carefully maneuvered something onto Eliza's plate, some sort of meat in a sauce. She poked at it delicately with her fork.

"Not a fan of turtle?"

Eliza's fingers flew to her mouth. *Why couldn't it have been chicken?* She'd never been particularly good at trying new foods, and though she'd read turtle was a Regency delicacy, she was loath to try it.

Lady Parcine broke in. "I do love turtle. It's so … succulent in the mouth. Don't you agree, Your Grace?"

My God, why don't you just strip off your dress and lie down on the table naked, offering yourself up as Deveric's next course?

Deveric's lips flattened into a line. *Good.* Perhaps he didn't care for Witchy's innuendos, either. Taking a quick sip of wine, he answered, "It is quite fine. What do you think, Mrs. James?"

"Um," Eliza hedged. "It's not a dish with which I'm familiar from where I come." She gave Deveric a pointed look.

"Fear not," Chance said. "If you don't care for the turtle, we have pigeon, as well."

Good Lord, what she wouldn't give for a good old-fashioned pizza. One with ham and pineapple on it. Not … turtle. Not … pigeon.

She sighed. At least she might slim down here.

"Is there something in particular you would like?" Deveric asked in a soft voice. "I could see if our chef could—"

"—No, no, I'm fine. Really. Please don't go to any trouble for me."

Lady Parcine looked from Deveric to her, a slight frown marring the woman's otherwise beautiful features. Evidently disappointed by whatever she saw, the Witch turned the full force of her grin on Chance, who, upon noticing her sudden attention, dropped a piece of turtle onto his cravat.

Eliza stifled a grin as he attempted to surreptitiously clean himself, all while flashing Lady Parcine his pearly whites. That boy would be a heartbreaker someday. All charm and good looks.

Deveric could use some of his brother's easy-going nature. He looked far too serious far too often. Of course, it was the intensity of his face that set those butterflies aflutter in her stomach … and elsewhere.

After several more removes, mostly of foods and meats Eliza didn't recognize or didn't care for, her mouth watered when a custard appeared on the table. She dug in with relish, closing her eyes at the smooth feel of the lemon cream on her tongue. Opening her eyes for a second bite, she caught Deveric watching her, his gaze smoldering. He dropped his eyes to her lips for a moment before looking down at his own plate, a muscle ticcing in his jaw.

She looked away, her own cheeks on fire. Did the man have any idea what those emerald eyes did to her?

"Ladies," the Dowager said, rising from the other end of the table, her voice sharp. "Let us leave the men to their port and cigars." She shot Eliza a dark glance, pursing her lips.

Great. Just what Eliza needed—a trip to the Dragon's lair. She'd never return if the Dowager had her way, Eliza was sure.

"Gentlemen, please join us shortly in the music room for a few pieces before our evening's entertainment, *The Sailor's Daughter.*"

The other women stood up and dutifully followed after

Deveric's mother. Eliza wished she could stay. How was she to get to know Deveric better if the men and women were always separating from each other? She hadn't even had the chance to show him her phone yet, to prove her claims, and share with him about things to come.

On the other hand, leaving took the pressure off of trying to attract Deveric's attention while holding off Chance's. Not that that seemed much of an issue anymore; Chance was staring at Lady Parcine, who was batting her eyelashes right back at him. *Lady, my ass.* But hey, if that's what a young buck wanted to chase, at least he knew he had a good chance of catching it.

Entering a room off the dining room, Eliza moved to a corner as Grace proceeded to the small piano in the front. Amara came to stand with Eliza, and together they listened to Grace play a wistful-sounding tune, before she turned to a more upbeat number Eliza recognized as a Mozart composition.

"She's quite good!" Eliza said.

"Yes, she is. Grace has always enjoyed playing more than the rest of us. Not that Mother would let any of us forgo the requisite lessons."

Another young woman approached the front after Grace had finished her second song, taking a seat at the harp near the piano. She was a brunette with a slightly over-sized nose, but with a pleasing voice. Too bad Eliza had always found the harp a dull instrument, too reminiscent of funeral parlor music to her.

She covered a yawn just as the Dowager made her way over to her, mouth downturned.

Men began filing into the room. As Deveric came through the door, followed by Arthington and Emerlin, the Dowager asked, "Do you play, Mrs. James?"

Eliza heard the challenge in her voice. "No, I'm sorry. We did not have a piano in my home." That was true—her parents never had been very musical. They'd preferred television to radio, which was one reason Eliza had spent lots of time in her room. She'd loved belting out her favorite songs in private, without the TV to distract her.

"I see. Do you play any instrument? The harp, perhaps?"

"Mother, leave her alone. I'll play if you'd like," interjected Amara. "Or Emmeline." She gestured to her sister, who'd joined them.

"Actually," Eliza found herself saying, desperate to prove she had *some* sort of the musical ability expected of any Regency lady, "I can sing."

Emmeline clapped her hands. "Wonderful! I do so love singing."

"As long as you're not the one doing it, sister dear," Amara said. A wry smile from Emmeline affirmed that perhaps that particular ability was not among her talents.

The Dowager regarded her. *Was that a glimmer of respect in her eyes, because I hadn't backed down?* "Please," Deveric's mother said, gesturing toward the front of the room. "Would you like Grace to accompany you?"

"Um, no. I don't think she'd know this song." As Eliza made her way forward, she frantically tried to think of something she knew well enough to sing that wouldn't sound completely out of place and time. She had the sneaking suspicion that *Moves Like Jagger* or *Super Bass* wouldn't cut it. Nor would the '80s songs she loved, though she longed to break out in some Wham!

Turning around to face the crowd, she took a deep breath. All eyes were on her. Her head swam under the scrutiny, so she closed her own, shutting out everything and everyone. After a small pause, she started to sing Michael Bublé's *Home*, the song she and Cat had sung together often the summer Eliza's parents had died, when both she and Cat were longing for the time before heartache.

The room hushed of all noise as her clear soprano rang out. Eliza hardly noticed—she was lost in the words, lost in the song. Thinking of Cat, a tear slipped down her cheek as she sang.

She'd always loved this Michael Bublé song, loved the beautiful plaintiveness of his voice. She'd sung it who knew how many times, but never had she felt it as much as she did right now, on the spot in front of people two hundred years and a whole culture removed from her.

As the last words drifted away, she opened her eyes to thunderous applause. At some point, Deveric had moved to the front of the room. His eyes locked with hers now, an inscrutable look on his face. She couldn't tell what he was thinking. Had he liked it?

"Bravo!" a male voice cried from the back. Several young ladies pleaded with her to sing another. The room fell silent again, however, as Deveric's mother approached her. After a moment, the Dowager Duchess of Claremont nodded. "Well done, Mrs. James. Well done."

Eliza smiled broadly. She had a way to go in her battle to win over Deveric's mother, but at least she'd won this skirmish.

Lady Parcine came forward and settled herself at the piano with flourish, obviously not pleased at the amount of attention Eliza was receiving. As pleasant notes spread through the room, Amara linked her arm in Eliza's and pulled her off to the side, where Grace was standing with that shy, endearing smile.

"Grace wants to compliment you," Amara whispered. "And it's always good to leave a gentleman wanting more." She inclined her head briefly toward her brother.

Eliza peeked at him. Deveric was still staring at her, his mouth tipping down. He gave her one crisp nod before walking back to his friends. *What was that about?* He seemed upset with her, but Eliza didn't know why.

After warm congratulations from Grace, Eliza held a hand to her forehead, pleading a headache. Really, she was just hungry, and ready for a break. The emotionality of that song had wrung every last bit of energy from her. She slipped out of the room before any of the sisters could stop her. *I want to dream of Dunkin' Donuts and Facebook and … and Deveric's lips on mine.*

Chapter 21

The knock at her door came late, so quiet Eliza barely heard it. She froze under the blankets. It had to be after midnight. Who could it be?

Stumbling out of bed, she pulled on the heavy robe Betsy had left on a nearby chair, grateful the glowing coals of the fire illuminated the room enough so that she didn't bonk into anything. Halfway to the door, she realized she probably could have just called, "Come in," and not had to leave the warmth of the covers. Oh well. Better safe than sorry, since she had no clue who was out there. She cracked the door open a few inches.

Deveric stood before her in his shirtsleeves, his cravat off, hair rumpled, a lit candlestick in one hand.

What on earth? He shouldn't be there. As he'd said earlier, no man or woman should be in each other's chambers, especially at night, unless they were man and wife.

"May I come in?" he finally said, his voice slightly slurred.

Eliza stared at him. Was he drunk? "Are you drunk?" Her

words echoed her thoughts.

"A gentleman does not get drunk. Mildly foxed, perhaps. But no, I am not." His eyes danced up and down the hallway. "Please? I should not be here."

Eliza opened the door wider, and he walked through, steadier on his feet than she expected. "Why *are* you here?"

"I …" He scanned the room, looking everywhere but toward her. "I don't know. You. That song. The pain in your voice."

Eliza swallowed.

"It hurt me to hear it, 'Liza. I can't stand the thought of you in pain. And that scares me."

"Scares you?" Her heart sped up at his words.

"All I bring is pain. To anyone I've ever let close. I can't. I can't bring pain to you." He closed his eyes.

"Come here, sit down." She walked over to the bed and plopped down on the mattress.

Dev's eyes widened, his pupils flaring.

"No, I'm not trying to seduce you," Eliza said. Though Lord knows she wanted to. But not now, not like this. This felt all wrong. She just wanted to console him. Whatever she hoped for between them, driving him to drink was not one of them.

"More's the pity," he muttered as he crossed the short distance, setting the candle on a bedside table before sitting down mere inches away from her. The smell of brandy and male tickled her nose—a not-altogether unpleasant sensation.

"I want to know," he said. "Know more. I want to see this tele-phone, as you call it. I want proof."

So that's what this was about. Disappointment flooded through her, even though moments before she'd said her goal wasn't seduction. Well, his could have been, damn it.

But maybe this was better. She stood up and walked to the armoire, seeking out the lockbox. She'd wanted to show him, to prove her story, to share her twenty-first century life with him. Now was her chance.

As she pulled the phone out of the box and pressed the power button, anxiety swept through her. What would he think of what she was about to show him? Would it send him running away? Would he accuse her of witchcraft again?

She knew what was in the phone, had experienced it all. But the things he was about to see were things he likely couldn't fathom. How would she react, if the situation were reversed, if someone had appeared to her in 2012, claiming to be from 2212? Not well, most likely.

She closed her eyes, sending a little prayer heavenward, before settling back down at his side. His eyes widened as the phone made its intro noise, and the screen illuminated, but he didn't freak out, didn't even move. Icons appeared, and Eliza pressed the one marked Photos.

The screen filled with the last picture Eliza had taken— the selfie with Cat of the two of them in their Regency finery. Eliza's eyes teared up at seeing her friend.

"I—I saw that woman," Deveric said, his body rigidly still.

"Yeah, that's Cat. My best friend."

"The one who sent you back."

"Yes." She looked up at Deveric. His eyes were fixed on the screen, soaking in the photograph.

"The detail is amazing. An exact reproduction."

"Yup. May I show you?"

He swallowed. "Yes."

She held the phone up and snapped a picture. The flash caught Deveric by surprise, given his startled expression, but to his credit, he merely blinked a few times to clear his vision. Flipping it around, she showed Deveric his photo. He reached for the phone, and she gave it up.

He studied the photograph for a minute, and then said, "So that's what that woman was doing. Show me how to do it."

She leaned over. "Hold it like this, then push this button."

Deveric raised the phone in front of his face and did as instructed. Whatever appeared on the screen had him chortling.

"What?" Eliza grabbed the phone. He'd taken a picture of her breasts. Or where her breasts would be, rather; the thick robe mostly disguised them.

Men. She arched an eyebrow. "Are you going to claim that was an accident?"

He shrugged his shoulders, his face adopting an innocent expression. "I consider it luck."

She bopped him in the shoulder. "Do you want to see this stuff, or not?"

Deveric grinned, cocking an eyebrow. "Oh, yes, but you'd better show me more of the tele-phone first."

She laughed. She couldn't help it. A slightly inebriated Deveric was adorable—in control enough not to worry her, but relaxed enough to be showing a new, fun side of his personality—a light-hearted, teasing side. He should show it more often.

She flipped through the photos. "Here. Here's Cat's car."

Deveric grabbed the phone, his eyes soaking in Cat's little Honda. "And it moves on its own power? Steam?"

"No, gasoline. Though I'm not an expert in the interior workings of the automobile. Sorry."

"Show me more."

For the next few hours—Eliza couldn't say how long—she showed Deveric photographs, grateful she hadn't erased them after downloading them to her computer. It was amazing, the things she took for granted that Dev noticed. He wanted to hear about the street lights, the paved roads, the McDonald's in the background, the airplanes and Space Shuttle pics from the Air and Space Museum, the laptop on which a guy was typing in a pic she'd snapped in the coffee shop she and Cat frequented. Anything and everything, he wanted information on.

It pained Eliza to watch the phone battery dwindle. She knew once it was depleted, she'd never see these pictures again. And yet, what better chance to convince Deveric once and for all she was exactly who she said she was?

She'd taken a picture of one of the pages of Cat's magical manuscript a few weeks ago, a beautifully illuminated portrait of a woman writing on parchment. At Deveric's request, she explained again how Cat's powers worked, dancing around the part about Deveric being created for her. He didn't ask, so she was glad she didn't have to answer.

As time passed, his speech grew steadier, his eyes clearer. The alcohol wore off, but his enthusiasm for talking with her didn't. He quizzed her not only about the technological things he saw, but also about Cat, about Eliza's family, about her husband. She hadn't wanted to talk about Greg, wanting instead to focus on Deveric, on the here and now—or here and the future, if one thought of it that way. But she'd shared, anyway. An open and honest relationship necessitated communication both ways. If she wanted him to reveal himself to her, she had to be willing to do the same.

At some point, she'd ask him about Mirabelle. She definitely wanted to know about his first wife, but now was not the time; tonight was for showing him who *she* was. Hopefully tomorrow, and in the days after, he'd reciprocate.

A noise in the hall startled both of them.

"Good God, what time is it?" Deveric leapt off the bed. "I should not be here. Alone, with you."

Eliza yawned, the lack of sleep catching up with her. It wasn't as if they'd done anything untoward—they hadn't. Nothing overtly sexual had happened since he snapped the picture of her boobs, and yet a startling sense of intimacy settled over Eliza. How amazing, to feel that without having had physical contact of any kind. She liked it. Liked it, indeed.

Not that she didn't want to jump him. Seeing him there, in his shirtsleeves, dark shadows of a beard gracing his face, and his eyes, so earnest, she wanted nothing more than to lean in and kiss him, to start something she now truly wanted to finish.

A second noise in the hallway dashed all thoughts of that from her brain. It really wouldn't do, being caught in bed with the Duke, even with both of them fully clothed. She didn't want to poke the Dragon—and she didn't want to force Deveric's hand. Would he feel compelled to offer for her? That's what all the romances hinted at. But she didn't want it that way. If she and Deveric were to become something, it needed to be of their own free choice, not dictated by circumstance.

Well, circumstance beyond the ones she'd manipulated to get here.

Dev ran his fingers through his adorably bedraggled hair. "I ... I must go, Eliza."

Something in his tone caught her attention, spreading unease through her, but he silenced it with a quick kiss, a brash meeting of mouths. Before she could say anything, he yanked open the door, and with one last look at her, dashed out and across the hallway.

Eliza sat back down, her phone clutched in her hand. Thirty percent battery power. Crap. She took one last look at the photo of Cat and her, and then powered the machine off, carefully securing it in the lockbox before lying back down on the bed.

Sleep. She just needed to snooze a bit. She'd find Deveric later, see how he was feeling after all he'd seen and heard.

Surely this was a great sign, that the hours they'd spent together had felt like minutes; that they'd talked like old friends, in spite of the energy surging between them. This was the kind of relationship she wanted, one full of passion, but built on friendship.

Tonight, Deveric Mattersley had felt like a friend.

What would tomorrow hold?

Chapter 22

A few hours later, Eliza woke refreshed, despite the small amount of sleep, happy to face the day. Surely last night signified a major step forward in building a relationship with Deveric. He knew her now, knew all about her—or as much as one could share in a few hours. They had their future to truly become intimate with each other. Not only did he know her, he believed her, accepted her story for truth—and had kissed her again, after all was said and done.

They'd mostly talked about her and her time period, true, but he'd shared small tidbits of himself along the way, discussions of his passion for science, his fascination with the potentials of steam, his frustration that ducal duties often prevented him from pursuing more information, from experimenting on his own.

But was it enough? She still had to win over his mother. Not to mention the rest of Regency society. At least the Dowager appreciated Eliza's singing. Maybe if she just sang all day long, she'd be in like Flynn.

Grinning, Eliza threw the covers off, then immediately pulled them back on. Brr! She wished she had her electric blanket—and Elvis, the cat, who'd slept on Eliza's feet every night, though he was technically Cat's kitty.

"Sure, steal my feline. It's not like he's my namesake or anything," Cat said once.

"Namesake?" Eliza had teased. "Your name is Elvis? Your parents must have had a cruel sense of humor, or been true fans."

"Very funny."

"Thankya, thankya verra much."

People kept pets in this period, too. She'd seen dogs in paintings, and occasionally a cat or two. What had happened to the dog she'd seen with Freddy that morning? Eliza had a hard time believing the Dowager would allow animals in the house. Which was sad, because in Eliza's opinion, companionship from an animal was one of God's greatest gifts. Oh, how she missed a snuggly warm body in the morning, something that loved her without reservation— and never criticized her. Exactly how she dreamed Deveric would be. She'd take him over a pet any day.

There came a knock at the door, and then it opened quickly. It was still disconcerting to know servants could enter at any time.

"Good morning, my lady."

"Morning, Betsy."

Eliza braced herself, threw off the covers, hopped up, and ran to the washstand. She quickly washed her face, thankful Betsy had brought warm water, and then ran to the fire, which Betsy had stoked up to a merry blaze.

"Thank you, thank you, thank you. I'm so cold. How do

you stand it?"

"'Tis a bit colder than many a March, but I don't find it so bad, my lady. Virginia must be warmer?"

"Um, in a matter of speaking."

"I brought another of Amara's gowns for you today."

Eliza examined the dress, admiring the intricate stitching on the bodice. This one, while still long-sleeved and fairly high-necked, was not nearly as dowdy as the first Eliza had worn. "She is too kind."

"I'm glad she is being kind to you. She has a good heart, but she's become so hardened, so standoffish." Betsy clapped her hands over her mouth, her eyes wide. "I'm sorry. I shouldn't have spoken so freely. I love the Mattersley family; they have cared for me and my family for many years."

"No offense to me, Betsy. I value your help in navigating the family dyn—relationships, since I'm new." 'Family dynamics,' which she'd been about to say, was certainly not regular Regency parlance.

Betsy hesitated for a moment. "We know much that goes on in this house." She held out Eliza's stays.

Eliza's eyes flew to the maid's. Was she implying … did she know about last night? Eliza turned around and looped her arms through the undergarment, attempting to act calm.

"We don't know *everything*, but many people speak or act in front of us as if they've forgotten we are there. It's as if we're invisible." Betsy tied the stays, and then lifted the morning gown.

"I shall have to be careful, then," Eliza joked as she settled into the dress. "No trysts in the garden, huh?" Why the heck had she said that? Deveric's face flashed before her, those green eyes doing all sorts of things to her insides. *Because I'm thinking about the master of the house, and yesterday's kiss, and last night.* Especially last night. What was he doing right now? She could hardly wait to see him.

"You are safe, my lady. You've already won us over because you treat us as if we are equals. We like how you have brought His Grace back to life, as well."

"Back to life?"

Betsy worked on the back fastenings. "He has been so dour for so long. Since the loss—" Betsy broke off, but Eliza knew to what she was referring. "It's nice to see a spark in his eyes again."

"I think you give me too much credit." Had he been so in love with his wife? Eliza didn't want to compete with a ghost the rest of her life. "What was she like? The Duke's wife?"

Betsy waited a moment before speaking. "Lady Mirabelle was an elegant lady, small and frail." She picked up the brush and motioned for Eliza to sit at the dressing table. "Impeccable in behavior and manners. She did not say much, preferring to keep to herself."

Eliza's heart constricted. She was the opposite of this Mirabelle in every way. "Did Dev—did the Duke love her?"

Betsy smiled over Eliza's head in the mirror. "Love is not usually a part in such high marriages, is it? But, no. I do not think he loved her. She definitely did not love him. Her maid often whispered of the things Lady Mirabelle told her about His Grace."

Eliza's eyes widened. "What kinds of things?"

"That he was a monster of a man, a giant, fierce and rough. Of course, we did not believe her, no matter that she was the Duchess. We saw no evidence of harm on her, heard nothing to indicate he hurt her. We saw for ourselves how His Grace looked after his son, his horses, and his dogs. No, most of us did not care much for Lady Mirabelle, Eliza. She drained the spirit out of all around her."

Relief surged through Eliza. Not that she'd wanted Deveric saddled with a horrendous wife, but Eliza certainly didn't want to compete with the memory of a perfect one, either.

"You're so kind to me, Betsy. It's nice to feel accepted by at least one person here."

"Oh, you've won over far more than that," Betsy said, tying Eliza's hair back in a ribbon.

What did she mean by that?

As Eliza watched her in the dressing table mirror, Betsy's face suddenly crumpled, fear etching its way across her forehead. "What is it, Betsy?"

"Beg pardon, my lady. I should not have said so much about the family, particularly the Duke's wife. I—I forgot my place."

Eliza turned on the chair and grabbed her in an impulsive hug, squeezing her tightly. "No worries. Your secrets about this family's secrets are safe with me."

Eliza followed the hallway to the grand staircase, pleased she was finally a bit more oriented in this enormous house. Her sense of direction had never been her forte.

After descending the stairs, she made her way to the breakfast room. Low murmurs of conversation and the tinkling of silverware on china greeted her as she walked in. She'd hoped to find Deveric, but was disappointed to discover only Amara, Emmeline, and Becca. At least the Dowager Dragon was absent.

Sitting down, she looked over the options on the table. There were several kinds of cold meat, but Eliza never could stomach it in the morning. She set a piece of cheddar and a chopped egg on top of a piece of hot toast, pleased when the cheese melted. *Not quite an Egg McMuffin, but it will do. At least it's not turtle.*

Becca's face wrinkled when she saw Eliza's plate. "Eggs on toast? Is that an American tradition?"

Eliza laughed. "Perhaps. I find it delicious." She took a quick bite, washing it down with coffee. "Has Dev—I mean, has everyone else eaten already?"

"Most people are still abed. We are rather early risers," Emmeline said. "Mother's already finished and has gone to confer with the cook on dinner."

"I don't know where my brother is," Becca said. "Well, Deveric, I mean. Chance will likely sleep until near dinner."

"He left."

CHAPTER 23

At Amara's words, Eliza's eyes flew to hers. "He left?" she exclaimed before she could stop herself.

"He got called away to London."

"*When?*" Was it before or after he came to her room? Is that why he'd come, because he knew he was leaving? What did this mean?

All three sisters looked at her.

Crap. Eliza didn't need hot toast anymore; she was pretty sure she could melt cheese on her cheeks at the moment.

Amara took a sip of her tea. "I overheard him talking with Arthington after the play. He said he'd received a message while the men were at their port; Uncle Desmond is in trouble again, so Dev had to leave for London first thing this morning."

Becca snickered. "When is Uncle not?"

Emmeline shushed her.

"Our brother is constantly bailing out those who make foolish decisions. They should be left to stew in the remnants of their own soup!" Becca's chin jutted out in a way reminiscent of her brother's. Must be a Mattersley thing.

"Easy for a seventeen-year-old who's never been into major trouble to say." Amara's voice was calm. "If it hadn't been for Dev, I'd have been blacklisted forever, or had to enter into a marriage I didn't want."

Becca looked down at her lap. "I'm sorry, Amara. You are right."

Eliza wanted to throw up. Dev had left? Left her here, on her own? Why hadn't he at least told her? Oh, sure, he'd said he had to go, but she'd thought he meant back to his own chamber. Not off the estate. Not all the way to London!

What did it mean, that he'd come to her, that he'd spent the night before he left? Had he wanted to forge a stronger connection to bind them together before his absence? Or had he merely wanted his questions answered, in case he weren't to return? He *would* come back, wouldn't he? Confusion swirled around her, enveloping her in its disheartening fog.

"Let us not argue," Emmeline interjected, her voice falsely cheerful. *The peacemaker of the family.* "Though the house party is over and our guests are leaving today, we still have ways to entertain ourselves. We should journey into Winchester and procure our cousin new dresses."

"Winchester? Eliza would have more fun learning to ride a horse than visiting silly old Winchester. There's hardly anything there."

"Becca, *you* may think there's nothing better than a horse, but that doesn't mean everyone does."

Eliza took a bite of her egg sandwich, hardly tasting it now. As bewildered and saddened as she was over Dev's sudden disappearance, though, she enjoyed the banter between the sisters, loved the affectionate edge she heard in their words. These women may bicker from time to time, but it was obvious they had each other's backs.

She wished she'd grown up with that kind of security, the built-in friendship siblinghood brought. She'd found Cat in her twenties, thank God, but for most of her life it'd been just her and her parents—and they'd focused on their own things so much she'd often had to fend for herself. Until she'd met Greg. They'd gotten married. Friends for life. And then he'd died.

Maybe that's what made it so easy to leave Cat. Maybe she'd never expected their friendship to last. Horror filled her. Had she really dismissed her best friend so easily? *No! Cat wanted me to go. She knew. She knew I couldn't stay stuck anymore, just as she couldn't either.* "I hope she's happy, whatever she's doing," Eliza mumbled as she traced her finger over the edge of her fork.

"Did you say something?"

Eliza glanced over at Amara. "No, sorry, nothing. Never mind." After a pause, she steeled her shoulders. Deveric would come back. He had to. For now, she should use this opportunity to get to know his sisters better. "Winchester would be delightful, actually. I've always wanted to see the cathedral there." Not really, but Eliza's mom had loved that terrible old Winchester Cathedral song. It seemed a good enough reason to go.

Amara stood up. "Let us go to Winchester, then. We won't find anything nearly as good as in London, but there should be one or two serviceable gowns we can find for Eliza until we venture back to Town."

"I think not," a voice called from the hallway. The Dowager strode into the room. "Mrs. James can make do with your older gowns, Amara. Frederick is ready for lessons today. Mrs. James shall attend him."

"But—" Emmeline started, before falling silent again.

"Yes, Your Grace." Eliza dipped her head toward the Dowager. She refused to let the Dragon intimidate her—*Eleanor Roosevelt, baby*—but she also didn't wish to make a permanent enemy by responding pugnaciously. *When I'm Duchess, we will be equals.*

She wasn't a duchess yet, though, if she ever would be, and so for now, she must cede the battle. Besides, she *had* volunteered to tutor the boy. "Could someone direct me to the nursery?"

"I will," Amara said, daring to shoot her mother a look. "Follow me."

The two women escaped the breakfast room.

"My pardons. Mother feels she must preserve the family name, so she is always on guard against potential scandal."

Eliza nearly snorted. She, scandalous? As if. Good Lord, she'd been called a Goody Two Shoes more times than she cared to count in Charlottesville. *Then again, Lizzie, she doesn't know you.* To Deveric's mother, Eliza was new, of an obscure background, with manners and mannerisms that didn't fit in. Hardly enough to raise eyebrows back home, but she wasn't home anymore, and those things meant everything in Regency society.

Pain shone in Amara's eyes. After a moment, she whispered, "It's hard for her to look at me sometimes."

"It's your mother who's missing out, you know," Eliza said. At Amara's questioning look, she continued. "You seem pretty wonderful to me. Bright, observant, caring. If she's going to lose her relationship with you because of something that happened years ago and that wasn't even your fault, well, that's her loss." Eliza shrugged her shoulders as if to say none of it was a big deal.

Amara gave a hoot of laughter. "I like you Americans. If only it were that easy."

"I like you, too, Amara," Eliza said, grateful for another moment of connection in the midst of emotional chaos.

"What is *she* doing here?" Freddy demanded as Eliza entered the room.

Nurse Pritchett slapped him on the knuckles. "A child does not speak to elders in such a manner. Not even a duke's son."

Eliza flinched. The boy stared at her mulishly, ignoring his nurse. "Please don't hit him!"

Nurse Pritchett glowered at her. "You are a stranger in this house, a poor cousin. I am nurse to the Duke's heir. You dare to command me?"

Eliza drew up her shoulders, preparing for battle. Normally, this scary old crow might frighten her, but her anger flared upon seeing Deveric's son struck. That was not acceptable to her.

It was normal in this time, a voice in her head said. Well, it wasn't going to be the norm in this house. Not if she had anything to do with it.

Would the Dowager throw her out over this? She glanced at the boy. He was small for his age, but fire sparked in his eyes, his jaw squarely set. *Just like his father's.* Her heart flooded with unexpected emotion.

"I do." Eliza's composed demeanor belied her inner turmoil. "As a governess, I have deduced if you want children to learn and behave, there are far better methods. And as a family member, I'm telling you, do not lay a hand on him again."

God, she hoped she was right. She was making all this up as she went. *Governess, my ass.* She'd never taught children in her life. But she *had* held Story Hour every week at the Treasure Trove, and saw how kids ate up compliments for good behavior.

On the few occasions she'd had a yeller, as she called them, she'd cringed. Most of the time, those children continued behaving badly, even after being screamed at. They'd grown immune to it.

The nurse crossed her arms under her chest, bristling with belligerence. "I've been a nurse longer than you've been alive." When Eliza showed no sign of backing down, she finally huffed, "I leave you to him," and stalked off.

Round One to the American.

Would Nurse Pritchett report this to Deveric's mother? Most likely. The Dowager was probably a firm believer in corporal punishment. *I'm sure she'd like to whip me.* Well, Eliza would cross that bridge—and Dragon—when she came to it.

Closing the door after Nurse Pritchett, Eliza made a show of exhaling in relief. "Whew, I'm glad she's gone."

Freddy glared at her, mutiny in his eyes. *So much for gratitude.* After a minute or so, he looked away. *So much bravado in such a little boy.* "I can handle a knuckle rapping," he grumbled.

"I'm sure you can, but I don't think you should have to."

He kicked at the floor.

"Does it help you learn when she does that? Does it make you want to work harder?"

He stuck his lower lip out, considering. "It makes me

want to hit back," he admitted. "But I know if I don't mind, it will happen again."

"I understand. But I think people respond better to kindness, don't you?"

His eyebrows lifted, as if he was surprised she'd asked his opinion.

"I suppose so," he said. "Jerome the stable hand always kicks at the dogs, saying that's what will make them stop chewing at his breeches. But the dogs never chew *my* breeches." He took a breath.

"Exactly," Eliza said. Sensing an opportunity, she continued. "You like dogs, don't you?" The joy on his face when he'd burst into his mother's chamber, dog on his heels, just a few days ago had said as much.

"Papa says I'm not to play with them, that they're for hunting."

"Hmm. Well, we had a dog when I was young, and I loved him. He was my best friend for years."

Freddy looked at her, his eyes round in surprise. "In truth?"

"Yes, really. Maybe you can take me down to where the dogs are? Perhaps we could pet one today." If she couldn't be with Deveric, at least she could get to know his son.

His face lit up. He stubbed his toe on the ground again. "But Papa—"

"—is gone for the time being. And I will deal with him if it becomes an issue."

Oh boy. Interfering with Deveric's authority wasn't the wisest tack to take. But come on; dogs made the kid happy. And wouldn't Deveric want his son happy and thriving? Wasn't that what all parents wanted?

The Dowager's stern face flashed before her. Maybe

she was wrong. Maybe in this period, appearances and conformity outranked familial affection. If that were the case, she was in deep trouble.

On the other hand, how much worse could it get? It was not as if Deveric's mother liked her, anyway, though at least she hadn't thrown Eliza out. *If you keep challenging her, she might, regardless of what her son said.*

Shaking off all the what-ifs, Eliza walked over to the boy, crouching down in front of him. "We have not been properly introduced." The rushed greeting from their first encounter didn't count. "My name is Mrs. Eliza James. I'm from the United States—Virginia, actually. I'm your cousin"—funny how she hardly tripped over those words anymore—"but also now your governess. You may call me … Miss Eliza." Mrs. James sounded too formal for a child that young, and Eliza too casual, so she took the good old Southern approach of slapping "Miss" in front of her first name.

"I am Lord Harrington," Freddy responded, his voice as supercilious as his father's.

Lord Harrington? Ah, the courtesy title taken from his father. He expected her to address him so? Perhaps he'd been taught to; she was a stranger, after all. "That is an appropriate title for an important lad such as yourself," Eliza said. "But since I have given you leave to call me by my first name, might you extend the same courtesy to me?"

Frederick—Lord Harrington—mulled that over, his brow crinkling in an adorable imitation of his father. "I suppose. My name is Frederick. Though my aunts call me Freddy. Since you are a relative, you may also call me Freddy."

"Thank you, Freddy." She wanted to scoop him up in a hug, this boy pretending at his tender age to be a man. "I am sorry it upset you to see me in your mother's chamber the other day," she said, her eyes fixed on his darling green ones. "I lost both of my parents. I know how hard that is. I want you to know I wasn't trying to take over her space—I didn't even know it *was* her space. It's just where they put me."

His lip trembled. "You did? You lost your Mama *and* your Papa?"

"Yes, I did. I was older than you are, but they died in a car—a carriage accident."

Freddy tentatively linked his hand with hers. "Let's go and see the dogs!" he said, clearly wishing to change the subject.

Her heart melted at the feel of his tiny fingers in hers. "Lead on, my little lord."

CHAPTER 24

As they exited the house, Eliza said, "I heard you've been sick. I'm glad you seem to be feeling better."

Freddy just nodded. So much for hinting for information—he was about as forthcoming as his father.

"May I ask what sickness you had?"

"Don't know." He shrugged. "I've had fevers. Everything was achy, 'specially my legs. And my throat hurt very much."

Eliza puzzled over that. Whom was she kidding? She was no pediatrician. "But you're feeling better now?"

"Mostly," he said. "I still get tired a lot. Nurse Pritchett always wants me in bed."

They neared a large stone hut not far from the stables. As yelps and barks pierced the air, Freddy started to run.

With an excited grin, Eliza gave chase. "Wait for me!"

Freddy was already on his knees inside the door, a foxhound jumping on him and licking his face. He laughed, his cheeks flushing with happiness.

"Who's there?" came a grouchy voice, as a tall, lean man came out of the shadows. "Oh, it's you, Master Frederick." The man's face was kindly, in spite of the brusque greeting, and his eyes brightened as he watched the boy.

"Hello, Mr. Johnny," Freddy answered absent-mindedly, giggling as the dog's tongue scrubbed his face.

"His Grace doesn't like for you to be here," the man chastised, but Eliza sensed softness under his tone. She warmed to him immediately, thrilled to see someone look affectionately upon the child.

"Hello," she said. Habit had her wanting to extend her hand to shake his, but she caught herself just in time. "I'm Eliza James. I'm … Frederick's governess."

"She's also my cousin, Papa says," the boy offered, before he went back to tickling the dog's stomach.

The man touched his fingers to the brim of his hat. "John Sayers, my lady," he said. "Master of the Hounds." As he watched Freddy roll on the ground with the dogs, he added, "His Grace does not like his son with the dogs."

"Why not?"

"The dogs are trained hunting animals."

"And?"

"They are not meant to play."

She eyed Mr. Sayers. Something in his tone caught her attention. "But you don't agree with that?"

He looked at the ground. "I would never disagree with the Duke of Claremont." His voice was strong, but he didn't meet her eyes.

"Of course not," she affirmed. "But it is nice to see Freddy smile, is it not?"

John gave her a measuring look. "It is, indeed. He is a fine lad."

Turning back to the boy, Mr. Sayers said, "Master Freddy, Althea whelped her pups. Would you like to see them?"

Frederick leapt up, dogs at his heels. "I would! I would!"

John gave him a kind smile. "Remember not to touch them. They are too little."

"I won't, Mr. Sayers, I promise!" Excitement laced the boy's voice.

Eliza followed them farther into the hut, her ears echoing with the sounds of myriad dogs barking as they passed.

The houndsmaster opened a door, and the majority of the hounds ran out. As she passed by, Eliza glimpsed the dogs romping in a small field surrounded by a wooden fence.

Gesturing to Eliza and Freddy, Mr. Sayers quietly approached a corner in the hut, where a foxhound lay on her side, nursing her new pups.

Deveric's son crouched down eagerly, getting as close as he could, but remembered to keep his hands to himself.

"Look, Miss Eliza!" he exclaimed. His green eyes, so like his father's, sparkled.

Smiling, Eliza bent over next to him. *Wow, I've never seen dogs this tiny.* She watched a teensy pup try to work its way into the mix of its brothers and sisters. "That one seems quite small."

"Ayup," John said. "He's a runt. Probably not going to survive. Even if he does, he'll never be a hunting dog. One of his eyes is damaged." He crouched down next to the boy. "I should probably put him out of his misery, but, well, it's not his fault he got the short end of the stick."

Eliza's esteem for this John Sayers rose by leaps and bounds. Hunting dogs in this era were not pets; they were business. To have a master of hounds be unwilling to kill a less-than-idea animal spoke volumes as to his character.

"Oh, can I have him? Please, Mr. Sayers, please?"

John's face twitched in a frown. "Master Frederick, the little pup most likely won't live. And I'm not sure what your father would say."

"Let me take care of that," Eliza broke in. "I bet I can convince him there are lots of educational lessons to be learned in caring for another creature."

Frederick looked at her with grateful eyes. Mr. Sayer's were more indiscernible.

"But like Mr. Sayers said, Freddy," she added in a gentle voice, "it may not survive."

He bobbed his head up and down. "I understand. But I will come every day to talk to him and encourage him—and hold him when you let me, Mr. John. That would be all right, wouldn't it?"

John Sayers held up his hands. "I can't argue with the future Duke of Claremont, now can I?"

Freddy drew up his shoulders, as if just now remembering his social position, and expectations. Eliza hated to see it; she wanted him to remain as carefree as he could for as long as he could. Life brought hardships no matter what one's position in society; children should enjoy being young.

Freddy nodded. "Thank you, Mr. Sayers." Leaning over the pups, he studied the one-eyed dog. "I shall call him 'Pirate,'" he said, his voice solemn. "Lots of pirates have only one eye. Isn't that right, Mrs. James?"

Eliza laughed. "So I hear. I've never met any in real life. And wouldn't want to."

"You didn't see any on your ship? When you crossed the ocean?"

Oops. She'd forgotten that part of the story. Hopefully, nobody would press her for many details. How could she speak convincingly of a sea voyage when she'd never actually been on one?

"In truth, I haven't got much of a stomach for sailing. I was seasick most of the time and stayed in my cabin." Well, that was a half-truth—if she *had* been on a ship, she most likely *would* have been sick, considering how ill she'd gotten the one time her family had taken a ferry from Maryland to New Jersey.

"Oh." Disappointment laced his voice. "I wanted you to tell me some adventures." He scrunched up his nose as he eyed her, as if trying to decide whether she'd ever be any fun or not.

"I can't tell you about sailing, but I can tell you a little about Virginia," she said, hoping she'd be able to keep it to stuff relevant to the Regency period. "Plus, I doubt most people encounter pirates at sea."

Freddy had already lost interest, and was watching the dogs again.

"It is unlikely His Grace will let Master Frederick keep a dog, my lady." John had removed his cap and was worrying the edges with his fingers. "I love to see the lad happy, but His Grace may fear the dog will not be good for his son, especially given the boy's frail health."

"He doesn't look frail right now, does he?"

Both of them watched the little boy, who was whooping with delight at the puppies as they crawled over each other. His cheeks bloomed with color.

"You said yourself you don't know if the puppy will survive," Eliza added. "So let's cross that bridge when we come to it. Besides, Deveric—I mean, His Grace—is not here right now. What he doesn't know can't hurt him, right?" She bit her lip, hoping Mr. Sayers hadn't noticed her flub with

Deveric's name.

"Be careful, my lady. He is a powerful man who does not like to be crossed. I would hate to see you turned away without a reference."

Eliza wrapped her arms around her middle, propping up one arm to chew at a fingernail. "Does he—does the Duke do that often?" She couldn't imagine Deveric being so heartless—he'd taken her in, after all—but it's not as if she knew everything about him.

"In truth, no. But his father did. He was demanding in his expectations."

"That's terrible!"

Mr. Sayers' eyes flashed in warning. "Don't let the Dowager hear you say that."

Eliza nodded. As if she needed reminding to be careful around that dragon. *Hold on.* John Sayers had known Deveric's father? Maybe he could shed some light on the family situation, on the Dowager, or Deveric himself.

"Did the current Duke and his father get along well?"

Mr. Sayers pinched his lips. "That is not for me to say, my lady."

Shoot. She'd take that as a *no, they didn't*, only she didn't know Mr. Sayers well enough to read him yet. "My apologies. I did not mean to overstep bounds. My American manner is often too direct, I know."

The houndsmaster dipped his head stiffly.

"May Freddy and I visit again tomorrow?"

"Of course."

"Come, Freddy, we should return to the house."

"Aww, do we *have* to?" His eyes were plaintive as he looked up at Eliza. The dog he'd been petting thumped its tail on the ground.

"We do. But we shall come back in the morning, provided you attend your lessons, and get the rest you need."

She grabbed his hand to pull him up off the ground, pleased when he didn't let go once standing.

"Bye, Pirate. Bye, Mr. Sayers. See you tomorrow!"

Hand-in-hand, they headed back to the house.

CHAPTER 25

Deveric groaned as he rolled over in the massive oak bed he'd had custom-made for his beloved St. James townhouse. The property was big enough to hold his entire family, but it provided much-needed respite from the constant commotion of his numerous siblings—not to mention his mother—and so he kept it to himself. There were definite advantages to wealth. He did, however, offer the house as lodging for his close friends when they were in town, though he was regretting that this morning. Arthington yelling for Collinswood was what had woken him.

They obviously hadn't drunk as much as he last night. He held his hand over his eyes, blocking out the sunlight streaming in through the windows. They'd started with port, but what had he finished with? Whisky? Scotch? He wasn't sure.

He'd only known he'd wanted to forget the images he'd seen that fateful night. And then on Eliza's phone. It was all real. All too much. And Eliza. Eliza was too much, with the way she'd winnowed herself in through his defenses.

What was she doing? It'd been a week. A week since he'd fled Clarehaven. A week of trying to drown his confusion, and his desire, in drink. It wasn't working. The only thing he thought of was her. Eliza, her eyes aglow as she regaled him with tales of the future. Eliza, her face a mask of pain as she sang so beautifully, so hauntingly, of wanting to go home. Eliza, who'd somehow wormed her way under his skin. The unexpected desire she sparked in him was difficult enough to battle, but this … this stirring of less base emotions was downright terrifying.

How could it be true? No one could travel through *time*, for Christ's sake. It was impossible. Except she had. *He* had. He'd been someplace else, someplace quite different from Clarehaven, with people he'd never seen who were wearing clothing that was not quite right, with objects he'd never encountered. He'd been two hundred years in the future.

He'd wanted to dismiss it as a dream, a quite creative one, though he did not count a vast imagination as one of his over-arching qualities. But it wasn't. Eliza proved that— proved it with her presence, proved it with her tele-phone. Some might have dismissed the object as some form of trick, some sort of sorcery. He knew better. It was an advanced machine, capable of things he'd never imagined. And what he'd seen on it …

Eliza James had traveled through time. With him. To him. *For him?*

His mouth watered as he recollected the first time he'd seen her, in that deliciously snug gown with the purple and green embroidery. She'd looked up at him as if it were Christmas morning, and he her gift. Had any woman ever viewed him like that? As a gift, rather than a prize to be claimed? Or a monster to be avoided?

He looked over toward the letter his mother had sent, which lay folded on the table near his bed. She'd made no mention of Eliza, which he found suspicious. He'd known how upset she'd been at this stranger appearing in their home. He'd known she doubted his cousin story, though he typically told the truth to a fault.

She'd written about what needed to be done to prepare the estates for the spring sowing—tasks his estate manager had well in hand, but on which his mother always felt it necessary to comment. She'd shared tidbits about his sisters—they were, of course, all fine, but Emmeline was restless now that the house party guests had gone home, whereas Grace was relishing the quiet and solitude, spending much of her time reading and playing the piano. Becca was out every day with the horses, in spite of the cold. No surprise there. His mother had even written that Freddy was thriving; he'd had no more fevers, and was showing great energy again. *Thank God.*

But no word on Eliza.

Surely he needn't worry. Surely if something had happened, if Eliza had … disappeared, his mother would have informed him.

He wanted to know what she was doing, what she was thinking, how she was feeling. Was she okay on her own there, without him? *Okay?* The American was wearing off on him, her vocabulary infiltrating his, much like she'd infiltrated his quiet, staid, predictable life. And he liked it. A little too much.

He hadn't focused so much on another person since Mirabelle died, and then his thoughts had centered on the daughter he'd never know, not the wife he'd lost, or even the son he still had. Remorse gnawed at him constantly over that.

He and Mirabelle were never a good match, especially after the first year, after Frederick was born. He'd felt a failure, not being able to build a true marital relationship with her. Not that he knew what that meant; his parents' own relationship had been volatile. At times, they'd held great passion for each other; at others, they'd reviled each other. Samuel and Matilda Mattersley had always maintained proper decorum in the presence of others, however, just as they had taught their children.

Did any of his siblings know how contentious their parents' marriage had been? Unlikely. It was he who'd often sneaked down to the library at night when he couldn't sleep, seeking solace in a book, only to wander by his mother's chamber or his father's study and hear them arguing. Occasionally, he heard noises of an entirely different nature. As a young boy, he hadn't understood them. As an adolescent, he'd been sure to hurry past, not wanting to acknowledge his parents were still driven by the flesh.

And then his father would disappear again, back to London, back to the city and the temptations the Duke loved, but which Deveric's mother did not. Much of their time after Chance was born had been spent apart, though three sisters had followed. Neither one of them talked of his father's unfaithfulness, of course, although it'd been common knowledge about Town, of which Deveric and his mother were painfully aware. To acknowledge it wasn't proper.

When once Deveric had asked his father for advice on matters of the heart, his father had shut him down.

"Focus on begetting heirs, my boy," he'd said. "You needn't feel anything for your wife; she's not likely to return it. Women are fickle." His father had eyed him under those ferocious eyebrows and commanded, "Find love where you wish. You are a Claremont. You may do as you please."

That had often been his father's guidance: "Do as you please." Except, of course, when that went against his father's other myriad commandments regarding how a gentleman, or a Claremont, behaved.

Deveric stuck a leg out from under the covers. Gingerly, he sat up, trying not to move too quickly, lest he worsen the pounding in his head. Had doing whatever he wanted, sporting with all those women, made his father happy? It'd certainly made his mother miserable.

Was his mother's sorrow over his father's carousing the reason Deveric had no interest in it? Besides the fact he didn't want to kill anyone else, of course.

Deveric didn't know. He *did* know what he wanted to do most was go back to Clarehaven and drink in Eliza's amazing blue eyes, run his fingers through her soft flaxen hair, kiss her luscious pink lips … and question her all over again about the future. It fascinated him, the things she knew that he didn't.

A knock came at the door, followed by Arthington bellowing, "Get up, lazy bones. It's near four o'clock and I thought we might take a gander through Hyde Park. I'm wearing my newest waistcoat."

Four o'clock? How was that possible? *It's possible*, his head screamed, *when you don't set the bottle down until after the sun is up*. He groaned. He wasn't ready to face the day. He wanted to be left alone with his thoughts, his fantasies about the amazing American at Clarehaven.

The door popped open a few inches. "Don't you know, you clot pole," Deveric snapped, "that no one disturbs a duke?"

"Except a fellow duke, perhaps," Arth quipped, ducking the goblet Deveric snatched from the table and lobbed at his head. It fell to the floor with a thud. "Amazing. It didn't even shatter. That must be pricey crystal."

"Be quiet."

Arth sniggered. "Never could hold your drink, could you? Not that I know many who could consume an entire bottle alone. And then a second. By all rights, you should be dead."

"I feel dead. Now leave me be. I shall be down in half an hour."

"Wonderful," Arthington said. "There is a certain lady I am hoping to see."

"And you need me?" Deveric muttered as he rose slowly from the bed.

"Good God, man, warn a fellow!"

Dev looked down. Damn, he was naked. When had he ever slept naked? He grabbed the bed covering and held it around him.

"Be off," he snarled at his friend.

The door closed, but Deveric could hear Arthington call, "Keep the rumpled hair and surly expression. I can only look better in comparison."

Exactly half an hour later, Deveric strode into the foyer, hair carefully combed and impeccably groomed.

"My, my, one would never guess you had single-handedly tried to drink all of White's under the table last night," Arth joked as he examined his friend. "Except perhaps for the eyes; they're a little on the red side."

"Cook gave me her amazing remedy. I don't want to know what's in it, and Lord knows it tastes like swill, but I know of nothing better for ridding the headache."

Collinswood sauntered into the hall, wearing a closely fitted coat of blue superfine wool enhanced with a red waistcoat.

"You look like a peacock!" Arthington poked his friend in the arm.

Coll's cheeks tweaked up in a grin. "Tell me that again when all the ladies are preening for my attention," he said in his lilting accent.

Deveric rolled his eyes. *These two.* He couldn't imagine better friends, or people more perfect for plucking him out of his doldrums than James Bradley and Morgan Collinswood.

The three men exited the back door and walked to the mews, where their horses were already saddled and waiting.

"Tell me why I'm doing this again?" Deveric said as he mounted his horse and they ambled off. "I've never enjoyed the Hyde Park parade. Too many people, too much horse dung."

"Because, as you know, I need to marry, to produce an heir, lest my dastardly uncle get his hands on the estate," Arthington said. "And so I must ensnare a fine filly. And because you need to get back up on the horse, as well, so to speak."

"I prefer an actual woman," Deveric muttered. One woman in particular. He'd like to ride her—or perhaps have her ride him. His groin pulsed just imagining it. *Ludicrous.*

"It's nice to hear you prefer anything," Coll said. "I'd feared we needed to procure you monastic robes."

The burning of his ears told Deveric they'd turned red. Great. As if these two needed more ammunition. He flicked his hat against his thigh, urging his horse forward so that he needn't respond.

They rode in silence, his friends' gazes on the people around him. Dev's thoughts flitted back to the people—person—at Clarehaven. How he wished he were there.

Arthington adjusted his cravat as they turned into the park, his eyes already scouting the ladies in nearby carriages. He grinned. "Shall we drop into Watier's for a quick bit after this?"

"A bit? Of what sort? Food? Female? Cards?" Coll's dimples were out in full force as he teased his friend. A young lady strolling to their side stumbled as she saw him, her cheeks pinking. *They drop like flies wherever he goes.*

Deveric sighed. He'd had enough of gaming hells. Between his uncle and his brother, he was forever dragging someone away from the tables. He'd managed to satisfy the creditors this week, promising he was good for his uncle's debts, but he wasn't happy about it.

All he wanted to do was return to Clarehaven, return to Eliza. If his friends knew of his obsession for his American "cousin," however, he'd never hear the end of it. He had to play his part, at least for now.

Cracking a grin, he winked at the two men. "Why limit ourselves, my friends?"

Chapter 26

*I*t'd been a week. The days had passed slowly. Agonizingly slowly.

Not that Eliza didn't enjoy her time with Deveric's son. She did; Freddy was an inquisitive, clever young boy who loved peppering her with questions about Virginia and the world. His winsome grin and enthusiasm for life wormed their way into her heart in no time. In spite of his initial distrust, he warmed to her rapidly, his eyes lighting up whenever she came to see him. If only his father were so easy to win over. She couldn't exactly forge a relationship with someone who wasn't there.

Every day, Freddy gained strength, though he still rested each afternoon, a concession Eliza had made to Nurse Pritchett. She and the nurse hadn't exactly mended fences, but they weren't openly antagonistic to one another, either. Eliza suspected Nurse Pritchett enjoyed having some time off.

When Freddy rested, Eliza had time to herself. Occasionally, she walked in the gardens with Amara, or discussed books with Grace, or listened to Emmeline plan for the upcoming London Season—the one the Dowager made quite clear Eliza wouldn't attend. Even the Dowager, however, grew less hostile in her interactions as the week went on, evidently satisfied with Eliza's efforts with her grandson.

In the late afternoons, Eliza and Freddy visited the pups. It quickly became her favorite time of day, not only because she herself loved dogs and delighted in seeing Freddy so happy with them, but because she and Mr. Sayers conversed on a number of topics. Eliza learned much about the care of hunting dogs, of horses, of local villages and the pattern of days, and seasons. If he was surprised at her lack of knowledge, he never showed it, never talked down to her, but treated her rather as a friend.

Occasionally, Eliza wondered if something more sparked in his eye. He wasn't an unpleasant man to look at, his face weathered from years of outdoor work, but his eyes a pleasing gray, and his chin strong and square.

Too bad she felt nothing in return. Her heart already belonged to Deveric. She missed his intelligence, his teasing wit, even his rather stoic demeanor, such a contrast to her own exuberant and expressive nature. She missed the nearly tangible current that flowed between them whenever they were in the same room, missed the butterflies of anticipation and nervousness that fluttered in her stomach whenever he was near.

Frederick sometimes told her stories of things he'd done with his father, such as when Deveric had let Freddy ride on the front of Lightning with him, or showed him the fish swimming in the nearby lake, or read stories to him before bed. The wistful tone in the little boy's voice told Eliza he missed his dad as much as she did.

Where was Deveric? It had been a week. Was he coming back? Or was he merely waiting for his family to join him in London? Amara said they were traveling there in a week's time, after all. Without her.

Uh, Cat? What went wrong? How is this conducive to building a relationship? Are we betting on an 'absence makes the heart grow fonder' deal?

She just wanted him to come home.

"Pirate's doing well, isn't he, Eliza?" Freddy pointed to the pup, which had grown at such a rate he was nearly the size of his brothers and sisters. Eliza suspected Mr. Sayers must have been taking extra measures to help the small dog.

"He is. Much like you, don't you think?"

Freddy grinned. "I do feel ever so much better!"

"A little love goes a long way." Goodness, had she said that out loud? Frederick didn't notice; he'd already sprawled on the ground so that the dogs could lick him, but Mr. Sayers tipped his head to her, a knowing look in his eye.

She'd grown so fond of the boy in just a week. It surprised her, this depth of feeling. She'd babysat often as a teenager, but that was for money, not because she liked kids. She adored little Freddy, however.

She bit her lip, worrying at it with her teeth. His father should be here, should be witnessing his son's transformation, his zest for everything around him. A boy needed his dad. "Deveric should be here," she blurted out.

Sayers raised his eyebrows, but said nothing. Did he

disagree? Or was it because she'd called Claremont Deveric again?

"Don't you think a boy needs male attention?"

John shrugged. "He has you. Me. Nurse Pritchett. And the sisters sometimes entertain him. I saw Emmeline spinning a hoop with him on the grounds just yesterday."

"Well, yes, they do, but it's not the same. Children need their parents."

She'd needed hers. Wanted hers. They hadn't been unloving, her mom and dad, just always busy. Dad's work as a management consultant had him traveling all the time for business, and Mom, as a school principal, had constantly been in meetings, dousing one fire or another. Not much time had been left over for Eliza.

If and when she had kids, she'd sworn it would be different.

"Did De—His Grace get along well with his father?"

She'd asked a similar question a week ago and he'd shot her down. This time, however, John sighed before admitting, "His Grace showed little interest in Master Deveric. According to Mrs. Wiggins, he only cared whether or not his son behaved in ways befitting his station. The old Duke had strong ideas about those behaviors."

Mrs. Wiggins was the housekeeper. Eliza hadn't spoken with her much, but the woman had never been less than polite, and Betsy said she treated the housemaids with respect. Good enough in Eliza's book.

John cleared his throat. "When His Grace decided he preferred London to Clarehaven, we were not displeased. The Dowager seemed happier to remain here without her husband, as well. She could turn more of a blind eye to his … indiscretions that way."

Dowager Dragon or not, no woman deserved a husband

who treated her like that. Unexpected sympathy flooded her for Deveric's mother.

Eliza studied Freddy, with his mop of auburn hair and darling square chin, trying to picture Deveric at that age. She thought of the knuckle rapping Nurse Pritchett had given him, how it had not fazed the boy. "Did the old Duke beat his children?" She clapped her hand over her mouth, not believing she'd asked that question.

Mr. Sayers' eyes clouded. "Lord Chance bore the brunt of his ire often, yes. I do not know about the current Duke. At least the old Duke left his daughters alone. I'm grateful for Lady Amara's sake, though, that he was not alive when ..." He stopped talking.

"Yes, I know about that," Eliza said. "Hardly her fault, and completely unfair that she should suffer so much because some jerk took advantage of her."

"Jerk?"

"An American expression. Basically a man without honor."

"A fitting word, then."

Eliza walked over to check on Freddy, who'd grown quiet as he leaned against the side of the stone wall to watch the puppies. "Why, he's asleep!" she said, her cheeks crinkling in amusement.

"He is still recovering. Perhaps he shouldn't be outside for so long."

"Or perhaps this is exactly what he needs. Being cooped up in that nursery all day with Nurse Pritchett can't be good for *anyone's* health."

"No, indeed," John said, a slight smile escaping him.

"What did Lord Chance do to displease his father so often?" She was being extra nosy, but she couldn't imagine that charming scamp ever being a true problem. He certainly didn't show any ill effects, as far as she could see.

"I don't know that it was anything he *did*. I think it was his mere existence."

Eliza cocked her head at him. "How do you mean?"

John shifted on his feet, tugging on the brim of his hat. "His Grace was convinced Chance was not his son."

"What?"

"He never publicly accused her. Thank goodness. Chance was born seven months after the last time His Grace had visited Clarehaven. The Duke had been gone before that for another five. Although Her Grace insisted Chance came early, His Grace had his doubts. Mrs. Wiggins overheard him demand the boy be named Chance, because there was only a chance he was Claremont's."

"That's *awful*!" Eliza exclaimed. "Although do you think? The *Dowager*?" Eliza couldn't imagine the woman indulging in passion with anyone, much less two different people.

"No. I don't. I was here, a young man at the time. It was an unexpected and messy birth. Both the Dowager Duchess and Chance almost died. He was exceptionally tiny. An exact image of the Duke, though."

Eliza mulled that over. Emmeline, Grace, and Becca were all younger than Chance. The Dowager had taken the reprobate back into her bed?

Mr. Sayers shuffled his feet, his mouth twisting down. "I have said too much. You make one feel … at ease in your presence, Mrs. James." His voice softened as he said those words.

Eliza avoided his eyes. She didn't want to encourage tender feelings on his part, but she was desperate for information. Asking his sisters didn't feel right, and she didn't want to put Betsy in an awkward position. Guilt tugged at her conscience.

Accused of infidelity by her husband and then her daughter's seduction made public? No wonder the Dragon adhered so rigidly to social etiquette, determined to never let scandal shadow the family name again.

What could be more scandalous than an unpolished, untitled American widow after her son? Not to mention the time-traveler part—not, of course, that Eliza would ever reveal that. *I haven't got a shot with her.*

Eliza's shoulders fell. What had she gotten herself into?

The mama dog yelped as a puppy bit her ear, and Freddy stirred.

"I should get Frederick back to the house."

Mr. Sayers pulled at his collar. "I should not have shared so much."

"Don't worry, Mr. Sayers. I will hold everything in strictest confidence. I would not dishonor our *friendship*." She emphasized the last word, hoping he'd get the message.

He touched his fingers to the edge of his hat, giving a grateful dip of his head.

Freddy yawned and stood up, rubbing the sleep out of his eyes.

"I think this has been enough of a lesson for one day," Eliza said. "You look like you need a nap."

"I've just had one!" Frederick protested as he stumbled sleepily toward the door. "Please take care of Pirate, Mr. John. I want him to live."

"I'll do my best, lad," Mr. Sayers said with an affectionate glance. "I want him to live, too."

With the way the houndsmaster's eyes trailed after the young boy, Eliza had a sneaking suspicion he wasn't referring to the pup.

CHAPTER 27

*D*everic nodded to every female they passed in the Park and engaged in polite conversation with more than a few, but his head and heart weren't in it.

"We might as well secure invitations to Almack's if you're serious about this, Arth, rather than freeze out here," Coll said. He rubbed his hands together and pulled the neck of his coat more tightly around his ears. "Why am I part of this, anyway? No proper English lass would seriously consider me."

Deveric arched a brow at him. "The flock of ladies ever-present around you says differently."

"Flirtation only. Even if a young miss were to take a true interest, her parents would not. You know 'tis true. I will go back to Ireland some day. My estates are there."

"And leave London?" Arthington asked, horror etched across his face.

"Not everyone loves this dirty, loud, stinking city as much as you do, Arth. I do not get there often, I know, but I miss the greenness of my home."

"Please don't tell me you miss the sheep, or I shall start to worry about you," Arth said.

"Ha ha. I miss the air. And the lassies, I'll admit. They're a bit freer than many an English woman."

Deveric gave a derisive snort. "Freer? If some of the women around here were any freer, they'd be naked." Several of the "respectable" ladies of the *ton* they'd come across had sported décolletages so low as to be practically non-existent, and had eyed the men in such a way that each was aware they need look no further for companionship that evening, should they wish it.

Deveric did not wish it. Oh, his pulse had quickened ever so slightly at a plump blonde who'd meandered down the lane, but upon approach, her rather dirty fair hair, lackluster brown eyes, and sallow complexion couldn't hold a candle to Eliza. No one could.

"Not an admirer of the newer styles?" Arthington quipped. "Would you rather the women wear the gowns of forty years ago, as my grandmother still does? Great monstrosities, with panniers so wide one has to turn sideways to enter a room?"

"I didn't say I didn't appreciate a low-cut bodice. I merely noted that many an English lady is not as decorous as they make out to be."

"I need to be meeting *your* ladies, then," Coll said with a wink.

"It's the Prince Regent."

Deveric looked up at Arthington's words, watching as

Prince George shuffled through Watier's front door and crossed over to a table of gentlemen involved in a raucous game of Macao. The Regent had never particularly impressed Claremont; he indulged too heavily in food, spending, and women for Dev's taste.

"How much do you think he eats in a day?" Arthington asked.

"Shh," Coll chided. "Even a duke can't get away with those kinds of comments."

"Eh, possibly." Arth shrugged his shoulders. "But it's a fair question, don't you think?"

Deveric's attention wandered as he surveyed the room. Dandies of every variety indulged in drink, food, and cards, their faces registering either great excitement, or boredom.

He didn't want to be here. He wasn't much of a gambler, not after dealing with his uncle and now his brother. Too many men lost their fortunes in houses like these.

He shouldn't be here. He should be home, at Clarehaven. He'd concluded his uncle's business; why hadn't he headed back? Mother had said they were journeying to London in a week's time. He could merely await their arrival. On the other hand, he could be home in a day. See his son. See Eliza.

The idea both elated and terrified him. It was the terror keeping him away. For what did he hope if he returned? Anything less than marriage wouldn't do, not for a woman like Eliza. She deserved more. But marriage was the one thing he wouldn't consider. He'd sworn never to marry again, never to endanger a woman in that way, never to relive the horror of losing a wife, and a child.

It was an impossible situation. Every inch of him ached for her. But lust was no reason, no excuse, to risk it all. Lust would pass. Wouldn't it? No, Eliza James was not an option, no matter how tantalizing she was, no matter how much she called to him. It would never, could never work. He had to let this obsession go.

"Lady Gertrude Featherstone was paying you quite a bit of attention today," he said to Arthington, desperate to distract himself. "She cuts a fine figure, comes from a respectable family, and, rumor has it, possesses an obscenely large dowry."

Arth winced. "Yes, but her name is Gertrude."

Coll let out a bark of laughter. "Seriously? You'd avoid a match because of a name you'd likely never call her, anyway? Duchess would do after marriage."

Deveric took a swig from the tumbler of brandy in front of him. Nothing like the hair of the dog to cure his lingering headache. Cook's remedy hadn't worked nearly as well as he'd claimed, though he was loath to admit it. "Do you *want* to marry?"

Arthington grew uncharacteristically silent. "At thirty, I'm more than of age," he finally said.

"That wasn't the question."

Arth shrugged. "I might as well. I need an heir. And I truly don't wish to see the estates pass into my uncle's family. Not that I would be alive to witness it if that happened, I suppose." He sipped from his own tumbler. "I had hoped ..."

"Hoped what?"

Arthington smiled again, as if the question were inconsequential. "I had hoped to find someone with whom I truly belonged."

"A love match?" Coll raised an eyebrow.

"I know it's silly," Arthington said. "We know what this society is like. Few couples are faithful to each other. Even those who start out so, well, look at Lord and Lady Effingham.

They persist in trying to outdo each other in the number of people they take into their bed."

"Better not to marry at all," Deveric grumbled.

"Do you truly feel that way?" Arthington took a deep drink from his cup, and then beckoned a waiter for another bottle. "I know yours wasn't a love match, but I always thought you and Mirabelle got along tolerably."

Deveric had hidden his marital woes even from his friends; there was no sense in burdening others with his failings. Plus, there'd been the Claremont reputation to uphold, especially in the wake of poor Amara's scandal.

"As long as I didn't touch her, we got along tolerably well. And my insisting on touching her is what killed her." The minute the words were out of his mouth, he wished he could call them back. He'd been brooding about Eliza when he should have been guarding his tongue. His sin wasn't something he'd confessed to anyone outside the family, outside Amara and Cecilia, actually. Ever.

Both friends stared at Deveric.

"Good God, is that what you think? That you killed her?" Arthington exclaimed. "Dev, you know as well as anyone that many women die giving birth. My own mother died birthing me. Do you blame me for her death? Or my father?"

"If I hadn't touched her …"

"If you hadn't, you wouldn't have Frederick," Arthington reminded him. "At least your bloodlines aren't in danger."

A bitter laugh escaped Deveric. "Yes, because that makes up for causing a death?" He ran a finger along the edge of his glass. "I was … I was too big for her, and yet I forced her."

"You forced her?"

"No, no. I never raped her. I would never rape a woman. She said she was willing, that it was her wifely duty. But I

242

knew. I knew she wasn't interested. Knew she took no pleasure in it. I shouldn't have."

"My God, man, you can't blame yourself. Have you been holding onto this all these years? You never said a word." Arth clapped a hand on his friend's back, his fingers pressing into Deveric's shoulder.

Deveric ignored it. "If I had tried harder, found a way to please her …"

Coll spoke up after a moment of silence. "Maybe it had nothing to do with you. Maybe she never would have liked that aspect of married life. Your Duchess never struck me as the passionate sort."

"You were thinking of my wife in that way?"

Coll held his hands up. "Not like that. But I notice things. I can tell which women are of a lustful nature, and which are not."

Deveric closed his eyes, exhaling. "And Eliza? What of her?" There. He'd admitted his attraction. He shouldn't have, but he couldn't deny it anymore.

"Eliza?" Arthington's eyebrows furrowed together. "Who is—Oh, Mrs. James, your cousin? Wait, are you?"

"I'm nothing. Nothing. Never mind."

"She looks at you. A lot." Coll said, ignoring Deveric's words. "And not in a familial way." He smiled widely, those deep dimples showing on both cheeks. "And you don't look at her as a cousin, either. Who is she, really, Dev?"

"I wish I knew." Dev stared into the now-empty glass in front of him. "I wish I knew."

CHAPTER 28

E liza rolled over and stared morosely at the floor, pulling the coverlet up around her ears for a bit more warmth. England was freezing. Clarehaven was freezing. How did these people stand it? She longed to be sitting on the couch in the Treasure Trove in front of a roaring fire with a cup of hot chocolate—really sweet hot chocolate—at her side and her laptop on her lap.

What had she been thinking? Who in their right mind would give up all they knew and travel *back in time* to a period where so much was different? Granted, she wasn't in ancient Rome or medieval Germany, where she would have had no shot with the language, much less everything else. She wasn't a beggar on the streets in India, nor a slave in the New World. She wasn't among the working classes here in Regency England, much less the poor.

She shouldn't be complaining. She'd gotten exactly what she wanted, as absolutely impossible as it had sounded, and should have been. She was in a duke's home, living a life of relative luxury. Servants waited on her, meals were prepared for her, and the family was pleasant and friendly with her. Well, except Deveric's mother, who, though not as harsh as she'd been at first, still reminded Eliza often of her position in the family: cousin or not, she was going to earn her keep as Master Frederick's governess.

She was a servant, but not a servant. She was family, but not family. And she was lonely. Desperately lonely.

Deveric had been in London for nearly two weeks. Two weeks! How was she supposed to get him to fall in love with her if he wasn't even in the same vicinity? How could she fall in love with him if he was nowhere to be found?

She'd asked Amara when he would return, but Amara had merely shrugged. "I don't know. It's possible he will remain in London until the family joins him."

If that were the case, and the Mattersleys didn't take her with them, then what? What was she supposed to do on her own in this cavernous house? Eliza was unused to the silence; there was little noise except for occasional sounds of servants cleaning, or the sisters talking.

She missed music. Thank God Grace played the piano every day; it soothed her. She wished now she'd learned to play when she was younger. She'd tinkered a bit one morning, but figured out only one line of *Wake Me Up Before You Go Go*, her favorite Wham! song. It'd take a long time for her to become remotely proficient; talent like Grace's she was sure she didn't have.

How much she had taken for granted the ability to flip on the radio and hear songs any time she chose! They'd always had music playing in the store—usually classical, but sometimes they'd switch it up with a day of '80s music or '50s rock and roll.

What she wouldn't give to hear those songs now. She sung to herself often, but it wasn't the same. She missed all the creature comforts of life she'd taken for granted in twenty-first century America. But even more than that, she missed Cat.

She'd spent several evenings in Amara's company, whom she liked more and more. The woman was clever, with a biting wit, and keen observations of the people around her. But their interactions were more formal than Eliza was used to; no lounging about on the floor in pajamas, no snapping each other with dish towels, no giggling over kooky customers in the coffee shop.

Would she ever again have a friendship like she'd had with Cat?

She sighed as she hauled herself out of bed and over to the fireplace, coverlet firmly in place about her. The fire was blazing, thanks to Betsy. Eliza wasn't sure where the maid was at the moment, but she didn't mind the alone time. Sulking was always better in private.

She hummed the lively tune Grace had played yesterday while the dance teacher was there, trying to distract herself from the hopelessness creeping in. Because Becca was coming out this season—she'd turn eighteen in just over a week—the Dowager had brought in a dance instructor from the City, and several afternoons, the sisters practiced their steps in the ballroom, with Grace on the piano.

The Dowager allowed her to attend once, when Freddy was napping. Eliza'd fumbled her way through a dance or two, the instructor almost comical in his over-the-top reactions to her ineptitude. She envied the grace the sisters displayed as they moved easily and familiarly through the steps.

Even Becca knew most of the dances by heart. She didn't need an instructor anymore, really, but Eliza figured it gave the women something to do while the cold winds raged outside; they were all getting restless in the house. Lady Mattersley likely also wanted to ensure her youngest daughter was a diamond of the first water her first season out.

She certainly could be. With her ebony hair and stunning round blue eyes, Becca would turn heads wherever she went. All of the sisters would, actually. Their beauty would have intimidated Eliza more if they'd been more stand-offish and if, well, Eliza had been less attractive herself.

She knew, in spite of her complaints about her rounded hips and poofy stomach, men considered her beautiful. They'd told her so all her life. It was a bit harder to feel attractive here, however, without the mouthwash or daily hot showers she'd been used to.

She was growing accustomed to her face without make-up, at least. She actually looked younger—though Becca's glowing, unblemished, unlined skin brought out her envy. Women thought aging in the twenty-first century was hard; try being twenty-nine in Regency England! She was far past the bloom of youth here.

"Over the hill, and I'm not even thirty yet. Great," she muttered, as she clutched the blanket around her shoulders.

Betsy entered the room as quietly as usual, bustling around with efficiency, stirring up the fire, pulling out a borrowed dress, and setting fresh water on the washstand.

What if I didn't want to get up at this time every day? What if I told Betsy to leave me alone so that I could stay in bed all morning, burrowed beneath these blankets? Could I get away with it?

Not that she'd ever be rude to Betsy. Eliza considered her a friend, though she doubted Betsy thought the same. Betsy still addressed her as Lady James half the time, and was always eager to do whatever she could to please Eliza. At least she was willing to chat with her, and Eliza enjoyed hearing about Betsy's family. Betsy'd also confided she was sweet on one of the footmen, although he didn't pay any attention to her, much to Betsy's chagrin.

Eliza could relate to that. Here she was, two hundred years away from her own life, trying to get a man to fall in love with her who was nowhere to be found.

She groaned. What her mother would have said about that.

"A relationship shouldn't be the center of your life, Eliza," Deborah James had chided often, especially when Eliza and Greg got so serious at such a young age. "You need other interests, something to do to give yourself your own identity."

That had worked for Eliza's mom. But was it so wrong if Eliza *wanted* to find her identity in her relationships with others? Her parents had found it in their work. She wanted it in people. Why was that so bad? Once upon a time, in *this* time, as a matter of fact, women were expected to center their lives on marriage and family. She was glad, of course, that women had far more choices in the twenty-first century, and no longer *had* to do that if they didn't want to. But what about those women who still did? Did they have to be devalued for those goals?

Once upon a time. Eliza had wanted to come here for the fairytale, for the Cinderella story. But not for the rags to riches part. No, for the part about finding where she belonged. Of being the center of someone's life in a way she never had been before. Of being able to make someone the center of hers, to devote herself to loving that person and building a relationship, a family, like she'd never had.

She grimaced. That sounded so anti-feminist. Maybe it was, if taken on the surface. But if feminism meant women had the same choices as men, shouldn't they be able to *choose* marriage and family, if that was what was central to them, without being made to feel lesser?

It's not that she didn't prize her intellect. She certainly did. Frankly, maintaining a healthy family and marriage while running a household required a great amount of smarts. *Especially a ducal household.*

She covered her chilled ears with the blanket. She just wanted to be loved for who she was, like the heroines in romance novels. The heroes loved those women exactly as they were, often exactly *because of* how they were. Okay, maybe she wasn't a Civil War spy or a duchess running a school for heiresses, or a viscount's daughter masquerading as a pirate. She still deserved love, didn't she?

And so did Deveric. So much pressure on him, as the leader of a great ducal family. A mother to deal with, sisters to help, a son to raise, estates to manage, duties to perform. He needed support, more than she was sure he ever got. Dukes were supposed to know exactly what to do at all times. But, come on, he was human. Surely he had doubts and worries and insecurities, too?

She could help him, could be there for him. She could be his touchstone. She could do that. If only he'd come home.

Eliza let out a large harrumph, blowing the hair out of her eyes. This wasn't quite the fairytale she'd fantasized it would be. Though she'd not wanted the outcome guaranteed, she had to admit she'd wanted Deveric to fall madly, deeply, instantly in love with her. *Guess I watched Cinderella one too many times. This feels more like Snow White, with an absentee prince and a wicked dowager mother.*

Come home, Deveric.

It'd been a good day, after all. It really had. She'd loved her time with Frederick. They'd visited Pirate, who was growing by leaps and bounds, and then spent time reading stories and studying the globe. She was doing a decent job of covering for her geographical faux pas, she hoped, having forgotten Italy wasn't wholly unified yet, and that places like Iowa weren't yet part of the United States. Frederick was a bright young boy, and she was grateful for his natural curiosity—while still wondering how long she could pull off this governess charade.

Dinner had been more stilted, since they dined in the presence of the Dragon. After a few questions about Frederick's studies, however, the Dowager left her to eat in peace, discussing plans for the upcoming season with Emmeline. Mother and daughter were in the midst of preparations for hosting a ball at their London home in a few weeks. Eliza had to admit, she desperately wanted to go to London. No matter the vast size of Clarehaven, cabin fever had set in big time.

If only she'd had a hamburger on her plate, instead of fish, which she'd never cared for. She longed for a salad, instead of over-boiled vegetables. *Guess fresh greens are hard to come by this time of year.*

The seasonality of foods was something Eliza had never thought about. Every grocery store in Charlottesville offered great varieties of fresh produce any time of year. To not have lettuce or strawberries because they were out of season was a foreign concept.

Of course, her local-food-crazy friends would love this era—everything Eliza ate probably came from within five miles, if not right here on the estate. But, as she lay in bed later, mulling over the day, how she wished for pizza. Or good old-fashioned apple pie. Or even just a fresh orange.

Her stomach rumbled. One positive thing about these Regency foods to which she wasn't accustomed; she was losing weight. The dress she'd worn the night she arrived was noticeably looser in the bust, much to her delight. She'd never be as tall and waifish as, say, Grace, but it was nice to feel less like a stuffed sausage in her borrowed gowns.

She fell asleep on that pleasing thought, until her stomach—and her bladder—roused her. She was hungry. And now had to go to the bathroom.

Dang, she missed modern conveniences. The chamber pot grossed her out—both using it, and knowing someone had to clean it. Who knew how much a good old-fashioned toilet and toilet paper would mean to her? *And don't even get me started on how much I long for a hot shower, to be able to stand under the streaming water for fifteen, twenty, thirty minutes, soaking in the heat and the relaxation!*

Huffing, she rolled over again, then gave up and got up to use the pot.

Her stomach growled. Turtle was almost sounding good, with how hungry she was.

What time was it? She had no idea. No light peeked in around the edges of the window coverings, but the fire had died down to smoldering coals. Early morning, perhaps.

Maybe there was something in the kitchen she could mooch.

She pulled the heavy robe on over her chemise, and left her room, making her way down as quietly as possible to where she thought the kitchens were. After more than one wrong turn, she eventually found herself in a large room, filled with pots, pans, and people. *Wow, they're up early.* "I'm so sorry. I didn't mean to disturb anyone."

A large, ruddy-cheeked woman hurried over. "Come

in, come in, lassie." A Scottish burr laced her speech. "I'm Rowena. Ye must be Mrs. James, the American," she said, more to herself than Eliza, apparently, as she kept talking without pausing to wait for an answer. "We're so happy the little laird's been eatin' more o' his dinners since ye've come, lassie. He needs fattenin' up."

Eliza couldn't argue with that. Frederick was still painfully thin, but he'd regained his appetite and had tucked away quite a bit of food in the past week or so.

"Thank you," Eliza said, unsure if an answer was expected. "I was, um, wondering if I might find something to eat?"

"Of course, my lady! The bread be rising fer baking an' not quite ready yet, but let's see. I have some cheese, an' a few cherry tarts fresh out o' the oven."

"That sounds delicious." Cherry tarts? They had cherry tarts? Had they served those before and she'd missed it?

"The Dowager, she likes me not ta make too many sweets; doesn't want her daughters leaning toward fat, but I say there be nothin' better in the world than a properly made cherry tart. His Grace and Lord Chance agree, so I bake 'em fer them. And extras fer meself." She chuckled, patting her large belly.

The cook indicated a stool and Eliza sat down gratefully. "Thank you," she said again.

Rowena beamed as she set a plate of cheese and tarts in front of Eliza. "How nice to hear a bit o' gratitude."

Eliza took a bite of the tart. The light crust melted in her mouth, and the mix of cherry and sugar exploded on her tongue. She wanted to kiss the cook, literally. It was delicious. Beyond delicious. Oh, how she'd missed sugar. "Rowena!" she exclaimed. "These are awesome!"

"Awe-some? That is no' an expression I've heard applied

ta food," Rowena said, "but I'm hoping 'twere a compliment."

"A compliment indeed!" Eliza took another bite. *Oh my God, these are insanely good.*

"They be His Grace's favorite, too," the cook confided. "Have been since he were a wee lad."

It hardly seemed possible Deveric was ever that small.

Had he been? She stopped chewing. If Cat had created Deveric for her, had he had an actual childhood, or had he sprung forth fully formed as an adult, like Athena from Zeus? Did Cat truly create Deveric, his family, the people around her, from nothing, or was it possible she'd somehow tapped into people who already existed?

Eliza's head spun from trying to figure out the ramifications of her friend's gift. It was incomprehensible to fully grasp how this people-creating power worked, or that time-travel was possible, and yet here she sat in a nineteenth-century kitchen, eating cheese and tarts, surrounded by strange utensils for which she didn't know the use, listening to the cook and watching kitchen maids prep food for the upcoming day.

She bit into another tart. She'd have to be careful, or she'd eat all of them she could find.

"It's nice ta see a lady with an appetite," Cook said as she bustled about, slamming a slab of dough onto a board and kneading it with her large, beefy hands. "Would you like a cup o' chocolate?"

"Oh, that would be heavenly. Could you add a bit of sugar to it, as well?"

"Indeed. Moira?"

A small, dark-haired maid nodded, setting down the knife with which she'd been chopping potatoes. Taking what looked like a brown bar of soap, she chopped it into small bits, and then added the bits to a pot that rather resembled a modern coffee pot. Pouring in some milk, she then held the pot over the fire, occasionally stirring the mixture. Removing the pot from the heat after a few minutes, Moira added sugar the cook had shaved off of a cone, and mixed it in with a spoon. She poured out the chocolate into a china mug another maid had brought over, and set it in front of Eliza with a smile.

Holy cow, that's labor-intensive. Nothing like popping milk in the microwave and adding hot chocolate mix. Remorse hit her for making the women go to so much effort when they were already busy. On the other hand, the chocolate was delicious.

"Thank you. You all are so very kind. Would you mind if I spent time here in the kitchens when I can? I'd be glad to help out, if you'd like." Not that she knew a thing about cooking in a nineteenth-century kitchen, but a girl could learn, right?

Rowena gave her a wink. "Ye be more than welcome, lassie, but I don't know that His Grace, or Her Grace, would approve."

"I'll take full responsibility if there's an issue. I like it here. It's warm!"

The women grinned at each other. "Then ye be most welcome anytime," Rowena affirmed.

Eliza munched on another tart, relishing the warmth of the fire as much as the food before her, a bit uncomfortable that she was relaxing while they worked. Not uncomfortable enough to leave, though.

A door on the other side of the room whipped open. Eliza dropped her tart in surprise when a deep voice echoed through the kitchen. "Rowena, have you got any of those cherry tarts for me?"

CHAPTER 29

*D*everic strode through the door, bundled up in a form-fitting coat, cheeks red with cold. He was taking off his gloves when he spied Eliza and stopped mid-stride.

"What are you doing here?" He eyed her up and down. "And what are you wearing?" His tone indicated disapproval.

Eliza pulled the robe more tightly across her body. Although, really, the robe was thick, and in her opinion the chemise she wore underneath was practically the same as a day dress—not exactly a Victoria's Secret type garment. Nobody could see anything. So why was he freaking out? And why was he here, anyway, so early in the morning, looking so damn luscious?

Where have you been? she wanted to chide, even as her eyes drank him in. Cat couldn't have done a better job of creating the perfect man for her, eye candy-wise, at least. The stubble gracing his face rendered him a little less perfect and a whole lot sexier to Eliza. She wanted to run her fingers over his chin, touch his upper lip, slide her hands across his cheeks.

She wanted to devour him.

His eyes fixated on her, burning into her, and her cheeks grew warm. *What would he do if I walked over there and kissed him?* At that thought, her ears, and other parts, tingled, and she shifted uncomfortably on the stool.

"I couldn't sleep."

He didn't say anything, just crossed the room and stood right in front of her, appraising her. He didn't seem to notice the cook and all the other maids had stopped working and were watching this exchange in fascination.

Eliza did.

She looked down at her lap. This would be so much better if they were in private. She didn't like being the morning's entertainment. On the other hand, Deveric was here. In front of her. And looking at her as if she were the cherry tart he'd asked for.

He reached out a hand, smoothing it over the side of her lip. Her skin came alive, shock reverberating through her at his touch.

"You've been sampling Rowena's tarts, I see," he said, showing her the tip of his finger, on which the crumb he'd wiped off her face rested. His green eyes smoldered as they bore into hers.

Eliza's mouth dropped open, and from the stirring in the room, she could tell Deveric's actions startled the servants, too. It was a surprisingly intimate touch, here in the kitchen.

"Yes, they are exquisite. I'm afraid I've eaten two or three." *Idiot! Why are you confessing how much you've eaten? Do you want to draw attention to the fact that you're not a dainty little thing like his sisters?*

"Have another. You've grown too thin." He frowned, scanning her up and down. "Have you not been eating?"

Eliza gaped at him. *Too thin? I've never been accused of being too thin!*

"I'm not as accustomed to some of your dishes," she managed to get out, glancing at Rowena guiltily. "Not that everything hasn't been wonderful," she assured the cook. "I'm just used to other kinds of food."

Rowena looked unsure whether she should say anything. At Deveric's glower, she quickly turned back to her bread dough.

"I'm sure if you let us know what you want, Rowena can make it for you," he said, his voice gruff. Or was that husky? His eyes devoured her, and she nearly forgot to breathe.

I want a hamburger. Pizza. Chocolate chip cookies! And you.

She sat up straighter, letting the robe fall open. "I'm fine, Your Grace, but I thank you for your concern." She put her shoulders back, bringing her breasts forward. *Brazen hussy,* her mind screamed. But she'd better start pressing her advantage if she were going to get anywhere with this man, and her advantage was her boobs.

Sure enough, his eyes drifted down. *Not much to see through these layers of fabric, but at least I've got his attention.* Moira moved within her field of vision, momentarily distracting her. The maid's eyes bulged, reminding Eliza they were not alone. Her shoulders shrank down again. She wasn't used to playing the seductress, much less with an audience.

"Shall I escort you back to your room, Mrs. James?" Deveric asked.

Eliza took a quick drink of cocoa to mask her astonishment. Moira dropped a pan.

"Uh, what?"

"There are matters we need to discuss," he said, his voice all business. "And surely you need more sleep."

"Um, okay." She stood up. He'd told her himself it was unacceptable for a man to take her to her bedroom, but then again, this wasn't any man. This was Deveric. This was the Duke. And this was his home. If he wanted to escort her to *his* bedroom, she didn't think the servants would say a thing. Truth be told, the way her body was shaking, her pulse racing, her skin tingling, there was no place she'd rather be but in bed with him. Right now.

The lust setting her aflame both astounded and thrilled her. It wasn't as if she'd become asexual after Greg had died, of course. She'd had feelings and desires, especially knowing what lovemaking was like. But she'd stuffed them down. Though body consciousness admittedly played a part, she'd realized she didn't want to be intimate with anyone she didn't love enough to be with forever.

She was old-fashioned, to say the least, for her era. Magazines, movies and television shows intimated something was wrong with a person if they weren't having sex every night. In multiple positions. Maybe with multiple partners. Even many of her girlfriends had no problem with one-night stands, or at least passionate short-term relationships. That didn't bother Eliza. It just wasn't for her.

But looking at Deveric right now, with his windblown hair and that damn stubble across his jaw, that tight-fitting coat and those breeches hugging his thighs, the thoughts filling Eliza's brain were anything but pure, anything but patient. *But I plan on marrying him, even if* he *doesn't know it. That makes it okay, right?*

Her eyes locked with his, the electricity pulsing between

them so powerful as to almost be painful. With great effort, she pulled herself together, securing her robe around her before walking ahead of him to the door, aware with every fiber of her being of the magnificent male at her back.

Deveric put his hand at her waist as they walked, as if politely guiding her in the right direction. Ha! He wanted to push her up against the wall and capture those sugar-sweet lips with his, wanted to wipe the taste of those cherry tarts from her memory and replace it with only memories of him, his mouth, his hands, his ...

His body had betrayed him the minute he'd walked into the kitchen. He'd used every ounce of willpower he had—and thoughts, however brief, of his mother—to keep his desire from making itself obvious to everyone in the room.

His visceral reaction to her shook him to the core. One minute back in Eliza's presence and he wanted to pull off that robe, rip off what lay underneath. He wanted to spread her across the kitchen workspace where Rowena kneaded bread, and knead Eliza's body in similar ways, wanted to caress her flesh, molding it beneath his fingers, wanted to pound into her as the cook's fists had pounded into the dough.

Desire raged through his veins as he passed through the kitchen door after her, her robe swaying back and forth over that delectably round derriere. Once they'd cleared the doorway and moved into a hallway farther off, he stopped.

"What do you do to me, Eliza James?" he murmured, yanking her to him before his lips swooped down over hers, his tongue invading her mouth as the pent-up passion of the last few weeks exploded through him. He lifted his lips momentarily, stunned and ashamed at his own actions, his own ferocity, hoping he hadn't hurt her, but he had no opportunity to think beyond that, as she wound her arms up around his neck, running her fingers through his hair and pulling his head back down to hers.

He wanted to weep in relief. Her lips moved as eagerly over his as his on hers, and he rejoiced in the satisfied sounds she made. She ran her fingers across his cheeks, and then moved her hand down, sliding it over his neck, running it across his chest and around to his back. The other hand she kept laced through his hair, keeping his face locked with hers, but he wasn't about to complain.

He moved his hand down, as well, fumbling through the open robe, desperate to reach her body. His torso pressed hers against the wall and he knew she could feel him, hard, pressing into her. But she didn't retreat. She arched into him, returning his kiss, running her tongue over his lips and seeking entry inside.

He reveled in it, the desire this befuddling American exhibited. His fingers traced their way up over a breast, joy running through him as he took an entire handful in his grasp at last. He loved those breasts, the fullness of them. He wanted to bury himself in them and luxuriate in all of her flesh. Sliding his fingers across her clothed nipple, he heard her gasp as it hardened under his touch.

He lifted one of her legs, urging her to wrap it around him so that he could press more closely into her. She readily complied. His hips matched the rhythm of their mouths, an exquisite back and forth that had both of them murmuring small sounds of pleasure into each other. He reached for the buttons on her chemise, grateful they were in front, and had just slipped the second one out of its hole when a gasp roused him from his lustful fantasies.

Suddenly Eliza was pushing against him, and he looked at her, eyes hooded, momentarily confused by her switch in attitude, until he followed her wide-eyed gaze to the Dowager, standing in the hallway, cheeks white and lips pinched as she glared at the two of them.

He instinctively moved in front of Eliza, as if to shield her from his mother's attack, realizing belatedly that gave his mother an ample view of just how much he'd been enjoying the previous moments. Not that it lasted long; he shriveled under her baleful gaze.

"Claremont," she barked, all starch and rage. "I expect better of you. One does not couple in a public hallway. And *you*. Trollop," she fumed, vehemence radiating from her as she addressed Eliza. "Pack your bags. No woman of loose morals shall remain under my roof."

CHAPTER 30

Eliza froze. *Oh my God. No. No. No.* What would she do? Where would she go? *I can't leave. This isn't the plan.* She clung to Deveric, panic inundating every inch of her.

"No," Deveric said, his voice calm steel. "I attacked her. The fault here is entirely mine." He took a small step away from Eliza.

"You didn't *attack* me," Eliza protested, incredulous, even as Deveric continued speaking.

"You will not refer to Mrs. James that way ever again, Mother, nor will you treat her with anything less than the respect owed to a member of our family. I apologize for my actions, to you, and to Mrs. James."

Eliza sensed it as he left her, emotionally as well as physically, his soul uncoupling from hers. It was as if he locked himself up behind some wall. *No!* she wanted to scream. *No, our connection is real. Don't do this. Why are you doing this?* But she could say nothing to stop him. If she said anything at all at that moment, with tensions sky high, she'd likely only make things worse.

She watched mutely as Duke squared off against Dowager. A long moment of silence stretched the air, until the Dowager tipped her head ever so slightly, raising her chin at Eliza. "As you command, dearest son. I will not speak publicly against Mrs. James in any way."

Deveric nodded, grasping Eliza by the elbow as if to lead her away, when his mother spoke again. "But in return, I remind you of your obligation to the family honor. Do not bring disgrace upon the name you and I have worked so hard to rescue from your father's and sister's actions."

With that, she turned, stiff-backed, her bearing as regal as any queen, and walked down the hallway from whence she had come.

Eliza exhaled a long, grateful breath. "I'm so sorry your mother saw us, Dev—" she started.

He broke her off sharply. "As I said, the fault is all mine. I am the monster." He let go of her elbow and stepped away from her. Staring straight ahead, he said, "It shall not happen again," his voice and face devoid of emotion. Without another word, he walked off in the direction his mother had gone, leaving Eliza stunned and heartbroken, alone in the hallway.

Dev stomped his way to his study, glaring at any unfortunate individual who happened to cross his path, which at this time of the morning was only one maid. She scurried away like a frightened mouse, and he made a mental note to apologize to her later, if he could remember who she was.

Thankful to see a fire had already been lit—word of his return likely spread the instant he'd left his horse in the stables—he threw himself into the ornately carved chair behind his desk and picked up a sheaf of papers. After staring at them blankly for a few minutes, he tossed them back down in disgust.

What had possessed him? What had possessed him to attack her, a gentle-born lady, regardless from which century she claimed to come? He'd pushed her up against the wall like a common prostitute and would have taken her then and there, had his mother not interceded.

He ran his fingers through his hair. *She'd responded. It was not as if she'd been unwilling.* Did that make it better or worse? What did he know of this Eliza James, anyway? She'd already said sexual relations were much more lax in her time. Had she lain with many men?

The thought saddened him, but at the same time, he didn't believe it to be true. *You don't know her.* "I know her well enough," he grumbled, thankful no one was in the room to catch him talking to himself.

He longed to go back, to apologize, to erase that wounded look in her eyes he'd seen before he'd run away. And that's what he'd done—he'd run away. He sighed, shame settling across his shoulders like a yoke.

What kind of man fled from a woman he'd disgraced? Where was his honor? Was he such a coward in the face of his own desire that he would abandon her the moment the truth was acknowledged?

His mother may have caught them, yes, but that wasn't the real reason he'd run. He'd fled because he didn't want to feel what she stirred in him. Desire … lust … a wanting so deep he didn't know how to cope with it.

But not just that. He wanted to possess her, he wanted to consume her, yes, but he also wanted to know her, to know all about her, to simply be with her. He wanted everything.

The thought terrified him. When his wife had made it clear theirs was not a marriage of connection, it had saddened him. But, he conceded, it had also been easier. He hadn't had to change his lifestyle much, hadn't had to take anyone else into consideration, hadn't had to expose any of his inner self.

That was how it should be, his mother would say. *A Claremont does not lower himself to vulgar displays of emotion.* He'd had that drilled into him since he was a child and his father had caught him weeping over a dead cat.

"A stupid animal is not worth your tears," his father had said. "Claremonts do not cry." He'd lashed Deveric with a belt to prove his point, not stopping until his son had ceased to shed tears.

Deveric had learned the lesson well. Stoicism was a better face for the world. It was what was expected of a man of his station, and it kept anyone from getting too close. Except for Eliza. She'd needled her way under his skin, and he hadn't even spent more than a few days in her company. How? How did she do it? He'd thought his walls impenetrable since the loss of Mirabelle … and Louisa.

Louisa. He tried not to think of his daughter. She'd been innocent, a tiny little thing, with a shock of red hair. She'd looked so peaceful as he'd held her, but it wasn't peace. It was death. She'd never drawn a breath. According to the midwife, the cord had wrapped around her neck and strangled her.

Deveric had wept that day, wept for hours, clinging to his infant daughter until his mother finally pried the child away and had his valet dose him with laudanum.

After that, he'd ceased to talk. The family assumed grief

kept him silent, grief over the loss of his wife and daughter. It was, to a point. But it was also shame—shame for what he'd done to Mirabelle, shame for his inability to save her and his daughter, shame for breaking down for the entire world to see. *A Claremont does not cry.*

He'd shut himself away from the world, throwing himself into managing the estates, into providing for his sisters, into whiling the hours away drinking with his friends, to all appearances detached, emotionless. *A gentleman of good breeding does not display an excess of feeling.*

Arthington and Collinswood knew the truth, though. They'd been with him since Eton. They'd seen him cry over finding an injured bird, seen him jump with joy over the attentions of a young lady at a ball, seen him rage at the injustices done to his sister Amara after that blackguard seduced her. They knew, but they did not judge him. Thank God. Arthington's willingness to feel, to show, to revel in emotion was one of the things that had drawn Deveric to him. But he couldn't be like that. He couldn't.

But Eliza … Eliza. She'd got under his skin from the moment he'd met her, from the instant she kissed him and sent them both whirling, literally, through time. Figuratively, as well, for his world hadn't stopped spinning since. She made him want things. Want more. She made him want to laugh and weep and question and rejoice. She made him want to live again.

He stood up from his desk and walked to the brandy decanter. It may only be seven in the morning, but he needed a drink. As he poured, his eyes fell on the settee near the fireplace, the one on which he and Eliza had awoken those few weeks ago. Had it only been such a short time? It felt as if he'd known her, had been with her, had wanted her forever.

Sipping the heady drink, he walked to the fire, staring into its flames.

"You have burned me, Mrs. James," he whispered. "Singed me to the core, and yet at the same time, brought me back to life. You've reignited me. I both hate you and love you for it."

Love. The word echoed through his skull. Love? Did he love her? Could he love a woman he barely knew?

He didn't think he did. Not yet. But he could see himself doing so very easily. He could see himself losing himself in her, opening his heart, letting her in. The thought brought waves of terror with it. He'd lost one wife and he hadn't even loved her. He'd been a monster to her.

He couldn't be a monster to Eliza, too. Couldn't get close to her, couldn't let her get close to him, or she'd see. She'd see his passion was too much, his emotions were too much. She'd see he wasn't a man. He was a mess. A mess of feelings too powerful to acknowledge, so he'd spent years tamping them down.

Leave the emotions to the poets, to Shakespeare and Wordsworth. He was Claremont. He was a duke. He didn't have time to be anything more. Or anything less.

With a sigh, he sat down on the settee, nursing his brandy, losing himself in the flickering of the fire. Why had he come back? It'd been easier in London, easier to immerse himself in insignificant things with friends than to deal with how this one woman had turned his world upside down.

But she'd drawn him back. He had to know. Had to know more about her, had to know if she still affected him like she had in those first few days. He needed to know if the desire she'd kindled in him still flamed as hot, or if it'd merely been a momentary spark of infatuation, a temporary bout of insanity. He had to know if he could control himself around her.

The throbbing of his cock told him he couldn't. He'd sworn he wouldn't lose control with her, wouldn't force her. Except he almost had. He threw the glass into the flames in disgust, listening with satisfaction as it shattered. What if he'd taken her there in the hallway? With no thought to the ramifications? What if he'd got her with child? His cheeks turned to ice as he pictured Eliza lying cold and pale in death, as Mirabelle had. As Louisa had.

No. No, he couldn't do that to her, couldn't do that to any woman ever again. He had to suppress his passions, had to regain control of his emotions, had to retreat behind the wall. Most of all, he had to go back to London. He couldn't stay here, not when he knew she was here. He had to go back to London, or his own burning need for her would consume him alive. That was unacceptable.

A Claremont never lost control.

CHAPTER 31

Eliza lay across her bed, tears streaming down her face. *This is not going to plan, Cat!* She wanted to scream, wanted to beat her fists on the pillow, but if she did, one of the blasted ever-present servants was likely to hear and would come to her aid. She didn't want anyone. Not right now.

What had gone wrong? She'd been ecstatic to see Deveric, even more ecstatic to register the look on his face when he'd seen her. Pleasure. He'd been visibly pleased to see her, and that had warmed her heart, made her feel as if she had a chance to make this fantasy come true. And then, in the hallway … She touched her fingers to her lips, covered now with salty tears, remembering the deliciousness of Deveric's mouth on hers, the feel of his body pressing hers into the wall, the desire to get closer to him, to wrap herself around him and in him.

No one, not even Greg, had roused this fierce need in her, this sense that something was missing, that the puzzle wasn't complete and wouldn't be complete until Deveric and she had fit together.

It went beyond sex. She wanted to know him in a way nobody else did. He obeyed social norms of behavior to a fault—in her modern opinion, at least. He preferred order and stability and calmness. But that interlude in the hallway was anything but calm. Anything but orderly. There was so much more to Deveric Mattersley than he let on.

Was it Mirabelle? Had his first wife done this to him? A cold fish, the servants had termed her. Ill-matched to a man like Deveric. What had happened between them to have such a passionate man draw such heavy walls around himself?

Now that she'd gotten a peek over the wall, she wanted to break down the door, unlock him, and discover exactly who he was behind the shield. Because she had a feeling she could love that man, love him truly, madly, deeply.

Oh, Cat. I need you. I don't know what to do. This mess was definitely not what Eliza had wished for. She hiccupped through more sobs. She'd been so selfish, asking Cat to send her here to find love. She'd abandoned her friend to pursue a fantasy.

On the other hand, Cat wanted her to be happy, to move on, to grow, instead of hiding out in the bookstore while life passed her by. And it wasn't like she and Cat had known this would work. A big part of Eliza had assumed it wouldn't. After all, while Cat had the power to create her own love interests, they'd had no clue whether she could craft them for others.

Yes, Eliza'd taken this crazy chance for a reason: she wanted love. She wanted to love and be loved. She wanted passion and desire. She wanted someone so enthralled with her, so intoxicated by her, that he'd never leave her—and vice versa.

She snorted through her tears. Maybe that kind of love wasn't realistic, no matter what romance novels claimed, especially in this society, where rules of propriety forbade all but the minutest of contact between single men and women, and where people were expected to follow the codes of conduct to the letter. Many didn't. But Deveric did.

If she couldn't find that kind of bone-deep connection in the twenty-first century, where men and women pretty much did whatever they wanted with each other without anyone batting an eye, why had she expected to find it here, in a society familiar and foreign at the same time, bound by countless customs and rules she couldn't keep track of, in spite of all the literature she'd read from the period?

At that, her thoughts turned to Jane Austen, and her tears slowed. Austen had written about all those rules, the social niceties, the pressures and realities on women in this time. But she'd also written about love, about grand, all-consuming love. About the kind of love that had led Darcy to declare to Elizabeth, "In vain have I struggled … You must allow me to tell you how ardently I admire and love you." That had had Wentworth confessing, "You pierce my soul. I am half agony, half hope."

It had to be real. Or was Jane as hopeless a romantic as Eliza, wanting something that could never be had, an impossible fantasy? Darcy and Wentworth were literary creations, after all. In real life, Austen had never married. If she'd been in love with Tom DeFroy, as many asserted, it'd never gone anywhere.

Were the characters Austen created just as unrealistic as modern romance novel heroes?

Bitter tears streamed down Eliza's face. Her eyes were red and raw, and her nose full of phlegm. This was reality. A mess of a face, a broken heart, trapped in a strange bed in a strange house in a strange country.

Could she have mucked this up anymore?

A few hours later, Eliza woke from the sleep into which she'd cried herself. Her eyes were puffy and raw, her lips dry and cracked. She was still in the chemise she'd been wearing since the night before. Where was Betsy? She hadn't come in, as far as Eliza knew; perhaps the maid had heard her sobs and decided it best to leave her alone.

"Buck up, Eliza James," she scolded herself. "You wanted this. And no one said it'd be easy." The Coldplay song *The Scientist* echoed in her mind, and she sang a verse out loud.

Did she want to go back to the start? Did she want to give up? Would Cat's escape clause even work?

Standing up, she crossed over to the dressing table and sat on the stool. The reflection in the mirror wasn't pretty. She took a brush and started to work it through her hair when a knock came at the door and Betsy entered.

The maid's eyes radiated sympathy. Eliza's sobs *had* been heard in the hallway, then. Good. She hoped Deveric had been across the hall and had had to listen. The jerk. Why was he fighting his attraction to her so hard?

Maybe because attraction is not enough, Lizzie. Maybe he's better at seeing—and understanding—the gaping chasm between your experiences and his. It's not like you've been trained to be a duchess since the day you were born, as have many of these upper-class English ladies.

And sexual desire was not the same thing as affection,

much less a wish to marry. If this had been a romance novel, he would have had to offer for her. He'd compromised her, after all. Hadn't he?

Did people really do that? Marry for something as innocuous as getting caught together in a hallway? Okay, she and Deveric had been doing more than merely lounging about, but still.

Well, if he *did* offer out of obligation, she'd turn him down. Marriage wasn't a prize won by default. She wanted all of him, or nothing at all.

"May I fetch you anything, my lady? A coffee?"

Goodness gracious, we're back to my lady? Betsy had taken to mostly calling Eliza by her name in the past week. *She must really be feeling sorry for me.*

"No, thank you. I shall have some when I breakfast."

Betsy held up the gown she'd brought in for Eliza. "Breakfast is long past, but I'm sure we can find something for you. Emmeline sent this dress today."

Eliza eyed the white gown. White. White. She was so tired of white. At first, she'd been mad with curiosity for each and every garment she saw, ecstatic to try on authentic Regency garb. Now, the authenticity was getting to her. She didn't want stays and petticoats and dresses with a zillion buttons, she wanted an exercise bra and a loose-fitting T-shirt with sweats. She wanted to curl up on the sofa in front of a fire, drinking coffee and zipping through Target.com on her laptop, Chinese food on the way.

"It's nice." What else could she say?

"And …" Betsy shifted uncomfortably. "The Dowager sent this cap for your head. She insisted you might be … cold."

Eliza's mouth twisted in a half-smile, half-sneer. She knew what wearing a cap indoors meant; it's what older women put on to signify respectability. *She wants to mark me as ancient, as unavailable, as an old maid. Someone who poses no threat.* Maybe as a widow, Eliza couldn't be an old maid, but she could refuse the cap.

"No, thank you. I've gotten quite used to the temperature." That wasn't exactly true, but she was not about to put that ugly thing on her head.

Betsy assisted her out of her chemise and into the day dress without comment, walking behind Eliza to fasten the lacings. Goodness, it was tight; she could hardly breathe. Emmeline was definitely smaller in the chest than she was.

Eliza tried to breathe in, looking down. Her breasts were smashed up so high as to almost overflow the bodice. Good. A satisfied smile teased at her lips. That would give Deveric something to think about when he saw her again. If he saw her again. He'd taken off for weeks before; was he was already on his way back to London now?

"Is that too tight?" Betsy asked, a nervous edge to her voice. "I fear Lady Emmeline is a bit, er, narrower than you are, my lady."

Eliza snorted. "Ain't that the truth." She smoothed her hands down over her hips. In spite of the tight-fitting bodice, she *had* lost some weight here. She had no idea how much; there weren't exactly bathroom scales lying around, something she found quite freeing. Not being able to try on her own jeans made it hard to know, but her stomach was slightly less round, her face a bit more angular. There was something to be said for not having food as readily available as it had been back home.

Home. She missed home. She missed Cat. She missed Presley, the big ol' furball. She sighed. *You can't always get what you want.* The Stones' song echoed through her head.

It'd been a favorite of her father's, so she'd heard it time on end, but never appreciated the sentiment as much as she did now.

She certainly hadn't gotten what she wanted so far. Was it time to go?

A maid entered the doorway. Lucy, if Eliza remembered correctly. "Beggin' pardon, my lady, but the Dowager Duchess has sent notice to all the ladies of the household that we will be leaving for London the day after tomorrow."

"London?" Betsy squeaked. "But I didn't think they were leaving until the end of the week."

The maid shrugged. "I think so; I heard it directly from the Dowager. She's planning Lady Rebecca's coming out ball, and has decided she needs to make the arrangements in Town herself. Or so I heard her telling her lady's maid." The woman flushed, as if realizing she shouldn't be admitting to eavesdropping.

"All right, then," Betsy said. "We will have to pack. Not that you *have* much to pack, my lady, but I'm sure His Grace will set that right in London. There are lots of modistes there."

"Oh, I'm not going."

"Not going?"

"The Dowager has made it clear my place, if anywhere, is here, with Frederick." Eliza fought back the lump of disappointment in her throat. She desperately wanted to see Regency London, to see the places she'd read about as they were in this era: Grosvenor Square, Berkeley Square, Hyde Park, Gunter's. Yes, she wanted to see all of those places. Almost as much as she wanted to stay with Deveric.

Betsy's face fell.

"What's the matter, Betsy?"

"Begging your pardon, Eliza. I did not mean to show

disappointment. I had looked forward to seeing London, 'tis all, going with you as your lady's maid."

"You've never been to London?"

"Oh, no, my lady. I stay here, at Clarehaven. There are plenty of servants at Claremont House; they've no need of a country miss there. I prefer the quiet of the country, anyway."

That was a big fat lie, if Betsy's crestfallen expression said anything, but Eliza didn't call her on it.

It certainly *was* quiet. Eliza missed the hustle and bustle of the first week, when the house had been filled with guests. She could see why house parties that lasted for days or weeks were so popular—otherwise one could die of boredom on such an estate.

She wanted to slap herself. *My God, I sound like one of the bored, entitled debutantes I so despise.* There were tons of things to do here. She'd sampled just a few. She certainly enjoyed her time with Freddy, and the dogs. She'd sat for hours in the library while Dev was away, combing through the volumes. She'd read a fair number of novels, some familiar from her twenty-first century studies, others not. She'd even tackled the *Flora Britannica* before deciding she wasn't that desperate.

And now that she'd met the cook, she wanted to spend time in the kitchen, getting to know more of the house staff and learning this century's methods of cooking. How *did* one make food without access to a microwave, or a refrigerator?

Yes, there was plenty to do here. If she didn't go home, that is.

An hour later, Freddy dragged her by the hand to the familiar stone hut. Though her own heart was heavy, she loved that his cheeks glowed with healthy exuberance as he chatted animatedly about Pirate.

"He licks me all the time!" Freddy exclaimed. "And even though he hasn't got an eye, he runs around just as easily as his sisters and brothers. And he's only a little bit smaller, you'll see!"

Eliza wasn't sure what the boy expected her to notice, considering they'd been down to see the dogs together every day, but she followed along dutifully, glad for some time away from the main house and the people—all the people—in it. She needed to think.

Deveric's son had run a few steps ahead when a booming voice called out over the courtyard. "Frederick! What are you doing out in this weather? You should be in the nursery, warming yourself under the covers."

Freddy froze in his tracks, his face anxious, though he tried to hide it. "Good afternoon, Father," he replied automatically. "Lizzie and I are going to visit the dogs."

Deveric turned to Eliza, arching an angry eyebrow. "Lizzie, is it?"

She shrugged. This? This is how he interacted with her after ditching her in the hallway that morning? By picking an argument over a nickname? Freddy had started calling her that a few days ago, and she'd decided she didn't mind, especially since when he said it, it was laced with affection.

He looked back at his son. "You should call her Mrs. James; it is what's proper between a governess and her charge."

"Yes, Papa." Freddy tucked his head down into his chest, his spirit visibly dimming.

She wanted to clobber Deveric over the head for stealing

his son's joy. And for referring to her as the governess. The man was erecting fences left and right. Sadness seeped into the hole in her heart.

"I told him he could call me that, Your Grace." She emphasized his title. "Freddy and I get along well. Our daily trips outside have done wonders for him."

Frederick gaped at her with wide eyes as she challenged his father. He nodded enthusiastically, his small head bobbing up and down. "I have, Papa. I haven't had a fever for weeks, Nurse says, and my throat hasn't been sore at all!"

Deveric paused before answering. "I am pleased you are feeling well, my child."

"Do you want to come see the puppies?"

"Puppies? Oh yes, Master Sayers informed me Bertha had whelped her litter." He paused for a second. "Wait, have you been playing with the dogs? Those dogs are hunting dogs, meant to be trained and controlled. They are not playmates."

"But I have my own dog now, Papa," Freddy protested, looking at Eliza for back up.

Great. I go up against his dad, and now Freddy tries it. That'll get me in trouble, for sure, teaching impertinence. She smiled at the boy. Deveric deserved all the impertinence in the world today, for the way he'd behaved. Could he not see how red her eyes were?

"Mr. Sayers and Liz—I mean Mrs. James—let me keep him! Come see!" Freddy ran down the path, obviously anxious to show his father his puppy.

"You gave my son a hunting dog?"

Eliza's eyes turned frosty. "No. Mr. Sayers let Frederick keep the runt of the litter, an adorable little fellow with one eye that your son has fallen in love with and spent a lot of time nurturing."

"A runt? Why didn't Mr. Sayers put it out of its misery?"

"Because that runt has saved your son from his."

"His what?"

"His misery."

Deveric scowled at her. "What do you mean? My son is not miserable. He has a good life."

"A good life? Are you kidding me? Yes, he's a duke's son, so I suppose he has most anything material at his beck and call. But do you know what he wants? What he needs? That boy wants love. He wants attention. And he wants it from his father!"

Her voice had risen until she was yelling at him, anger surging through her. How dared he come out here and treat her so formally, so coldly, as if she really were nothing more than a servant. How dared he act as if nothing had happened between them, as if he—and she—could bury the emotions, the desire, the connection between them.

"He's been sick for months now, and what do you do? Coop him up in a room with that ghastly Nurse Pritchett." Her chest heaved with every word. "And instead of spending time with him, you run away for several weeks. I didn't know—I mean, *he* didn't know if you were ever coming back!"

Chapter 32

*D*isbelief immobilized him, left him frozen, as he stared into the blazing eyes of one very furious Eliza James.

His own anger sparked. How dared she accuse him of neglecting his son? He always made sure the boy had everything he needed. He visited Frederick at least once a day, sometimes more, didn't he? When he was here, at least.

He shouldn't feel guilty. Rest and quiet were what the doctor said, what Nurse Pritchett said, were best for an ailing child, so he'd been careful not to stay too long and overtire the boy.

He did better than his own father, didn't he? Samuel Claremont had never paid much attention to *him,* beyond drilling principles of proper behavior into his brain, not until Deveric had reached his majority and needed training in the running of the estates, anyway. And in truth, the estate manager took on the majority of that task. His father had preferred Town life, even off-Season.

Deveric hadn't *wanted* attention from his parents when he was younger. Most of what he got came in the form of disapproval, whenever he'd made a wrong step, whenever he'd not comported himself as a duke's son must. He'd quickly learned to stop wishing for their attention and to start being grateful when they left him on his own.

Eton had been an escape, as had Oxford. It was why he preferred his townhouse in London to Claremont House— fewer people underfoot, and less criticism from his mother.

"I always come back. Frederick knows that!" he bellowed. "I would have come back sooner, but I … I …" He faltered. He couldn't admit, shouldn't admit *she* was the reason he'd stayed away so long.

She stalked off ahead, clearly uninterested in his self-justification. He watched in disbelief, hands on his hips. She dared leave him, Claremont, a duke? *Isn't that exactly what you wanted? For her to stay away?*

With a growl, he headed toward the kennel, his long strides ensuring he and Eliza reached it at the same time. Deveric stopped in surprise. His son was rolling around on the floor, giggling, a tiny puppy trying to jump on him and licking him everywhere it could. Mr. Sayers stood off to the side, watching the boy with a fond expression.

"Frederick!" Deveric bellowed. "Sayers! What is the meaning of this?" It was one thing for his son to visit the dogs against his wishes; it was quite another for the boy to roll in the dirt with the animals. What if he took ill again?

The houndsmaster's back went rigidly straight at the harsh voice, before he reached down to pull the puppy off of the boy. "My apologies, Your Grace. I know you don't like Master Freddy to play with the pups. I should not have allowed it." Sayers ducked his head as the puppy squirmed in his arms, wanting to get back to the boy.

Frederick scowled at his father. "Why do you have to ruin it? Why do you have to ruin *everything*? You don't even care! You don't care about me! You wish I'd died when Mama did!" he shouted, tears streaming down his face. He turned and darted out the door.

Deveric made to go after him. Eliza caught at his arm. "Maybe you'd better give him some space."

"How dare you—" Deveric thundered. Then, suddenly, he grew eerily quiet. No one said a thing as he stood, hand on a hip, his gaze never leaving the squeaking pups crawling around on their mother.

Closing his eyes, he exhaled, willing himself calm. He looked at Mr. Sayers, at Eliza, at the puppy.

"You are right," he said. "You are right. I am grateful to you both for providing my son with some joy in his life, seeing as I have failed to do so."

Without another word, he exited the hut.

Eliza and Mr. Sayers stared at each other in confusion.

"I've never seen His Grace do that," Mr. Sayers said.

"Seen him do what?"

"Back down. Admit wrong."

"Well, he should have. He *is* wrong."

"But he's a duke," Mr. Sayers said, as if that explained everything. "For you to challenge him …" He looked at Eliza in wonder. Shuffling over, he placed the puppy back in the pen with his mother. Pirate whined, clawing at the dirt.

"He's a man, a human being. Same as you or me. And

he needs to be a parent to his boy." Eliza didn't care she was imposing twenty-first century values on a nineteenth-century situation. Frederick deserved better, and frankly, so did Deveric. *Let not the sins of the father …*

She walked over and picked up Pirate, who licked at her fingers. "I think I'll take him to see Freddy. I'm sure the boy could use some comforting."

"You're playing with fire, my lady." Sayers' eyes held a mixture of respect and concern.

"Probably. But it just might be His Grace who ends up getting burned."

Deveric fled to the stables, needing time—and speed—to clear his head, to get these overpowering emotions under control, to determine his next course of action. He rode Lighting hard for more than an hour, desperate for clarity, for answers. How had his world gone topsy-turvy so quickly? *Because of a certain blonde-haired, blue-eyed force of nature.*

He still wasn't sure what to do about Eliza. His mind urged him to stay away, to enforce distance, lest he hurt her. He couldn't risk that. Wouldn't risk that.

His heart, however, pulled him to her with its every beat. He needed someone like her, someone to speak plainly, to call him out in a way no one else dared. Someone who fired his blood like no one else ever had.

But first, he needed to make amends to his son. There was truth in what Frederick had said. Not that Dev wished he'd never been born. Certainly not that. But in avoiding and shutting off everything and everyone since the loss of his wife and daughter, he'd shut his son out, too.

And then when Frederick had been so sick, Deveric had nearly gone out of his mind with fear of losing him. He'd wanted to drop to the ground, scream his anger and grief at God, plead for his son's life. He'd tried it before, bargaining to save his wife and daughter, but it hadn't worked; God had taken them anyway.

Instead, he'd thrown himself into work, into riding, into punishing himself every way he could think of. He'd brought in the best doctors, commanded Nurse Pritchett to tend him around the clock, kept the boy's room warmer than any in the house, but he hadn't done what his son had needed him to do most—be there for him.

When Freddy was born, Dev had taken one look at that tiny, red, bawling face, and sworn he'd love him better than his parents had loved Dev, that Frederick would never want for anything, would never have to labor more than have fun. Societal expectations be damned.

And yet what had he done? Abandoned his son at his greatest time of need. *I truly am a monster.*

Sliding off the horse, he threw the reins at the stable master, not even staying to brush Lightning down, but racing toward the house. He needed to change—he was drenched in sweat from the intense ride—but then he was going to make it up to his son, whatever it took.

Eliza stayed with Freddy until he fell asleep. He'd sobbed in her arms for a good half hour, hiccupping and asking Eliza why his father didn't love him. She assured him repeatedly that the Duke did indeed love him, but when Freddy demanded, "So why hasn't he come now?" she had no answer.

When he finally dozed off, she laid him back in the bed and covered him carefully with his blanket. She wanted to stroke his cheek, to wipe the remaining tears away, but was afraid to, lest she disturb him. *Who knew that when I traveled through time for a duke, I'd end up loving his son, instead?*

Because she did love Freddy, loved him dearly. She'd started to think of him almost as her own son, which was a mistake, if for no other reason than things weren't working out with his father.

Could she stay here? Could she stay at Clarehaven if Deveric never returned her feelings? Could she spend days, months, years, watching him, living with him, loving his son, but never having him?

She bit her lip in frustration. This wasn't the happy-ever-after she'd longed for. This was no fairytale ending, no midnight waltz at a ball. Instead, every time they took two steps forward, her Prince Not-So-Charming took twenty back.

Deveric didn't want her. Yes, he desired her physically; of that she was certain. It was something. But it wasn't enough. She wanted the deep, all-consuming love of which she'd always dreamt. And she didn't want to constantly have to chip away at someone else's iceberg to find it.

She carefully stood up, tiptoeing her way to the door so as not to wake Frederick. Walking down the hallway, Eliza was at a loss. She didn't know what to do.

She longed to be sitting in The Grounds with Cat, nursing a cappuccino and talking about what kind of Easter activity to plan for the kids at the Treasure Trove. She wanted to be bowling with Shannon and Jill. She wanted to be where she fit in, where she didn't constantly feel judged as lesser. Or worse, she didn't want to *feel* lesser, which was certainly the case when she was in the Dowager's presence.

Maybe a book would help. They'd always been her escape in times of trouble, her friends when she hadn't had any. Changing direction, she headed toward the study she'd found herself in that first evening. Under Deveric.

Once there, she thumbed her fingers across the titles, grateful the room was empty as she looked for something, anything that would distract her. She could read Dalton's *Atomic Theory*, or Davy's *Elements of Chemical Philosophy*. They were bound at least to put her to sleep.

Her eyes unwillingly bounced to the settee where she'd lain with Deveric, trapped in his arms, staring into his deep emerald eyes. She'd been so hopeful then.

A small book casually discarded on the far end of the settee caught her eye. She strolled over and picked it up, opening to the cover page. *Sense and Sensibility.* Ah. She'd thought the binding looked familiar—it was the copy Grace had been reading those few weeks ago. She sat down, leaned back on the settee's arm, and started reading, the opening paragraph well known and welcoming.

> *The family of Dashwood had been long settled in Sussex. Their estate was large, and their residence was at Norland Park, in the centre of their property, where for many generations, they had lived in so respectable a manner as to engage the general good opinion of their surrounding acquaintance.*

The words were as comfortable as they were comforting. She didn't know how many times she'd read this book, but it was the closest thing she had right now to a dear friend, and she let herself sink into it. She didn't notice the sun setting until a maid came in to draw the window coverings.

"Oh, I'm sorry, my lady. I thought it were empty in here." She was a pleasantly plump young girl, all cherry cheeks and big eyes.

Eliza yawned, setting the book down. "No need to apologize. I lost track of time. What time is it?"

"Six o'clock, my lady. Would you like for me to stoke up the fire again?"

"No, no. I'd better go. Thank you, —?"

"Dora, my lady." The maid gave her a nervous curtsy.

"Oh, no need for that." Eliza winked at her. "Please, call me Eliza."

Dora smiled again. "The governess?"

"Yes."

"Betsy says Master Frederick's been ever so much better since you've been here."

"Thank you." *Freddy!* She'd been in here for hours—she should have checked on him long ago. Poor kid, deserted by everyone on the same day. "Excuse me, Dora," she said, grabbing her skirt in her hand, "but I have to go!"

Eliza ran out of the library and raced toward the hallway with the nursery. As she coasted around a corner, she ran smack dab into a tall, imposing figure. "Oompfh."

Both women staggered back. The hat the Dowager was wearing slid off her head and landed with a thud on the floor. That thing must weigh twenty pounds, Eliza thought, as she gazed at the elaborate millinery creation, her head spinning.

A noise similar to a hiss emanated from the Dragon. "It is not seemly for a woman to … to *run!*" she huffed as she straightened her skirt.

"I'm so sorry, Your Grace," Eliza said, wanting only to get past her. "I was going to see Master Frederick."

Down the hallway past the Dowager, the door opened and Deveric emerged, followed by Freddy. Eliza's eyes widened, a tremulous smile crossing her face, as Dev picked up his son and enfolded him in a deep hug, his back to Eliza and the Dowager. Freddy's lips curled up in a smile. Whatever had happened between him and his father had ended happily, and Eliza's heart swelled with hope that Dev and his son might have a closer relationship from this point forward, regardless of what happened with her.

Deveric's mother turned, following Eliza's gaze. Both women watched as Deveric walked down the hallway in the opposite direction, his son clasped firmly in his arms.

She whipped her head back to Eliza and snapped in a low voice, "Hear me now, *Mrs. Eliza James*. You will not have my son. You will never have my son. Oh, he may want to bed you—and given the way you look at him, I daresay he will succeed—but he will not marry you. He will never marry you."

Eliza stared at her, momentarily cowed by the menace in the woman's voice. Her face drooped and her shoulders slid toward the floor. *No,* an inner voice cried. *Eleanor Roosevelt. Eleanor friggin' Roosevelt, baby!*

She pulled up her spine and thrust her shoulders back, her stance confident, her eyes calm as she returned the Dowager's direct gaze. "I don't believe that is for you to say, *Your Grace*. Your son is a grown man and I daresay he can make his own decisions."

Triumph entered the Dowager's eyes. "Aha! You admit you're trying to ensnare him!" She fixed a shrewd look on Eliza.

"No. I'm not."

"You just said—"

"I said he can choose whom he wishes to marry. And, yes, I have hoped he would choose me. But I never, not for one minute, have tried to ensnare him."

The Dowager frowned, as if what Eliza was saying simply didn't compute.

"I want his heart," Eliza confessed in a small voice, almost more to herself than to Deveric's mother. "But only if he gives it freely."

"Rubbish," the Dragon said, hurling the word at Eliza. "You are a fortune-hunter seeking to gain one of the highest positions in the land. Don't think I don't know your kind." Her eyes snaked into reptilian slits. It would not have surprised Eliza if the woman breathed fire next.

"I do not know why you hate me so much! If you think so poorly of me," Eliza responded, her voice rising, "why don't you throw me out?"

"Don't think I haven't wanted to. The only reason you're still here is that family takes care of family, and Claremont insists you are a long-lost cousin. My son does not lie."

Eliza wasn't sure how to respond to that. Should she insist Deveric *had* lied? Because he had. She was no more related to him than she was to the Queen of England, and they both knew it. Surely that meant something; that he'd covered for her at the cost of his own honesty. Except he'd had to, because really, how else could he account for her sudden presence, an American widow at Clarehaven? Nobody would believe the truth, and any other explanation begged for a scandal.

Eliza's shoulders rose and fell as she stared down the Dowager. How was this to end?

"Mother. Mrs. James."

At Deveric's deep voice, Eliza literally jumped. When had he returned? How had she not noticed him approach? And where was Freddy?

"Claremont," answered the Dowager with a tight nod, her eyes never leaving Eliza.

Eliza said nothing, instead pulling and twisting the tendril near her ear with such force it hurt. The air was so thick with tension, she could have cut it with that clichéd knife.

Deveric's brow knit as he looked back and forth between the two women. "Is there some—" he started to say, but apparently thought better of it. He took a deep breath. "May I escort you both to dinner?" he asked, extending an arm to each of them.

"Thank you," Eliza responded, her voice tight, "but I wanted to check on Frederick. Is he in his room?"

It was all Eliza could do to hold it together. She wanted to rail against his formality, his distance. His mother. She wanted to bring back the man who'd spent the night in her bed—platonically—discussing airplanes and taking raunchy photographs. Attempted raunchy photographs, that is. That man, and that night, seemed so far away now. Her dream was slipping through her fingers.

"No. He is down in the kitchen, stealing cherry tarts from the cook."

Eliza nearly smiled at the image of Freddy with cherry smeared across his face, but the Dragon's hawk-like stare stopped her. "Maybe it would be better if I took a tray in my room this evening," she said, breaking eye contact with the Dowager. Perhaps that was an admission of defeat, but she was tired of the battle. Tired of everything.

"Of course," Dev answered. "I will have someone bring up dinner for you." Concern flashed across his face, but he instantly reverted back to a blank expression as his mother linked her arm through his.

"Thank you," Eliza said stiffly, her heart in her throat.

He gave her the barest of nods. And then mother and son walked off without another word, leaving Eliza in the hallway, alone.

CHAPTER 33

*E*liza stood a few minutes longer, shaking from her altercation with the Dragon. She cast her eyes to the ceiling, willing her insides to stop roiling. *I will not let that woman have power over me. I will not.*

She'd met viragos like Deveric's mother in Charlottesville, embittered women whose sole purpose in life seemed to lie in making others miserable. Occasionally, she'd caught glimpses of the hurt, of the vulnerability lying beneath their caustic exteriors. It'd given her empathy toward those women, where others often had none. She wasn't feeling empathetic now. Then again, she'd never herself been the subject of such viciousness.

The Dowager Duchess will not steal my sunshine.

Question was, if Eliza remained under the same roof with that thundercloud, would she have any left?

Ugh. Regardless of what happened with Deveric, regardless of what happened with his mother, what Eliza needed was some time off, an evening free of worry or care.

An evening with *Sense and Sensibility*. It'd be better with ice cream, but she'd take what she could get. Returning to the library, she grabbed the book before going back to her room. She didn't want anyone to disturb her, wanted to pretend she was back in her own bed, in her own apartment, living vicariously through Austen's prose, and forgetting for a while this mess of her own creation. Well, hers and Cat's. Life was so much simpler in novels—especially when the happy-ever-after was guaranteed. No wonder Eliza had wanted to live that fairytale, Austen-esque romance; reality was messy, uncertain, painful. Better to return to the familiar, the expected, the beloved. Fiction.

She'd only been reading a short time when a knock came on the door. *Who could that be?* She quickly brushed her hair back behind her ears. Deveric?

"Eliza? It's Emmeline. May I enter?"

"Sure." Not Deveric. She stuffed down her disappointment. So much for her personal Darcy. Apparently Dev's feelings *could* be repressed.

Emmeline walked in, her face alive with excitement and some sort of magazine in her hand. "Mama said at dinner that Becca and I are to get completely new wardrobes in London. My brother insisted you are to get new dresses, too! I brought *Ackermann's Repository* for us to look through for ideas. I have seen the most delightful spencer, of such a fine green."

"Wait. De—I mean, His Grace—wants *me* to have new gowns?"

"Yes!" Emmeline plopped down on the bed and opened up the magazine to a page showing a sketch of a woman in a blue dress. "Mother protested you didn't need anything, the silly goose, but he absolutely insisted, going so far as to say you should have *carte blanche*. He said he expects you to participate in all social events with the family, and so you must look the part."

Eliza gaped at her. "What? But I'm not going to London." Had Deveric had a change of heart? Was this the sign she was looking for?

"You are, indeed. You get to come to the balls! And the theater! And Almack's. I'm sure he can secure you a voucher; my brother knows all the patronesses, of course." Emmeline bounced on the bed. "I can't wait!"

"But why would he do this?" Giddiness enveloped Eliza, in spite of her doubts. Emmeline's enthusiasm was contagious. Almack's? *The* Almack's? She looked at the page to which Emmeline had flipped. And a gown like that, just for her? She couldn't even imagine. London. With Deveric. Her heart swelled.

Emmeline shrugged. "You're family, of course."

Guilt crept across Eliza's shoulders like a heavy coat. No, she wasn't.

"Mama finally agreed maybe it was a good idea, to help you catch a husband. She said you didn't even look all *that* old."

Eliza nearly choked. A husband? Deveric wanted her to find a *husband*? All this time she'd been hoping, believing, and he'd been finding a way to get rid of her?

It was as if he'd punched her in the stomach.

No wonder the Dowager was willing to go along with it— then she'd be rid of the nuisance, too. Eliza deflated like a balloon, her eyes welling with tears. *He doesn't want me. He wants to get rid of me.*

Or could it be all the Dragon's idea, this desire to marry her off? "Did Dev—did your brother say he wished me to marry?" Eliza asked, surprised at her own bluntness. But she had to know.

Emmeline shrugged again without looking up. "I don't know, I wasn't paying close attention. Oh, look at this bonnet! Don't you love the way the brim rises up, and how the flowers match the pelisse?"

Eliza pretended to share Emmeline's enthusiasm as she bent over the illustration, but she wasn't focusing on it, fighting instead to keep the tears back. In spite of her best efforts, one slipped free and dropped onto the page.

Startled, Emmeline looked up. "What's wrong?"

Another tear fell. Eliza shook her head, unable to say anything.

Emmeline's eyes widened, her mouth rounding into an O. "It's Deveric, isn't it? You wish to marry my brother!"

Eliza remained silent, emotions coursing through her.

Emmeline clapped her hands, but then grew somber, the sides of her mouth turning down. "But it will never work, Eliza. Even if my mother would approve—and I dare say she would not, since you're not of high enough social position— Deveric won't marry again."

Her eyes were sorrowful as she set a hand on Eliza's knee. "He says he'll never repeat that pain. It saddens me so. He could find a happy match if he wished, I'm sure of it. Our sister Cecilia secured one. But he's adamant. He says he has his heir and needs never marry again; he just needs to marry *us* off. He claims that will be a challenge in and of itself!" She giggled a bit at the last part, but then stopped, looking sheepish.

Misery crashed down on Eliza, sucking her into its giant black hole. It had all been for naught. She was here for naught. How could Cat create someone who wasn't emotionally available? Wasn't that exactly the opposite of what Eliza had wished for?

Had Cat done it on purpose, so Eliza would use the escape clause and come home to her? Was this her ultimate way of proving to Eliza romance novel dreams didn't come true?

No. Cat would never do that to her. If Eliza was here, it was because she was supposed to be here. Deveric was supposed to be hers. Then again, in creating such a backstory for Deveric, in having him lose a spouse like Eliza had, maybe instead of linking them through something in common, Cat had given him something he couldn't, or wouldn't, overcome.

Eliza fought to breathe. The Dragon hated her. Deveric was fighting whatever attraction he might have for her, tooth and nail. And Emmeline had just confirmed he wasn't going to change, not for Eliza. Not for anyone.

She sighed. She'd been an optimist her entire life, determined to muddle her way through any odds, but this was too much. How hard was she supposed to fight? How much more did she need to go through? When did she get a break?

"I'm tired," she said out loud. It was exhausting, watching her dreams crumble to dust.

I'm tired. Tired of fighting this battle. Tired of longing for what I can never have. Tired of wishing things were different.

Emmeline grabbed Eliza's hand. "I'm sorry. I would love to have you as a true sister. But I don't think ..."

Eliza sucked in a breath. "I know. Your mother is right. I don't belong here. I don't fit in here. And even if I did, your brother ... His Grace ... You're right; he won't love me. Not the way I want to be loved. Not the way I deserve to be loved."

"Perhaps going to London for the Season is what you need. You can find a new suitor!"

Eliza gave a pained laugh, one that echoed like daggers through her body. *Oh, Emmeline. You are so young.* Clearly the girl had never been in love, or she'd know people couldn't switch affections as easily as they switched shoes. At least Eliza couldn't. Love didn't work that way. And she did love Deveric. She knew it, felt it in her bones, in every inch of her. She did. Not just because Cat had created him for her to do so. Not even because she thought she should, but because she did.

He was fierce, strong, every bit a man, but she had no doubt his stoic manner and reserved nature masked a man who felt deeply. She'd sensed it in the few times he'd kissed her; a well of passion, emotional as well as physical, lay below that calm exterior. She loved his quiet confidence, loved his love for his son—which she hoped he'd now show more openly. He was committed to those he cared for, as evidenced in how he interacted with his family, his sisters, even his mother.

"Maybe." *Crying over spilt milk won't clean up this mess. Chin up. Attitude out.* Wiping a tear from her eye, she gave Emmeline a weak smile. "Why don't you show me which is your favorite dress?"

Emmeline clapped her hands before thumbing through the pages, chatting exuberantly about each dress she saw. Eliza sat next to her, not paying any attention.

I think it's time for me to go home. This is getting far too painful. If she was going to be lost in a sea of unrequited emotion, she'd at least like to do it on common ground, with friends around who knew and loved her. With heat and Internet and coffee and cars.

"Oh, here's a lovely riding habit." Emmeline peered more closely at the page. "Perfect for an outing in Hyde Park. Don't you love the deep green of the velvet? I'd add some epaulettes at the shoulders, but I'm sure Mrs. Shabner can do that."

"Riding?" Eliza sat up straighter. "You're right. Hyde Park. I need riding lessons." Turning to Emmeline, determination setting in, she said, "Do you think Becca would teach me?"

"I'm sure she'd love to. She'd much rather ride than pick out dresses. She'll be thrilled if you ask her, rather than having me talk at her about gloves and shoes and spencers all the day. The poor girl. She's hopeless. As if a man will ever want a wife as wild as she." Emmeline clucked under her breath.

She would ride for the monolith, the mini-Stonehenge Cat had penned in as the place to which Eliza needed to go if she wanted to come home. Becca had told her last week it lay on the northern boundary of Clarehaven, some ten miles hence. Luckily, the young girl hadn't thought to ask Eliza how she knew about it, or why she was asking; she'd merely rattled off the info. Eliza herself had hoped learning the location was just a case of 'forewarned is forearmed.' So much for that.

She swallowed. The Escape Clause, as she and Cat had called it, capital letters and all, stated Eliza just had to sit on the center stone and wish with all her heart to be back in the twenty-first century, in the arms of William Dawes. If she did, Cat had written that William would fall madly in love with her, like he'd done with Cat.

Eliza had wanted to pick Jesse Parker, the fellow grad student she'd had a mild crush on last year—he'd seemed a good pick—but Cat reminded her it had to be a fictional character, one Cat had created. William was as good a choice as any. Unless Cat had decided to be with him after all. Eliza wrinkled her brow. Hopefully that wasn't the case.

Sure, a love story with William would be formulaic. Eliza would never know if he loved her for *her,* or loved her because Cat had written he would, but at this point, she didn't care.

She just wanted love and security and the realization of *some* sort of a happy-ever-after.

It wasn't politically correct of her, to want the fairytale happy ending, but she didn't care about that right now, either. She wanted release from longing for a man who would never love her, for a man who affected her like no other man ever had, but who wouldn't—or couldn't—set aside his earlier experiences and take a chance on love again. She deserved more than that. She wanted to be Cinderella for once and land the Prince. Happy Ever After. Boom. Was that so wrong?

Emmeline was so excited about dresses she didn't notice Eliza's lack of attention. That suited Eliza fine; she needed time to make plans of her own.

Deveric sat at his end of the dining table, swishing the port in his glass. He glanced to his right, at the spot where Eliza typically sat, but it was empty.

He'd been mostly silent during the meal. Not that his siblings had noticed, as busy as they were plotting their plans for London, each excited to be heading there for the Season. Except maybe Amara.

He understood. His sisters were always happy to come to Clarehaven after the non-stop whirl of the Season's social events, but a few months here, especially when the snow piled up and made it hard for them to visit anywhere, and they were ready to go back. He'd always been the same, too.

He didn't want to go to London now, though he knew Arth and Coll awaited his return. Normally, he, too, liked the hustle and bustle, liked the temporary escape from the pressures of estate management. Now, it all felt empty, meaningless. Especially if he had to be with Eliza, but not *be* with Eliza. The idea of watching her, watching her flirt, watching her possibly fall in love with another man, maybe even accept a suit, tore at him. But what could he do? He could not offer for her.

He exhaled loudly. His sisters had all left, anxious to finish travel preparations, but his mother remained at the opposite end of the table. She watched him silently, her lips pinched, her brows folded over her eyes, puzzlement etched on her face. Raising an eyebrow, he took a bite of the beef still on his plate, but didn't taste it. His eyes wandered again to Eliza's empty chair.

He would find her tomorrow. They had to talk about this, this … passion, or whatever it was, that flared between them whenever they were together. He had to make her understand he could not, would not follow through on it. He wasn't interested in marrying again. He'd suffered enough the first time, and Lord knew he'd never risk impregnating someone. But he wouldn't, couldn't ask Eliza for anything less.

She was a widow, and therefore had more social freedom than other women. Many a widow carried on affairs without repercussions. But he wouldn't disgrace her—or himself— by asking her to enter into such a liaison. He wouldn't give in to the feelings he had for her. They were feelings of lust, no more, he told himself for the hundredth time. He wasn't stupid enough to fall in love with her.

In love with her? He wasn't in *love* with Eliza James, this wondrous creature from the future, who talked with strange words and treated servants, treated everyone, as if they were not only equals, but also friends. Who'd taken his son—*his* son—under her wing, loving Frederick as he deserved to be loved, even when Deveric had failed to do so. This woman who not only fired his blood, but piqued his intellectual curiosity like no woman ever had. This exquisite, bewildering, tempting, exasperating American with whom he wanted to spend every minute—in and out of bed.

No. He was not in love with her. He *could* not be in love with her. It was lust, the lure of fantasy, the magnetism of the unknown. That's all. And he was the Duke of Claremont, with a myriad of responsibilities and pressures. He had no time for distractions, for fantasizing about women.

Not women. Woman. One woman. Eliza. Oh, how he wanted her. He wanted to ravish every inch of her, to lace his fingers through her starlit hair, kiss her honeyed lips. He wanted to squeeze those voluptuous breasts, run his fingers over her nipples, feel her tremble as his hand moved up her thighs. He wanted …

Good Lord, he needed to get a hold of himself. Perhaps literally, to get this vixen out of his head. Surely easing the lust would erase these other emotions, the ones dangerously close to those the poets had always described.

No, love was not for him. Love meant risk. Love meant losing control. Love meant vulnerability, the possibility of blackness after bliss. He couldn't do it, couldn't let her in, couldn't let it all out, all he'd fought so hard to contain after the loss of his daughter. He couldn't risk hurting Eliza, couldn't risk losing her. Better to never have her at all.

He looked to his mother again, his expression hard. She gave a slight nod, as if satisfied with what she saw in his face.

Yes, Mother. You have won.

CHAPTER 34

The next morning dawned cold and breezy. Not the best day for a ride, perhaps, but Eliza was determined. She needed to go, needed to escape, needed to run back to all that was familiar, to where she knew she was loved, at least by one person. Cat.

Freddy's face popped into her head. *He loves you, too, Lizzie. You know it, and you love him. Now you're going to abandon him?* It couldn't be helped. Life lessons were often painful, but Freddy would survive. He wasn't supposed to get attached to his governess, anyway, and that's all she was. She wasn't his relative, wasn't really his cousin. She certainly wasn't his mother. She had to let him go.

Her heart nearly ripped in two at the thought.

Steeling her shoulders, she walked down to his room. His door was open and he was playing with some small metal soldiers on his floor. He looked up warily upon hearing her footsteps, and then grinned.

"I thought you were Nurse Pritchett." His eyes revealed

how much the idea displeased him.

Eliza kneeled on the floor next to him. "Freddy," she said, her voice wavering slightly. "There may come a time soon when I have to go."

Freddy dropped the soldier he'd had in his hand. "I know you are going to London with everyone else. It's all right. I'll be okay here with Pirate."

She smiled at both his use of okay, and at his attempt to cheer her up—cheer *her* up, when he was the child and she the adult. *What a precious kid. I hope he never loses that kind heart.*

"I'm sure Pirate will love you as you love him." She leaned across and drew Freddy into a hug. He tensed, momentarily startled, and then threw his arms around her. She buried her nose in his hair and squeezed him back. "As I love you," she whispered.

"Papa says he will bring me to London when it's a little warmer. He says he'll take me to see the Menagerie!"

Eliza fought to keep the tears from falling. "I'm sure you will have a wonderful time." She smoothed her hand over his hair. "Freddy?"

"Yes?"

"Thank you for being my friend. It was hard to come here all alone, but you have brightened my days for me."

He gave her a grin. "Really?"

Another word he'd adopted from me. "Really."

"Look, Lizzie," he said, sliding out of her arms and back onto the floor. "My front tooth is wiggly!"

She watched him move it back and forth. "You're growing up!" she proclaimed as she stood up. "Take care of yourself, Frederick. Don't forget me."

He gave her a wry glance. "It's not like you're leaving *forever*." *Except it is.*

Becca beamed with delight when Eliza asked her for a riding lesson at breakfast. "I knew it!" she said. "I knew you'd fall in love with horses, too! How can you not?"

"How not, indeed," Emmeline murmured. "Maybe when you get close enough to smell them, and realize they'll bite or kick you, or throw you off their backs if they can."

At Emmeline's words, Eliza momentarily reconsidered her plan. Horses scared her, too. But the monolith was too far away for her to walk, not without her absence being noted, at least. *Not that anyone would care.*

"Oh, Emme, not all of them are like that and you know it. You just need the right horse. Hasn't Buttercup been fine for you?"

Emmeline nodded. "I suppose. But I prefer traveling by carriage—so much more civilized."

With a roll of her eyes, Becca rose from the table. "Are you ready, Eliza?"

No, her heart screamed. *I'm not ready. I didn't even say good-bye.* But her mind locked those thoughts away. *You need to go home, Eliza James. You don't belong here. It was a freak of nature, a trick of time that you ended up here anyway, and clearly the Universe has told you it's a mistake.*

"Yes." Standing tall, she followed Becca out of the room. "Yes, I am," she said in as strong a tone as she could muster. Which didn't feel very strong at all.

Eliza pulled at the folds of the riding habit Becca had loaned her, once again feeling the stuffed sausage, as Deveric's sister was definitely of a thinner build than she. How did women manage to ride a horse while draped in so much fabric? As they approached the stables and a horse whinnied, doubt enveloped her again. *What am I thinking? I've never been on a horse. Like, ever. How am I going to stay on one all the way to the monolith?*

Becca walked in and immediately over to Otto, stroking his nose before offering him an apple. A stable hand brought over a sidesaddle and hitched it onto the horse as Becca spoke to the animal in loving tones.

Eliza's eyes widened. *Crap.* Sidesaddle? That thing looked downright dangerous. Becca started talking, explaining how to mount a horse, how to sit, how to hold the reins, but Eliza barely heard a word.

I can't do this. I can't do this. She closed her eyes, forcing herself to breathe, in and out, in and out. Only that brought the pungent scent of horse rushing through her sinuses and she sneezed. *See? I'm allergic to them. I'm allergic to escape. I shouldn't be running away.* Opening her eyes, she squared her shoulders, trying to restore her confidence.

Was she giving up too easily? Deveric was obviously attracted to her. Wasn't that at least something? *Not enough,* her brain screamed. *Not enough.* She couldn't keep fighting this war on so many fronts—the social gulf, Deveric's mother, Deveric himself. Not to mention the time period issues. Their entire life experiences and expectations were so different. She was tired and wanted to go home. A heavy sigh escaped.

Becca turned to her. "Are you nervous?" she said. "Don't be! You're going to have so much fun. That's Petunia." She gestured to the horse on which the stable hand had just attached the saddle. "She's so gentle. Here, Sam will help you up. Watch me first."

The stable hand nodded without saying a word. Eliza watched as he assisted Becca into the saddle, noting the way she hooked her leg around the saddle's front. When Sam came to her, Eliza smiled grimly and stepped onto the mounting block, swinging her leg in what she hoped was the correct manner. To her surprise, she got it on the first try, even if the sitting position was extremely awkward. She looked down to thank Sam, but he was blushing as he averted his eyes.

"Oh, your dress!" Becca burst out, a twinkle in her eyes. "It's caught up around the pommel!"

Eliza glanced down. She was revealing a great deal of leg. Clothed leg, as she did have stockings on, but leg nonetheless. Who knew such a mild sight could elicit such a reaction in a young man? Like any man in her era would have paid attention. It was actually refreshing, the idea that a clothed leg could cause such a stir. She yanked on the fabric, finally disentangling it.

"Shall we go?"

Eliza looked toward Becca, who was giving her an encouraging grin. "Uh …"

"You'll be fine. Just hold the reins and Petunia will follow after me. She'll follow Otto's lead, so all you have to do is sit and relax, I promise."

Sure enough, the horse ambled after Becca's at a slow and easy pace. *Well, this isn't too bad.* Eliza clutched the reins, risking a quick peek over her shoulder at the estate. Deveric was somewhere inside. At least she assumed he was; it was possible he was also out riding somewhere.

How long before he noticed she was gone? Would he care? Or would he be relieved that this burden, this distraction, this intrusion into his well-ordered and socially correct life had disappeared?

She chewed the inside of her cheek, thinking of Freddy again. Oh, how she would miss him. She prayed the thawing of the relationship between Deveric and his son would continue, and that the little boy would grow up with all of the love that he deserved, Regency peerage expectations be damned.

She gave a final nod of acknowledgment and turned around again toward Becca, her eyes fixed firmly on the path ahead … and the future.

"Let's ride to the pond," Becca called over her shoulder. "I don't believe you've been there yet, and it's a beautiful spot."

"I was hoping to visit the monolith. I've never seen one," Eliza answered, relaxing into the easy rhythm of the horse. *How long until my leg cramps from sitting in this weird position, though?*

"We will," Becca promised. "The pond's not far from the old stones." As they neared the edge of the woods, she called out, "Hold on to the reins. I'm going to kick Otto into a canter; he's itching to go faster."

Eliza gripped the ropes in her hands, her heart racing as Petunia sped up to match the horse in front of her. Trees flew by on the left and right.

"Uh, Becca," she tried to yell, but the wind ripped her voice from her. *We're not going that fast,* she reassured herself as she closed her eyes. *Petunia will keep me safe. Petunia will—*

A rustling sound came from the right, and Eliza's eyes flew open in time to see a fox race out from the underbrush, darting across the path in front of her horse. Petunia snorted and threw her head back, catching Eliza by surprise. She dropped the reins and Petunia bolted. Eliza grasped wildly for the reins and then the pommel, seeking something, anything, to keep her secure as she bounced along.

"Eliza!" Becca screamed, as a tree branch caught Eliza across the forehead. Her leg wrenched loose from the saddle, and she felt herself falling, falling. The ground rose up to meet her, and everything went dark.

CHAPTER 35

*D*everic rode Lightning hard, pushing them both to their limits—anything to ward off the combustible emotions he so wanted to keep at bay. He didn't know what to do about the delectable Mrs. James. Honor dictated he not go near her again, not with how the mere sight of her made the blood race in his veins, not with how he wanted to nibble on her ear every time she looked his direction, not with how, no matter how hard he tried, nothing sated the ferocious desire within him to claim her, to possess her, to make her his in all ways.

All ways except one. He couldn't marry her. He couldn't. Not only because his mother—and likely the rest of the *ton*—would never condone it. A duke and a nobody wasn't done, even if that nobody was allegedly a relation. *You could change that,* an inner voice insisted. *If your family accepted her, everyone else would, too. Surely your mother could make peace with it eventually, especially if she saw you were happy. Couldn't she?*

If that were the only deterrent, he'd have Eliza before the local vicar in an instant.

The image of Eliza, looking up at him with love shimmering in those wide blue eyes as she spoke vows, slammed into his heart, making him grasp his chest with the power of the aching there. He fought to catch his breath. Marry her? Impossible. He wanted her in his bed, no doubt about that, but that was impossible. Just like marrying her was impossible. He'd reaffirmed that last night.

He wouldn't do that to a woman again, wouldn't do that to himself again. He couldn't bear to see the fear in her eyes, couldn't bear the rejection sure to come when she realized they didn't fit. He couldn't hurt her.

And heaven forbid she get pregnant. Deveric's heart constricted again at the thought of Eliza heavy with child. His child. His mouth went dry at the memory of Mirabelle lying on the bed, the life seeping out of her, her face mingled with Eliza's face.

He couldn't. He couldn't. Better to take her to London, to find her a husband, a different man. Someone who would cherish her, who would love her, who wouldn't hurt her. Someone who wouldn't kill her.

He pulled Lightning up short and they both stood there, sides heaving. What was he to do?

A scream rent the air, somewhere ahead of him in the woods. He immediately kicked Lightning into a gallop, racing toward the sound.

"Eliza! Eliza!"

Oh Lord, that was Becca's voice. *And she's screaming Eliza's name.* What were they doing in the woods? Eliza didn't ride. She'd told him herself she'd never been on a horse. She was downright scared of them.

He caught sight of Otto ahead and steered Lightning in that direction. As he neared, he could see Becca on the ground, leaning over a prone form. When she heard his approach, she turned to him, terror written all over her face.

"I'm so sorry!" she said. "I'm sorry! I'm so sorry!"

Deveric leapt off the horse before it had even come to a full stop, racing over to the two women.

"What happened?" he roared as he went down on his knees, examining the wicked scratch across Eliza's forehead. She was pale and eerily still. He bent his head down to her chest, listening for her heartbeat.

"I—I—she—she wanted to go for a ride," Becca exclaimed, tears seeping from her eyes. "I was taking her to the pond, but a f—a fox scurried out from the brush and Petu—Petunia was unnerved by it."

Deveric willed himself to stay calm as he checked to see if Eliza was breathing. Her heart was beating, thank God. Once he could see her chest moving up and down, he felt around to determine if anything was broken. He breathed a sigh of relief that her legs seemed fine, but a large lump had formed on the back of her head, presumably where she'd struck the ground.

"Has she said anything? Has she opened her eyes?"

"N—no. She's going to be all right, right, Deveric? She's going to all right, isn't she?"

"I don't know," he bit out as he lifted Eliza carefully into his arms. He'd seen others die from what seemed like simple falls before. He looked down at her closed eyes. *You will not die. You will not. I won't let you.* He started walking back toward Clarehaven.

"What are you doing?" Becca demanded. "You can't carry her the entire way back!"

Deveric stilled. She was right, damn it. It was too far. Carefully, he lowered himself to the ground, cradling Eliza in his arms.

"Get your horse and get help. Get Chance or Sayers to bring a wagon," he barked over his shoulder. "Go. *Go!*"

Deveric stared down into Eliza's deathly pale face, willing the woman in his arms to wake up, to look at him, to smile and tell him it was going to be all right. *Okay,* he amended. *She would tell me it was going to be okay.* But Eliza didn't stir.

He tenderly, carefully ran his fingers through her hair, smoothing the back of a hand against her cheek, whispering to her she was safe, that he had her, that she would be fine.

He paid no attention as Becca raced past him. He only had eyes for Eliza.

Pain. Pain was all she felt, in every part of her body. Well, her head and right side hurt most, if she could quantify the agony lacing through her. *Percocet. I want Percocet.* Voices murmured around her and a cold cloth pressed against her forehead. *Nice. That was nice.* Fingers traced their way down across her cheek. *Is that you, Cat?*

She winced and groaned. *What had happened? Why did she hurt so much?* A hand slipped behind her neck and a cup touched her bottom lip. She thought a deep voice said something, but she couldn't make out the words. She was grateful for the cold liquid pouring slowly down her throat, though; she was so thirsty. *A soda would be nice,* she thought, before all went dark again.

"Damn it, man, it's been two days! Why isn't she waking up?" Deveric paced back and forth across his former wife's bedchamber, glaring at the doctor before looking back at Eliza. She seemed so small, nestled in that large bed. She hadn't stirred since he'd brought her back home. He wanted her to open her eyes, those gorgeous blue eyes, and look at him. Smile at him. Tease him. But she didn't. She just lay there, breathing in and out, in and out. Slowly.

Hell, at least she's still breathing.

Amara approached him, setting her hand on his shoulder. "I'm sure the doctor is doing everything he can," she said. "You need to rest, brother. We will care for her. Becca and I are here."

"Becca is the one who got her into this mess," Deveric barked, shrugging off Amara's hand. Upon Becca's devastated expression, he swallowed hard. It wasn't her fault. She'd told Dev how Eliza had insisted on riding that morning, how she'd said she needed to learn, if she were going to fit in. How she'd asked to go to the monolith.

Why the monolith? He'd asked himself that question time and again. How had she even known about it?

"I'm sorry, Becca," he offered, pinching his nose with shaking fingers. "Please forgive me. It's not your fault. Truly."

Becca nodded, wiping tears from her eyes. "But it is," she whispered. "If I'd never taken her out, never tried on the first day to go to the pond. We should have stayed in the ring."

"What's done is done," a brisk voice said from the doorway. Deveric looked up as his mother entered the room. She eyed him up and down. "You look terrible," she announced. "You are in need of a bath and a shave. A gentleman should never look so unkempt, even in the presence of family." She waved her hand toward the door. "Go. Mrs. James is well cared for. She does not need you."

Deveric balled his fingers into fists, seriously tempted for the first time to strike a woman. "I am no longer a child to be commanded, Mother," he said, clenching his jaw. "She is my duty and I shall care for her." *And I need her.*

His mother drew her chin up. "You are correct. You are not a child. Nonetheless, you are behaving like one. You cannot ensure Mrs. James' return to health by endangering your own. I assure you we will wake you if there is any change."

He considered. He hadn't left Eliza's side since he first laid her in the bed, dozing only occasionally in the chair next to her, but he knew he was about to drop. He wanted nothing more than to crawl into the bed beside her, hold her, will her awake, but that was not an option, not with all these people here. He nodded crisply to his mother, his green eyes locking with hers.

Her normally hard expression softened unexpectedly as she reached out, smoothing an errant lock of hair off his forehead, even offering a half-smile, which elicited a gasp from Amara. "Your sense of duty to those in your charge is admirable."

As she swept out of the room, he could have sworn she murmured, "And your love for that woman obvious."

He slept for fourteen hours.

Enraged upon wakening to learn he'd spent that much

time away from Eliza, Deveric leapt out of bed, hastily pulling on breeches and a freshly laundered shirt, ignoring his valet's efforts to assist him. He wanted to leave off his waistcoat and jacket, but knew his mother would have a fit if she caught him in such a state of undress, so he shrugged them on before bolting out the door.

Entering Eliza's room—for it was Eliza's room; he no longer thought of it as Mirabelle's chamber—his gut constricted, seeing her still lying there, deathly white.

Amara looked up from the book she'd been reading.

"Has she woken?" Deveric walked to Eliza's side and reached for her hand. It was cool to the touch, but no longer ice-cold. He gave a brief prayer of thanks; surely this was an improvement.

"Not exactly."

"What does that mean?"

His sister stood, setting the book on the small table near the bed. She smoothed her skirts before answering. "She talked off and on through the night. But I don't think she knew what she was saying. She was calling for a cat. And something called 'perk a set?' I couldn't make sense of it. She mentioned an aero-plane and something called a phone, and about a vampyre writing a diary?"

Crossing to him, Amara reached out, rubbing her brother's back. He stiffened. Amara never touched anyone. "She said she wanted to go home, Dev."

His face paled as he clutched Eliza's hand tightly. She wanted to go? Not that he blamed her. He'd been an ass to her, desperate to convince himself they could never be. Still, his heart thundered at the thought of her leaving him. *Don't leave me, Eliza. Please don't leave me.*

"She also said," Amara continued, her hand still moving

in slow, calming strokes, "she loved you." After pausing to let that sink in, Amara left the room.

Deveric stood there, his shoulders heaving and shuddering, his fingers clasping Eliza's, tears streaming openly down his face. He could hear his father's voice chiding him. *A Claremont does not cry.* It didn't stop the sobs from coming. She looked so pale, so tiny, so close to death. For a second, Mirabelle's face superimposed itself on Eliza's, and it was if he were standing in the same spot he'd stood three years ago, watching the life bleed out of his wife. *Eliza is not Mirabelle. Eliza is not Mirabelle.*

"And she will not die," he declared, his voice strong in spite of his weeping. "She will *not* die."

Wiping the tears from his eyes, he sat down next to Eliza, applying a cool compress to her head. His hands lingered on her face. He traced her eyebrows with his fingers and ran his thumb over her bottom lip. "I love you, too, Eliza James. God help me, I do."

CHAPTER 36

he doctor clucked as he leaned over Eliza, checking her pulse. "I don't understand it. Her heart is strong, her breathing has returned to normal. I see no reason for her not to have awoken." He held a hand to her forehead, his mouth turning down. "It's possible her brain sustained hidden damage from either the branch or the fall and cannot recover."

At the expletives Deveric uttered, the doctor cleared his throat and backed away from the bedside. He bent down for his bag.

"Shall I return in the morning?" he asked, the bobbing of his Adam's apple indicating his nervousness.

Don't bother, Deveric nearly snapped, but he checked himself and nodded. He turned to Eliza, ignoring the doctor.

"If I might, Your Grace," the doctor said, hesitation lacing his voice. "You need rest, too. Either she will recover, or she won't; it won't do you any good to take ill in trying to keep her from the grave."

Dev's eyes swung back to the doctor, piercing him with a murderous glare. "She will *not* die," he insisted, before commanding the doctor to leave.

As Deveric settled himself in by Eliza's side, Amara knocked at the door.

"He's right, you know," she said as she entered, obviously having overheard the doctor's words.

Deveric snarled. "She will not die. I let Mirabelle die. I let my daughter die. By God, Eliza *Will. Not. Die.*"

His sister was quiet. She walked to him, crouching down before him. She took both of his cheeks in her hands, forcing him to look at her. "You didn't kill Mirabelle, Dev. It's not your fault she died."

Deveric's whole body stiffened at his sister's words. Coll and Arth had argued the same thing. "Yes, it is," he bit out. "If I hadn't touched her, hadn't forced her."

Amara's eyes widened. "You actually believe that?" She shook her head. "You would never force yourself on a woman, brother. It's not who you are."

Deveric stared at the ground. "She didn't enjoy it," he whispered. "I shouldn't have."

"That is different. Some women are like that. But I don't think most. Mirabelle *was* fragile, but that was not your fault. She might have been better suited for a nunnery; she was not cut out for this world." Amara smoothed the hair back from his forehead. "You have to let it go."

His heart pounded. "I can't let her go," he admitted, his eyes flashing to Eliza.

"Not Eliza," Amara said. "This guilt that has consumed you, trapped you. You couldn't save Mirabelle. Nobody could. And you couldn't save Louisa. None of it was your fault."

His sister's words washed over him. He wanted so badly

to believe them. Truth be told, Amara had always been his favorite, though of course he loved all of his sisters. But Amara shared his volatile temperament.

At times, he'd been jealous she could display her emotions more openly than he could. Or so he'd thought; after her disgrace, he'd realized how much greater the restrictions were on women than men. Women who followed their hearts often got burned. As his sister had.

How he wished Evers hadn't fled, hadn't denied Dev the satisfaction of avenging Amara. Not that it would have done any good; he might have been able to redeem the family's honor, but his sister's was gone forever.

He rubbed his eyes with his fingers. "I can't," he whispered. "I can't lose her, Am."

Amara leaned in and folded her arms around him as they both looked at Eliza. "You won't."

Eliza's head hurt. She was so tired of her head hurting. "Make it stop," she whimpered. "It's like someone is beating a bass drum in there, Cat."

A soothing voice coaxed her into drinking some tepid water. "Can't I have ice?" she protested. "Or a Coke?" The scratchiness in her own voice irritated her. Why wouldn't her eyes open? "What happened?"

"You fell," the kind voice said. "But you're going to be all right. You're going to recover and be all right."

The voice sounded familiar, but Eliza couldn't quite place it. It wasn't Cat. Or Jill. Shannon? No.

She blinked as her eyelids opened, her eyes straining to

focus. "I'm hungry," she said to the figure standing at her side. "Can I have some pizza?"

At first, Eliza didn't recognize the woman standing near her. The woman's odd costume made her want to giggle, but her face was gentle. Familiar. *Amara,* her mind whispered. *Deveric's sister.*

At the thought of Deveric, Eliza's eyes whipped wide open. All was suddenly clear again. "I'm still here?" she exclaimed, grabbing at Amara's hand.

"Yes. Where else would you be?" Amara held the cup to Eliza's lips again.

"I, um. I thought maybe I was home," Eliza said before taking a sip.

"In Charlottesville? With your cat and your Facebook and your phone? Whatever those are." Amara's eyebrow rose, a smile tickling at the corners of her mouth. "I am glad you are awake. We have been quite worried. I need to go alert my brother. Rest now. Betsy will look after you."

Eliza turned her head to the maid, acknowledging her with a weak smile before drifting off to sleep again.

"She's awake?" Deveric exclaimed, leaping from his bed. He'd been resting for an hour, and that only at Amara's insistence she would remain by Eliza's side. "Why didn't you get me?"

"I just did, brother."

He made to run out the door, but Amara grabbed at his elbow. "She has likely fallen back asleep, but I promise you, she was awake. She spoke."

"She did?"

"Yes." Amara's eyebrows popped up and her lips pursed. "I think you have some explaining to do."

Dev's head whipped back around.

"But first, let us have something to eat. You need nourishment."

Reluctantly, he allowed his sister to lead him to the breakfast room, glad to see when they arrived that he and Amara were alone.

"No one else is up; it is only six in the morning." She buttered a slice of toast. "Now, I want to know the truth. Who *is* this Eliza James?"

He froze. "What do you mean?"

"It's clear she's not who you've said she is. Oh, not about the cousin part." Amara waved her hand dismissively. "I don't care about that. But it's something more than that, isn't it?"

Deveric said nothing.

"She talks about things of which I've never heard. *Pizza?* Some fellow named McDonald, and of something she calls a computer. She claims she can send an instant post through it to someone across the world."

"She said all of that to you?" His eyebrows rose.

"Not knowingly. At first, I dismissed it as delirious ravings. But she kept talking about you being there and knowing it was the year 2012, that you'd seen it with your own eyes. It made me think perhaps there was something deeper, something stranger, going on. Given your reaction, I'm right." She leaned forward on her elbows. "Would you care to explain?"

Deveric looked around the room.

"There are no servants," Amara assured him. "I sent them all to the kitchen."

He pulled at his rumpled neck cloth. "Yes."

"Yes? That's it? What does that mean?"

"Yes," he repeated. "There's something more going on. Eliza ... Eliza claims to be from the year 2012."

Amara stared at him with rounded eyes.

"She says her friend Cat has a magical manuscript which lets Cat write stories that come true. She insists Cat wrote a story that let Eliza travel through time to be here."

At that, Amara burst into loud guffaws. "She said this all *before* she struck her head? Good Lord, the woman is *mad!* She needs to be committed to Bedlam." She took another bite of her toast, her eyes twinkling with amusement. When Deveric remained silent, she swallowed, hard. "You're not serious, Deveric? You're teasing. You must be teasing."

He shook his head. "No, she truly said those things. And I believe her."

"What? That's preposterous!"

"I believe her. Because I *was* there, Amara. In 2012. I saw a number of the things of which she spoke. And the phone she mentioned? She has it. Here. She showed it to me; could show it to you. There are pictures on it, photo-graphs, they're called, of things the likes of which you could never imagine. I, too, fought long against it, but there's no other explanation, unless the both of us belong in a sanitarium."

Amara sat in stunned silence. At length, Deveric told her of the New Year's Eve ball, how he had been at Clarehaven and then suddenly not, of seeing the black box that played music, of the lights flashing through the window at blinding speed. He told her of the kiss, and how he had woken to find himself on the library settee, Eliza in his arms.

When he had finished, neither one of them said a word for quite some time.

When Amara did speak, her only words were, "But ...

why you?"

Deveric tapped his fingers together. "I had suspicions, but did not figure that piece out for a long time. Not until Eliza's accident, until how I nearly died, seeing her there, lifeless, on the ground. Now I see, now I believe, the part Eliza left out was that Cat wrote a story in which Eliza came here to find *me.* That's why I went forward to her, to bring her back here. It was so she could fall in love with me, and me with her. We needed each other for the story to work."

"I don't see how …" Amara finally whispered.

"I don't, either. But it is."

The door swished open and Becca and her mother entered the room.

"Promise me," Deveric whispered, his voice urgent, "that you won't reveal this. To *anyone.*"

"Your secrets are safe with me. Always."

CHAPTER 37

"You're awake! You're awake!" Freddy's excited squeals bounced around the chamber.

Eliza winced from the noise, which reverberated in her skull like a thousand hammers. She smiled, however, when she saw Freddy next to the bed, holding Pirate in his arms. The puppy wiggled to get down, but the boy gripped him to his side. "Told you she'd wake up, Pirate."

"Hi, Frederick."

"Why have you been sleeping so much?" His lip jutted out in a pout. "I haven't been able to visit the dogs much. I had to sneak Pirate in here today. Nurse Pritchett almost saw me!"

Eliza laughed, even as it made her head pound. "I didn't mean to be sleeping. How long has it been?"

"A week," came a deep voice from the entrance way as Deveric strode into the room.

"A week?" Her eyes widened. "What?—"

"You fell off that blasted horse. Hit your head." His voice was gruff, but tinged with worry, not anger.

I fell off a horse? How very Jane Austen, to secure a gentleman's attention through injury. For Deveric was definitely attentive; his eyes never left hers, the fierceness in them enough to weaken her already uneven pulse. She cringed as a stabbing pain pierced her head. *Not exactly the smartest way to go about it, Austen heroines. This sucks.*

"Frederick," he chastised, though his voice was gentle. "You should not be disturbing Mrs. James, much less have brought your dog into the house."

Frederick gulped at being caught by his father, but Eliza interjected. "It's all right. I'm happy to see a friendly face. Or two friendly faces, rather."

"Nonetheless, outside you both go. Return the dog to the kennel, and see Nurse about a bath. You smell of … stables."

Freddy flashed a sheepish grin. "Pirate ran through horse manure on the way here," he admitted, before ducking out the door.

Deveric remained a few feet from the bed. He wanted to throw himself at Eliza, to smother her with kisses and thank her for not leaving him, for not dying. She was still weak, however. Plus, truth be told, he wasn't sure where he stood with her, or what he ought to do.

"Dev." Her eyes brimmed with emotion.

"Eliza."

She swallowed. "I'm still here."

She's still here? What does she mean? "Of course. I knew you would pull through."

"I mean, I'm still here. In 1812. With you." A tear rolled

down her cheek.

Deveric sucked in a hard breath. What was she saying? That she didn't want to be with him? That she had been trying to leave? He could feel the blood drain from his face.

"I'm so glad," she said in a soft voice. "So glad." Her eyes closed and she drifted back to sleep.

Something shifted in Deveric's heart. It cracked. It expanded. It flew wide open. Tears pricked his eyes as he watched her chest rise and fall. He'd come so close to losing her. So close.

And yet, he didn't know what to do. He loved her. He knew that now. He loved this American with her bewildering tales of the future, this American who obviously loved his son, and had helped breach the distance between them. This American, whose happy attitude soothed his dour disposition. Her warmth, her tenderness, her love for his family that she wasn't able to hide; it was all he'd ever wanted. Yet so many things stood in their way. His mother. Society's expectations. And his fears.

How could he love her, how could he marry her, how could he ask her to be his wife, when he couldn't be a full husband to her? He wouldn't risk hurting her. He couldn't go through that a second time.

Yet the thoughts, the images, the possibilities cascaded endlessly through his head, crashing over him again and again like the tide beating at the shore.

Deveric darted from the room, desperate for something, anything to take his mind off Eliza. How cruel was the Universe, to send him an angel he couldn't have? He stalked down through the main entryway, ignoring the startled looks from Emmeline and Grace, who'd stood conversing there.

Once outside, he ran for the stables, desperate for escape,

for release. He saddled Lightning by himself, not waiting for a stable hand, and leapt on the horse's back, kicking his heels into Lightning's side, heaving a sigh of relief as the horse took off. He didn't know where he was headed; he just knew he needed to go. He needed to clear his head. He needed to forget it all.

Eliza blinked at the bright sunshine streaming in through the window. She looked around the room. She was alone. *I must have fallen asleep again. Deveric was here, talking to me, wasn't he? Freddy, too.* Maybe she'd been hallucinating, but she swore Dev had been at the foot of the bed, looking at her with the tenderest expression she'd ever seen.

She sighed. Things hadn't turned out as planned. By now, she thought she'd be back in Charlottesville, back in 2012, back with Cat … and William.

You could try again. You never made it to the stones. "No!" Eliza burst out, chasing away those thoughts. She wouldn't try again. She couldn't. She'd known when she opened her eyes and saw Deveric there, his eyes shadowed and his cheeks hollow, worry oozing out of every pore, that she couldn't leave him. There was something between them, something strong. Something she believed could be love.

Not only that, but she loved Frederick. She loved this family. And they liked her. *Except for Deveric's mother.* She ignored that voice in her head, shutting out the negative thoughts. She finally had the big circle she'd always wanted. How could she leave that?

Sure, she missed Cat. She missed her best friend terribly.

But Eliza hoped Cat had found the happy-ever-after she deserved. And if so, there wouldn't be space for Eliza anymore, anyway. She was okay with that; she was where she belonged.

She bit her lip. Was it enough? Was it enough that she'd fallen in love with the Duke of Claremont, with his son, with his family? One-sided love could never last. If he didn't return her feelings, if he wasn't interested in building a life with her, what would she do?

She could stay on as Frederick's governess, if the Dowager allowed it. But eventually, that wouldn't be enough. She wouldn't be able to stand on the sidelines day after day, wanting to be a part of this family, a part of Deveric, but never achieving it. It'd be like darts to the heart. That was why she'd run for the monolith.

"Are you okay, my lady?" Betsy asked as she entered the room.

Eliza smiled at Betsy's use of Eliza's expression. "Yes. Yes, I'm fine. A bit thirsty, though."

Betsy poured her a cup of water from the pitcher on the table to the side of the bed, and then handed her the cup. After a few sips, Eliza asked, "Was Dev—I mean, the Duke in here earlier? I could have sworn I was talking with him, but perhaps it was my imagination."

Betsy bobbed her head. "Yes, my lady. He hasn't left your side, matter of fact. Lady Amara has had to force him to rest at times. He's been nursing you himself, not allowing most of us near you."

Eliza's heart raced at Betsy's words. He had? Surely that was a sign that he loved her, wasn't it? Why else would a duke sacrifice himself, when he had plenty of servants who could have tended to her?

"I'm surprised he's not here now," Betsy added as she

offered Eliza her tooth stick and baking soda. Eliza took them gratefully and rinsed out her mouth. "I'm sure he'll be back any minute. Is there anything else you need, my—Eliza?"

"No, thank you, Betsy," Eliza said, fatigue overtaking her again. "Just rest."

Deveric stood within the circle of stones. He'd often come here as boy, had relished the peaceful feeling it gave him, a peace he sought now.

Who had put the stones here? What purpose had they served? Had others come here through the millennia to seek answers, as well?

Why had Eliza wanted to come here? How had she even known about it, this sacred place? He made a face. There were so many things he didn't know, didn't understand.

He sat down on a flat rock in the middle, watching as Lightning roamed around him, munching on grass.

"What should I do?" he asked the horse. Lightning whinnied in response. "Should I marry her? Could I possibly build a life with her, a life better than I had with Mirabelle, a marriage better than either mine or my parents'? Could it work?"

She certainly had responded to him in the few intimate moments they'd shared. Was it possible Coll was right, Amara was right, and that it hadn't been him, but Mirabelle? Could Eliza be different, be not only able to take but give as passionately as he? She was not the fragile flower his first wife had been; she was solid, strong, full of life. "Is it possible, Lightning?"

At those words, a ray of sunshine rose over the eastern rock, striking him full in the face. The warmth soothed him, even as the brightness blinded him. His body flooded with unexpected energy, as if illuminated from the inside out. He closed his eyes, letting the feeling run through him. *Yes*, the sun seemed to whisper. *Yes.* The simple word echoed through his head. *It's worth the risk. Yes.*

He sat a while longer, his body resonating with joy, his heart swelling with love, his mind convinced of what he needed. He needed Eliza.

Springing up, he called to the horse. "Let's go, boy. I have a question I need to ask her."

CHAPTER 38

everic bounded through the front door, eagerness causing him to take the stairs two at a time. Several maids stared at him, but he ignored them, racing up to the landing and down the hallway toward Eliza's chamber.

He ran directly into his mother.

"Oh!" she exclaimed as he reached his arms out to steady her.

"Mother," he said. "My apologies. I didn't see you there. I was—"

"—Rushing to see Mrs. James?"

He grinned widely. "To see my future wife."

The Dowager's jaw dropped. "But—but she's a commoner."

"Yes."

"She's—American."

"Yes."

"You're the Duke of Claremont."

"Yes."

Her shoulders sank. "Think of the family."

"I'm always thinking of the family," he growled. "I thought of the family when I protected Amara from scandal. I thought of the family when I married Mirabelle, wanting to satisfy Father's wishes, though he was already dead. I thought of the family when I covered for his peccadillos, when I ensured nobody knew he had died in his mistress's bed, Mother. I think of the family all of the time, and yet grave things keep happening." His eyes pierced hers. "Don't I deserve a chance at something good?"

His mother pinched her lips, looking away from him. "Of course," she whispered, after several tense, silent moments.

It was all Deveric could do to keep his mouth from falling open. He'd expected protest, not affirmation.

"I'm sorry, my dear," she went on. "I've watched you this past week, watched how you've fretted, how you've suffered. As much as I have fought against this Eliza James, wanting to keep her from hurting this family, from hurting you, my heart ripped in two, seeing you in such pain.

"I didn't think you'd survive after Mirabelle, and my granddaughter. I couldn't bear for you to go through that torment again. I thought I was protecting you, like I wish … like I wish I'd had someone to protect my heart from your father."

She walked over to a portrait hanging on the wall, a picture of his father in his youth. Staring at it, she said, "I'm sorry I've let my own disappointments turn me into who I've become."

She touched his father's painted hand. "I was not always this hard. I wanted a grand love, too, you see. I thought I found it in your father. He was all I ever wanted. But I … I was not enough for him. Never enough." She broke off for

332

a moment, her eyes flicking back to her son's. "When he stepped out on me, it nearly killed me. I loved him. I loved your father, Dev."

He made to walk over to her, but she held up her hand and shook her head. "Let me finish. I convinced myself if I was the best duchess I could be, if I followed every rule and observed every bit of decorum, I could win him back. And if not that, at least no one else would be able to find fault with me, not like he clearly had.

"It didn't work. He said I had become … boring. Not only that, I found myself accused of adultery by my adulterous husband." She bit out a caustic laugh. "As if I could ever do to him what he had done to me. And yet, I was still weak. I couldn't refuse him when he returned home, even though I knew he'd been with other women. I loved him too much."

She walked back over to Deveric, smoothing his hair off of his forehead, just as she had done when he was a small boy. "I told myself if I grew strong, if I grew hard, that he would no longer have power over me." She exhaled slowly. "I was wrong. He still has power over me, and he's long dead."

She sucked in a breath, her shoulders shuddering. "I thought I was shielding you, shielding this family, by trying to keep you away from this Mrs. James. She was too different, too foreign, a commoner; everything I thought you didn't need, everything I thought would only make life harder."

A single tear spilled down over her cheek. "I have seen in these last days just how much the American means to you, seen that this is much deeper than simple desire. I see now you are a different man than your father. You are like me. You are faithful. You will love only once. What kind of mother would I be to keep you from your chance at happiness?"

Deveric crushed her into his arms. It was the first time

they had embraced in years.

"It will take me time to accept this, dearest. To accept her. But I will not attempt to stop you any longer. Go to her," she said, the tears flowing openly now.

His own eyes threatened to spill over. "Thank you, Mother." He wiped a tear from her face. "Thank you."

Eliza stood at the edge of the bed, clutching the post, praying for the dizziness to subside. She was so tired of lying around. She wanted to get up, to *do* something.

The door swung open and Deveric strode through. When he saw her standing there, unsteady on her feet, he raced to her. "What are you doing?" he chided, fear lacing his voice. "You need to be lying down!"

"All I've been doing is lying down," she grumbled, even as she grabbed on to his shirtfront for support. She was so close to him, his delicious woodsy scent enveloped her. She closed her eyes and breathed in, savoring his nearness. Leaning her head on his shoulder, she sighed as he wrapped his arms around her.

"Ah, Eliza. My sweet Eliza," he said, his lips brushing her hair.

She pulled back and looked up at him, drinking in those vibrant green eyes, which glowed with emotion. She said nothing, the expression on his face, so gentle and yet so fierce, hypnotizing her.

He leaned down and brushed his lips against hers. She knew he meant it to be a light kiss, nothing more. But as he tried to lift his head, she snaked her arm up and around his neck, sinking her fingers into his hair, pulling him back down to her. She kissed his chin, then the corner of his mouth, then settled her lips on his, tasting him, teasing him, darting her tongue out and licking his lower lip. He groaned and opened his mouth, returning her caress, drinking her in. She let him. His hand slid up her side and around to her front, over her breast. Her nipple puckered as his fingers traced it, and she moaned.

At the sound, Deveric's eyes flew open and he released her mouth. "Oh, God, Eliza, I'm so sorry." A muscle in his cheek ticced.

Eliza grimaced. "Will you stop apologizing every time you kiss me, you big idiot?"

"Idiot?" he repeated.

"Yes. Idiot. I like you kissing me. I want you to kiss me. For Pete's sake, I need you to kiss me."

He brushed a piece of hair out of her face. "But you're still recovering. I don't want to hurt you. I never want to hurt you."

"The only way you hurt me is when you stop, dummy."

He chuckled. "Your choice of vocabulary is making me doubt your claims."

She nipped at his lips. "Get used to it, blockhead."

He laughed, a full, rich bellow. She loved it, the joy she heard in his voice.

Eliza let go of him and sat back down on the bed. "In truth," she confessed, "I am a little dizzy. While I think that might just be the power of your kisses, I probably should lie down. Will you lie with me?"

She moved higher on the bed, patting the space next to her.

"You want me to lie with you?" he repeated.

She smirked. "What? Do you think I'm going to impugn

your honor?"

"I might impugn yours," he teased.

"A woman can hope."

He stalked to the door, and for a moment, she worried he was leaving her, that she'd gone too far. Instead, he thrust the bolt in the lock and then drew the curtains closed over the windows, before returning to her, his eyes dark, expression inscrutable.

Deveric settled himself on the bed next to her, lying on his side so they were face-to-face. He reached out and traced a finger down her cheek, a myriad of emotions skittering across his face. "Eliza, why did you ask Becca to go to the monolith? How did you even know it was there?"

She stared into his rich green eyes, mesmerized by the pulsating orbs. "I … I … Cat wrote about it. She told me if I ever wanted to go home, I should find the monolith."

He said nothing, waiting for her to continue.

"I was to sit on the rock in the middle of the stones and wish to be with William Dawes."

Deveric's eyes widened. "Dawes? Everett's brother?"

"Not *your* William Dawes. The one from Virginia. *My* William Dawes."

He didn't like the sound of her calling any man hers. *Except me. I want her to call me hers.*

"If I wished hard enough, Cat said, if I pledged my whole heart to loving William and having him love me, she thought that might bring me back."

Deveric's whole body went rigid. She'd wanted to leave

him that badly? For another man?

"But I already knew after only a few minutes on that horse I couldn't do it, Dev," she said, her eyes glistening as she traced a finger across one of his eyebrows. "I couldn't. My heart isn't with Mr. Dawes. It never will be. It's with—it's with Freddy. And Amara. And Becca and Emmeline. It's with Clarehaven. It's with this family. But most of all, it's with you. I love you, Deveric Mattersley. With all of my heart."

He could see the sheen of moisture in her eyes, a sheen he knew was reflected in his own. He should be careful, shouldn't touch her, but it was as if a force beyond his understanding pushed him toward her. For a second, his brain recognized it *was* a force beyond understanding that had brought them together. Then he was dipping his lips to hers, tasting her sweet essence, and all thought was forgotten.

Her fingers dug into his hair, pulling him closer. He gladly acquiesced. He peppered her lips with kisses, and then moved over her cheek, nipping at her earlobe. "What you do to me, Eliza," he whispered, before returning to her mouth.

She said nothing, merely stroking his face before moving her hand down, unbuttoning his waistcoat, each release sending surges of anticipation through him. Who knew the mere act of unbuttoning could feel so erotic? And then she was tugging at his shirt, pulling it from his breeches. Her fingers slid up underneath the cloth and over his belly, sending shivers through him. It had been so long since anyone had touched him there.

"I love that you have hair here," she said as her fingers danced across his chest. "Too many men in my era shave all their hair off. It looks weird."

Shave chest hair? He hardly had time to ponder that curious statement before she was undoing the buttons on his shirt, as well.

"Eliza," he said, the last bit of reason reminding him now was not the time or the place. He didn't want to hurt her, to endanger her fragile health.

"Mmm?" she murmured as she planted kisses along his pecs, stopping to lick his nipple.

A zing of electricity went through him even as he tried to pull away. "We can't."

At that her fingers stilled. "Why not? Because we're unwed? I'm not a virgin; I've been married before." A fingernail traced its way across his bellybutton, distracting him. "I know what I'm doing."

"No. That's not it. I mean, yes, that's it, but no." He sighed, rolling over onto his back. "I can't."

She eyed the bulge in his breeches. "Other parts of you tell me you can."

He coughed, unused to such frank talk. "I want to. Believe me, I want to. But I can't. I don't want to hurt you. There's … too much of me."

Eliza laughed out loud. Color flooded his cheeks.

"I know men like to boast about their size," she said. "But I highly doubt that you are too much."

"You don't understand," he insisted. "Mirabelle didn't care for the intimate side of marriage. She said it hurt."

Eliza arched a brow. "She's not the only woman you've ever been with, right?"

Deveric closed his eyes. "I should not be having this conversation with a lady." Running his hand through his hair, he admitted, "No. Of course not. But a few others expressed … concern, too." Though they hadn't complained after, he had to admit.

"I'm not concerned. If a woman can birth a baby, she

can accommodate a man. Even a well-endowed one." She waggled her eyebrows at him.

When he said nothing, she frowned, her brow creasing. "Is that why—" She hesitated, her fingers reaching out to stroke his side again. "Is this what's kept you from being with me, kept you running? You think you'll hurt me, if we have—if we make love?"

His throat constricted, and he swallowed before answering. "I'm afraid I'll do more than that. Even if you … tolerated intimacies with me, the idea of you—" He broke off, overwhelmed by a vision of Eliza swollen with his child. It sent jolts through him, unexpected thrills as much as terror. "Mirabelle died giving birth, Eliza. She died because I insisted on a physical connection, on trying for another child. If I hadn't done that—"

Eliza's delicate brows twisted. She was quiet for a moment. "Dev, are you saying you think you killed your wife?"

He squeezed his eyes shut, his mouth flattening into a harsh line. "My wife. My daughter." He swallowed again. "I can't, I *won't*, do that to someone else."

She traced a finger over his eyebrow, her eyes brimming with emotion. "But she gave birth to Frederick. Were there problems in that birth?"

Dev frowned. "No." The midwife had assured him everything had gone splendidly, in fact, though Mirabelle had used different terms.

"Then how can you blame yourself? That makes no sense."

Tears pricked the back of his eyes. "Amara said the same. Coll, too. But don't you see, Eliza? Don't you see I can't risk it, won't risk you?"

"No, actually."

His eyes widened at her simple, matter-of-fact response.

"Frankly, I think these hips were made for child-bearing." She snorted before her face grew utterly serious.

Stroking her hand down the side of his face, she cupped his cheek as her eyes burned into his. "If we live our lives always assuming the worst is going to happen, that's not living. I lost my husband. I lost my parents. But I never lost hope I would find happiness, Deveric. I couldn't. I wouldn't have been able to go on if I had. It's what … it's that hope that brought me to you."

Deveric lay still, his thoughts and emotions tumbling over each other. He couldn't believe she was so nonchalant about it all, so unconcerned about the risk to her person. And then what she'd said about not living, about hope … It rang so true.

At length, he said, "You astound me."

Eliza rolled over to him, climbing on top and pressing her full body into his. "You intoxicate me," she said before kissing him again.

He groaned as she moved her lips down across his neck, reveling in the frissons of electricity ricocheting through his body. Could she be right? Mirabelle had birthed Frederick, after all.

He wanted to believe so badly.

Or at least one part of him did.

CHAPTER 39

is hands reached for the laces on the back of her gown. He loosened them and those of the stays underneath, pushing them down over her shoulders.

She sat up so she could pull her arms out of the top of the dress, allowing her breasts to fall free. His eyes widened as he drank in the sight of her.

"You're so beautiful." He reached to stroke her breast with one of his hands. "So beautiful, Eliza."

He pulled her forward again, just enough so that his mouth could taste one of the orbs. She sighed in satisfaction as he moved from one to the other, licking her, suckling her, absorbing the deliciousness of her.

"I want to see you, too," she said after a moment, her voice coming in small pants.

His groin jumped at her bold statement. Mirabelle had never wanted to see him unclothed. He had frightened her. But Eliza—Eliza was different. Thank God Eliza was different.

"All right." He hardly believed his own voice. *What was wrong with him?* Surely he wasn't going to seduce this woman, wasn't going to risk hurting her. *Trust in this,* a voice echoed in his head.

As Eliza's fingers pushed his shirt off of his shoulders and then skittered to the buttons on his breeches, he realized he wasn't exactly the one doing the seducing. He lay back, watching her face to gauge her reaction to the full of him. When he sprang free from the constraints of his smalls, he was sure she'd recoil in disgust. She didn't.

Eliza, his Eliza, smiled, a gentle smile at first, and then one that turned quite saucy. "This ought to be fun," she said as her fingers traced up one side of him and down the other. His cock constricted and flexed under her ministrations, and it was all he could do not to flip her over onto her back right then and there.

Slow down. Slow down. "Slow down," he said. "I want to see you. I want to savor you."

Eliza's eyes widened as if surprised, but she stopped, her hand merely holding him. "Slow down? That's not something I've heard often," she said, chuckling.

A bolt of jealousy streaked through him. "Have you been with so many men?" he said, more sharply than intended.

Her eyebrow winged up. "No. Only two. Not that that's any of your business, really. How many women have *you* been with?"

After a moment, he said, "Five. And you're right; I had no right to ask that. It's just—the thought of someone else holding you, someone else touching you drives me mad."

"Right back 'atcha," Eliza answered. "But you're with me now. And you're the only one I want to be with." She leaned down and kissed him again, her lips opening over his. For long moments, they savored each other, tongues dancing and retreating, a meeting of bodies hinting at delights to come. *And of souls,* he thought.

"Forever," he said, surprising himself. "You'll be with me forever."

Eliza pulled back, an astonished look on her face. But before she could say anything, he whipped her over onto her back, pressing the full length of his body into hers. She moaned.

Instantly, he rolled back off. "I'm sorry." He scanned her face. "Did I hurt you?"

She bopped him on the shoulder. "No, you idiot. I liked that. I want more of that!"

She reached for him, but he was tugging at her dress, pulling it and her undergarments up and off as she leaned forward to aid him. He drank in the sight of her, his own Eve, a temptation grander than anything Eden's serpent could ever have offered. "Oh my God, Eliza. You are perfect. Simply perfect."

Eliza flushed. "Am I not a bit too much?" she said, her voice small and unsteady as she self-consciously touched her stomach.

"No!" he declared, running his hands up her thigh, over her hip, and over the small mound of her belly, moving her fingers away. "You are all woman. Luscious. Ripe." He ran his fingertips up her abdomen to her breasts. "I'm particularly fond of these. Leave the apples to Adam, I say; I prefer melons."

She chortled at that, and he was glad to see the doubt leave her eyes. She reached out to him. "Come back to me. I want you." She wiggled an eyebrow in comical fashion. "Also, it's darn cold."

She grinned, her eyes dancing, as he pushed his own clothing off and shoved it over the side of the bed. "Cheeky wench," he said, covering her once again with his length. He reached for the quilt and pulled it up over them both. "There. Satisfied?"

"Oh no." She ground her hips against his. "I'm just getting started."

A guttural sound emerged from Deveric's throat. Her enthusiastic directness excited him like nothing else. He buried his face between her breasts, delighting in their warmth. Her hands roamed over his back and down over his buttocks, his nerves firing wherever she touched. He pressed against her and in response she made the most delicious sounds, arching up against him.

"Please, Deveric," she whispered.

Surely she wasn't ready yet? Surely it was too soon? He reached down between her legs and was surprised to find her soft and wet.

"Yes," she breathed into his ear. "Yes."

She moved her hand from his rear to in between them, grasping him and guiding him. He hesitated for a fraction of a second, and then slid into her, slowly, so slowly, as she panted and mewled against him. He gritted his teeth to keep from plunging full in. *Please, God, say I'm not hurting her.*

"Oh, Dev," she said. "You feel so—you feel so—"

He waited for her to tell him to stop, waited for her to say it wasn't going to work.

"—*good*," she finished, as she placed both hands on his buttocks and pushed him all the way in.

"Oh God, Eliza," he cried, relishing the full length of him inside of her. "You're all right? You're truly all right?"

"Yes, silly man," she panted. "More than yes. Now can

344

we stop talking and …" She thrust her hips up against him, letting him know without a doubt what she wanted.

He pulled back and then buried himself in her again. Her skin was flushed, her eyes closed, a blissful expression on her face. "Yes, yes, yes," he said, punctuating each thrust. "Yes, Eliza, my Eliza, yes."

Her fingers slid in between them again, pressing against herself just above their joining. He slowed down. "Do you want me to do that?" he asked, his chest heaving.

"No," she exclaimed. "Just … harder. Harder!" The sight of her touching herself, the feeling of being in her, the idea that she was relishing this as much as he was, drove him over the edge. Pounding into her, he could feel her constrict around him, heard her own shouts of pleasure. Ecstasy flooded through him. Leaning down, he drew her lips into a fierce kiss.

"I love you," he chanted against her mouth as the spasms overtook him. "I love you, Eliza James."

She clutched him to her, savoring every last instant. *Oh Lord, Cat, what a man you made for me.* She smiled sleepily, chiding herself for thinking of her friend while she lay in the arms of this man. Or underneath this man, really.

She felt his belly contract as he pushed up on his arms before rolling off to her side. Pulling her close, he nuzzled her hair. "I pray you are not laughing at my performance," he said. "Next time will be better. It had, uh, just been a long time, and—"

She laughed outright before he could finish. "You think

I'm complaining? That was awesome. *Better* than awesome." She snuggled into his warmth. "I was just thanking Cat for giving you to me."

"Likewise," he said with a yawn. "I am full of awe." His eyelids fluttered closed.

She watched him as he settled into a relaxed sleep. She was tired, too, and knew she should rest. All she'd done for the last week was rest, though. And as if she could go to sleep now, after sharing the most intimate emotional and physical connection she'd ever had.

A flash of guilt zapped her when she thought of Greg. She'd loved him, too. But this was different. This was beyond special. This was a connection surpassing time, a love for eternity. She closed her eyes and settled in next to Deveric, vowing she would find a way to repay Cat for all her friend had done for her.

Deveric awoke to a warm body pressing into him. Eliza. He rolled to his side and snaked an arm around her waist, pulling her close to pepper her shoulder with light kisses. "Good morning. Or evening. Or whenever it is," he whispered, his voice husky.

Eliza turned toward him, her eyes flying to the window. Sunlight peeked out from the edges of the curtains. "What time is it? How long have we been in here? Does everybody know?"

Deveric chuckled at the panic in her voice, his fingers dancing over her hip. He'd thought *he'd* have been the one panicking in this situation, but he felt oddly calm.

"It's all right, dearest Eliza. Or perhaps I should say, it's okay. No one will begrudge me a little time with my Duchess-to-be."

At that, Eliza sat up and stared at him. "Duchess-to-be?"

"Well, of course. I've now thoroughly compromised you."

"We thoroughly compromised each other," she retorted. "But just because we made love doesn't mean we have to get married."

His face stiffened. "You don't wish to marry me?" Fear constricted his breathing.

"Of course I do." Exasperation showed through in her tone. "But I rather expected to be asked, not informed." She sighed, brushing the hair out of her face.

Deveric watched her, this goddess, *his* goddess, sitting upright in bed without a stitch on. He leaned in and pressed his lips to her stomach. She shivered, goosebumps rising on her skin. He looked up with a devilish grin.

"Oh, get off it. I'm just cold!" She shoved at his shoulder, but the side of her mouth quirked up. She winked at him before lying back down, burrowing under the blankets and up against him.

He stroked her back, pondering all that had happened in such a short time. Had someone told him a month ago he'd reconsider all of his thoughts on love, on marriage, on society, he'd have laughed in their face. He was a Claremont. Claremonts behaved in expected ways.

And then this whirlwind entered his life. Against all possibility, against all logic and rationality, he found himself ensconced in bed—naked—with a woman two hundred years younger than he was.

At that thought, he winced. That hadn't sounded good. A woman opposite from him in so many ways, but one who had managed to make him feel complete again. It was as if the final piece of the puzzle, missing for so long, had fallen into place at last.

He pulled himself away from her and exited the bed. Eliza gasped—perhaps as much from the absence of warmth as from his unexpected departure; he didn't know. Worry etched across her face, but before she could say anything, he dropped to one knee.

"Dev!" she exclaimed. "You're naked!"

"So I am," he said. He glanced down at himself for a moment and then back at her. "And from the look of things, all of me would like nothing better than to hop back into bed with you right now."

She giggled, clapping her hand over her mouth.

"But I find myself with a question to ask you." He pressed his hand to his chest, looking for all intents and purposes like a lovelorn Shakespearean character—albeit a naked one. "Mrs. Eliza James, time-traveler, unpredictable American, adopted cousin, charmer of children, speaker of odd phrases, and other half of my heart. Will you do me the highest honor and consent to be my wife?"

Eliza's mouth had fallen open as he spoke. She leapt from the bed and bowled him over, the two of them rolling onto the cold floor. "Eek!" she shrieked before springing back up.

Deveric raised himself slowly to his feet. "That was not exactly the answer for which I was hoping," he said, as he reached for the blanket on the bed.

"Yes." She wrapped her arms around him as he settled the blanket around them both. "Yes, Deveric Mattersley, Duke of Claremont, eater of cherry tarts, rider of scary horses, master of my destiny, my own personal Mr. Darcy. I will marry you."

He frowned. "Who is this Mr. Darcy of whom you speak?"

"I'll tell you later," she said, before she pressed her lips against his neck and her hands to parts farther south.

"Much later," he agreed, as they rolled onto the bed. They said nothing else for hours.

CHAPTER 40

"Oh, I'm glad you're well enough to come to London with us, Eliza!" Emmeline hopped up and down, clapping her hands. "We shall have such fun!"

"I'm glad that we shall be sisters," Becca said, gazing at Eliza fondly. "I'm so dreadfully sorry about Petunia."

Eliza waved off Becca's apology with one hand. "For the last time, Becca, it was not—"

A small voice broke in from the side. "I'm glad I'm going, too. I want to see the menagerie!"

"Frederick, do not interrupt your elders," the Dowager said, but she tempered her words with a smile. "Now let's be out and into the carriages; I want to reach Town by sundown."

The Mattersley family filed out of Clarehaven and into the small caravan of coaches awaiting them. "Goodness, how many books did you pack?" Emmeline said to Grace.

"For heaven's sake, we all know it's *your* dresses taking up all the space," Grace muttered, pulling out a small tome from beneath her arm.

Eliza smiled at the women surrounding her. Deveric, Frederick, Chance, and the Dowager were riding in the carriage ahead of her. While Eliza missed Dev, she was actually grateful for the time with the sisters; had Dev been here, she'd only have been thinking of kissing him, and touching him, and …

Emmeline tilted her head. "What are you thinking about, dearest cousin? Soon-to-be sister?"

"Given the color of her cheeks, I'd say nothing of *your* concern, surely," Becca interjected.

Grace had her nose in her book, but the corners of her mouth curled up in amusement.

As the horses took off, the countryside meandered by, rather than flew. It was certainly a different pace of life, traveling by horse-drawn carriage instead of car. Had they been on an interstate, Eliza wouldn't have appreciated her surroundings nearly as much; they'd have passed by too quickly. Here, she could admire the trees on the horizon, the occasional small house, the sheep grazing in pastures.

Of course a car would be far more comfortable, considering how the carriage lurched about. How had any of them bought her story about sleeping the whole way from London? She didn't think anyone could sleep through this.

When they finally arrived, it was all Eliza could do to keep her jaw off the ground. She'd been in London before, of course.

But not Regency London.

A few buildings were familiar, but much of the city looked

vastly different from her twenty-first century recollections. She soaked in everything she could as they made their way slowly through the noisy, bustling streets, the cacophony a sharp change after weeks in the country.

The Mattersley sisters were anxiously discussing the night's social event—a ball thrown by the Earl and Countess of Redbury. Eliza listened to their animated conversation with amusement. Emmeline knew gossip about nearly every debutante and potential gentleman, and speculated on who might become engaged to whom. Becca only cared how often she could go riding, until Emmeline mentioned several Regency bachelors who were known to be in possession of a fine stable. Grace insisted she cared not a whit what eligible men might attend the ball; all she wished was to visit Hatchard's, to see what new books they might have.

"There it is!" she exclaimed, as they passed the bookseller on Piccadilly.

Amara said nothing. None of the sisters took note, but Eliza, who was sitting next to her, touched her hand to Amara's knee. "You okay?"

A ghost of a smile crossed her soon-to-be sister-in-law's face. "Yes. I am thinking of something, something perhaps with which you could aid me. I should like to talk with you about it at greater length in private, if you are amenable."

Eliza couldn't imagine what she could help Amara with, but she was more than ready to do so; she'd grown so fond of Deveric's sister. *Cat would like her, too. I just know it.*

"There it is!" Emmeline clapped her hands. "Oh, I'm so ready to be done in this carriage. Any longer, and I fear my brain would be jarred loose."

"Who says it hasn't been already?" Becca said, poking at her sister.

Eliza pressed her face to the small window, staring at Claremont House as they approached. Good God, could it *be* any more magnificent? The house surpassed her wildest imaginings, a glorious mansion in the middle of Mayfair.

She wondered briefly on which street they were—she didn't remember any mansion as grand as this when she'd visited in the 2000s. It saddened her to think this house would ever disappear. She preferred to imagine it hadn't; that she just hadn't ventured to that part of London at the time.

The carriages stopped in front of the home, servants gathering immediately to help the ladies out.

"We should hurry—we haven't much time to prepare for the ball," Emmeline said, as she alighted.

Guilt tickled at Eliza's skin; they'd planned to arrive in London far earlier, until her accident. When she tried to apologize, though, the Dowager interrupted her. "Nonsense! It's more important that we arrived together, as a family."

With her children watching her as if she'd grown two heads, the former Dragon smiled—a true smile. "If anyone is going to challenge Mrs. James, it shall be me. And having already done that, and lost, I shall now ensure that not a word is spoken against her rather less conventional ways. Because in my losing, we all won." She beamed at Deveric.

Tears threatened to spill over Eliza's cheeks at how much had changed between her and the Dowager—and between the Dowager and everyone else—since Eliza's accident. Deveric's mother had even promised to help Eliza with the ins and outs of navigating the *ton*. Eliza wasn't quite sure what had happened to bring about the transformation, but she wasn't complaining.

As everyone else climbed the few stairs to the house, Eliza asked Deveric if they could walk a bit first. She wanted to stretch her legs—and she wanted a few minutes alone with him, before she was thrown into what she was sure would be an overwhelming next few weeks and months. It'd been one thing to interact with the relatively small number of people at the Clarehaven house party; rubbing elbows with the entirety of the *ton* in London was a daunting prospect indeed. *Eleanor Roosevelt, baby. Just keep telling yourself, "Eleanor Roosevelt."*

"You don't wish to rest? The trip didn't do you ill?" Dev's face was so adorably concerned, she had to lean in and press a kiss to his cheek.

"No way. I want to see everything! I want to see what's different and what's the same. But for right now, I really want to walk in Grosvenor Square. It's the most famous romance novel setting in many of the books I read, and while I strolled through it in my era, I want to see what it looks like now."

He chuckled. "Your wish is my command," he said, extending his elbow. "It is only a street away." She placed her arm through his, and they walked along, Eliza uncharacteristically silent as she took everything in.

"Oh, it's beautiful!" she said upon reaching the Square. Many a gentleman tipped his hat to Deveric, and several women passed by in open carriages. "Much of it feels the same, surprisingly. Except, of course, that the American Embassy isn't at the west end."

"The Americans build an embassy here? In Grosvenor Square?" Indignation fired in Deveric's voice.

Eliza merely clasped his arm with hers, and breathed in deeply. *Eww.* Perhaps that wasn't the best idea; the smells of animals and coal laced the air, even in this part of town. "I can't believe I'm here. I can't believe I'm standing in London, in 1812. I can't believe I'm with you. Deveric Mattersley.

Duke of Claremont. My future husband."

"I wouldn't be anywhere else, my love."

Over the next month, Eliza visited nearly every place she'd ever read about, plus many she hadn't. Miss Walters in Cavendish Square provided her with an entirely new, unbelievably luxurious wardrobe, not to mention hats, bonnets, and other accessories from Mrs. Bell.

She rode in a barouche in Hyde Park with the Mattersley sisters, doing the best she could not to gape at the *ton* who passed, debutantes and dandies, Regency bucks and portly bachelors, matrons and young misses alike. Of course Emmeline knew them all, and regaled the sisters with the latest *on dits. It's like celebrity spotting in America.* Minus the paparazzi, at least.

They'd bumped into Deveric's friends there, the Duke of Arthington, the Marquess of Emerlin, and even Everett Dawes, Earl of Stoneleigh. He bore a startling resemblance to the Dawes Eliza had met in 2012, though even better-looking. She understood why Dev said all the ladies were mad for him.

The gentlemen had exchanged quite polite conversation with each of the ladies, but if Eliza wasn't mistaken, Emerlin's eyes lingered a little long on Becca. *Now wouldn't that be interesting? Probably shouldn't tell Dev, though—nothing like an overly protective brother to sour a relationship's prospects.*

It was strange at first not to see the double-decker busses or London taxis she loved, strange to see not paved but cobbled, gravel, or even dirt roads, strange that much of what she associated with modern London—the Houses of Parliament, Big Ben, Trafalgar Square, hadn't even been built yet. But then again, she got to see things long since gone by her era, including Astley's Amphitheater and the well-known—and here newly opened—Egyptian Hall.

They ate ices at Gunter's, meandered through Green Park, shopped at Fortnum and Mason, and strolled down Bond Street, where Deveric pointed out the infamous Gentleman Jackson's boxing salon.

"Do you take lessons?" she'd asked him.

"Lessons?" he'd answered in mock disgust. "I could *give* lessons, my lady." Given his muscular chest and arms, she had no doubt he was right. *Thank you, Mr. Jackson.*

Though disappointed she wasn't allowed to walk down St. James's Street—it was definitely the province of men in this era—she delighted in shocking Deveric by telling him that not only did White's and Brook's still stand, and were still gentlemen's clubs, but that she'd peeked in the windows of both. "Sacrilege, Eliza," he'd said, as she dissolved into giggles.

Frederick begged to visit the Tower of London, to see the Royal Menagerie there, so on a sunny afternoon, they went. For Eliza, it was quite the experience to see lions and baboons roaming the grounds; when she had visited, the only wildlife left had been the ravens.

As they strolled along Piccadilly one early May afternoon, Eliza asked to turn down Albemarle Street. They'd passed it many a time, but never ventured in. "John Murray has his offices here," she said to Deveric, by way of explaining her interest.

"John Murray?"

"Oh, he published Jane Austen's works. Although, wait—that was her later ones." Eliza paused for a moment, thinking.

"Thomas Egerton published *Sense and Sensibility*. Next year, he will publish *Pride and Prejudice*—which I suppose means Miss Austen is working on its final touches."

It thrilled Eliza from head to toe to think that Jane Austen was, right now, working on what would arguably become her masterpiece. "Could we go visit Mr. Egerton? I would so like to thank him for publishing her amazing books."

Deveric nodded. "Of course. I admit, however, I don't know where his office is."

"Thirty, Charing Cross," Eliza replied promptly, eliciting a chuckle from Deveric.

"You do know quite a bit about this Miss Austen," he said. "Perhaps I should warn her she has a crazed admirer."

Eliza whacked him on the nose lightly with her purse. *Wait, no, reticule.* Purses were reticules here. He kissed her in response, much to the astonishment of the group of young ladies passing by with their maids. Giggles trailed behind them as Eliza and Deveric walked on.

It was perhaps unusual for a duke to travel such a distance on foot, rather than by coach, but Eliza couldn't get enough of the sights and sounds of the city, and often stopped to examine a building, carriage, or anything else that caught her fancy. Luckily, Deveric indulged her.

As they approached Mr. Egerton's place of business, a tallish woman with brown, curly hair exited the front door, holding a thick passel of papers to her chest. Next to her walked a tall, vaguely familiar-looking man of similar age.

Eliza's heart raced. "Is that ... Is it? No, it couldn't be."

Deveric's eyebrows puckered. "Whom do you see? I see no one of acquaintance here."

"I think—I think it's Jane Austen herself!"

CHAPTER 41

    liza gasped, halting herself before she could run forward to greet her idol. How likely was it, after all, that she would run into *the* Jane Austen here in London? Granted, London wasn't nearly the size it would become, but it was still a large city. And who was to say Miss Austen was even *here?* It was far more likely she was at Chawton Cottage. Right?

Eliza had to know. "Pardon me," she burst out as they neared the man and woman, who were engaged in rapid conversation. "Are you Jane Austen?"

The woman stopped walking and looked first at Eliza, and then at the man, whom Eliza thought she recognized as Henry Austen, Jane's brother. The long nose and receding hairline reminded her of a portrait she'd seen of him. The man nodded at Eliza and Deveric, but said nothing.

"My apologies for the interruption," Dev said. "I am Claremont. And this is my fiancée, Mrs. James."

The woman's eyes widened at his name, and she dropped

into a curtsy.

"It is a pleasure, Your Grace, ma'am," the man said, bowing. "I am Mr. Austen, and this is my sister, Miss Jane Austen."

Eliza's cheeks blazed with excitement. "Oh, my God," she burst out. "I love *Sense and Sensibility*. I've read the novel countless times. I can't believe I'm standing here in front of you—*the* Jane Austen!"

Jane gave her an uncertain smile. "How did you—" she started. "I didn't—"

"I can't wait to read your next one. It's my—" Eliza broke off, realizing she was about to make a major faux pas in her giddiness; *Pride and Prejudice* hadn't been published yet. "I'm sorry, rather, I mean I'm sure whatever you write next will be a big success."

Jane nodded, confusion written across her face. "Thank you, Your Grace."

Eliza waved her hand. "Call me Eliza. I'm not a duchess yet." At that, she leaned into Deveric and gave him a tender smile. He dropped a quick kiss on her lips, right in front of Jane and Henry. Eliza blushed, but added, "And I'm American, anyway; we don't do the whole title thing."

Jane gave her a warm smile. "I appreciate your compliments, Your—Mrs. James," she said. "But I beg your pardons; we are to meet my sister shortly."

Eliza nearly said Cassandra's name, before realizing that that would most certainly freak Jane Austen out. And freaking out Jane Austen was the last thing Eliza James wanted to do.

"I do hope," she said to Jane, "that you might allow me to call on you. I would love to hear you discuss your writing."

"I do not wish to offend, Mrs. James, but my sister and I return to Chawton tomorrow."

Eliza's face fell.

"Chawton?" Deveric said. "That is not so far from Clarehaven. Perhaps Miss Austen might allow you to visit when we are back in residence? Or, of course, the misses Austen would be most welcome to join us at Clarehaven for any length of time you choose."

"That would be my pleasure," Jane replied, hesitation evident in her voice.

Eliza clapped her hands, giddiness still racing through her. "I shall visit Jane Austen at Chawton! Did you hear, Dev?"

Deveric chuckled at his fiancée's excitement. "We look forward to it, Miss Austen. If this first impression has not scared you off from us."

Eliza winked at Jane, nodding toward the papers Miss Austen held to her chest. "It can be difficult to overcome first impressions, can't it?" She grinned slyly. "Why, Claremont here had to overcome his prejudices and I my pride after our first meeting, and yet here we are. I dare say it was a most unexpected match."

"Yes, first impressions can be … quite indelible," Jane murmured.

Eliza knew she was behaving like an idiot, fangirling over this not-yet-famous author who hadn't a clue as to who Eliza was. She didn't care. As they said their farewells and moved on from each other, Eliza touched her hand to her heart and whispered, "Thank you, Cat. For yet another dream come true."

A month later, the bells of St. George's in Hanover Square pealed in announcement. Inside, Eliza Mattersley, new

Duchess of Claremont, greeted well-wishers as her husband, the Duke of Claremont, beamed at her side.

It had been a whirlwind of a month, with numerous soirees and balls and morning calls and afternoon rides. Eliza wasn't sure she'd ever get all the etiquette down, but luckily having a fiancé—now husband—scowling at anyone who raised so much as an eyebrow had helped her through more than one occasion.

When she'd fretted about successfully fulfilling the duties expected of a duchess, he'd shrugged, as if it were of no concern. "Any details you need to know, I or my family will teach you. You needn't worry about a thing."

She'd crushed him to her, whispering of the numerous ways she intended to make up for her lack of qualifications. His ardent response was all the affirmation she needed: she could handle any challenge polite society threw at her, as long as Deveric was at her side. Being with him was enough, no matter where she was.

Still, she looked forward to the end of the Season and removing back to the country; as much as she loved London, she was exhausted.

Frederick, at least, was thriving. He'd had no more fevers, and his color was bright, his energy boundless. Deveric had taken the boy out on numerous occasions to show him the sights. Freddy had been particularly taken with the horses at Tattersall's, and Dev had promised his son he'd teach him to ride once they were back at Clarehaven.

Nothing could move Eliza more than father and son so obviously adoring each other. Until the morning of her wedding, that is, when Frederick had come to wish her well before the ceremony. He'd eyed her in her new dress, an ivory gown trimmed in beautiful green ribbon, a green that matched the green of Deveric's eyes.

"You look beautiful," he'd breathed, as if he could hardly believe it was her.

"Why, thank you, Freddy. You don't look so bad yourself." He was wearing a miniature copy of Deveric's own wedding garb; white trousers and a blue tailcoat, with a green and blue embroidered waistcoat underneath. It was uncanny how much he resembled his father. "You surely will break hearts when you are older," she'd teased him.

Frederick had only wrinkled his nose in disgust, thoughts of young ladies clearly years from entering his mind. "Lizzie," he'd said after a moment, his voice hesitant.

"Yes?"

"Would it be—could I maybe—would you mind if I called you Mama now?"

Eliza's eyes had swelled with tears as she looked down at the earnest young boy. "Oh, Freddy," she'd said. "I could never take your mother's place, nor do I want to. But maybe you could consider calling me … Mom?"

He'd tested out the unfamiliar word. "Mom … Mom. Okay," he grinned. "I shall call you Mom!"

She stood now on the front steps of the church, Freddy's hand in one of hers, Deveric's in the other. She looked at the smiling faces all around her: Amara, Emmeline, Becca, Grace. Even Deveric's mother's face glowed with happiness for her son and his new wife. Deveric leaned over and kissed her, murmuring of what he couldn't wait to do with her later. Her heart swelled.

"A matter of time," she whispered, closing her eyes and thinking of her best friend. "You were right, Cat; I would find my true love. It was just a matter of time."

EPILOGUE

*D*everic Mattersley, Duke of Claremont, paced the hallway in front of his chamber, his son walking in his footsteps right behind him. Moans echoed from within, and Deveric's throat constricted. He whirled on Frederick. "You shouldn't be here, my son. This is no place for a boy."

Frederick gave his father a pat on the back. "It's going to be all right, Father," he said.

"How do you know?" Deveric burst out, unable to control himself at hearing Eliza moan again.

"Because she told me so," Freddy said. "She said it will hurt a little when my brother or sister is born, but that she would be fine, and I was to reassure you of that. I am doing my duty."

Deveric looked at his son. When had the boy starting acting like a man, like a duke? "Remember, it's all right—it's okay—to be scared sometimes. Right?"

"Yes, Papa," Frederick answered. "But I'm not scared now. Mom told me she'll be fine. That it was *you* who was going to have the harder time with this."

Deveric resumed his pacing, marveling over his son's resolute faith. Not that Dev didn't have faith in Eliza; he did. It's just that God sometimes had other plans. But surely God wouldn't bring Eliza into his life, only to take her away again. Would He?

After a particularly loud groan, Deveric pounded on the door, demanding to be let in.

His mother opened it a few inches. "You shouldn't be here," she said. "It isn't seemly."

"She's my *wife*. Nobody can keep me from her." He pushed his way into the room. "Take Frederick back to Nurse Pritchett. I'm not leaving Eliza."

Eliza lay on the bed, her face a grimace of pain as another contraction tore through her. "Get over here, Dev," she commanded. He ran to her side.

"Oh, Eliza, I'm sorry. I'm so, so sorry," he murmured, holding her head against his chest. He stroked her face, tears running down his face. "I never should have. We never should—"

"Shut up," she said. "I admit, I'm ruing the lack of epidurals available." She squeezed his hand in a vice-like grip as another contraction hit. "But I'm fine. And you're about to meet your child." She panted. "Don't. Leave."

Deveric glanced down at the midwife, who wasn't looking the least bit concerned, although she avoided Deveric's eye. He knew it was unheard of for a man to be in the room during childbirth.

"Push," he heard her say to Eliza, and he watched as his wife grit her teeth and bore down.

"That's good," the midwife said, coaching her through several more contractions. "I can see the baby's head. The baby is coming!"

Deveric clutched Eliza's hand, his grip possibly tighter than hers. "Please, God," he whispered. "Please." He closed his eyes.

Suddenly, the sound of an infant wailing reached his ears. His eyes flew open. He looked at the babe, a squalling mess, but a very alive, very red and healthy-looking mess. He looked back at his wife, Eliza, who had tears running down her face as she held her arms out for the baby.

"See?" She cuddled the infant to her chest. "I'm fine. We're fine. And you have a healthy daughter. We have a daughter, Dev."

Deveric released the breath he hadn't realized he was holding. He watched as the babe worked to latch on to Eliza's breast, joy bursting through him. He ran his hand over the babe's head, marveling over her tininess, her hardiness.

"Shall we name her Catherine?" he said. "Catherine Rose."

Eliza gave him a tremulous smile, her eyes flashing with raw emotion. "Thank you."

"No," Deveric said. "Thank you. You gave me my life back. You gave me my son back. You gave me … you. I love you, Eliza James Mattersley. For all of time."

He brushed a gentle kiss onto her lips.

"Yes," she said. "For all of time."

Coming 2016:
A Scandalous Matter –
Amara and Matthew's story

Independent, feisty Amara Mattersley may live under the shadow of scandal, but at least the Regency society judging her is familiar, if not exactly beloved. That's all about to change when this nineteenth-century duke's sister finds herself in twenty-first-century Charlottesville, Virginia – and locking horns with one very befuddling, very male, University of Virginia professor.

Computer science professor Matthew Goodson has no time for love – no time for anything, actually, but his quest for tenure, his obsession with the screen. The last thing he expects is to get sideswiped by this adorably odd British miss. Yet something in her calls to him, pulls at him, in a way unfamiliar to him – and unwanted.

Can this odd couple blend the past and the present into a mutual future, or will old wounds and new complications sabotage any chance at a twenty-first century happily ever after?

Don't miss Cat's story in
A Man of Character.

Available now at **http://bit.ly/AManOfCharacter**

What would you do if you discovered the men you were dating were fictional characters you'd created long ago?

Thirty-five-year-old Catherine Schreiber has shelved love for good. Keeping her ailing bookstore afloat takes all her time, and she's perfectly fine with that. So when several men ask her out in short order, she's not sure what to do…especially since something about them seems eerily familiar.

A startling revelation – that these men are fictional characters she'd created and forgotten years ago – forces Cat to reevaluate her world and the people in it. Because these characters are alive. Here. Now. And most definitely in the flesh.

Her best friend, Eliza, a romance novel junkie craving her own Happily Ever After, is thrilled by the possibilities. The power to create Mr. Perfect – who could pass that up? But can a relationship be real if it's fiction? Caught between fantasy and reality, Cat must decide which – or whom – she wants more.

Excerpt from *A Man of Character*:

Cat stood there, breathing slowly to calm her flaming senses. Anyone would react to that man, right? Right? That mouth. She'd wanted to touch it, to feel those lips on hers. Goose bumps prickled her skin.

She didn't understand what was happening to her, why she was suddenly so aware of men, when before she'd managed to convince herself they were just part of the scenery. No doubt her sister would say it was her biological clock, tick, tick, ticking away.

Cat wasn't so sure. Maybe it was her stories, the ones Eliza had unearthed from that box. She had written them, after all. Perhaps reading them again had sparked something within her, made her realize that at one point, at least, she'd been very, ahem, interested in men and sex. And love.

ACKNOWLEDGMENTS

"There is nothing I would not do for those who are really my friends." – Jane Austen

Thank you to the Shenandoah Valley Writers critique group and my beta readers for helping me shape and refine Eliza's story into something of which I am proud.

Likewise, thank you to my marvelous editor, Tessa Shapcott, for giving me the tools to chisel the sculpted story out of the marble holding it down.

Thank you to the RWA's Beau Monde group, for answering my numerous questions regarding Regency period details. Any errors are my own, but I know there are fewer, thanks to your guidance.

Thank you to Lankshear Design for the gorgeous cover and visually appealing formatting – my books look ever so much more beautiful because of your efforts.

Thank you to my family for putting up with me when the deadlines hit. Kids, you rock. Brett, you are my rock. Thank you for everything.

And finally, thank you to my readers. Your encouraging comments and enthusiasm for my writing mean the world to me. I can't tell you how touched I am when someone says they love something I've written – it's this giddy little author's dream come true!

About the Author

Don't tell her mom, but Margaret Locke started reading romance at the age of ten. She'd worked her way through all of the children's books available in the local bookmobile, so turned to the adult section, where she spied a book with a woman in a flowing green dress on the cover. The back said something about a pirate. She was hooked (and still wishes she could remember the name of that fateful book!).

Her delight in witty repartee between hero and heroine, in the age-old dance of attraction vs. resistance, in the emotional satisfaction of a cleverly achieved Happily Ever After followed her through high school, college, even grad school. But it wasn't until she turned forty that she finally made good on her teenage vow to write said novels, not merely read them.

Margaret lives in the beautiful Shenandoah Valley in Virginia with her fantastic husband, two fabulous kids, and two fat cats. You can usually find her in front of some sort of screen (electronic or window); she's come to terms with the fact that she's not an outdoors person.

Margaret loves to interact with fellow readers and authors! You may find her here:

Blog/Website: **http://margaretlocke.com**

Facebook: **http://www.facebook.com/AuthorMargaretLocke**

GoodReads: **http://www.goodreads.com/MargaretLocke**

Pinterest: **http://www.pinterest.com/Margaret_Locke**

Twitter: **http://www.twitter.com/Margaret_Locke**

Interested in being the first to know about Margaret's upcoming releases, or hearing about other insider information not shared on her website? Sign up for her newsletter! **http://bit.ly/MLockeNewsletter**

What did you think of *A Matter of Time?*
I would so appreciate it if you'd leave a review on
Amazon (**http://bit.ly/AMatterOfTime**) or
GoodReads (**http://bit.ly/GR-AMOT**).

Word-of-mouth is still the best way for indie authors to gain readers, and the online version of word-of-mouth is reviews. Thanks so much!

Made in the USA
San Bernardino, CA
24 November 2015